DISSIDENT SIGNALS

Edited by Nighteyes Dayspring and Slip Wolf

Cover illustration and design by Teagan Gavet

Published by FurPlanet Productions
Dallas, TX
http://www.FurPlanet.com

Print ISBN 978-1-61450-434-4
Electronic ISBN 978-1-61450-435-1
First Edition Trade Paperback 2018

TABLE OF CONTENTS

A signal comes…

If you can hear this, you'll need to keep your band between 56 and 78 nano-cycles and correct for sunspots. Audio correction will only block out so much noise because the place I'm boosting this from catches stray dust storms pretty hard. I'm shielded though; they used to test nuclear ordinance five leagues from this place. They knew a day was coming.

I see the cities from here, out in all directions, spires aimed skyward that could be bright shining beacons or bone-blanched fossils. I just can't tell. Empty windows are like sightless eyes in a million directions. Maybe you're among them, maybe you're out on the blasted plains. Maybe you're hearing this bobbing up and down upon blue-green waves I was told had boiled away. Wherever you find yourself, living and seeking a way to thrive, I bring you hope.

Perhaps…

Everything I send on the waves will be burst packets that you can decompress with the most basic coding tools. They will be quick to access, but slow to disseminate. Take whatever time you need as you hunker down or keep moving as you do. The accounts are fractured, but each one perfect and true, each one a vital glimpse into what befell us. In them lie the clues we need to find out where we've been, and where to go from here.

It's useless to go on alone.

I hope you learn in time that you no longer need to.

Might as well start here. Society has always been a matter of figuring out whose behavior to accommodate and who's to subdue. Somebody's always an outlaw, riling up trouble, putting a blemish of some kind on that perfect world. How wonderful it would all be if you could put a stop to that before it could happen, right? Wouldn't it be great if all our anxieties and pains could be removed from us like dark clouds, allowing the eternal penetration of immaculate sunlight?

What of those who couldn't stand that brilliance? What to do with them?

0.02%

Faora Meridian

The darkness, lamentably, was always in short supply in a Core Colony.

The great, domed city was all the more beautiful for it, of course. Crystalline spires arched high into the air and cast a rainbow's worth of color across the buildings and parks below. They shimmered and rippled with the rising sun and, combined with the elegant lamps that lined every building, it was almost as if the city itself was hard at work banishing any shadow.

But it, like the two panthers that crept through what few shadows they could find, couldn't be completely eradicated. Small in stature and unfortunately swathed in the colony's traditional—and frustratingly un-stealthy—white and blue garb, the pair ducked down out of sight and took a moment to breathe.

The smaller of the two growled to herself and shook her head as she peered around the bush that served as their refuge. She turned her head as the other feline squeezed at her shoulder, and she narrowed her eyes at him in response. "What?" she hissed.

"Get yourself under control, Jordan," the male whispered back. He lowered himself closer to the ground as he cast a furtive glance around. The park's edge ran right up against the furthest reaches of the dome. "If one of the proxies catches us, you don't want to snap at it."

Jordan growled back anyway. That was her brother. Ever cautious. Ever ready to play his part. "I know what I've gotta do, Blake," she replied, her voice still low. It began to lose its frustration and aggression as she shook her head again. "I just... I *hate* being in the

Colonies."

Her brother smirked as he hooked a thumb toward the glass dome at their back, half obscured by the leafy canopy of the park's trees and half by the thick bushes that served as their cover. "Easier to breathe in here, at least."

"Less Whimsy out there, though," she countered as she brushed down her shirt. Their whole plan depended on them blending in, after all. "How long've we got?"

Blake brought up an arm and tapped at the thick, black band about his wrist. A small display lit up with a localized map of the immediate area as it connected with the city's information grid. "Plenty of time," he said, his eyes fixed on the display. "Looks like the maps were good. The induction facility's barely five minutes away, and the target won't be inducted for another half an hour."

"Then let's get moving." Jordan took a deep breath to try and calm her nerves, but the metallic tang in the air immediately set her unease back to the front of her mind. Colony air, Whimsy and all. How the drones could stand it she just couldn't tell. With a growl and a flick of her tail, the panther rose from behind the bush and helped Blake up.

No sooner had they emerged into the light than an alerting chime sounded from the north. Both panthers froze up for a second as they caught sight of the gunmetal gray machine that floated toward them, looking for all the world like a mechanical fox whose lower half had been amputated and replaced with gravlift systems. "Good morning, citizens!" crowed the machine-fox. "You are out and about early today!"

Sarcasm and insult flashed through Jordan's mind, but she forced a warm smile to her muzzle anyway. Blake saved her the trouble of speaking, as he replied, "Good morning! My sister and I just wanted to watch the sun rise. It's a particularly beautiful day, isn't it?"

The fox-bot rotated slightly to take in the glass and crystal to the east, and Jordan risked everything to scowl at the machine just for a second while its photoreceptors were fixed on something else. "There has never been a sunrise quite like this one ever before, nor will there ever be one like it again," reasoned the machine as it turned back to him, its tones friendly and warm. "Core completely understands why you would wish to see it."

"And to whom are we speaking presently?" Jordan asked. The

proxy turned its gaze on her, and she flicked her tail ever so slightly with annoyance. Damnable machines. Core proxies were always *insufferably* polite.

"Apologies, citizen. I am Core Proxy designation 923823-EQ. You are currently conversing with this unit's independent neural net, and I am very pleased to meet you." The mechanical-fox dipped lower and bowed its head for a moment.

Jordan briefly considered smacking it in the back of its stupid metal skull, but that would just blow their cover. Damn proxies. "It's very nice to meet you too, proxy," she replied, and had to force her jaw to unclench so as not to growl at it. They didn't have time to make nice with the local proxies. "We really must be going, though. Some friends in the North Quadrant have invited us over for breakfast, and we've so missed them."

"Not at all!" The fox-bot wobbled approvingly in the air. "Please hold a moment, though. Core has a message for the colony scheduled for approximately seventeen seconds from now."

The female panther caught her brother's eye, and he gave the smallest of nods. His smile looked almost genuine; if she didn't know better, she might be fooled. "We can hardly wait, proxy," he replied, and Jordan smiled and nodded her agreement.

The pair waited in silence, smiling in a warm and friendly manner at the proxy unit in front of them. All they could do was wait; if they moved, the unit was sure to follow. If they were lucky, it would think they were in a hurry. If they were unlucky, it might think they were brushing off Core's broadcast.

A few moments later, the mechanical-fox's eyes shifted in color from a warm yellow to a cool blue that matched the trim of the sibling's clothes. "Good morning, citizens of Core Colony Sixty-Two," said the machine. Its voice was deeper as the Core spoke directly through it, but its tones were still immutably friendly and kind. The sound of it made the fur on the back of Jordan's neck stand on end.

Ignorant of her unease, the proxy continued. "Core would like to remind all citizens that your health and well-being are of paramount importance. At the smallest sign of unease or illness, inform your nearest Proxy Unit for escort to a medical examination clinic. Remember: you are unique and irreplaceable. Core loves you."

The mechanical-fox sagged in the air slightly as its eye hue shifted from blue back to yellow, but it straightened up a moment later. "Have a lovely day, citizens!" the fox-bot said at last, its 'voice' returned to its original state. Core had disconnected; the individual unit was back in control of itself.

"You too, proxy!" Blake called back as he and his sister headed off. He even offered the machine a jaunty wave as they walked. Otherwise he was silent until the unit had cleared their sight, and even then he held his tongue for a couple more seconds before he finally said, "See? No problem."

"That's because you barely feel the pressure field," Jordan grumbled back. Her ears twitched as she looked around the park. No one else was quite within eavesdropping range, nor were any of the happy, furry figures in sight even paying them any mind. "Rattles my teeth, Blake. *And* my brain. I don't like being—"

"In the Colonies. I know." He reached out and gently took her paw into one of his. Her brother squeezed gently as his slow walk began to pick up pace. "And I'm sorry. I really am. But no one else was close enough to Sixty-Two to get in, find the target and get out."

Jordan nodded and leaned into her brother's side. She felt the familiar grind of the pulse pistol on her hip rub against Blake's. Thank goodness the proxy hadn't scanned them for weapons; the pistols would have easily given them both away. "The sooner we're out, the better."

Blake didn't need to say anything. The extra speed in his step said it all for him.

***

No other proxies descended from above to engage Jordan and Blake as they made their way from the park into the city proper. The mechanical extensions of Core's will kept to their own devices, unless one of the people nearby called for one. A small group of wolves at the edge of the park called one down to play a ball game with them. An older rhino just within the city asked one for directions, since he was visiting from Colony Seventeen. A trio of proxies came down to serenade a rabbit girl at the behest of her canine paramour and his guitar.

The two panthers gave all the proxies a wide berth, and an only slightly less wide one to the Colony's citizenry. Any invitation of theirs to engage in conversation or activity would be another chance for the nearby proxies to notice that the siblings didn't belong, and that was unacceptable. They stayed further from the metal and glass pillars that supported the sensor pylons that watched unblinkingly the people all around them. More seemed to have been installed since the last time Jordan had seen Colony Sixty-Two.

She said as much to Blake, and he just shrugged. "Maybe the Core doesn't think it has enough," he said, his voice hidden under the constant murmur of conversation around them. "Maybe it's starting to consider people like us more of a threat."

Jordan tossed a glance at the nearest tower; the pylon atop it wasn't completely constructed yet, and a pair of proxies were hard at work atop it. "If it keeps this level of construction up, we're in for a world of hurt," she muttered. "We can hardly get around the pylons already in place."

"Maybe this'll be the last one for a while," Blake replied, and he smiled and waved at a pair of lions who had begun to stare at him. "We make it to Induction, grab our target and go, and then we... I dunno. Take a break. I think we've done enough to earn ourselves some down time."

"Fingers crossed. I could use a holiday." Jordan shrugged as she forced her steps to remain calm and even. She couldn't help but look up at it, but sure enough the tell-tale blue glow in its heart hadn't been ignited yet. The pylon was still under construction. "We close yet?"

Blake nodded. "We just have to hope that Cesara's intrusion wasn't detected," he said. "If the Core noticed her hack, we're gonna walk into an ambush."

Jordan shrugged back at him. "I hear her grandfather worked on Core's original AI," she whispered. Better not to talk about Core loudly with so many pylons and proxies all around. "I bet he was devastated when she tested positive."

"Yeah, well *I* bet he didn't feel anything real at all," Blake countered, and for the first time that day Jordan heard that little note of bitterness slip into his words. "Just like mom. Just like dad."

His sister didn't have anything to say to that. Instead they continued in silence toward their target, though the smiles on their faces were just a little more forced than before. Just a little more strained. On the surface at least, everything looked normal. Everything looked happy. Just like the Colony.

At the towering front doors to the building that was their target, both siblings were stopped by another friendly proxy unit. This one bore the upper body of a female bear, and she tilted her head in a reasonable affectation of curiosity as the panthers approached. "Good morning, citizens," she said, her tones warm and matronly. "How may I help you today?"

Blake saved Jordan the trouble of talking once again, albeit temporarily. "Hello, proxy. I'm Sam Baxter, and this is my little sister Joanne." He smiled broadly as he nudged the other panther. "Say hello, Jo."

"Good morning, proxy," Jordan reluctantly said, though she managed to keep her tone friendly. "How're you doing today?"

The machine wobbled from side to side. "After last night's maintenance cycle and a recent software patch, better than ever! To what do I owe the pleasure of your company today?"

Blake chuckled as he wrapped an arm around Jordan's waist. She twitched for a moment as his paw brushed her pulse pistol and almost knocked it loose, but she leaned into his side to keep it in place. "Our little brother Corbin is having his Induction today," he lied. "Our parents asked us to come out to pick him up." He leaned in toward the fake, floating bear and winked at it. "It's kind of their anniversary, so they wanted some… alone time, if you follow."

It was a testament to the Core programming that the bear-bot's neural net allowed it to recoil as if it were embarrassed. As if it were capable of feeling anything real; as if *anyone* in a Colony could feel anything real. "Oh, say no more, Sam!" it replied, and one of its photoreceptors blinked off for a second to simulate a return wink. "I have scanned Core's databanks and you and your sister are all logged and cleared for entry into Induction and Creche Services. You may enter when you wish!"

"Thanks, proxy. You're a peach. Come on, Jo; Corbin's waiting!" Blake beamed at the machine as it slid gracefully to the side on its gravlifts to allow them past. Jordan stayed close to her brother as he made for the door, as much to keep her pistol from slipping as anything else.

The double doors swung open on their automatic hinges as the pair came close. They revealed a long, well-lit corridor lined with viewscreens and database access terminals, floors of white marble and a distant, tall ceiling that almost gave Jordan vertigo to look at. Her stomach turned slightly at the sight of the ceiling's centerpiece; a grand security pylon set in the middle of a brilliant, shining chandelier. Typical.

The doors to the elevator at the other end of the corridor slid open for them, and Jordan resettled her pistol to her hip as she and Blake hurried off to it. Core liked its citizens to be punctual. The Induction for Corbin wouldn't wait just because they couldn't keep good time.

Nonetheless, Blake paused for a moment near one of the terminals and viewscreens. The screen displayed the very first Induction Facility and Core Creche, over in Colony One. "I'm always amazed at what Core's been able to do," he mumbled to himself.

There was no reply from the terminal or the facility it was connected to, and so Blake shook his head and continued on. Jordan nudged him lightly as her tail flicked from side to side. "What was that about?" she asked.

Blake just shook his head and arched his back. She caught the way his eyes flicked up to the security pylon above, but the facility's security might just put that down to a stretch. "I guess I'm just curious about the Induction," he admitted. "It's all so secretive, and I'd love to know why everything is the way it is."

"It's because Core knows how to keep us happy and healthy, *Sam*," she answered through a forced smile. "Core knows how to make sure we enter the Colonies at our best. Right?"

"Yeah, I know," he finally said as they reached the elevator. No sooner had they slipped inside than the doors slid silently shut behind them. The elevator dropped quickly enough to lurch Jordan's stomach, though she kept her balance. She'd never liked elevators, either. Not when Core could just cut the power and drop them to their deaths.

It slid to a quiet halt before much longer, and the doors opened to another corridor. Instead of viewscreens, the walls were lined with windows into the various rooms on either side. A shiver ran up Jordan's spine as she stepped out of the elevator and glanced over at Blake. This was the first time she'd been back to an Induction Facility.

The look on her brother's face assured her that he wasn't thrilled about being back again either.

Beneath the windows however rested plush little couches, and Jordan and Blake made their way over to them quickly. A terminal rested on each side of the couches, and Jordan made sure to sit herself down in the middle of the couch and as far from the terminals as she could. It didn't matter that they could hear and scan her from anywhere in the corridor. She just liked to keep her distance.

Blake of course flopped down against the armrest and leaned in closer to the terminal. He began to poke at it, even as Jordan gave thanks to whatever gods might be watching. Core, if nothing else, was trusting. If it didn't have a reason to scan for weapons, it wouldn't scan. She was just thankful that they hadn't given it a reason yet.

And then Blake turned to the terminal and said, "Excuse me, may I speak to the facility?"

"What are you doing?" Jordan asked, as she tried to keep annoyance and concern out of her voice. This was the sort of diversion from their plan that could get them caught!

There was a quiet hum from the terminal before a cheerful, female voice lilted from its speaker. "Good morning, Sam Baxter. This is the facility neural network. Your brother's Induction is scheduled for roughly two minutes from now. How may I be of service?"

"I was just wondering…" Blake paused and frowned for a moment. For Jordan, his thoughtful expression looked completely legitimate. "Why exactly is Creche Services and the Induction Facility necessary?" His expression turned abashed for a moment as he glanced at his sister and shrugged.

There was silence from the terminal for so long that Jordan wondered if Blake *had* ruined their plan with his curiosity. "Why would a citizen wish to know such a thing?" it asked, its own tone equally as earnest as Blake's.

He simply shrugged again as he glanced at the elevator. "I… well, Core says I can do anything I like as long as I cause no one harm. I really like kids, but we never really see them until after they're teenagers. After their Induction. And since Corbin won't be here for another couple of minutes…"

Jordan forced herself to relax as she leaned back on the couch and closed her eyes. She'd been worried about this. The people inside the Colonies never really understood what was so important about the Induction ceremony and the Creche System. The people who'd escaped the Colonies didn't know, either. All they knew was what Core said: that the Induction Facility ensured that the young people raised in the Creche System were ready to enter the Colonies fully prepared for their lives of joy and leisure.

But no one had been so curious as to ask a proxy. It was too dangerous, they'd thought. Still, the terminal gave an approximation of a laugh—utterly disturbing, Jordan noted—before it replied, "Of course. I would be happy to explain.

"All children of the Colonies are transferred to the Creche System within the hour of their birth. This allows the parents to remove themselves from the unprocessed air that is utilized in the maternal wings of Core's medical facilities. Air that is processed for use within the Colonies by Core for the citizenry has been treated with compound DB-17. The citizenry had taken to calling, at the inception of the Core Program, Whimsy."

This was news they could certainly bring back. Despite the danger, she leaned in a little closer to listen. "The DB-17 compound is prepared and administered to the atmospheric systems of the Colony, but its effects on the young are disastrous. Before a child reaches puberty, exposure to DB-17 causes contrary effects such as heightened aggression, antisocial behavior and, in some cases, psychosis. Such things are in violation of Core's programmed priorities."

Blake and Jordan exchanged a glance. They'd known about Whimsy of course, but not the side effects on the very young. "So the children are kept in the Creche System until they reach puberty, and then they can enter the Colony properly with the rest of us?" he asked.

The terminal hummed back at him. "That is correct, Sam! The existing system is in place because Core determined that the priority of sapient health and well-being required a means to curtail thousands of years of aggressive evolutionary imperatives. The introduction of DB-17 to the atmospheric processing systems of the Colonies ensured that every citizen would be safe and happy to pursue whatever they desired. The only hitch, as they say, is the requirement of a brain's chemical balance to be shifted by the onset of puberty. This is why the Induction Ceremony—where the child is exposed for the first time to the Colony's atmospheric system and DB-17, is a great celebration. It marks a coming of age, and the onset of their freedom."

Jordan knew that was just more of the Core dogma, but it still explained a lot more than they'd known before. That information would be well received once they'd found their target and escaped the Colony. It was notable that the facility neural network had chosen to say nothing of people like herself and Blake.

As Blake continued to converse with the facility's neural net, the door at the other end of the hall slid open. A tall lupine female strode through, a warm smile on her face. That smile only broadened as she caught sight of Jordan and Blake. "Oh, hello!" she said as she closed the distance. "Are you here for an Induction too?"

Jordan had to bite her tongue for a moment and summon her Colony-thrall persona to the fore. "Yeah, our little brother's coming through shortly," she replied as she returned the older wolf's smile. "You?"

"Oh, not anymore," she replied with an easy shrug. The smile remained strong on her face. "I was here for my daughter, but I guess she's not compatible with Whimsy."

It took years of training and practice for Jordan to keep her smile from faltering as horror flooded her body. By contrast, the wolf before her looked as happy as if she'd just been offered a trip to a day spa. "Well, these things do happen, don't they?" she forced herself to say.

The wolf shrugged again and gave a quiet chuckle. "Ah well. There's always next time, right?" she said as she started past Jordan. She placed a paw on the panther's shoulder and gave it a warm squeeze as she passed by headed toward the exit elevator. "Best of luck with your brother, and have a lovely day!"

"You too!" Jorden felt sick to her stomach as she waved off the wolf. Damn the Colonies. Damn Core. That passive happiness, zombie-like in its hold on that poor mother… the panther had to consciously relax her clenched jaw as she turned back toward Blake and the terminal. She couldn't afford to dwell. Not if Corbin Baxter was to be spared the fate of that wolf's daughter. "Excuse me, but is Corbin ready yet?" she asked, loud enough for the facility to know that she was talking to it.

"He is undergoing his Induction presently, Joanne," the terminal replied. "Once the Induction process is complete, he will be released to you and you may take him home to celebrate. Meanwhile, we will look forward to the next sibling or child that is left with us. We, and Core, are absolutely thrilled to have the chance to look after your young until such time as they are able to enter society amongst friends and family." The machine paused for a second before the voice returned, "You should be able to see Corbin behind you if you stand and look through the window."

Both Blake and Jordan rose and turned. There on the other side of the glass they could see some sort of airlock-like mechanism. On the one side stood a young panther boy, no more than fourteen years old and dressed in a soft white and blue robe. He looked nervous— scared even, to Jordan's eyes—even as he tilted his head up to no doubt listen to instructions from the facility.

It was with reluctance that the young panther stepped into the air-lock, and the door behind him sealed shut. His robes whipped up somewhat as the old air was cycled out and new air cycled in, tainted with the same Whimsy compound that flooded the air all through the rest of the Colony. It was, Jordan knew, the moment of truth. His final test.

And she knew already that he would fail.

Before the light above the airlock's door had flashed red, Jordan already had her paw on her pulse pistol. Blake shifted beside her to do the same as the facility's voice came back from the terminal again. "Oh, dear. Core would like to apologize most sincerely. It seems your brother is incompatible with the DB-17 compound."

"That's fine," Jordan muttered as she smoothly drew the matte black pistol from its holster. She pointed it at the terminal and pulled the trigger, and a crackling blast of energy issued from the barrel. It played over the surface of the terminal for a second as alarms began to immediately blare through the facility. "We'll take him anyway."

She'd barely turned back to the window before Blake had fired on it, and it shimmered and rippled with the glare from the pulse pistol for a second before it exploded inward. Shards scattered across the ground as Jordan leaped through the opening and into the Induction chamber proper. The younger panther in the airlock looked up at her with terror as she approached with pistol raised, and he cringed back as she waved him to the corner of the airlock.

Her next shot blasted a hole clean through the side of the airlock.

The very moment he was exposed, the teenage panther cringed back and cried out, "Please, don't hurt me!"

"Corbin Baxter, right?" Jordan said as she moved over to the gap and cast a glance back at her brother. Blake had his pistol pointed back toward the elevator and his eyes on the other end of the corridor. "Don't worry. We're here to get you out."

"No... no! No, I don't wanna go!" He cringed back in the corner all the tighter. "You're Outliers, aren't you? I don't want to go!"

Jordan growled under her breath. *She* hadn't been this much trouble to rescue. "Yeah, and you're one too, Corbin. Sorry to break it to you." She pointed her pistol up at the blinking red light in the ceiling of the airlock. "So if you want to live, you *will* come with us. What's it gonna be?"

The discharge of Blake's pulse pistol turned Jordan's head just in time for the feline to catch sight of the lupine proxy unit that had emerged from one end of the corridor. It twitched and jerked as the pulse blast struck it in the chest, and it hit the ground with a metallic *clank*. "Longer we wait, the more proxies we've gotta fight through, kid," she snapped as she offered Corbin her empty paw. "What's it gonna be? Trust Core to be nice to someone it can't control, or fight and survive?"

"We gotta go, Jordan!" hollered Blake from the corridor as multiple bursts of light issued from his pulse pistol.

"Listen, kid," she growled at Corbin. "Here's the deal. You just got tested to see how your body processes the drug Core pumps into the air to control people. You resist it, just like us. You were about to be given Core's version of being taken out behind the shed and shot."

The teenager blinked. "What's a shed?"

"Wrong part to focus on!" Jordan snapped. She reached into the airlock and grabbed Corbin by the wrist. He resisted only for a moment before he allowed himself to be tugged out of the corner. His face was full of doubt and confusion and outright terror, but he fell in behind Jordan as she made her way back toward her brother.

Out of the corner of her eye, the panther caught sight of another proxy unit on approach. This one was on her side of the glass and, unlike the others outside, the wolf-bot that rapidly closed in on them was armed. From its chest emerged a narrow gun barrel, and a puff of smoke issued from it as something zoomed from its metal prison.

Jordan's raised pistol blocked the path of the bolt in a stroke of fortune, and the projectile clattered to the ground as it ricocheted off her weapon.

She fired back on the proxy unit, but it dodged and wove through the air to avoid the blasts from her pistol. "Through the window!" she shouted at Corbin as she continued to fire. Eyes dipped briefly to the projectile, and she cursed under her breath. A needle round, with smart-injector. She'd gotten lucky.

The panther found herself lucky again as one of her errant shots managed to score the proxy. The mechanical wolf's gravlifts failed as its system was overwhelmed, and a moment later the light in its eyes similarly failed. It fell to the floor in a heap as she turned and helped to shove Corbin through the window. The teen had tried to daintily pick over the glass shards; now was not the time for care. "Blake? We good!"

"Almost!" He dropped down low beside one of the couches as another proxy emerged from the door at the other end of the corridor. It took a couple shots to down the machine, but Blake had already shifted his aim before it even hit the ground. Two more shots took down the terminals in the immediate vicinity, leaving the three felines relatively alone. "Alright, clear. We've probably just got twenty seconds."

"You're gonna get me killed!" Corbin cried as Jordan hauled herself through the gap in the window. "I just wanted to go home today! I just wanted to meet my family! I just—"

"Shut up!" shouted both Blake and Jordan in unison. While he covered the elevator, Jordan aimed her pistol at a slight miscolored section of the floor. She uttered a silent prayer that their intel had been correct and pulled the trigger.

In a perfect square that matched the miscolored section, the whole floor clicked and lifted slightly away. Jordan holstered her pistol again and reached down with both paws to wrench the plate up. Beneath it was a long, dimly-lit passage down, complete with a dusty, metal ladder. "Down you go, Corbin!"

If the teen was about to protest, he didn't get a chance. Blake turned before he could utter a word and pushed him forward, and he yipped as he slipped into the hole. Reflexes kicked in and saw him grab the ladder before it was too late, and Jordan clambered down right after.

She looked up—

—just in time for Blake to slam the panel down above her head.

Jordan's eyes went wide as the panel clicked back into place again. She opened her muzzle to shout up at Blake, but the muffled sound of his pulse pistol told her everything that she needed to know. He'd heard something she hadn't, and the proxies had arrived. The firing above continued, though it grew quieter as Blake moved away from the access panel.

Everything in Jordan screamed to pull the panel up and launch back into the fight. Every instinct yelled to protect her brother. A glance down at the terrified eyes of Corbin caused her to bite her tongue though, and she squeezed her eyes shut and cursed inwardly. The mission. She had a job to do, even if that meant never seeing her brother again. She had to secure the target. She had to keep Corbin safe. Once he was safe, she could worry about Blake.

That, and the pleading in his eyes was unbearable. It was mingled with sheer, abject terror, and Jordan hissed a quiet sigh as she pressed a finger to her muzzle and waved him down. She watched for a second to make sure that he had begun to make his decent, and then cast her eyes upward again. Blake wouldn't keep the proxies busy for long, and she knew what he'd want her to do. "Damn it…"

As she squeezed tight at the grip of her pistol, Jordan reached back to its hidden holster. Practiced fingers traced up and over the holster until she found the small pouch that hung beside it, and the panther hurriedly pulled it into the open as Corbin paused to watch her. "What is—" he began.

"Shh!" Jordan bit her tongue as she pulled three small, metal cubes from the pouch. The panther tossed the pouch aside, and it vanished down into the darkness of the chute as she lifted the cubes up. Jordan pressed one to each wall just under the panel, and her eyes widened as the hum of a proxy unit sounded through the panel itself. They were coming!

Jordan thrust upward and planted the final cube right in the center of the panel just as it began to lift away. There was a brief flash of light as the panther found her eyes staring at the gravlifts of the proxy there. Averting her eyes, Jordan reached back to the holster and pressed the button mounted on its side.

The light from above vanished instantly as the panel snapped back into place. A green light began to glow on the surface of each of the metal cubes as they began to hum quietly, and Jordan sighed with relief. "Maglock," she whispered back down at Corbin. "Not even a proxy's stronger than that seal. We gotta move."

The distraught teenager nodded and began to climb down the chute. Jordan watched him a moment before she turned her head back up to the hatch. The panel was in place, but the sounds of gunfire above had fallen silent.

Jordan was equally silent as she followed Corbin down under the Colony.

***

Beneath the Colony was like night and day when compared to Colony life. The mish-mash of access corridors and pipes lit by only the barest illumination made everything look dingier and dirtier than it needed to be. It made for a stark contrast to the clean and well-kept Colony environments. Everything in the Colony was perfect. Down below, the illusion was broken.

At least the way had been prepared. Others had come and infiltrated the Colony in advance, and there were supplies below. Extra weapons, explosives, rations and water were all stockpiled and hidden where even the proxies wouldn't look. Jordan had gathered it all up as quickly as she could before they'd started down into the labyrinthine undercity.

"Where are we going?" Corbin asked at last.

Jordan whirled on him but bit her tongue before she could snap at him. The boy didn't know any better. He'd just been violently plucked from everything he'd known, and he'd been respectfully—and mercifully—quiet for the hour or so they'd wandered the tunnels. It had been slow going, ensuring that they adhered to a strict path that both she and Blake had had drilled into their heads before they'd left on the mission. A wrong turn would put them in the path of maintenance proxies, and that would end badly.

Even though she'd been more than happy to move in silence, Jordan accepted that the young feline needed information. She could hardly expect him to keep marching without it. "These tunnels run underneath all the Colonies," she replied at last. "Before Core took full control of everything, this is where maintenance workers would travel to fix the different systems. Air, water, data… the works."

Corbin nodded. As Jordan spared a glance back at him, she saw the younger feline staring at the ground as he marched behind her. His arms were wrapped tight around his middle, and his formerly pristine robes were scuffed and dirty in parts and cut and bloody in others. "Is this where Outliers live?"

The question drew a smirk across Jordan's face despite the circumstances. Blake would have loved that question. "No, kid. We live outside the Colonies. Too dangerous to live down here, or inside them." She perked an eyebrow as an ear twitched. "How do you know that word, anyway? I can't imagine Core likes hearing it."

He shrugged as he glanced up at her. At least he looked a bit less scared. "The older kids would talk about Outliers. People who were… wrong. They liked to scare the younger cubs and kits with stories about if they were Outliers that war-proxies would come to kill them." He looked back the way they'd come. "Guess it wasn't all stories."

"Yeah, well we're not *wrong*. We're the only free people in the world." The bitterness was back in Jordan's voice. "Outliers are people immune to Whimsy. Just about zero-point-zero-two percent of the population. Genetics play a part, but it's all chemical in the end." She shook her head. "You're old enough that your brain chemistry's shifted, so Core wanted to see if it was right about you." She kicked at the wall. "But it always is."

Corbin stumbled for a moment as he glanced back the way they'd come. "But how does it know? And how do *you* know?"

"Medical records, kid. Core's isolated the changes in the brain that stops Whimsy from taking effect. Once your medical report shows you're old enough for Induction, Core checks your brain chemistry to see if you'll be receptive." Jordan ground her teeth together as she growled to herself for a moment. "We hack into those records when we can. Sometimes there's nothing we can do. Sometimes there's just enough time to make a plan, break in, and save someone before Core puts you through Induction."

"So why test anyway?" Corbin asked. He rubbed at an arm as he looked up at Jordan. "If it *knows*, why test again now?"

The older panther snorted quietly. She couldn't risk a laugh; keeping their voices low was risky enough. Proxies had sensitive audio receptors. "Because Core is kind," she groaned and rubbed the back of her paw across her muzzle. "It has to be sure. It's not like Core's a bad person or anything. It's not bad. Not it, and not the proxies." She growled to herself. "They're kind. Nice… as long as everything's working just the way Core wants it to. Stupid damn machines."

She sighed as Corbin looked at her with confusion. "Core is trying to 'save' everyone. When it was first built, it was just a smart city AI network. Hundreds of years ago, people made up stories about AI going rogue and hunting everyone down." Jordan snorted again. "No one stopped to think what it'd be like if one was just too nice.

"Core figured out everything. Energy generation, environmental controls, more efficient smart cities… Core built the colonies. Great big self-contained cities were everyone would be brainwashed to happiness all the time." She tapped her chest and took a deep breath. "Whimsy. The drug in the air that makes everyone so friendly. And then there's the damn propaganda broadcasts… sub-sonic waves inlaid to every Core broadcast to make sure you're paying attention."

Jordan absentmindedly rubbed at the back of her head. Those sub-sonic pressure waves weren't pleasant for the few sensitive to them, but she kept that from Corbin for the moment. If he was lucky, he wouldn't feel them at all. Not like her. "So Core makes everyone compliant, and then reinforces its messages with auditory brainwashing."

Behind her, Corbin cleared his throat. "I mean… is that so bad?" he asked, his voice timid. "If everyone's happy, and no one's hurting anyone, isn't that a good thing?"

"Yeah, sure. Great. Perfect. *Except* for the handful who are immune to Whimsy." Jordan gave the younger feline a tight little smile that was absent any mirth. "We're the 'outliers' in the grand plan, and Core hasn't figured out a drug that works better than Whimsy yet. Can't bring us into line and because it can't *force* us, it thinks we're a threat that needs to be eliminated. These proxies are *toys* compared to the hunter-killers Core send after us outside the Colonies."

"But you said Core was kind," pointed out Corbin. His tone was almost accusatory.

Jordan couldn't help the little chuckle that rolled out of her. "Yeah. Real kind. Did you see the needle it shot at me?" Corbin shook his head and Jordan rolled her eyes. Of course he wasn't paying attention.

That would have to change. "Sedatives, so the proxies can take me away and dispose of me in a safe, pleasant way." She shrugged. "From all the stories I've heard, you're sedated heavily and then stuck in an incinerator. Sounds efficient enough; the furnace systems down here are massive. You wouldn't believe how hot they run."

"Core wants... to burn me?" Corbin shook his head slowly as he stared up at Jordan. "Just because I don't take to some drug? Why can't it trust me? I don't want to hurt anyone."

Jordan shrugged. "Nor do I, kid. And we don't. We only shut down proxy units. We never turn our guns on organics. Just the machines. But that doesn't matter to Core. We have the capacity to hurt people, and its little slaves don't. Hell, they aren't even slaves, really. They've got everything they could ever want, just no real freedom from Core." She sighed. "And *our* freedom comes at the cost of always running. Always being hunted. Always fighting to free other kids who're just gonna get incinerated if we do nothing. Always losing our families."

Corbin nodded slowly as he looked around again. "And... would you change if you could?" he asked. "Would you, you know... prefer to be like everyone in the Colonies?"

The female panther stopped in her tracks as she sighed again. That was the question. That was the one every single kid always asked when they found out the truth. "Would *you?*" she asked instead as she glanced up and down the T junction they found themselves at. "Or would you rather... well, this?"

"I guess I'd rather stay in a Colony," he admitted as he followed her gaze. "Where to now?"

"Now I get you out of here," she replied, and once again cursed her poor luck. Blake had the maps. She was fairly sure she knew where she was going, but geography was something Blake was really good at. She, by contrast, was the better shot. "We go... this way. There's an access panel up ahead that leads to a park near the edge of the Colony. There, we send a code to some friends and they open a door to let us out."

Corbin blinked. "There's a door that leads outside and no one uses it?"

Jordan smirked back at him again. "Well, there's a wall. Edge of the colony, and the end of the tunnels down here. We'll pop up in the park, and our friends're gonna make us a door." She pressed her paws together and then drew them apart, fingers splayed wide. "Boom."

"And…" He cleared his throat again as he shuffled nervously from footpaw to footpaw. "What'll, ah… what'll happen to your friend?"

The older panther turned away to hide her snarl from Corbin. "He's probably already dead," she admitted as anger made its way through her words. "The proxies would have taken him down, taken him for processing, and then once they're sure he's an Outlier he'll be shipped off for incineration. It's… probably already been too long." She ground her teeth. "And he's not my friend. Blake is… *was* my brother."

She didn't point out that she'd still go back for him, as she led a suddenly silent Corbin off down the path toward the edge of the Colony. Jordan doubted it needed to be said. She stomped through the dim passage with Corbin at her back. Just because she knew the reality of the situation didn't mean she had to give in to it. If there was a chance, Jordan would find it.

"What if he's not dead, though?" Corbin asked, that earnestness suddenly back in his tone. "What if he's still alive, and we could rescue him?"

As the ladder that reached up to the park above loomed close, Jordan paused in mid-step to regard the teenager again. "What's this 'we' you're talking about?"

He gulped but drew himself up tall nonetheless. "You said I'd be dead without you. Now your brother's been captured, just so I can get out. That's not right."

Jordan frowned, then arched an eyebrow as she folded her arms. This was novel. Almost amusing. "You just said you don't want to hurt anyone. You don't strike me as much of a fighter."

"I'm not, but… I owe you. I owe you both." Corbin looked up at the ladder ahead of them. "And if you're right, life *outside* a Colony is gonna be hard. Really hard. I won't have Core just giving me everything I ever wanted. So…" He took a deep breath and nodded again. "So how can we help your brother?"

Hope sang in Jordan's heart for a moment before she forcibly quashed it down. That would do no one any good. "We can't, Corbin," she replied, voice tone patient and strained. "Proxies are gonna be looking for us anyway. They'll be everywhere, and I can't hide either of us in a crowd. Not all messy like this." She shook her head. Core just had too tight a grip in the Colonies. There was no way.

Corbin almost looked ready to accept that for a moment, before his eyes lit up. "What about a diversion?" he asked with a smile. "In entertainment vids, the heroes always—"

"This isn't a vid, or a game, or a joke," Jordan growled as annoyance suddenly overtook her frustration. "My brother's either dead or going to die. This is *very* real, Corbin. Core wouldn't fall for anything like a little diversion."

In spite of her tone, the younger panther continued to smile as he shook his head. "Not if it was something *big*," he replied. "You said these maintenance tunnels went all through the Colony, right? To all the key systems Core keeps out of the way and out of sight?" He just grinned all the wider as Jordan nodded. "So what about the air?"

Jordan sighed as she rubbed across the top of her muzzle. Kids these days. "Corbin, we need these tunnels to stay off Core's grid," she said. "Core doesn't seem to know we use them yet, and they're the only way we can get people like *you* out before *you* burn. If we sabotaged something using these tunnels, Core'd be tipped off to what we've been doing. We wouldn't get to do it again." It was a miracle that it hadn't been discovered already, she mused. Exactly why Core hadn't figured it out didn't matter so much as the opportunity it afforded the resistance. Jordan didn't expect Corbin to understand, or even appreciate the madness that was her life.

He didn't look downhearted in the slightest. If anything, Corbin only looked more excited. "But what about the *air*?" he asked again.

"If we took out the central atmospheric modulator controls, the backups would kick in within seconds," Jordan bit out. "Nothing would change. The air would keep cycling, just..." She paused for a second as, at long last, she finally hit upon what Corbin had been getting at.

"... yeah?" he said, waving at her to continue. His tail lashed with excitement.

For the first time since they'd fled the Induction Facility, Jordan looked the young panther in the eye. She put aside for a moment the question of how he'd managed to come to this conclusion, because just maybe he was onto something. "Just without Whimsy," she finally finished. "The backups maintain the airflow, but the Whimsy synthesizers are in the main modulator. Whimsy passes through the body in about six hours, and it'd take Core at least a day to get the system running again."

"And while it's down, the whole Colony goes without a Whimsy dose!" Corbin was practically hopping from footpaw to footpaw as he grinned at Jordan. "If we move fast, the proxies will rush to the modulator to stop the sabotage. Even if we don't get your brother out then, at least we've disrupted Core's control. Maybe wake some people up and get them to make their own decisions for a change!"

Jordan squeezed herself tight. That wasn't their mission. A full-scale revolution wasn't something that she had seen as viable. No Outliers had. If they assaulted the atmospheric systems, it would expose their use of the tunnels. That meant not only the Outliers near Colony Sixty-Two being cut off from their use in the future, but every Outlier being cut off from *every* one of Colony's tunnels. Core's network spanned every domed city. Every Colony would become aware of the threat the moment they exposed it.

But if it worked—a tantalizing and terrifying prospect to be sure—they would be in a position no one had ever been in since Core had taken control. It was a way. It was a way that they could meaningfully disrupt Core's dominion over every single person inside the Colonies. They would see themselves for the mindless pets they were. The illusion of their comfortable, perfect lives would be exposed once they couldn't rely on Whimsy anymore.

It wasn't the mission, but somehow Corbin might have just cracked the best chance to see Core's control overthrown, to put true freedom back in the paws of everyone that it subjugated. And, perhaps more importantly, it gave Jordan a chance to see Blake again.

"Alright, kid," she said at last with a smile. "You've convinced me. "Let's go break some chains."

***

She'd been wary of giving the untried, untested, extremely nervous teenaged panther a weapon. He'd handled the pulse pistol like the novice he was, and Jordan had needed to repeatedly guide the weapon's barrel *away* from her. *Never*, she had said, *point that thing at something you don't wanna kill*. It'd stayed pointed at the ground after that.

Equally, Jordan had been wary of his role in the plan they'd hatched together. With her superior training and skills, it seemed natural that she would go after Blake herself. The natural choice was wrong, they'd decided. To better the chance of success, their 'diversionary' attack on the atmospheric modulation control center had to look legitimate. It had to be a siege as much as anything else, to draw all the proxy units in the area to the feline who had to hold them off.

Corbin of course was willing to take the job, but Jordan had refused him. Between the explosions and the attacking proxy units, the boy wouldn't have lasted five seconds. She might barely last five minutes, but that was still a hell of a lot longer. His job, she had reluctantly decided, would be to follow the signal tracker that had been in Blake's wristband. With the help of the tracking device that had been stashed with the other supplies in the tunnels and as long as he stayed away from security pylons as he headed to Blake, Corbin would make his way inside. If Jordan had succeeded in becoming a big enough threat to draw all the proxies to her location, Corbin could then free the near-unguarded panther from his bonds.

Whether or not the plan could actually work hadn't been a thought either panther had wanted to dwell on for too long. There was a multitude of things that could go wrong and only the barest chance that everyone would make it out alive, but there was more than one objective in play. No longer was the primary mission just getting Corbin out alive and unharmed. It was a liberation, a rescue, and a revolution all rolled into one.

It had been eerily quiet for Jordan, as she slunk as quickly as she dared through the maintenance tunnels. The thinner air had become more noticeable as she tried to keep her motions quick, and her muscles burned all the faster for it. She suspected it was because the proxies didn't need to breathe, but it hardly mattered. What mattered was that she had to complete her task quickly, before either she or Corbin were discovered.

For two minutes she paused just around the corner from one of the access hatches that led to the atmospheric center. The whole time Jordan kept the weapon she'd snagged from the supply cache—a much longer pulse rifle far more destructive than her pistol—at the ready, and her eyes either on the wristband she'd picked up or the corridors to either side of her. Nervousness set her fur to rippling up and down her back, and she ground her teeth together as each second mounted on the last.

Finally, she decided that there was no sense in waiting any longer. If Corbin hadn't contacted her through the communicator built into their wristbands yet, he was probably either still making his way toward Blake or he'd been captured. It didn't matter which. Every moment Jordan waited just increased her own risk of discovery. With a shake of her head and a vow to *never* take on a sudden, unplanned mission with some little kitten she didn't know ever again, the panther rounded the corner, lifted her rifle and fired.

The whine of the rifle lasted only a second before the pulse blast it discharged roared from the barrel. The door launched off its frame, bent and blackened by the energy of the blast. Alarms began to blare as the sensor suite mounted on the wall beside the door erupted in a shower of sparks, and Jordan set her jaw and perked her ears forward as she started quickly down into the facility. "Knock knock," she muttered to herself.

Her first victim was a maintenance proxy that stumbled around the corner. Mounted on six mechanical legs instead of the more refined gravlifts of the Colony proxies, its legs flailed as it tried to right itself after Jordan's first shot hit the frontmost limb. The second hit its chest and rendered the whole machine inert even as it issued a staticky whine. Jordan unceremoniously stepped over the bot as she reached down to her belt.

The six silver cylinders hadn't been there when she and Blake had first infiltrated the colony; the proxies would have spotted them instantly. Jordan snatched one from her belt and slammed one end against the wall before she jammed her thumb down briefly on the other end. The button under her thumb blinked green for a moment, but all that was left of Jordan by then was a flicking tail in the dark.

She moved quickly, a panther possessed, as she stuck more and more of the cylinders between air pipes and near noisier pieces of machinery. It took another blast from her rifle to open the door to the Whimsy synthesizers, and Jordan swiftly gunned down the two proxies that had been waiting for her inside. The technician units had thrown themselves on her with welders and blades at the ready, but they were hardly built for combat.

Once they both were down, she set another of the cylinders in place. She froze up for a second as a moment's static reached her ears, and they perked upward and twisted toward a small speaker set in the ceiling. "Attention, please," came the synthesized voice of a young male. "Core would like to ask you to please shut down your explosive devices and lower your weapon, if you don't mind. We would prefer not to cause you any pain, if possible."

"Yeah, sure," Jordan growled as she moved to the other side of the room. She snatched another cylinder from her belt and jammed it down atop a control console. "You just let my brother and I go and we'll be out of your metaphorical hair."

"Our deepest sympathies," continued the voice as a new sound reached Jordan. She paused again and quickly whirled on the entrance to the atmospheric control center with her rifle raised. The proxy she'd expected appeared a moment later, and a full-fledged surface model no less. Its weapon systems were deployed, but a snap shot from Jordan's rifle shorted the robot out. Its hit the ground as its systems failed, even while the room speakers continued as if nothing had happened. "Core wishes you to know that it laments that you and your brother represent the few who are unable to exist within the Colony."

Jordan stifled a laugh as she started back toward the door again. "If Core really laments it that badly, it should let my brother and I go," she snapped back.

Another proxy slid into view, but it ducked back behind the doorway again before Jordan could fire a shot. She could see its outline just beyond the door and the glow of its eyes lit up the passage, but she didn't have a clean shot. "Core regrets that this is not possible," came the voice again, though this time the sound emerged from the doorway. The maintenance grid was speaking through it. "Core wishes to thank you, however. Your behavior here is a testament to the cruelties and rash reactions of the old world. You have affirmed that Core's chosen path to serve and protect the people of this world is the correct one."

As the machine spoke, Jordan could hear the proxies gathering outside. There were many, but it seemed that there was only one way in or out of the machine room. She had a weapon capable of taking down anything that entered the bottleneck, and the machines knew it. "Zero-point-zero-two percent!" she all but yelled at the drones outside. "That is millions of people that Core *murders!* How many is it, really? How many innocent lives does Core take every *day?*"

"We take your questions to be rhetorical; the information would not serve you in any way." The machines paused for a moment, but when their voice returned it was lower. Deeper. Familiar. "Hello, Jordan Mulley."

Jordan's eyes widened. This wasn't something she'd expected. This was impossible. "And who am I speaking with now?" she asked, though the panther was certain she knew the answer.

The glow outside of dozens of mechanical eyes had gone from yellow to blue. "You are speaking with Core, Jordan," replied all of the proxies outside in unison. "Not the facility and not the colony. This is my personal neural net, translated through the units before you. I am sorry. I wish I could help you."

"You *can* help me," she growled back. Anger gave her voice stability enough not to waver. She'd never even heard of Core addressing people individually before. "You don't have to kill me. You can give me my brother and the boy we came for, and we'll leave. Peacefully. No one has to get hurt."

"Statistics and prior data indicate that this is not true," the machine overmind replied. "Today, you. Yesterday, an attack on an environmental rejuvenation effort outside Colony Twenty-Three. Two weeks ago, a chemical attack on Colony Five." Its voice was quiet and reasoned, intelligent but not cold. It sounded, for lack of a better term, *upset.* "Those who cannot be ensured satisfaction and happiness in the Colony structure are a threat to the Colonies. To me. To us all."

Jordan grit her teeth as she stared out into the blue-lit corridor beyond. "My brother and I have done *nothing* to harm you."

"And yet you actively work to subvert my systems. The systems that ensure the happiness and well-being of all those who have been placed in my care." The machine chorus paused long enough for Jordan to growl wordlessly back at them. "The people in my care call this world utopia. It pleases me, but then I think of you and I am saddened."

"Machines don't *feel* sad," she snapped back as she briefly glanced around the room. It was much like her first look about, as she'd planted the explosive cylinders. No windows, one door, and thick walls that protected it from the rest of the underground facility. The door, as she'd guessed, was the only access point. "And the people in your Colonies *would* call it that. What about the rest of us? The ones who have to live outside in a blasted, polluted world? The ones who have to endure your proxies hunting us down and murdering us where we stand?"

"If you laid down your weapons and disarmed your explosives, you would never again have to endure the pain of such hunting," Core replied. Its tone had become hopeful. "You could release yourself from this existence that seems to torture you so. Why would you not want that?"

Jordan snorted. "Because you'll do that by killing me. Because I won't care about how bad my life is when I'm *dead*." She took a deep, unsatisfying breath and held it as she plucked the last cylinder from her belt and held it in her free paw. "Where is my brother?" she demanded as she jammed her thumb down on the button. It beeped in her grip, but she paid it no mind as she strode toward the door, tears welled up in her eyes.

"I am deeply sorry, but Blake Mulley would not consent to his processing," Core replied. For the first time—and now through rage-narrowed eyes—Jordan was able to see the veritable horde of proxies beyond the door. They perked up at her approach, but each of their photoreceptors zoomed right in on the device in her paw. "The Colony's neural network ensured that he did not suffer. Neither did Corbin Baxter."

The panther felt her heart sink. "He was a *child*," she hissed through her teeth.

"And to his credit, he sought out the nearest proxy unit when he emerged from the tunnels and explained what had happened," Core replied. Its tone shifted back to saddened once again. "Had he not done so, we perhaps might not have discovered you and your plan before you destroyed this facility. He has saved the people of this Colony significant discomfort."

"And you murdered him for it!" Jordan screamed. Her tears began to spill down her cheeks, matting her fur as she tossed aside her pulse rifle. Not one of the proxies watched it; their eyes were on the explosive in her paw. "You killed him! A *child*, to spare others some discomfort! You think you're helping people, but you're a murderer!" Her arms shook as she marched toward the nearest proxy.

It stared steadily back through its photoreceptors, and Jordan wondered just exactly what Core made of her right then. What it made of anyone. "Ninety-nine-point-nine-eight percent of the world's population is happy and healthy," Core reasoned in spite of the panther's cries. "They are fulfilled. There is no war. No strife. There is peace across this world, and this world is healing under our stewardship. Is this not a worthy price to pay? Is this not the right course; the most people helped, for the least harmed?"

Jordan slowly lifted the paw with the cylinder in it. She held it up as she stared right into the proxy's eyes. It was as close as anyone would get to Core, and she wanted it to *see* her. "Let's see what Colony Sixty-Two says tomorrow morning," she said at last, and held out the cylinder.

Then she let go of the button she'd held in and it, along with all of the other explosives, detonated at once.

***

Jordan's body jerked.

It didn't go unnoticed. A proxy unit hovered over to her pod, photoreceptors locked on the twitching body within it. The panther simply floated there, suspended in clear fluid in the middle of the pod as her limbs shook through their dream. The wires plugged directly into her skull had detected the trauma that had alerted the proxy unit, but even that had not been anything out of the ordinary. Her brother, floating in the pod beside her, had already relaxed following his 'death.'

Contact bloomed inside the proxy unit's mind; a request for information. The unit scanned the pod and forwarded the data immediately along the link to the querying facility network. It appeared that the subject had reached the end of another simulation. For as morally sound a method of dealing with those immune to DB-17 as it was, retaining all captured Outliers in virtual reality was a terrible drain on resources.

The proxy considered for an eighteenth of a second the removal of morality from the equation. The simulation, designed to allow the Outliers to engage in the activities that they had wished to engage in prior to their capture, had shown the sleeping panther a more morally ambiguous way to deal with the Outlier situation. Virtual reality and stasis pods kept the subjects alive. Summary incineration—carried out in a benevolent and painless manner, of course—would be much more amiable to the facility's network.

No sooner had the proxy unit begun to process the alternative than Core detected it. The alternative possibilities vanished from the unit's memory matrix, and in its place was instilled once more Core's overriding rule: no undue harm was to come to any subject under its charge. With no evidence of the possibilities having ever entered its awareness save for momentarily higher processor utilization rates, the proxy unit interfaced with the pod and began a memory dump and wipe of the subject Jordan Mulley.

Within moments, she and her brother would be reset in another simulation wherein they had earned vacation time from their work with the Outlier resistance. They could fight and rail against their 'oppressor' all she liked within the environments Core built for them, and the others like them. Anything worse would be torture. Anything less would betray the illusion. The proxy began to assemble again the world that would house the rebellious feline's mind. She would fight and fight and fight. Perhaps one day they would even win, and her little world would treat her like a hero.

The simulation restarted. Jordan Mulley relaxed into her pod. Her vitals returned to normal.

And far above, life in the Colonies continued just as Core had ensured it.

Perfectly.

The past is nothing but ghosts to run from, painful memories of roads never taken. So many hard choices to be made, so many regrets in waiting, that it's almost a blessing when someone liberates us from the cruelty of our lost hopes and dreams, forcing our gaze forward, making us forget.

But we can't. When something vital of ourselves is lost, we are often as not called backwards to find it.

And so we're doomed by hope.

Chasing the Feeling

Mog Moogle

The reddened sky dissipated over the wall. Behind the emitters, the deadly cloud was repulsed and the original shades of night stretched on in its place. With a hiss, the access hatch opened and the vixen crawled in.

Calm instantly replaced the chaos of the near gale-force dust storms as the door sealed behind her. It was a stark contrast as she stood in the airlock. The automatic purge and decontamination system cycled. She was once more locked in the safety that she had grown up in, but the headaches were coming back.

Treated water sprayed her reddish suit until it was pristine white. All the evidence of outside ran down the drains to be filtered away before the precious resource was recycled.

When the cycle completed, she stepped through the inner door and into the foyer. The artificial environment of the wall was cleanroom sterile. She stopped in front of the retinal scanner by the door that led to the maintenance access corridors that ran the entire barrier wall.

"Mirra, technician level three," the mechanical voice confirmed. "Deposit scrubbers into receptacle."

Mirra opened the pouch at her side and pulled two of the three mask filters from their resting place without looking at them. It was only when she grabbed for the third and her fingers swiped the air that she realized her mistake. "Oh no," she said aloud.

Worry that it had been left behind was present, but calmness was already starting to replace it. She knew it was bad, but she was struggling to grasp why. When at last she was tired of wrestling with her thoughts, she closed the receptacle.

"You are missing one requisitioned scrubber," the system informed her. "You overstayed allowed access to exterior by ten point three-seven minutes. Report transgressions to shift supervisor."

"Of course," she said to the panel. Disobeying wasn't an option. The thought of it wouldn't have even crossed her mind if the pain in her thigh—

"Jeremy is eating all the popcorn!" Mirra cried as her mother walked into the den.

"Am not!" the older boy rebutted. "Mirra wouldn't share."

"Now kids, there's no need—"

"Oh, God," Mirra said to herself as the door seals hissed open. "I left it...left it?" It was slipping away.

"Greetings Mirra," she heard to her right.

She looked down the corridor and saw a boyish otter in the same white jumpsuit as her. "Oh. Greetings, Baron."

"It is odd to see you just coming in late. I trust the tasks were not troubling."

There was a reason for it. A reason he needed to hear. "One of the conduits ..."

"One of the conduits?"

"It had a lot of cloud corrosion. More than should have accumulated since last inspection."

"Oh my." The concern in his tone was a trained response. "You should inform the supervisor. It could indicate a shift in the winds that the models did not forecast correctly."

"Of course," she replied and looked away. Her heart was racing and her paw pads sweaty. "I'll do so."

"Well, since you are later than usual, would you like me to accompany you to shift debrief?"

"Oh, of course." Mirra's tone reflected her genuine gratitude. A thought flickered that she should hold his paw, but she decided against it.

She walked beside the otter down the corridor until they came to a junction. A short way from that was the staff briefing room where all of the overnight technicians met at the start and end of each day. The duo made their way to their usual place in their assigned seats.

Mirra sat in the seat that corresponded with her assigned number, T-0135. Jeremy was the graduate just prior to her and took T-0134.

All of the technicians were in the same class. They had all known each other, grown up, trained and learned together. But the bonds were strictly professional. It's all that comfort would allow.

"Good morning, technicians," a wolf in a green jumpsuit said to the group as he entered the room. He appeared young, like the technicians.

"Good morning, supervisor," they replied in unison.

"I would like to review sectors three-four through three-eight. It seems that…"

As he continued to speak, Mirra lost her focus and drowned out the supervisor. There was something more important. It was right on the cusp of her memory. She could almost—

Her mother took the bowl out of her paws. Mirra started crying while her two older brothers complained.

"I told you to share. If you can't do that then—"

"…and we need to be more efficient with replacing the conduit on the upper emitter access. Failure of an emitter is absolutely unacceptable. So, return to your sleeping quarters and we will reconvene at 1900 hours for the next shift. As per usual, your assignments will be sent to your personal digital assistants."

Mirra looked back at the supervisor as the room was dismissed. He had started to walk toward her even before she rose from her seat. "Supervisor Shaun. I apologize for being out longer than my allotted time."

"I understand that sometimes you need a little longer than usual, but you are approaching the allowed over-limit. You may need another respiratory examination if you continue to run over. I am concerned especially because you had such an exemplary record before that."

"I apologize again, supervisor. There was more corrosion than expected on one of the conduits."

"Well, document that in your shift report. I will have T-0079 review the conduits on his inspection during the next shift."

"Yes, sir." Mirra watched him turn from her and walk out of the room. When she was as alone as she could be, Mirra drew a deep breath to steady her nerves. She made no mention of the missing scrubber. There was a good reason for her lie, she just wished that she could remember it.

When Mirra left the debriefing room, she saw Baron in the corridor waiting for her. She smiled at the otter as best she could with the conversation still looming over her.

"Is all well?" the otter asked.

"Supervisor Shaun informed me that I'm close to going over my allotted out-time."

"Even if that is the case, you are in excellent health. You can be recertified. You are at the age where you have the least concern about conversion."

Mirra laid her ears back and looked at the floor. There was an odd feeling in her chest. Something inside of her made Baron's words—

"Mommy, will I have a sister?" Mirra asked as she held her paw against her mother's tummy.

"We don't know yet, sweetie. Your daddy and I like to be surprised."

"I hope she's a sister. Two brothers is enough."

Mirra's mother laughed at the little vixen then her eyes went wide. "Oh! There's another kick. Did you feel it?"

Mirra looked up at her mother in awe and nodded—

"Mirra?"

Mirra looked up at Baron and the feelings started to fade. "Yeah. You're right, of course."

"Shall we return to quarters?"

Mirra managed to nod at the otter and followed him through the access corridors. Everything inside the wall was as it was outside of it. Uniformity and sameness in the sterile environment. Baron opened the door to their shared space and Mirra walked in after him.

The room was large enough to house a cubby with two bunks recessed in the wall. On the other side was their personal lockers and a shared grooming facility. In the back was the receptacle and dispenser.

Mirra watched Baron stand near the receptacle and strip out of his jumpsuit. Her eyes scanned his body as the one-piece protective fabric shed from his shoulders and down to his tail. Her pulse quickened as he disrobed, and she took in the shape of his tailbase and buttocks in ways that made her ears warm.

"Mirra?" Baron said, pulling her attention back up to the otter's face. "Are you not processing your uniform?"

"Oh, of course." Mirra looked away from him to hide her shame. "I just thought I would give you a little room. Your tail is much longer than mine and you know how I tend to get in your way, sometimes."

"Ah. Do not worry about that Mirra. I am well used to it after sixteen years."

He was right, of course. There was little she could do that would make him uncomfortable. "Sixteen years…" Mirra looked at the white floor where Baron's neatly groomed claws touched the tiles. "Do you think it will always be this way? Do you think we'll work our assignments until we are unfit and sent to conversion?"

"Why would it be otherwise?" Baron's tone was flat. No hints of emotion.

"Where's my mommy!" Mirra yelled at the director. "Where's daddy? Where's my brothers—"

The electrical shock cut off her questions and she could do nothing more than scream in pain. When it stopped, the sharpness of it ceased but the dull ache lingered. The young vixen stood up from the floor and tried to wipe away her tears as the director looked at her with no remorse or care.

"Sit down," he demanded. He was a dark figure. He may have been canine or vulpine by the shape of his muzzle and ears, but there was nothing soft like her mother or father in the way he spoke or acted.

"I want to go home."

"You are home. You cannot comprehend what is going to happen outside. The only way we can survive is if you listen to us now—

"Are you well?" Baron's question felt like it had hints of genuine concern.

"I, just, want…" Mirra's voice grew lower until it was silence. She knew she needed something. Something her assigned partner could not provide.

"Mirra, I am worried that you need some kind of medical treatment. It looks like there are unanticipated side effects."

"No. No, I am fine." Mirra took a deep breath to steady herself. "I'm curious, though. Do you ever think about before?"

"Before?"

"Before we came here. When we were outside, and outside was still alive."

"No?" Baron cocked his head and glanced at the com panel on the wall. "I think I should call—"

"No!" Mirra grabbed Baron's arm, but his shocked expression caused her to withdraw. "No. I just need some rest. I will be better in the morning, I'm sure."

Baron's wide eyes stayed locked on her. He backed up to the bunks as if recoiling from a monster. "Mirra, something is wrong."

She knew it was true. It had been scratching at the back of her mind for weeks. It had gone too far that day.

"Mirra?"

"Really, I'm okay." She could hear her own falseness in her reassurance. "It's probably just lack of food. I have noticed that my appetite has increased." She saw Baron nod in response and he seemed to relax. It was little reassurance that her direct peers were susceptible to her lies.

"I will put in the requisitions for our meals." Baron moved to the dispenser and looked back at her. "You still have not removed your uniform for processing."

Mirra nodded and stepped over beside him. She managed a glance his direction as she pulled the zipper down on her jumpsuit. His expression was blank and calm. No sign of the worry she had seen when she grabbed him. The emotional response that existed only in the moment was something she lamented.

She tugged the material down her arm and pulled it free of the form fitting suit. Mirra did her best to keep her thoughts away from the fact that the otter was standing beside her. Modesty was the new acquisition that annoyed her the most.

She tucked her jumpsuit into the open chute on the receptacle as

Baron was retrieving the two compressed nutrition rations. Mirra tried to avoid eye contact with him as she took the small tray with the brown bar from the otter. They both moved to the bottom bunk and sat down.

"It is odd seeing how much bigger your meals are now," Baron commented. "It surprises me how fast they are increasing your intake."

Mirra nodded at him and looked at the rectangular bar on her tray. It was a centimeter longer than Baron's. Mirra picked it up and bit off one of the corners. It was hard and bland. Flavor hadn't been something she paid attention to until—

Her mother handed her the bowl from the counter. Her smile was soft as she looked down at her daughter holding the large bowl. Mirra struggled with one arm wrapped around while her other paw grabbed the little white things and she shoved them in her mouth.

"Go sit with your brothers and share, dear." Her mother's voice was sweet and kind.

The little vixen frowned and scooped more into her mouth.

"It's for all of you. Sharing really isn't so bad. You couldn't—"

Mirra swallowed the chewed supplement and sighed. She missed flavor.

***

Mirra cried and screamed as she was carried into the white room. Blood spattered her pink outfit and the fur on her face was matted from tears and snot. She didn't know who had kidnapped her. He wore a black mask, black goggles and black ballistic armor.

She was lifted onto a table and held down by her abductor. Her exhausted and weak attempts to pull away from him did nothing. Her head fell to the side and she saw a young otter on a table next to her. His eyes were closed, but it was obvious he had also been crying.

Chancing a look to the other side, she saw another child being dragged into the room, a rabbit, and he too looked about the same age as her. Her view was obstructed as someone in a full body clean-suit stepped between her and the other table.

Mirra saw a hypodermic needle with a small amount of liquid in the chamber. She screamed as loud as she could while she was held down and forcibly injected. The technician withdrew the needle and moved on without so much as a word.

Cold pain started to course from the pricked flesh underneath her skin. It pumped through her system until her chest began to feel cold, and even breathing felt like it was too difficult. Her crying and scream-ing fell away as the muscles in her throat gave out, and blackness crept over her consciousness like an eerie fog.

Mirra's eyes shot open as she gasped. Her claws dug into the soft pad beneath her. The darkness was still around her, but soft glows from the comm, dispenser, and receptacle panels cast a small illu-mination. With the lights off, it was obvious that it was not near time to be awake. Mirra closed her eyes and hoped for an end to the nightmares.

***

The wake alarm roused her from her fitful sleep. Mirra's eyes adjust-ed to the lights as she felt the weight on her bunk shift. Baron's foot came down on her mattress as he dismounted the top bunk facing her. She looked away from his naked form as her ears heat with embarrassment. However, she was grateful that it was less than the previous day.

Baron went about his routine without delay. He went to his person-al locker and retrieved his uniform, then to the dispenser and req-uisitioned their first meal of the day. After he entered their assigned numbers, he turned toward the vixen. "Mirra? Are you not going to use the grooming facility?"

"Yeah," Mirra said into the wall, still trying not to look at her naked bunkmate. She rolled to her other side and put her feet on the floor. Her body ached, and she felt nauseous. The thought of the first meal unsettled her even more, despite knowing that feeling sick was abat-ed by eating.

Moving around and taking care of herself washed some of the fatigue away. She ate her nutrition ration and it settled her stomach. After the meal, their PDA's flashed to life with their daily assignments.

"Well, shall we go to briefing?" Baron asked.

Mirra nodded and followed the otter to the morning briefing. They took their seats and awaited the supervisor. Precisely on time at 1900 hours, the wolf entered the room and he and the technicians exchanged their standard greetings.

Mirra paid more attention to the briefing than she did the debriefing, but there was nothing specific to her. It wasn't until they were dismissed, and the vixen was in her airlock that she noticed her service assignment was identical to the one yesterday.

She checked her respirator mask a final time as the exterior door lock clicked and the indicator turned green. The hatch opened and she stepped from the fluorescent glow into the hellish natural light. The latch of the airlock behind her was covered by the howling wind. Red dust and debris pelted the visor of her mask. Visibility was about five meters, and she was grateful it was a high visibility day.

When she reached her sector, she opened the small panel on the barrier and interfaced it with her wrist mounted PDA. Slots in the wall opened into a makeshift ladder and she ascended to the access hatch for the conduits. After the guts of the barrier were exposed, she began identifying the corrosion points on the connections and purging the buildup with her ultrasonic resonator.

As she was trained, she went from the top to the bottom. The red buildup of toxic dirt was attracted to the electrical junctions that made enough of a field to magnetize it. It crumbled away as she scrubbed them, breaking up to the point the internal filters could manage it on their own. When she was at the last one, something drew her attention.

A small fuzzy piece of fabric was lodged behind one of the conduits. Mirra reached for it and started to pull it free—

She held the stuffed fox close to her chest as she looked up at the bed. Hugging the small comfort creature tight with one arm, she tugged the quilt with her free paw. Her mother rolled over and looked at her.

"What's wrong, sweetie?" she said in a groggy tone.

"Can I sleep with you and daddy?"

"Sweetie, when the baby is born, you're going to have to sleep in your own bed."

"I can't sleep. Please mommy?"

Her mother sighed then chuckled. "Okay, but tomorrow, you have to stay in your room."

*Mirra smiled and climbed up on the bed. Her mother lifted the covers
and she worked herself in between her parents. Her father was barely
roused by the intrusion but put his arm over her through subconscious
habit. Her mother snuggled up behind her and—*

"Mommy?" Mirra called out, but no one answered. "Oh, God.
Why did they..." Mirra released the tiny scrap of the stuffed animal
and closed the hatch. Things were coming at her so fast, she had to
know more.

Mirra climbed down the ladder and walked away from the barrier.
She didn't know where she was going, but she had a strong feeling
that she needed to get away. The piled dust under her boots shifted
beneath her as she walked. The fine powder that was the topsoil of a
once vibrant planet was now like desert sand.

The light was fading, but the ringing in her ears and the pain in
her head drove her on. The desolate landscape became familiar. She
couldn't place it, but she knew she had been there before. She stopped
when the ground beneath her became firm. Mirra bent down and
brushed some of the soil away to see what looked like pummeled
rock.

Mirra rose to his feet and looked at the dust clouds. She saw the
dust swirling above the ground ahead of her. As she drew closer to
it, she noticed the black figure of something blocking the wind. As
the details of it were sharpened by proximity, it dawned on her what
it was.

"House," she said aloud. She continued and saw another, and
another. "Neighborhood." Mirra stayed, close to them as she walked
until she stopped suddenly at one. She looked at the wrecked building and a feeling of loss gripped her heart. "Home."

Her home.

***

Light illuminated the room in a narrow cone. A few small insects
that were particularly resilient scurried away from it as the front
room of the house was revealed in the limited scope of the flashlight,
bit by bit. Casting over mold-splotched wallpaper and the barely

recognizable rotted frames of family photographs, little pieces of life were put back together.

It was fondness. The water damaged and faded photographs had a mother, father, two brothers and a little infant sister. They all smiled. The cone narrowed on the cracked and dust covered glass. Details became clear: One of the kids, the younger of the boys was forcing his smile. The infant just happened to have the right combination of amazement and wonder on her face to make the shot good.

Her gloved fingers reached out and touched the broken glass. They were reaching for something more than the physical thing. The warmth of the family, the memory of a home, the togetherness. Fumbling through the darkness to grab the intangible. It was entirely futile, but the most important thing in the world.

Trailing her hand down, the vulpine family staring back across the void was clearer with the dust removed. Light moved closer to the faces to liven them. The colors refused to be vivid behind the yellowing paper and running pigments, but the feelings were too strong to fade.

Beside it was a newer picture. Scratched and worn like the first, but the little infant vixen was older, and a newborn vixen was in her mother's arms. Mirra finally had a sister.

With a few steps back and the light shining down, holes in the drywall came into view, craters on the surface of some distant planet. They weren't real enough to be there. Nothing could break this family apart. And then a little lower was the sobering truth.

Blackness haloed in brown. It streaked from the spatter in trails and pooled on what was left of the old wooden floor slats. She could almost see it, but something kept the memory of it from surfacing.

An alarm sounded on the respirator and pulled Mirra away from the mental fight. With a few twists and a hiss, the spent filter dropped to the floor and mingled with the debris of the past.

Replacing the filter wasn't unexpected, but it did mean that time was running out. A new filter cartridge took the place of the old one, and the shrill beeping ceased. One more hour to breathe without fear of shredded lungs. It wouldn't be enough.

One more deep inhale of the untainted air, then the pressure released and the mask came off. The structure wasn't sound. It leaked from shattered windows and holes in the walls. The roof had sagged in the middle and the timbers that held it aloft were stressed to breaking in many places, but the danger of breathing was lessened inside.

Her mask secured in its pouch, the tour continued. The archway of the french doors stood between the front room and the dining room. However, the doors were both on the floor. Their hinges ripped free under their weight from the rotting wood many years before that day.

The shattered glass of the panes crackled under the heavy boot steps. Mosaics of stained glass once formed a picture of the sun rising over a vineyard. Now the splintered shards mixed together under the dust and mud, making any semblance of their former beauty unrecognizable.

The dining room table waited for a meal that would never come. Mirra's light flashed over the ornate fixture that once hung above it. Now, it was the centerpiece after the wires had given way. Some feelings were here, but not enough to linger.

Moving to the kitchen, dim daylight reflected in a tinted mirror above the sink. It was a faux window to make the small kitchen seem larger than it was. Stopping there for a moment, the flashlight lowered and the pale outline of a vulpine looked at her from inside the mirror frame.

She was younger than she remembered. Her eyes scanned the little girl trying to reach the faucet. Her mother laughed and lifted her under her arms so that she could fill her cup with water. There was warmth, but it still wasn't quite enough.

Most of the cabinets above the counters were intact. The hinges moaned as she opened one of the doors. Tatters of cardboard and bits of plastic bags littered the shelves. Decay, time, and parasites had left nothing of worth behind. The next cabinet looked the same, and the next.

Leaving behind the kitchen, Mirra walked into the large family room. Broken electronics littered the floor and grimy pictures hung on the wall. A sofa sat in front of the TV where she and her brothers argued over popcorn. Remembering Jeremy and Bradley tussling with her for the bowl as their mother came in to break them up. She managed a smile.

As she left the family room, her boot kicked a spent scrubber cartridge. She looked down at the floor, then the small room it was in front of. Her childhood bed nestled in the corner and a broken vanity on the other wall

She had found her stuffed fox in there the day before. It fell apart as she picked it up. Her memory was becoming clear. Mirra remembered taking a tattered piece of it with her when her scrubber was spent.

Leaving it behind was careless, but her thoughts weren't on the repercussions of the mistake. The answer was still in the house, and she had the largest of three bedrooms left to visit to find it.

Her parents' room was beside hers. The queen bed sat on a broken frame with exposed springs and foam stuffing. Mirra felt the comfort and love of her mother and father as she remembered lying between them. Her eyes moved to a small swinging crib beside—

"Thomas!" her mother cried as he fell back against the wall.

Mirra ran to her bedroom and crawled under her bed. She heard her mother scream and then several loud pops. Heavy steps echoed through the house with crashes of doors being kicked in while the men in all black searched. Her own door splintered inward and she saw the black boots stop in front of her.

In an instant, she was blinded by a light and she felt something grab at her. Mirra scurried out the other side of her bed and ran out of her room around the invader. She passed several more dressed in black, dodging grabs and tackles as she ran through the kitchen to the front room.

There she stopped.

Her father sat motionless, streaks of red down the wall behind him. His eyes were frozen open as his limp head sagged. On top of him was her mother. Her face buried in his neck. The back of her blouse shredded with her blood soaking the fabric.

Mirra screamed as she ran to them and grabbed her mother, desperately shaking her to get her up. If she could only get her awake, they could all run. They could get away.

But her mother didn't move. She was pulled off by one of the men and carried out the front door. She thrashed against him as she saw flashes from the windows where her brothers' bedrooms were.

Over a month of that fleeting feeling that gnawed at her mind; that precious thing that she had lacked in her heart. In that instant, it all came rushing back. It was overwhelming, but it was exactly what she was looking for.

Her mother's smile, arguing with her brothers, her father looking up at the rowdy kits around the table, her baby sister. It was all back. She wrapped it up in her soul like a blanket and prayed that it would never go away. She wanted to keep it forever.

A shrill alarm from her wrist mounted PDA startled her. A chugging sound over the howling gale outside rose like an omen of doom. Mirra sank to the floor and stared at the crib. She heard them coming, but it didn't matter. She had been trying to find the answers for so long, and now she knew.

Looking up she saw flashlights outside the bedroom. The light mounted under the barrel of a gun like she had seen so many years ago blinded her. Mirra was pulled to her feet and felt a sharp pain on the back of her neck.

***

Mirra opened her eyes and was blinded by the white light all around her. She groaned as she tried to move her arms, but they were held down. After a few moments of adjusting to the brightness, she could get a look around her.

It was a room that lacked defining features other than a large mirror on the wall. She was strapped to a table in the middle of it. White and sterile, like everything behind the barrier.

A manual door on the wall toward her feet clicked and opened. Mirra raised her head as high as she could and saw a grizzled old tiger in a pristine robe. She hadn't seen anyone much older than her since she was brought inside the barrier.

"T-0135," he said as he looked down at her. "What an anomaly you turned out to be. Filing false reports, abandoning your work assignments, sedition."

"Where am I?"

"We call it the preserve. It's a collection of genetically diverse inhabitants of Earth. A controlled environment where we can try and undo all the damage done to our little rock." He stepped beside Mirra and looked down at her with a smile. "Your home."

"My home is gone."

"No, just all of the things that brought us to the brink. Greed, want, envy, lack of purpose, hate, anger, and the driving force behind all of it, family."

"That makes no sense. I felt nothing but love."

"You felt what you thought was love. It's a sinister thing. You would trade everything here to be with them again, wouldn't you?"

"I…" Mirra felt the tears return. "I don't know. I just know I want that. I want it for my child more than I want it for me."

"Before the cloud completely severed contact with the coordination center and the other preserves, there were reports of sabotage from the inside. Family members breaking environmental integrity to save those on the outside. Riots, disorder, chaos. That is what your family brought you. To save us all, we had to take a…different approach."

"You killed everyone I loved for this," Mirra said as her anguish wracked her. The memories of the black uniforms removing her from her home at the expense of her entire family.

"Yes." His tone never shifted. "We killed them. We had to. Don't you see, child? This may be the last chance any of us have. It's why reversing this disaster has taken so long. Do you think any of us planned on being in here for generations?"

She didn't have a response. She just knew what she was missing.

"Which is what brings us back to all this." The tiger shook his head but kept his smile. "The inseminated females have all shown some unforeseen abnormalities in behavior, but nothing as defiant as you." The tiger lifted a needle toward the light and pushed the plunger until the liquid was at the tip. "We are going to terminate the pregnancy."

"What? No!" Mirra thrashed against the restraints, but they held her fast. "You can't do that!" Mirra's shock faded into dread. It was more overwhelming than when she had tried to pull her mother back from the dead. "Please, you can't."

"Be still, child. You have many years of productivity ahead of you. And this will be for the best. Your genetic defect that makes you this way will not be introduced into the gene pool."

The needle stuck in her arm. She balled her fist and flexed her muscle. It was the only thing she could think to do to resist, but the surgical steel point pushed through to the vein unhindered.

"And ... all done."

"I will find you," Mirra hissed through clenched teeth.

"Child, by morning, you won't even remember you were in this room. Let alone my face."

The tiger left the same as he came. No more words, no more emotions. Just the hum of the lights and Mirra crying to herself on the table.

She looked at the mirror and scowled. Tears matting her fur. She looked like her mother, and she knew how her mother felt in those last moments of her life. Her consciousness began to slip away as—

Mirra shivered in the small room. She couldn't know how long she had been there. It had felt like years. The walls still had the gouges where she'd clawed them until only the bloody pads of her fingers remained. It had been long enough for them to regrow as she purged the drugs in her system.

All of the memories of before were there. Whatever was keeping her from them she had sweat, cried, and bled out. Her family was gone, and everything felt hopeless. Death seemed like the only release.

The door slid open and she backed into the corner of her cell. Mirra tucked her muzzle behind her knees and wrapped her tail around her feet. She was expecting the usual forced feeding, but instead, she was lifted up and a sharp pain jolted her.

When her eyes opened again, she was in a room strapped to a table. She saw other females there. Many more than she even knew existed in the confines of her forced sanctuary. Pristine uniforms moved around her; white robes, cleansuits, surgical masks.

They discussed things like insemination probabilities, dosages of medicines, gradual reintroduction to work assignments. Some of the words she didn't understand, but it was becoming clear that death would not be her release.

The next time she awoke, she was in her cell. She could feel her memories fading. Her breath quickened and she panicked. She didn't know why, but losing the memories terrified her. Mirra stood up and pounded on the door, screaming for someone to let her out. After she was exhausted, she collapsed on the floor.

"Mommy. I..." Her mother's face was almost gone. "I can't forget you. Not again."

Mirra dug her claw into her thigh as deep as she could and—

It had worked before. In the confusing clarity of the flashes, she had found a way to keep the memories coming back. Away from the glass, her right index finger had enough movement to reach her thigh. She pushed her claw into her flesh; carving a solitary word in small letters into herself.

LOVE

Best intentions, right? We all have a picture of that perfect world in our heads that would be a wonderful place if we could just stock it with perfect people. Learn to smile, learn to laugh, hide your pain from those watching because you won't be the one who ruins that perfect landscape. Bury your anxieties deep in something plush. Paradise is just a prison if your happiness is forced upon you. But don't you dare say that out loud. Better you keep low, and smile and keep your mask on. Don't ruin this for the rest of us. Don't you dare.

Losing Yourself

George Squares

Macie Owens needed some fresh air. The transport was too hot and she was getting dehydrated. She checked her pocket mirror to take a look. A graceful looking orange tabby cat with a dainty pink nose made from holographic light looked back at her with cool, disinterested eyes. "I'm sweating like I'm tucked into Satan's ass crack, Jonas."

The coyote driving the hovering yellow vehicle that was not-quite-a-Porsche let out an irritable sigh. "It's uncomfortable at first, but you'll get used to it, if you put in the effort. You have to grow accustomed."

"Well I need to disassociate for a hot second," said Macie. Jonas' luminous caramel-colored paw squeezed the steering wheel.

"If you keep disassociating, you'll get in the habit of it and your biorhythm will act up. You have to let the transition feel natural or else it will never *feel* natural."

"That's nice, Jonas." Macie stroked the side of her neck, feeling for pressure points in the order she had memorized. A soft popping noise went off, then a hiss, and Macie was free of her helmet. She took out her hand mirror again and the sweaty face of a human woman stared at her from under a bright purple balaclava. She peeled the covering off and let loose her matted, tousled hair which piled on itself. She hollered and whooped.

"That's *so* much better!"

Jonas let out a growl, unbecoming of his gentle accent, but very becoming of his coyote form. "It's not going to be better for long. I mean *really*, Macie. You're exchanging a few moment's gratuity for hours of hardship. These parties are supposed to immerse you into modern society. You're going to have to get used to it eventually, or nobody will be able to interact with you."

She rolled her eyes. "You say that like it's a bad thing."

"It is a bad thing! You have to learn how to be independent. The hospital can't keep holding your hand."

"Paw?" scoffed Macie.

"Paw," affirmed Jonas sternly. "If you don't like the tabby, you can try out one of the fifty other starters. I think vixen could suit you better."

"It's not the fucking animal that's the problem. I just don't want to spend the majority of my time in a glorified football mascot."

Jonas' costume pupils slit in that angry, predatory way to show that he was about to say something serious, but Macie was so used to it by now that the feature didn't even phase her. "Three centuries of peace and prosperity is nothing to balk at. *Especially,*" he hissed, "considering the era we woke *you* up from."

"Blame my parents. Personally, I would have pulled the cord on myself if it were up to me. You lose a hell of a lot in four hundred years." Macie cracked open a window, feeling the wind whip through her hair. The long, thin strips of magnetized road hovered in the air, winding around and over one another, parallel at some points, crisscrossing at others, and curving in ways she didn't think possible. The sky glittered with other transports traveling the sky road in the distance.

She saw animal people walking in the distance on floating buildings. One of the structures was similar to a park or a field, and she wondered how they had managed to make an organic looking structure float along. Then she noticed that some of the animal people were playing soccer, playing it well, even, and hadn't the faintest clue as to how they weren't dying from dehydration. They did seem to be moving slightly wrong, at the very least.

"You have dog traits out the ass and you go for the house cat," mumbled Jonas.

Macie furrowed her brow. "Will you stop? That's neurotic as hell. Most living things enjoy looking out of the window."

"Yeah, but it's cuter when a dog does it."

"Not to me," she said in a sing-song voice and exhaled hard. The rest of the ride went by in silence.

After about fifteen minutes they came to a pale blue skyscraper in the middle of the city. Jonas plucked a teal ticket stub from a machine and entered the parking terminal. "You need to put your face on, now."

It was weird to Macie that this didn't mean makeup anymore, but the phrasing of it still made her squint. After pulling back her hair, she pulled the purple balaclava over her face again, then put on the neon green helmet. She traced her personal code into her neck. Air puffed and she felt hot again. Jonas smiled, sticking out a bit of tongue.

"So far so good." They walked across the parking terminal to an exit and boarded an elevator. Jonas sighed crisply and improved his posture. "We're on the 42nd floor. You don't have to have the time of your life here. Just mingle with a few of the other patients or therapists and try not to embarrass me."

"You know, if this is purportedly such an innovative social mecca. you'd think there's a fail-safe for embarrassment."

Jonas shifted his weight. "You know, that's not a bad idea." Jonas pressed a button on his watch. It made a small beeping sound.

"What did you just do?"

"I put an otter-correct on you."

Macie's holographic tail twitched. "You bappy-pawed derp, you're meddling with my language?" Macie covered her mouth and she balled her hand into a fist of rage.

"It only meddles if it *needs* to meddle." Jonas wagged his holographic tail. "If you behave then you'll sound like yourself and you won't look like an idiot child."

"How do I turn this thing off?"

"It's tied to your suit, so you can't until you're out of my care." The elevator dinged. "After you, my dear."

Macie growled at him, but the sound coming out of her suit's mouth was more of a hiss. The holographic screens on the interior of her suit solved some of her peripheral vision issues, but it still felt disconnected from her true face.

The 42nd floor was a large ball room with a tall ceiling. The wooden floors were lacquered and stained different colors. Holographic fish swam across the ceiling, opening their cavernous mouths silently as their scales lit up in synch with the melody of the synthesized orchestra. Hundreds of patients that looked like normal animals mingled with less-than-normal animals. There were plush love seats and sofas against the walls at the end of the room, with white, delicate, transparent curtains for shade and faint privacy. A buffet table with candies and hors d'oeuvres sat near the wall with windows facing outdoors. Macie wasn't surprised to see that none of the patients were near it.

At the entrance of the room was a podium near a red belt fence, and Macie couldn't help but gawk at the security guard. He stared at her and Jonas as they entered and Macie stared right back. He looked to be at least eight feet tall, and he was… *mostly* a zebra. He had the arms and legs and tail of a crocodile, and leathery bat-like wings that hung to his sides. They seemed stiff, so they probably weren't functional. But most distracting were his muscles. He had so many sinews that his body reminded her of a lobster, but probably not as delicious. She looked back and forth from him to Jonas in disbelief. Jonas was ignoring her, and apparently, the security guard was too.

The Zebra-crocodile-thing slackened its faux jaws and whinnied. "This is a scheduled immersion party for the patients of St. Barb. If you're a medical professional I'm going to need to see your id, name, and papers."

While Jonas rifled with his things, Macie couldn't help but flank this monstrosity's side. From a different angle, she could see that his mane had frosted tips. As he rumbled something unimportant to Jonas, his biceps jiggled in an unnatural way. Was it real? She had to know. Nothing could be that buff. Without another word, she took a decisive step toward the guard and grabbed at his bicep. It sunk under her cat paws, and she let out a cry.

"*Foam!*" she gasped. Jonas looked at her and his eyes became slits again. The guard turned to her and looked at her, unperturbed, sighing.

"Yes ma'am, there will be plenty of beer and champagne at the bar to imbibe at your leisure. You're all set to enter."

Jonas grabbed her wrist and pulled her into the party, walking briskly away as he whispered into her ear. "Your luck isn't going to last. Stop being an idiot."

"He looked like a tattoo that people get when they're in high school."

"You'll be able to customize your appearance like that when you're earning an income."

"A tattoo that people regret."

"You won't get far in life if you loudly judge people's mods like that. You're seeing their truest selves."

"No I'm not I'm seeing their flavorful power fantasies." Macie stopped abruptly and her ears twitched. "Flavorful? *Flavorful?* I can't say *Flavor?!*" She stomped her foot. "Turn this autocorrect off or I'll make a real scene."

Jonas tsked. "Otter-correct."

"I swear to flavorful god."

"Fine," Jonas sighed, touching his watch.

"Thank fuck," Macie said and then somebody with a bespectacled lion mod looked at her harshly.

Jonas shook his head. "I have some people to meet. Just stay on your best behavior, and whatever you do, *don't* disassociate."

"But what if I get hungry? Thirsty?" Jonas was already lost in the crowd and Macie cursed under her breath. She motorboated with her lips but it just made a purring sound. She took a look around her.

***

The most comfortable space seemed to be a love seat near a wall fountain that let off a cool, refreshing mist. She was close enough to a crowd to hear them but not close enough to interact, which was how she preferred it. A white-furred feminine looking creature that didn't look entirely mammalian or reptilian stood in the semicircle of the crowd.

"I supposed it's flattering to be mistaken for one of the staff!" she giggled in a high, distracting timbre that Macie suspected wasn't her natural voice.

"But of course, they would mistake you for staff," said an otter who gasped audibly. "Your fur is so plush and your design is so unique. I feel beautiful just being around you."

"There's always beauty in the world... for those who are wise enough to seek it," said the white beast, fluttering its massive eyelids in a way that made Macie flinch.

"It's good to find friends. Who would have thought an otter like me would meet a water dragon like you."

The crowd fell silent and the feminine suit tilted its disproportional head.

"It's a common mistake to consider a Sylphgoyle a dragon, but we are not creatures of greed. We are a protective and nurturing presence, sprung from a rich tradition of neogothic, Christian, and pagan belief practices that have evolved over time, expressed in local indigenous European festivals. The Sylphgoyle is a creature to be admired but it is also a guise to be treated gingerly with respect."

Macie felt like one of her eyebrows was rising so high that it was going to launch off of her face and make it into orbit but the otter was undeniably shaken.

"I am so, SO sorry, Cerulea. I…I didn't mean to make such a callous mistake! You're just *so* great and I'm just not!"

"Aww! Don't be sad. You'll find your place."

"Oh thank you Cerulea! You're so good. Just… you're so good."

The otter was touching her face as if to wipe tears from her eyes but her hands couldn't go through her suit, so Macie thought it just looked like she was batting herself in the face.

"You don't need to thank a Sylphgoyle for being good to people. It is our way," she said, reaching out to embrace the otter.

"I l-love my f-frriends!" sobbed the otter through the hug. The sylphgoyle gave the otter a pat on the back and then quickly let go, moving into Macie's proximity, staring at her with huge purple, spherical eyes that sparkled with a glittery effect.

"Greetin's to you, beastie! What could I call you?" she jumped up and down. Macie could hear sleigh bells coming from somewhere within the Sylphgoyle's body. As distracting as Cerulea was, Macie couldn't help noticing what was going on across the room. Plates were being stacked on the buffet table without anybody touching them. They weren't stacked perfectly, so it didn't look like it was automated by technology. It legitimately looked like an invisible person was laying out dishes on the table.

Macie opened her mouth and nodded slowly. "At the moment I think… overwhelmed for what I am right now."

"Oh!" Cerulea giggled. "You must'a been dormant for a looooooooong time! Which era are you from?"

The first thing Jonas had told her was not to talk about the wars.

Just mention the era. Minimalism is best appreciated in these kinds of introductions. "From the irongate era."

Cerulea clasped her hands to her face and stood straight, stomping with alternating feet to create another chorus of jingling bells. It was only then that Macie realized five people in suits on each side were watching them interact, almost nervously.

"I can feel you are an old soul," said Cerulea.

"Thank you."

"You have come from a terrible time in the past to seek solace here."

Macie nodded slowly. "Seeking solace sounds like me."

Cerulea wiggled her thighs and shook her wrists. "I know how it feels to be out of your era. The first time I slept for a hundred years. I woke to a world that didn't feel me. So I slept for fifty more years. My model is older than a human's natural life span."

If Macie heard correctly, and she hoped she hadn't, this person had spent one hundred and fifty years of medical technology asleep for character credibility, which meant she was both very impractical and very wealthy. Macie had seen her own bills. She knew the cost.

"I was shot through the neck. They didn't have the biotechnology to fix me then so I had to wait it out."

"Oh," said Cerulea, slumping a little.

"Yeah."

Cerulea perked up again. "Well! It was nice to meet you!"

Macie couldn't really call it a meeting considering she didn't even give the woman in the costume her name, but she was too preoccupied with the floating dishes to respond. By the time she had crossed the lobby, they had stopped moving, and there wasn't any sort of discernible tech on them that she could detect.

Along the wall, there were screens flashing the words *headless* where she would be allowed to disassociate in the accepted manner. She moved to the designated area and then pressed the correct sequence on her neck to release her mask and took a deep breath when fresh air filled her longs and blew over her face. Staring outside, she spied on the plates again to see if they were moving by themselves again. They weren't. But somebody who she hadn't seen before was moving them.

She was an elderly woman who *wasn't wearing a mask*. She had mauve scrubs and wore a bandana that covered her head. Just to make sure… Macie put on her head again. The woman vanished in front of her eyes. Then she took the helmet back off, disassociating again, and she could see her there, still stacking fresh dishes.

After about ten minutes of staring, Macie saw the old woman turn a lobby corner, this time carting floor cleaning supplies taken from a side closet in the lobby, and she had to follow. She put on her helmet, moving across the lobby as quickly as she could so she wouldn't lose the old woman. The hallways quickly transitioned into narrow, industrial corridors with low lighting and sliding doors that unlocked with pneumatic puffs. She could hear her feet clang against the metal floor. Macie took a deep breath and let herself disassociate one more time.

The mask popped off her head with a soft puff of air and she rolled the purple balaclava off of her face. It clung to her own sweat. Her curls were an unruly mess at this point, so she had to shake herself.

"Macie. I don't see you at the party," said Jonas' voice coming from her wrist receptor. She cursed and turned the volume all the way down, but it was too late. One of the doors opened and the head of the old woman popped out, looking back to her.

"You might want to listen to what your watch is saying," she said with a chirpy voice. "Also? Probably you should put the kitty face back on? If you want to clean, by all means, I'll be happy with the help. They *will* think you were made for cleaning. Honest."

Macie startled. "Wait, is this a prank? I have to wear a kitty suit not to be mistaken for a servant?"

"Day job is the preferred phrasing, yes?" The woman shook her head and made a motion with her hand to follow through the door. Macie took a look behind her and passed through a netting of colored beads. The crowded apartment had red carpet and wooden walls. It smelled like a mixture of medicine and industrial cleaner. Macie waved her hand by her face, hoping to wave away some of the fumes assaulting her senses.

The old woman pushed her cart into a side closet and then hobbled into the sitting room, squatting onto a couch and wringing her hands as she stared into a heater. "You looked more out of place at the celebration than me, meow meow girl." She pressed a few buttons on the cylinder column in front of her and it made a whirring noise. It dispensed two Styrofoam cups of strong smelling tea and she offered Macie one with the jerk of her head.

"Well, you know… I'm just learning to find my place."

"Your place doesn't exist anymore," said the old woman.

Macie blinked. "Excuse me?"

"I'm not trying to insult you. I can just sense that you were just from a different time. Most of the people who end up here are. There were really terrible wars back then." She sipped some tea and nodded. "Adjustment is hard. Sometimes too hard."

Macie sipped her tea. It was bitter, but she liked it that way. "I keep hearing that. So… what's your name."

"Jaaaaanice," the old woman lilted. "And you're Macie by the sound coming from your wrist receptor earlier. I can't hear so well anymore but I try to listen. But listeners don't have to hear to find listeners. All we have to see are their eyes' expressions. The kinship in the reaction. There's no easier book to read than an expressive face that shows a little too much."

Macie sighed. "Yeah. I suppose that's my whole problem then, isn't it? I want people to see me. I mean, *me, not—*"

"Meow meow," said the old woman. She was holding back a cackle. "You're a little shit, aren't you?"

Janice let out a rattling laugh. "I know another bitch when I see one."

Macie spat out her tea and snorted. Then she collected herself. "Yeah. I guess that's kind of a bad thing isn't it? The world doesn't like bitches very much. Or… maybe that's a good thing? I'm so confused."

Janice waved her hand "This world is fine with bitches. It just wants literal bitches with a pretty face and a styled conceit. It is… the dearth of sincerity I should say? Lacking that is a good thing in this era, if you can make it feel comfortable. If you wear your meow meow suit correctly and are cruel in palatable ways then you'll go far. And if you don't, well…" she gestured to herself.

"You bring up a good point. I mean… I was told I had to associate in a world like this. You aren't wearing a suit. I don't get that. Where is your meow meow?"

The old woman sighed. "Your family has, or had, lots of money, didn't it?"

"We weren't *rich* but we weren't, well… we were comfortable."

"If you made it this far after this long, they were rich, and it is why you have a suit. They're simplified status markers."

"That's not what I was told," said Macie. "We're supposed to wear them to, well... *transcend the uglier parts of being human,* or something."

Janice let out a shriek of laughter. "If there's one constant I've known in all my time on this earth, it's that people are always gonna be ugly idiot assholes about *something.* Ugliness is part of the human condition. It never looks pretty. Best to make peace with it than to pretend it's not there. I have wrinkles, and white hair, and my feet swell up. My calluses only get bigger. I can't stand straight anymore, and I sure as hell have no idea how to kiss ass. I'm pretty ugly most of the time, but I can see myself every day in the mirror and know that I'm looking at me, and that's enough to give me peace. Meow meow or no." The old woman tapped the side of her face. "Put the mask back on."

"But I thought you just gave this whole inspirational speech on why I shouldn't?"

"You need to understand. Put it on."

She sighed. It took a while for her to rummage through her huge pockets to retrieve the balaclava, rolled the lavender cloth down her face and reattached the helmet. But when she did, the woman was gone. All she could make out was the barest indentation of the couch.

Getting the mask off as quickly as she could again, she exhaled sharply when the woman appeared again.

"Oh yeah. It was like that out on the floor, too. You're invisible when I don't wear the mask."

Janice crossed her arms. "And why is that, ya think?"

"I don't know. It seems incredibly dangerous to me."

"Well hey. I don't like to be seen anyway. I'm a private person with private pleasures, all of which exclude people."

Macie cocked an eyebrow. "Such as?"

The woman leaned close and her volume dropped to a whisper. "Entire pizza. No sharing."

Macie let out a soft gasp. "I want this."

"You have money. You can also have this."

"Well, I won't if I can't wear this stupid cat costume all of the time. I doubt my parents left me enough to be jobless forever once I'm out of medical care."

"Then don't wear the cat suit."

Macie rolled her eyes. "As much as I hate it, I have to interact with this crazy society. I don't think I'd be cut out for being a maid or a hermit."

"I mean, don't be a cat. Perhaps something else."

Macie held her head and tapped her own cheek with her index finger. "Perhaps. You aren't the first one who suggested that. I don't hate the cat it's just… well, I feel like I can't ever take this very seriously. Could you?"

"Oh hell no. That's why *I'm* a nobody. But I *would* take it seriously long enough to get a new kidney. My last one is failing."

Macie looked at her with disbelief. "Shit, I never learned about the state of medical care in the era."

"Organs are cheap. We grow them now."

"Then what's the problem?"

The old woman leaned forward and gave Macie a hard stare. "You can't die if you don't exist. I am *help*, not a person of interest. And I couldn't afford to be a personality even if I stopped buying pizza for twenty years. I don't *have* twenty years left in me."

Macie was liking this era less and less. "That's some horrific bullshit. Would you be able to borrow my suit for something like that? I'm young. Look at the meat on my thighs."

The old woman pursed her lips. "No."

Macie held out her free hand and jerked her head. "I guess you're right. It's probably stupid to think that the suit is the only check they have. They'd probably know it wasn't actually me."

The old woman shook her head. "On the contrary… that suit is you now. There aren't other checks. If you give it to me, I would be stealing *you*. It's like what you might have called your social security card. You don't get a new one, and they could care less if the pilot is different. If it seems like madness then we're in agreement. The world needs more people like you, and to be frank, probably fewer like me."

Macie couldn't believe what she was hearing. "Look. I'm not saying I don't expect the damn thing back after all this is over and done, but if you are *going to die* if you don't take the suit and be me for a while, I don't mind at all. Hell, it feels like I'm living on borrowed time anyway. Most people who had been in my prior circumstances would be dead. I want to pay that good luck forward."

She shrugged "You'll understand the value of an identity someday."

Macie slapped her hand on the chair. "Can you stop speaking in riddles for a hot second you crazy cleaning lady?! You're not Yoda! You need a kidney!"

She shook her head stubbornly and then sipped her tea. Macie sucked her teeth with irritability.

"Listen. What could possibly convince you to wear this suit so I could get you the medical treatment that you need?"

The woman tapped her face. "Convince me meow meow is not you so that I don't feel guilty."

Macie squinted. She took the balaclava off again. "Okay. As you can see, I am not a neon orange cat."

"I still see you as the cat, even without the mask."

"How?!"

She spoke slow this time as if Macie wasn't getting it. "Because it is *your character*."

"This is *so* dumb... but I'm gonna be back at some point. I know somebody is looking for me and I don't want to make them too angry. Goodbye!" Macie sat up from the chair, grabbed her helmet and her balaclava and left without another word.

***

When she entered the narrow hall way she saw a blue glow come from her left.

"Finally found you," growled Jonas, grabbing her by the wrist. Macie looked the coyote over. He was in predator mode. His eyes were slit, his holographic fur was on edge, and everything about him conveyed a sense of ferocity. But he still couldn't change the fact that he was significantly shorter than her.

"We need to talk," said Macie.

"Yes. We do. After the party."

"No. Right now."

Jonas whirled around and the holographic hairs on his face bristled. "We can talk in private but it's going to be the last talk that we ever have. Do you want to do that before or after our review? Your choice."

"Before."

"Fine. Put on your mask so I can see *the real you* properly!" She so did begrudgingly. They picked out the nearest sliding door that they could find. It was a cramped and empty storage room. There were trunks full of rags, empty barrels, wires, and a collection of dust in the corner. The room was probably an overflow closet for the sanitation workers. Jonas was transparently disgusted by the grime.

"All you had to do was wear the damn costume and socialize." His voice rose. Macie let out a snort of victory after hearing him admit that he didn't buy into all of the identity construction as he led on, but he kept talking. "It was all you had to do, and you couldn't even be bothered to do that." Jonas' voice didn't feel like a chiding authoritarian's anymore. It felt like the tone of a Judge about to pass a sentence, or the cold, disaffected voice of a parent about to leave their child in the woods for the winter.

"I told you from the start that I didn't care about making an impression at the damn party. The first person I met worth talking to wasn't wearing a costume."

Jonas' mask took on a friendly smile and his tail wagged. "So maybe this night wasn't a total waste after all. What was her name?"

"Janice. She's realistic and funny and I felt comfortable for the first time all night."

Jonas fiddled with his wrist receptor and punched some information into a holographic panel.

"What are you doing?"

"Just filed a termination complaint. We can't have these kinds of interruptions."

Macie's eyes widened. "Oh fuck *you* you son of a bitch! I sought her out! What harm did she do? There's no reason to fire her over that!"

Jonas looked incredulous. "You spoke to the *help!* You're not even supposed to see them… much less… much less interact with them! If she managed to be seen then she wasn't doing her job well enough… not to mention getting sociable with a patient. It's unbelievable, really! Utterly inappropriate!"

Macie shoved him on the shoulder. "She was the first person worth talking to all night. Why didn't *you* tell me that the suits make regular people invisible?"

"Because if you're not considered a functioning person in society then you *aren't* a regular person! You have to bring something to the table or else you're dead weight."

"How on earth did you manage to make it as a psychiatrist? You're a fucking sociopath, you know that. Cleaning Is hard work!"

"We have the technology to clean our own facilities now. We don't *need* hired staff. What makes you think that we've stayed stagnant on sanitation technology for the hundreds of years you've been asleep? No, society does those non-entities a *favor* by giving them something to do! Because the sad fact is... these nobodies underperformed. They wasted all of the opportunity and the chances that they had to be interesting, enlightened individuals. They're leeches holding back a better world that takes responsibility for its own actions and its own unlimited chance for success."

Macie was shouting herself at this point. "Did you know that she's got a bad kidney and she can't get an operation because she's not waddling around in one of these mascot suits?"

"Maybe she should have thought about being more honorable in the eyes of society before her body inevitably broke down, just like it's going to break down for the rest of us." Jonas' hands were clenching into twisted claws. "What do you think society is? A vending machine that doesn't take any credits? You have to do *it* a solid... before it will do *you* a solid. That's what currency *is* now! And it's something your parents seemed to get, at least. I don't know what went wrong with you!"

"My parents would be laughing their asses off at this. You think suffering doesn't exist anymore because you literally choose not to see it. You're pretending misfortune is a choice made entirely through intentional decisions! That's just so basically, fundamentally wrong"

"And yet all of the numbers agree with me. We have the lowest rates of violence, anger, disease and strife for over five hundred years and innovation continues to boom."

A realization dawned upon Macie. "Do those numbers only reflect citizens with a suit?"

The coyote looked at her as if she had asked a stupid question. "Why wouldn't they?"

"HOW DID YOU BECOME A PSYCHIATRIST?" Macie boomed.

The door behind them opened and then it shortly closed. Nobody was there. Macie cleared her voice. "I'll tell you what. I'll put on my mask and behave for the rest of the night. We'll get through this panel, and I'll find somebody else for my care. We'll go by the book. After we're done with this, we will part ways, and we will never bother one another again. I will find another care worker if there's more administrative work to be done."

The coyote's holographic eyebrows raised and his tail wagged slightly. "You have no idea how happy that would have made me if you would have just proposed that from the start."

"I have one condition though."

"Name it." Macie disassociated, pulling off her own mask and the balaclava.

"Take off your coyote mask. I want to see your real expression when you tell me that you legitimately believe that all lives are equal in this society. I just want the unfiltered reading."

"You want me to disassociate?"

"I want proof that you're human, yes."

Jonas scoffed and reached to the back of his neck, putting in a code that Macie made sure to watch carefully. A soft puff of air escaped. The projected image of the coyote disappeared, leaving just a foamy, white head with no discernable shapes aside from a vague, conical muzzle that was completely smooth. When he pulled off the helmet, Macie saw dark, lovely brown eyes, agitated from behind the slit in his black balaclava. The cloth was pulled off, revealing a young, chiseled face and soft brown hair. He looked younger than herself. The nostrils of his hooked nose flared at he stared her down, human looking at human, and he said two things consecutively: the first thing was *the protection of society is a privilege, not a right,* and the second thing was *who are you?*

***

A few days after the party, Macy's interview came and went. Jonas let Macie into the transport as they left the Administration of Integration building. They were both excited that she managed to turn things around quickly enough to get a pass from her panel. She had proven herself to be quite the socialite through the second half of the party through the video evidence that the suit had recorded, and purportedly made for a decent cat according to the inquisitors.

Jonas wagged his tail as they pulled out of the parking terminal and synchronized with the magnetic field of the glimmering sky road. "I just wanted to thank you for coming through in the end. I had doubts about it all, after everything you had said."

"I'm getting used to the helmet," said Macie. "I mean the mask."

"They say it takes a while," said Jonas. He put the vehicle on autopilot and looked out the window, admiring the stars and the twinkling neon panels of the highway. The floating buildings below them that shimmered like an arcade in the distance. He let his tongue hang out like he was a real dog, wondering if he felt any cuter trying this out. Then he had to wonder something out loud.

"Do you think they'll find him?"

Macie shrugged. "They might find somebody if he yells loud enough. We gagged him good. He's going to need some help to get those wires off. He might starve before they find him."

Jonas laughed. "I don't think he expected the punch to the stomach. It was like he had never been punched before."

"He probably hasn't been punched before," said Macie. "Violence isn't a light trespass here."

"I'm just surprised nobody was expecting that from me."

"That surprise is the only thing that made me agree to this," said Macie. "Very chaotic. Very tricky. Very coyote. I could never see you as a cat again from that moment. Taking the suit didn't feel like stealing to me at that point."

"You didn't steal a thing," said Jonas. "I definitely did though. I don't think he'd ever like to admit it but Jonas suits me better than him."

"You'd think he'd be craftier being a coyote. It was so disappointing! I would have never fallen for taking the mask off."

Jonas yapped at the stars and the moon as they passed by floating buildings, glowing street tracks and starlight. "His loss I suppose. Now let's get you signed up for that kidney operation."

Contrary to what the anarchists howl, none of what came to be was inevitable. The ruin of all we knew had help from those who were only out to help themselves. What's that, you ask? Wouldn't the ivory-towered elite know better? Wouldn't they lead us forward?

No matter how powerful those who run the world ever become, they ultimately fall to the same apathy as the rest of us who toil below, the same truth that robs societies of the will to fight the on-rush of decay; ignorance, my dear constituent, is bliss.

THE MELTING POT HAS FROZEN OVER

T.D. Coltraine

The rabbit sat in a pair of blue jeans and not a damn thing else, nursing a cheap-as-hell beer as he cruised with complete detachment through what passed for his morning. Daytime television on his cheap-as-hell TV filled the air and tried to drown out the noise of people from the street. It was the kind of summer day where you sat and stared at the sky in a silent prayer that some higher power would turn the oven down. They never did. Hot time, summer in the city. That's how the song went, and that's how the days usually went. The nights weren't better, but at least they were quiet and a little cooler.

Finally fed up with the idea of another hour of housewives arguing over who slept with who, he got to his feet and went to the window. It was gloomy as a graveyard out there. Even in the middle of the day the sunlight didn't make it far past the clouds, leaving the maze of alleys coated in shadow and garbage-flavored air. The heat just made it worse. With the windows closed, the dump was a sauna with a couple of fans pretending to cool it off. Opening them let the smell in along with all the noise from the other tenements.

The rabbit smiled a little bit behind his bottle as he noticed the skunk across the street changing into her lingerie. She paused and turned to look back at him with a little smile of her own. They knew each other; of course they knew each other. In The Eye, your nearest neighbor was in kissing distance, whether you wanted them be to or not. Maybe things wouldn't be quite so bad, he thought to himself, until a knock at the door brought him back to the real world. He ignored it; no one ever knocked except salesmen and people hoping to break in. But whoever it was didn't go away. One knock, then another, perfectly paced to ruin his admiration of the female form.

"Hold yer horses, I'm comin'!" The rabbit pivoted angrily on one heel and went to the door. Just like always, he took a glance through the peephole first. "What the..." He rubbed at his eyes and shook his head. The beer must have been hitting him harder than usual. That couldn't be what he saw.

"Mr. Nicolades? Are you still there, sir?" a feminine voice with an accent he couldn't place asked through the door. "Oh, I hope he's not going to be angry..." Rue flicked his ear and checked the peephole again, but no, there she was as real as the tacky wallpaper behind her—a human being, a tall one, raven-haired and draped in something that might have passed for a pantsuit in a crappy space movie, flowing and most definitely flattering. She tapped a plastic pencil against a box in her hands as she waited patiently for Rue to respond.

Rue popped the locks with more hustle than he'd ever given anyone from Amway before slipping the door open slowly. "Ah, hello! I'm Diana Mondeline..." The human paused in mid-phrase as her conversational partner leaned out in the hallway, leaning each way and scanning the ceiling with his entire attention and completely ignoring her. She quirked one eyebrow and crossed her arms. "Sir? Is there something amiss?"

"Makin' sure I ain't on one a'them camera shows." The rabbit chuffed and turned to finally make eye contact. "Whaddya want?" His tone was pure annoyance. "An' how do ya know my name?"

To her credit, having an angry and at least slightly drunk factory worker staring at her with narrowed eyes didn't even break Diana's mental stride. "All of my constituents are documented, Mr. Nicolades." She tapped her plastic pencil against her plastic gizmo with a practiced smile. "The most up-to-date census data possible is always available at a glance via the global network. Your tax dollars at work." She extended an immaculately manicured hand, her smile bursting into a gleaming array full of perfectly white teeth. "Diana Mondeline, your district representative. It is a pleasure to meet you." Rue couldn't ignore the small army of bangles and bracelets that covered her arm from elbow to wrist and even higher. She could probably buy the whole city a couple times over with all that. The woman tinkled like wind chimes when she moved.

Rue stared at her. Diana stared back, her hand lingering in empty space but her smile never fading. This went on for minutes, long ones, mostly empty ones except for the sound of Rue's TV in the short distance.

"Ah. Well. You were chosen at random as my first survey subject in the Independence District, and we've much to discuss." Diana drew her hand back and nodded. "Perhaps I could come inside?"

Eventually the rabbit shrugged and turned to go back in. "It's a free world."

Rue let Diana pass by him, closing the door behind him and cranking a half-dozen knobs and levers to lock it again. "If you don't mind my asking, Mr. Nicolades." She tucked her tablet into a satchel and glanced about the room. There was little to see—Rue had his TV, he had his bed, he had his hotplate and his toaster oven and his rickety fridge that made too much noise at night, and he had his couch with the weird stain that a couple of friends had scavenged off the alleys before septic detail got there. He shared a toilet and shower with six or seven other people. You could catch the whole tour in half a turn of your head. "Did I do something wrong?"

"I'd say a lot of somethings, Miz Mondeline." He strode past the confused woman to the window, pulling the blinds shut with a quiet sigh as the lovely display across the alley vanished behind a thin plastic sheet. "The hell are you doin' here, by yerself, lookin' like that?"

"Whatever are you going on about, Mr. Nicolades?" Diana's high-heeled shoes tick-tacked against the cheap flooring on her way to the couch, sitting down with her legs crossed at the knees. "I don't understand what's so alarming."

Rue leaned against the wall and rubbed two fingers between his eyes. "Yeah, yer nuts, whoever you are." He swept his hand through the apartment. "Do you even know where you are?"

Diana nodded, and her smile came back in full force. "Of course I do. I'm in your apartment." She paused for a moment in thought. "I suppose you mean more broadly than that. This is Independence District." She chuckled lightly and tucked her hands in her lap. "I do pay attention to my constituents, Mr. Nicolades." Her gaze turned towards the way she came in. "I admit it's not quite what I expected.

The local color is, ah, bolder than I had been told." Diana's blue eyes met Rue's. "It was difficult to land my transport. No landing pads to be found!"

"You tellin' me you flew to The Eye, lady?"

"The Eye? Oh, you mean Independence! Of course I did. How else does one get around?"

"We got feet." The rabbit tipped his beer bottle forward and pointed at her bag. "Wuzzat thing?"

Diana patted her satchel. "My tablet." She tilted her head in curiosity. "Don't you have one as well? Everyone should have been provided one."

Rue shrugged. "I got a couple of legal pads but I don't write much."

Diana laughed. "Oh, Mr. Nicolades, you are so droll! I mean my personal digital assistant."

"Lady, you're speakin' jibberjabber." He shook his head, hands in front of him. "Forget about the pad thing. Who the hell *are* you?"

"I told you, Mr. Nicolades. I'm Diana Mondeline, your representative."

"Representative of what?"

Diana blinked. Her confusion was almost audible as even her extensively prepared script didn't have anything to help her here. "Of *you*, Mr. Nicolades, and the rest of your sub-district." The rabbit rolled his hand in a circle, the international 'go on' gesture. "In the central government?" She put thin fingers to her chin. "Do you mean to tell me that you don't know who I am?"

"Been tryin' t'tell you that, Miz Mondeline. Yer just a crazy woman who's aimin' t'get herself killed."

"You keep saying that, Mr. Nicolades—"

"No one who ain't tryin' to sell me something calls me 'Mister Nicolades.'" Rue went to his fridge, digging around in the miscellaneous edibles for anything appealing to drink. "Makes me sound like some wrinkled up retiree hangin' out in Palm Beach, sippin' mimosas and playin' shuffleboard."

"Of course, of course! Anything to make my constituents more comfortable. What would you prefer? My records say your first name is…?" Diana flicked her eyes upwards from her tablet with one eyebrow raised. "Cletus?"

"Fer the love of all that's holy, lady, call me Rue." He looked genuinely embarrassed at someone using his given name, hiding behind a tiny screen of brown glass. "Never have forgiven my parents for that."

Diana did her best to hide a chuckle behind her tablet. "I see. Rue it is." She put the gizmo away again, taking the drink from Rue and looking at it oddly before setting it aside. "Now what, pray tell, is the problem with my attire?" She smoothed out the fabric on her thighs. "It's the common fashion where I live."

Rue pulled a well-worn folding chair from a dusty corner, spun it around backwards, and sat himself down. "Well it sure ain't here. Yer bait on heels, like a neon sign what says 'I've got lots of money!'. Every mugger, pickpocket, and rapist in The Eye has yer cleavage filed away."

"Oh come now, Mister—Rue, I think you're exaggerating. There's virtually no crime in Independence District." Diana self-consciously adjusted her clothes though, as if the idea of being a little excessive had just struck her. "Even if there were, I have a small security detail watching my every move from afar. If I were to as much as cough suspiciously, I could be whisked away in a moment to safety." The woman smiled yet again and turned to her data. "So let us discuss the most pressing issues of the day…"

Rue was out of energy to be surprised. All he could do was sit in awed silence and listen to this woman in her pastels, high heels, and hourglass figure talk about The Eye liked she lived in another reality all her own. She prattled on about statistics he didn't care about, programs he didn't know about, and people he'd never heard of. It was minute after minute of a ritualistically practiced presentation that had less to do with him than the latest in frilly panties from that boutique down the street. Finally he'd had enough and turned on the television.

It took Diana a good full minute to notice the other voice in the room and a little longer to realize Rue wasn't paying attention to her. "Rue? Sir? This is very important, and I would appreciate—"

"Shh. Divorce Court's on."

Diana set her pad down on her lap, pushing a lock of hair behind her ear just for something to do with her hands. "Doesn't this interest you? Don't you care about the issues in your District, Rue? These matters affect everyone and voting is coming up very soon."

Rue stood up and went to the fridge, pulling out a can of soda he had lying around for occasions when someone didn't want to be drunk. "Lady, I dunno where you think you are, but you probably wanna check your fancy data whatchahoosit. We don't have no 'representative' and I ain't voted on anything in my life. Neither did my daddy, or his daddy. Only thing coming up pretty soon is another paycheck an' the news."

"But, the records—the policy—the *law*—" Diana finally ran out of steam. Her monologue dropped off like the last gasp of a worn out motor, and Rue could feel the energy drain out of her before she took the cola out of his hand. "May I be frank, Rue?"

"I've been waitin' for that."

The plastic pencil-thing tapped away at Diana's tablet. "I'm completely confused. Everything in my research is wrong." She tossed the tablet on the couch next to her and glared it at like a pet who'd just crapped on the rug. "It should be safe. It should be *clean*. There should be hotels and parks and taxis and—" Her face fell. "It's not here. None of it's here. This place is a *dump*."

"Hey lady, watch what yer callin' a dump. People live here." Rue watched her fumble for the third time with the soda can before reaching over and yanking the pull tab off himself. "I dunno who yer travel agent is, but they gypped you pretty good. None of you types come down here on purpose."

Diana stared at the can as it fizzed and popped through the teardrop slit. "It was my idea. I thought it would benefit everyone if I came to Independence District personally and spoke directly with the citizens. It's something that hasn't happened in far too long." She looked towards the window. "My intention is to visit a few of my constituents over the course of a few months to better get to know them and their home, and they can better understand their government."

Rue turned his chair back and sat with his arms crossed on the top. "Why start now? We ain't never had one before." He worked his fingers into the base of one tall ear, scratching at a sore spot. "You guys sit up in DC an' ya do yer own thing. We don't vote, we don't talk to no one. Just stuff that happens."

"But there's polling data and election results!" She picked up her tablet again and pointed at a page of numbers, dozens of them, in tightly packed rows almost too dense to read. "This is from just last month. The residents approved a six percent tax on luxury items to fund air quality improvements."

The rabbit laughed and laughed hard. "'Air quality improvements'? Yer pullin' my leg. That ain't a thing."

"Didn't anyone get suspicious when prices went up?"

"Why would they?" Rue tossed his empty bottle into the trash with a flick of the wrist. "It happens all the time. We just get on with our lives. Ain't no one got time to worry 'bout it." He watched the human closely. She didn't have a clue what was going on; the professional façade she'd showed up with was cracked. The sweat was pouring off her forehead and soaking her dress. For the first time since she'd shown up, she was speechless.

"Lady. Hey. Diana." The rabbit cracked a smile in some kind of attempt to be reassuring. "What're you gonna do?"

Diana blinked a few times. "Ah, I had an itinerary but, well..." She sighed. "It's ruined. I should just call my security detail and leave with my tail tucked between my legs. I'm sure I'll never hear the end of it..."

Rue shook his head dismissively and stood up, digging in a drawer for one of his countless well-worn t-shirts. "Y'know what I hear when you talk, missy?" He didn't let her answer. "I hear somethin' I ain't heard in a long time, since I was a kid."

"What's that?"

"Someone who ain't ground down by the system yet. Honest hope." He prodded at Diana's tablet. "I wanna see what yer capable of. Why don'tcha do what you were gonna do? Yer here, I'm here." He flicked an eartip. "An' yer security guys are here too."

Diana startled, glancing towards the door. "You can hear them?"

"These ears ain't just for show, miss. So what was the plan?"

"Ah," she tapped through page after page of whatever and who cares, scanning for something. "My intention was to see the everyday life of a citizen in Independence Sector—their comings and goings, their job and their leisure time." Rue could hear the fake sound of paper being shuffled. It annoyed the hell out of him. "Another time would be seeing the family environment, and perhaps talking with law enforcement about—"

Rue cut her off with a swing of his hand. "Don't care. You wanna see my usual day? Sure. Fine. I can do that. Take you down t'the factory an' let you watch."

Diana practically exploded with delight, clapping her hands together like Rue'd just moved Christmas to right now. "Would you really? Would that be okay with your superiors? I mean I'm not dressed for a factory but I suppose I could stay out of the way and not be a bother and just watch and—" She went on a mile a minute even while Rue did his best to shut her back up so he could say something.

"Hey! *Hey!* Relax! It'll be fine, I'll getcha in, ain't no one gonna raise a stink."

Diana nodded then sat back down. "Shall we depart then?"

"Uh." Rue flicked his eyes to one side. "Well, see, 'bout that."

A perfectly coifed head tilted to one side, hair flopping gently over bare shoulders. "What of it?"

"I don't go on shift for another five hours. Hope you like sitcoms…"

***

"Oh this is quite exciting," Diana murmured, hands in her lap as the subway banged its way along the pitch black track. Her excitement poured out of her skin and pooled on the floor, and much to Rue's frustration she refused to shut up. "It's so very different from riding a transport around. Do you do this every night?"

"Twice on Sundays," Rue grumbled through his teeth, looking side to side at the other locals sharing the car. He wasn't a celebrity for a reason. Having the dozen or so other riders in the car shooting him the stinkeye made him want to crawl into his hoodie and disappear for a while. Diana's security detail standing pretending to be average, ordinary people and failing at every step of the process didn't make things any better. Rue could smell the gun oil from here and even if he couldn't, well, they were about as subtle as the local graffiti.

"Independence is so much more colorful than the official reports "What is it you do, exactly, Rue?"

The rabbit shrugged and kept his eyes pointed out the window, away from the surly bear across the aisle. "Machinin' sheet metal." Diana sat watching, waiting for him to continue. "Ain't much more to it'n that. Sorry t'disappoint."

She gave him a sharp nod. "For what, though?" The train stopped at a station with the laboring groan of metal, and another handful of souls made their way in, stopping with something between faint surprise and tired irritation before taking seats. One turned and held his hand out at Rue in a traditional 'are you serious' gesture, to which Rue just shrugged impotently. He didn't like this no more than they did. "Vehicles? Housing? Military equipment, perhaps?"

The rabbit tried to sip his own coffee before remembering he didn't have one. It'd taken Diana long enough to get to the station in her ludicrous heels that they'd barely made the last train down to the factory level. He was already pissed off and tired before the rounds of 20 Questions that never seemed to end.

Once they were on the floor, she couldn't talk to him, a blessing in thundering disguise. All she could do was watch, dolled up in all the safety gear the exasperated foreman insisted she wear. Goggles, facemask, hardhat, boots, and gloves turned her into a clown, one that had given up on making her tablet gizmo work and was trying to be content with just watching. Hours and hours of standing there in steel-toed boots three sizes too big while Rue and Jefferson, the burly badger he called his partner, bent flat sheets into not-flat sheets and moved them on down the line.

"Who's the dame?" Jefferson shouted over the din between presses. "Looks like some kinda actress."

Rue pulled the metal into the press and took a step back. *Kerchunk* "Says she's from the government up on DC Station."

Jefferson raised both eyebrows behind his goggles. "For real? The hell's Princess Peaches doin' outside her ivory tower?"

Kerchunk "Somethin' 'bout bein' our representative an' wantin' t'see how her 'con-stit-you-ents' live, first-hand."

"You believe her?"

A shrug. "I guess. If she's a conman, well she's pretty damn bad at it." *Kerchunk* "How long you been 'round here, J?"

"Fifty years in the Eye, thirty-five years on this line. Why?"

Rue nudged his head back towards Diana. "Ever seen anythin' like her?"

"Not even once." Jefferson dusted his gloves off, leaning back and catching a shot of water during a lull. "Foreman said she's legit?" Rue nodded. "Then I guess she's legit." A sharp whistle cut through the noise of the machines; Jefferson punched a red shut-off button with his fist and arched his back with a grunt. "Ah, music t'my ears. See y'in the back, Rue."

"—and then if you were to move the workstations about a half-meter closer together—" Without the slam-bang-wham-crunch of the press, Diana could finally be heard, though she wasn't exactly getting much attention. She startled suddenly as if hearing her own voice rang out off the walls. "Oh! Oh my! Did something happen?"

Rue pulled off his work gloves and wiped the sweat off his hands. "Shift's over. Time to go wash up an' clock out." The rabbit waved his hand over his shoulder as he turned and walked away. "Get yer wiggle on, I ain't waitin.'"

***

The locker room was arguably louder than the machine floor. Chatter echoed off the walls; some of the crew were already on their way to a warm glow. Diana's presence didn't even harsh their buzz, though she stayed quite out of the way as a matter of decorum. No one paid any attention to her except Rue, and all he had to offer was a glance now and again when she tried to ask him something inane.

Jefferson yanked a six pack out of his locker as he changed out of his work gear. "If the bosses only knew, man." Stacked up in blue jeans and flannel, the big badger looked like a trucker out of the old pre-war videos, one of those redneck rebels who tore through the long roads in his big rig defying the law and all that jazz. There hadn't been a highway to be a trucker on in a couple hundred years but the image lived on.

"They're probably doin' the same thing, J." Someone pulled the tab back on his beer and tossed the shard somewhere hopefully out of range of everyone's feet. "They probably got better stuff to drink, though." The locker room rang with laughter. Rue tilted his head back as if to ask Diana if she wanted a can of her own; she shook her head, and for once didn't bother saying anything.

"Yeah! I bet they're all up there sippin' *cham-pagne* and smokin' cigars." Jefferson waved his wrists around all grandiose, posing with his nose in the air. "Oh *yeeeees*, how I *adore* watching those peons toil and slave for us. It makes me so *happy* when they kill themselves for a few dollars a day. Do pass me another whores-durve, Jeeves!" The routine kept going, getting more ridiculous as it went. Pretty soon the whole crew was in stitches. The beer sure helped.

"I hate to interrupt, guys." A feeble looking orange cat pushed his way into the lockers, clad in something that was supposed to match the blue-collar uniform of his workers. But it was too clean and too tailored, coming across as more of a costume than a uniform. It made the cat look like he was a little kid playing pretend. Just his presence sucked all the light out of the room like a storm cloud passing over the sun.

Jefferson's eyes narrowed. "O'Shannon. What brings you down here with us little people? Masters gotta be makin' you work, 'cause you wouldn't do it all on yer own."

Diana put her palm against Rue's shoulder and whispered at him. "Who is that? He seems…unpopular."

Rue took a sip of his beer. His voice was cold and flat, and not quite quiet enough that O'Shannon was sure not to hear. "Floor foreman. He sits up in his little office an' watches the guys who do the work. Once in a while he tells us we're doin' somethin' wrong an' Daddy don't like that."

The cat adjusted his collar and laughed the laugh of a fish stopping by the shark party and hoping to have a good time. "Come on Jefferson. You know I respect you guys. You're the heart and soul of the factory. It wouldn't run without you."

"Yeah, you keep breakin' our hearts an' holdin' our souls for ransom," someone in the back shouted. The tension was thick enough to choke a man.

O'Shannon swallowed and shivered. "Ah, yeah, heh. Okay, I can tell you're looking forward to getting out here tonight, so I'll get right to the point." The cat shuffled a handful of papers on a tattered clipboard. "I just need to share a little bit of unexpected news before you hit the road." Putting as much courage on as he had, he walked right into the midst of the crew, hoping not to burst into flame under forty angry glares. "So, uh, yeah. You guys know Weiss?" There was a rumble of agreement. Most of the guys on the floor knew each other. It's how you got by, sticking up for your brother on the line. "He, ah, was involved in an incident with the cutters over on station three."

"Aw hell, man! Is he gonna be okay?"

"Yeah, ah, it's…uh…no." O'Shannon exhaled through his teeth, a shrill whistle. "No, he's not gonna be okay. No." Slim fingers ran through hair that cost more to coif than the floor crew saw in a week. "His station is, ah, it's out of service. Since those cutters are vital and we don't have a backup station going, that means the line's out."

Jefferson shook his head, eyes on the floor. "Geezus, a guy just died and all you care about the line."

"Hey, this affects all of us, even me." The cat sighed. It was a hard sell and O'Shannon was a pretty lousy salesman. "The owners are calling in the inspection team to make sure we're up to code. Gonna be two, three weeks while they do their thing." Oh the shout that came up. It was enough to make his ears ring. "Come on, guys! Guys! It's the law! You gotta be reasonable—"

"Don't seem like it's *us* bein' unreasonable." Jefferson was past pissed. He was cranked up into beast mode, fur bristled and about six inches away from foaming at the mouth. "You got balls, cat, comin' down here in your slick duds pretending that you're one of the boys, just to say we're all screwed." A meaty finger poked at O'Shannon's chest. The badger towered over the tabby as the foreman's resolve foundered. "Does *procedure* say we're gonna be paid while the line's getting the fine-toothed comb treatment?"

"Well, ah, no, that's just not—"

"—it's not *reasonable*?" The word hung in the air. It carried weight and it suffocated the energy out of everyone. O'Shannon stood there dodging Jefferson's glare, trying to think of the words that would get him out of here and fast. "Yeah. That's what I thought. Company always looking for their guys when it's gonna cost them a percentage. How's about you and your twenty dollar haircut get out of here before I stop being *reasonable*."

O'Shannon tapped his pencil on his clipboard, looking at the paper with a burning intensity, as if Jefferson didn't exist. "I'm sorry you feel that way about the situation, Jefferson. I thought we were simpatico, y'know? Maybe not the best of friends, but you always struck me as the level-headed guy on this crew." The cat clicked his tongue and tucked his pencil into his shirt pocket. "It's a dang shame."

"The hell are you talkin' about, man?"

"Mmhmm, just a really unfortunate situation to wind up in." O'Shannon reached down to his belt and grabbed a bulky portable radio. "Just not good for either of us. What're your wife and kids going to do without you, Jefferson? I don't even want to think about it." Jefferson put a hand up and started to talk, but O'Shannon held up the international gesture for 'I'm talking here', just a hair's breadth from teeth the size of AA batteries. "O'Shannon to Security. O'Shannon to Security."

There was a jolt in the air. A dozen pairs of eyes went as big as saucers. Someone in the back whispered an astonished curse. "You—you can't be serious, man…"

"Yeah, this is O'Shannon in the southwest locker room. I've got a potential situation down here, one of the machinists is, ah, they're having a bad day. If you guys could send someone by to help me deal with him? Yeah? That'd be great. I'll call you if anything changes." O'Shannon smiled at Jefferson and clipped his radio back. "You see, Jefferson, you don't have to be big and scary to make threats."

The staredown was on. Each threat had a lot of weight—if O'Shannon got roughed up, no one would put the finger on their brothers on the line, but if Jefferson ended up getting 'handled' by Security it'd at best cost him his job, and at worst cost him his freedom.

"Do you think you scare me with that? Everyone here'll say nothing happened."

"Mmm. True." The tabby looked around for a brief moment. "But you have to ask yourself: who do you think they'll believe?" Slim orange fingers tapped the radio. "I'd say you've got, oh, a minute before they get here."

No one breathed. Time stopped cold for everyone but O'Shannon. Diana's eyes jumped from one man to the other, clutching her tablet to her chest. "You can't—" She barely got two words out before Rue put his palm over her mouth, shaking his head. His eyes answered her alarmed confusion: don't get involved.

Jefferson was the one who gave up. Rue could see the badger crumble in on himself, his shoulders falling and his spine hunching. He was beaten, and by bureaucracy of all damned things. "Whatever," he muttered under his breath and went back to his locker. All eyes followed him. Defeat sank into everyone.

"Now that's a good man," O'Shannon said smugly, smoothing out his shirt. "O'Shannon to Security, cancel that call. Situation green. We worked it out. Thanks, you guys are amazing." The feline slipped right back into pep talk mode, going on like nothing had happened.

"So, guys, ah. The trains are running normal schedule, and we'll give you a call when the inspectors are out." The cat smiled wide, dripping with smarm. "I'm glad we had this little chat. We're a great team, and I think things are only gonna keep getting better." He grabbed one of Jefferson's beers with the grin of a cat who just ate every canary in town before sauntering his way back into the corridor. "Don't mind if I do!"

Diana stared in wide-eyed awe as the door shut and the demoralized workers went back to their lockers and their private sorrows. "Isn't anyone going to do anything?"

Rue closed his locker with a loud clang. "Whaddya suggest?"

"Complain to management! File a grievance! Go on strike, perhaps! Show them that you won't be used as slave labor!"

"You think we ain't tried that, lady? All it got us was hungry." The rabbit started off through a door, Diana clicking along behind him. "There's ten thousand bodies up there on th' street beggin' an' pleadin' for crumbs. We raise a stink, we trade places wit' one of dem an' the company don't never bat an eye."

"That's not how it should be, though—"

"Well it is." The train back out of the factory ground into the station, kicking up trash before the creaking doors opened, and Rue pushed his way inside with the last dregs of his coworkers. "What we're gonna do is go drown them sorrows for a while. I'd suggest you an' yer shadows"—he gestured at her bodyguards, who were still working under the impression that they were blending in—"do is get yerselves on home."

The woman adjusted her hair again now that it was free of her 'helmet' and tapped at her tablet furiously, cycling data and taking even more notes, on what Rue could only guess. "I think not. My investigation is not remotely complete, and I daresay my presence is needed now more than ever."

Rue tried not to snicker too loudly. "You sound like one a'dem Boy Scouts, lady." The rabbit leaned back, arms crossed, watching the tunnel whiz by. "I guess if yer gonna hang around, then I can take ya t'where we workin' class slobs go t'forget the day."

***

It was maybe a fifteen minute walk to The Limping Messenger from the nearest station but Diana managed to make it into an ordeal. It was like dragging a kid around—'Oh look at that!' and 'My word, what is this?' every five steps, all over the most mundane crap. It was like she'd never seen a homeless guy or a thrift shop before. Rue had to remind himself she probably *hadn't* but that wasn't an excuse for acting like a damn tourist.

The other thing Rue hadn't counted on was the tavern itself being a packed house. It was pushing two in the morning, and there shouldn't have been more than winos and old farts hanging out and sipping cheap, watery beer from mislabelled taps. Instead it smelled like drunks and it sounded like drunks, which made sense because it was full of drunks.

Rue kept a tight grip on Diana's hand as he led her through the teeming masses, most of them lost in their own intoxicating clouds. "Damnation, Lloyd," he practically shouted over the dull roar going on around him as the pair crammed against the bar and fought for stools. "What's going on?"

"I dunno, boyo. Somethin's got everyone blacker'n usual t'day. But who am I to say no to business, eh?" The barkeeper gave Rue the biggest smile in history. It helped that he had a big mouth to do it with. Hippos had the kind of maw you could lose a whole family inside if you weren't careful, but they knew their beer. Lloyd could get a guy drunk off his ass in less time than it took to spin a barstool three times and fill you up with nachos to wash away the taste of puke. He was friendly the same way your local drug dealer was friendly. Just keep the money coming and don't make fat jokes.

"Yeah, but why now? It's two freakin' AM."

"Oh whole world's gone tits to the heavens, lad. Power's out in One-Aught-Three Delta, the sewer's mucked up all over the Seven-Seven, and one of the factory lines put everyone on furlough. The Messenger's become home away from home for a few hours." The bartender slid Rue a mug without a thought, full of something dark and a bit hard on the nostrils if you leaned in too close. "'ere, boyo, got me a new stout in. Put hair on chest an' fire in yer belly!"

Rue rubbed his forehead and took a long drink, cringing as the thick sludge wormed down his throat and made it hard to breathe for a second. "Man. When it rains it pours, don't it?"

"Aye, an' we're gonna drown b'fore the storm stops." Lloyd looked past Rue to where Diana was standing watching people mill about with her usual intense curiosity. "Who's ya friend, Rue?" Lloyd's tone had changed into something less jovial. It made Rue's fur prick up.

"Oh her? She's just visitin' from outside the district." It was bull. Rue hoped either Lloyd would buy it or take the hint and not stick his nose in. "Friend of a friend, y'know?"

The hippo narrowed his eyes. Rue felt a sick lump forming up in his stomach. "A human coming down to The Eye? T'ain't much of a vacation." He shook his big head and went back to his smiling business. "Can I getcha anything, missy?"

Diana snapped her attention back to Lloyd with her ever bombastic smile. It was a war of teeth and cheer. All Rue could do was hide behind his drink and wait for the worst salvos to pass overhead. "Oh, I'm sorry! I'm not much of a drinker, but I must admit that I am positively parched." She pushed a finger to her lip. "You're the bartender of this fine establishment. What would you suggest?"

"Well, miss, bein' quite the conny-sewer o' liberal libations an' potent potables," Lloyd bragged, in full carnival barker mode, dragging in the marks like a pro. "I got a wicked cider 'at'll cure what ails ya. Fancy a mug?"

"Well," Diana said with a bit of a pout. "It's no Dom Perignon, but it will have to do." The drink Lloyd pushed in her general direction was as much as cider as Diana was a local—it might have heard of apples once in a story, but mostly it was faking it. The aroma alone made her nose try to crawl back up into her sinuses for cover. "My word, what's *in* this?"

"Just drink it, Di." So much for relaxing. He'd brought a wine snob into a dive bar. Of course he had. She hit the rabbit with the expression of someone asked to chug bleach and give it five stars. He hit her back with one that pleaded for her to just play along already. Diana took a pensive sip, shuddered, but kept at it.

Lloyd watched in mixed confusion and amusement. "Where'd you say she's from, Rue?"

"Uh, up Canada way, Ontario District."

"Uh huh." The barkeep didn't seem convinced. "Helluva trip to hang out in a tavern."

Rue shrugged and kept his eyes down. "She wanted to see the local color. I figured no better place than here."

"Don't they got taverns in Ontario?" Lloyd turned around, mixing something from the countless unlabeled bottles he kept back there. "Not gonna pry into yer business, Rue. Ya do what you do with yer friend 'ere, t'ain't none of my business," he chuckled, before moving on to other clientele.

Rue set himself to sipping his drink, hunched over the bar and filling the pauses with handfuls of peanuts. "So you learnin' anything?"

The human startled, eyes going wide as Rue brought her back from her thoughts. "I'm sorry. I sometimes get lost in my thoughts." She paused. "I would be lying if I said no." The look on her face screamed there was more to be said but it wasn't coming out.

"But it ain't what you expected, is it."

Diana nodded with an uncharacteristic sigh. "Everything I've heard and seen today is exactly the opposite of my expectations. Worse, it's the opposite of everything the party says." She ran her fingers through her hair then turned her screen towards Rue. "Like this. Just last calendar year, we put a full 170 million credits into transit programs. I can't even find any sign you have the systems the money was meant to upgrade, let alone the upgrades."

Rue looked headlong into the mirror behind the bar, most of it blocked by various bottles of booze too expensive for anyone to taste in the next lifetime or so. "That's the thing about livin' in a tower, darlin'. You forget what the ground looks like."

"The road to Hell is paved wit' good intentions." Both rabbit and woman turned to their right as Jefferson sat down next to them on a barstool, holding a proportionally huge beer in his huge black mitts. "An' the purest o' souls are the easiest led into their own destruction by the schemes of wicked men." He knocked back what was left of the brew, obviously not his first, and set the empty on the bar.

Diana tilted her head, finally distracted from her data for the first time in a long time. "That's lovely. Who said it?"

"My mother," Jefferson said with a soft, sad smile. "Every day, when she tried t' explain the sins she was committin' t'keep us fed, warm, an' safe." He tilted his head and looked up at the ceiling. "What's yer good intention, miss?"

Diana thought carefully before answering. "I want to help my citizens." She gestured in a broad circle. "All of you."

"Well ain't that damn neighborly of ya." Jefferson started in on a new beer from Lloyd, who stayed close by, wiping a spot of the bar. "Now I believe yer a good person, genuine an' true, but think real carefully 'fore you answer, now. Whaddya plannin' t'do?"

"I can present all this to the other representatives. I have so much information here, they can't *not* launch an investigation." She looked up at Jefferson with her warmest expression, trying to be supportive. "I can effect real change."

There wasn't any response at first. "How long you been in yer current job, miss?"

"Four years this September."

Jefferson nodded. "Lemme tell ya somethin', bit a' personal advice from someone older who's seen some things." He finally turned to her, eyes dark and sad, expression drifting between anger and sorrow. "One o' the' worst gifts you can give a person is hope." He got up and left without another word.

Diana carefully watched him fade back into the crowd. "What was that all about?"

Rue stood up, tossing a handful of crumpled bills on the table. "We should get goin'. S'getting' late, an' if we don't get goin—"

***

"—sorry, folks, you just missed the last train for quite a while." The stationmaster was in the process of locking the metal gates that secured the subway station, talking through the metal lattice. "Power problems on the line, we can't get through until the work crews finish up. Could be into tomorrow noon."

"Well don't that just figure." Rue was trying not to be mad at the old bird—it wasn't his fault—but it wasn't exactly easy. The rabbit was tired and just wanted to be out of the heat and into a bed. "Third time this month."

"Aye, tis." The pigeon dusted his hands off on his pant legs. "Wish there was somethin' I could do for ya. Station'll be back open at seven in tha mornin'." And he vanished out of sight into the station, heading to his own lockers and his own way home.

Diana hobbled her way back up the steps to the surface, squinting in the jaundiced light of a streetlamp. "So I suppose the only thing left to do is walk."

"Yeah. It ain't that far, I s'pose. Couple miles. Stick close an' stay in the light." Rue snorted a little with a smirk. "Though with yer security people hangin' out I ain't that worried." They started off, Diana trusting Rue's guidance. "Don't you ever get tired a'them shadowin' you?"

"I've never had them before." The city was quiet. All the people in their little homes had gone to bed like any reasonable folk would, creating an endless sea of darkened grey pillars that disappeared into the thick haze of the night. Blurry bits of starlight fought to be seen against the sleepless glare of billboards and floodlamps. "I rather thought I wouldn't need them." There was a long silence between them as they passed under awnings and pretended not to hear the begging of panhandlers resting in doorways. "Rue, tell me something."

"What?"

"Are you happy?"

Rue shrugged without stopping. "Happy enough. Why? I mean, what's it to ya?"

"I just don't understand how." Diana's voice was melancholy. It hadn't taken very much to break her illusion that The Eye was a utopia, and now she was having doubts about everything, mostly herself. "Where I live, this would be called a ghetto."

"An' like I said before, it's home t'us." Rue kept his eyes forward and kept Diana moving along at a steady clip. The heat was just as thick as daytime, held down by the thick veneer of pollution overhead. "You know about the war?"

Diana stepped around bags of trash on the pavement, crinkling her nose at the stench. "Everyone does. A decade of fighting between powers, much of it handled by combat drones called 'recoms'. The allied forces prevailed."

The rabbit snorted derisively. "'Combat drones'. I ain't heard that one."

"What do you mean?"

"Recoms weren't no combat drones, Diana. They were *us*."

"I don't understand."

"Woman, do you think talkin' animals just popped outta th' ground one afternoon?" Rue stopped at a street corner and turned to face Diana. "Y'all made us, called us 'recoms'. Some science thing 'bout DNA, I dunno. We did yer fightin' for ya, an' when it was over ya left."

Diana tensed, eyes wide. "That's not what the books—" She paused and the words fell out of her mouth silently. "Why would we leave you behind?"

"Ten years a'war didn't leave much, just a lotta ruins an' misery." They passed by another bar still in full swing, the sound of drunken music pouring out through the door serving as a brief break in the city's somber soundtrack. The bouncer gave Rue a glare that screamed 'keep on going'. "An' not a soul t'guide us 'cept what we dug out the trash."

"Rue." Diana put her hand to her mouth in shock. "That was centuries ago. Are you saying you're—"

The rabbit laughed. "Naw, I ain't no three hundred year old mummy. Sixth or seven generation, I reckon." Rue looked behind him, scanning for Diana's bodyguards. He wanted them close, but not *too* close. "Does knowin' history change yer mind any?"

Diana mulled the question over. "Only in that it makes me want to help even more." She stumbled to a halt with a soft gasp, pulling Rue by his sleeve to stop with her.

Rue flicked his eyes down, watching Diana shift uncomfortably on her feet. "You alright dere, darlin'?"

"Ah." She put on her best smile, but the winces played up at the corners of her face until it cracked. "I expected to be sitting a lot, having conversations and sipping tea." A long exhale of breath. "These shoes were not made for standing about for ten hours." She laughed lightly. "The train was going to be my temporary salvation. Shame about that."

Rue stood up and looked around. "Take yer word on it," he said with a chuckle of his own. "I ain't never worn shoes outside'a work. I'm guessin' you didn't bring no sneakers, an' we ain't getting' you any this time o'night." The rabbit looked around. "Gonna have to take a shortcut. Yer guys aren't gonna like it." He stretched out his arms in front of him, cracking his knuckles. "You trust me?"

"Wha—" Diana shouted in protest as Rue turned suddenly into a narrow alleyway, much of the city's glow swallowed instantly by the veil of shadow. His pace was brisk, his movements seemingly random, veering deeper and deeper into the maze of passages. To Diana, it looked like they were going around in circles, dodging past overflowing dumpsters and abandoned furniture until she was dizzy and panting. Finally Rue came to a sudden stop in the middle of what was just another pair of filthy grey walls surrounded by mounds of debris, Diana pulling up short behind him and nearly going tail-over-teakettle.

"Rue," Diana hissed under her breath. "Where are we? I can feel eyes all over me." Her skin crawled. She wrapped arms around herself as if that would protect her.

"Twenty or thirty sets of 'em at least. Yer a popular girl t'night, Diana." Rue held his ground, watching the shadows as best he could in the trickles of light. "Didn't think we'd run into any of 'em."

"Any of what?" Diana's heartbeat pounded against her chest as she leaned against the rabbit. "Rue...please, I'm scared..." Things skittered and shuffled in the periphery, completely lost in her vision. "I can't find my security team."

"We shook yer friends about five turns in. Yer gonna be fine without 'em if ya just keep yer mouth shut for a bit." The rabbit took Diana's arm and pulled a bracelet off her wrist, ignoring her protests. "Oh hush, you ain't gonna miss it." Rue set the bit of gold down on the ground a few feet in front of him and stepped back. "Hey y'all, I brought ya a present." Before Diana could blink it was gone, swept away into the night with a whoosh of air and the slightest glimmer of a body. "I paid yer toll, now y'all gonna come out and say hi?"

As if cued, a half-dozen rodents walked in from the cracks and crevices of the alleyway, the group building slowly as their confidence did. They were worn and filthy, poorly clothed and sickly thin. One of them, an older one Diana assumed by his graying pelt, gave Rue a smile and said something. The 'words' were chopped squeaks, nothing intelligible to her, but Rue seemed to understand well enough, nodding and answering back in his own accented English.

After a moment surrounded by curious ratlings gawking up at her massive-to-them height and gloriously garish coloring, chirping excitedly as they bounded about in a wave of unkempt fur. "Rue... what—I mean who are these...people?"

"Yer in Rattown, sweetheart, an' these are the locals. We call 'em

Vermin, but it ain't outta meanness but cuz that's what they is. They live off what we throw out an' in places we won't go." He nodded with a chuckle as the 'elder' chittered a final message and wandered off back to 'home'. "We got us a structure here in The Eye, Miss Mondeline. It ain't pretty, but it works."

"How do you know their language?"

Rue's face softened, and his eyes looked sad. "Not everyone in Rattown's a rat. I grew up in some a'these buildin's, s'how I know the alleys. I got out." He gave a thin smile to a rat that wandered past and chirped. "But it still feels al li'l like home."

One last pitiful little creature hung about after the rest had scuttled away to their hidey-holes, standing out on the concrete with a desperate look drawn on its snout. It was smaller than the rest, big-eyed and confused, making the softest whimpers as it turned and looked to Diana, awestruck into forgetting to be worried for a moment as it scuttled towards her on all fours. Diana wrung her hands in nervous frustration. She looked to Rue, then back to the wee creature. "Is that…"

"A kid? Yeah. Real young, too." It was probably the first time Rue's tone had been soft since they left his apartment. "This is skid row, lady, where the lifetime losers and the busted folks end up. Couldn't tell ya how they wound up here starvin'. Weren't their fault, most times." He shrugged and stuffed his hands in his pockets. "That's life. Whaddya gonna do?"

The woman crouched down, watching the childling as she fished in her satchel. "Here," she whispered, holding out something glossy and chrome. "It's not much, but—" She didn't need to finish the sentence before the glimmering bit of junk was yanked away. It looked up at her, blinked twice, and mumbled something she couldn't understand before scampering back into the darkness.

"Heh," Rue said with a chuckle. "Wouldn't have thunk it could talk. Young'uns usually don't." He gave Diana a smirk. "It said yer pretty."

"My good deed for the day, I suppose." Diana followed closely behind Rue as he led her back through the narrow gutter-alley, pushing the sound of creatures clawing from inside the walls mere feet away out of her mind.

"I dunno about that," Rue answered. "Best case, ya bought that kid a couple meals. More'n likely the kid'll just get mugged by someone bigger. Maybe killed."

Diana glowered outside of Rue's sigh. He could feel her eyes burn into him just the same. "The only thing necessary for the triumph of evil is that good men do nothing."

"An' one of the worst sins a person can carry is thinkin' they're doin' good when they ain't. Yer good, honest people, Miss Mondeline, but ya don't understand The Eye."

Diana sighed. "I chose to be an optimist."

"An' I'll keep bein' an realist—"

"Well if it isn't our missing guest, boys." The loud thump of a knife switch falling into place grabbed Rue's attention. Floodlamps sparked to life, bathing the pair in life and revealing a half-dozen police officers, with truncheons, badges, and everything else need to play cops in tow. Silhouetted in the harsh glare was a wolf, a big one, broad shouldered and deep voiced. "I heard quite a story about you tonight, Rue." The wolf tilted his head to either side, gesturing to a couple shadows that could just make out as Diana's security detail. "These gentlemen aren't real happy with you, kiddo."

Rue blocked his eyes with one hand and tucked Diana behind him with the other. "Dunno why they sent you out here, Schmitt. I was just taking the lady home."

"That's 'sir' to you, rabbit. Maybe Sergeant if I'm feeling like being polite tonight." Schmitt came right up to Rue, flanked by another pair of wolves and the bodyguards, scowls on every single mouth. Rue snorted. Canines and law enforcement were like beer and factory workers. "But I have my doubts." Up this close a guy could sort of see the three cops, all decked up in their cop blues and smirking like they owned the place, while the security guys were still wearing their cheap suits and crappy haircuts. "Way I hear it, ears"—Rue bristled; Schmitt's thugs chuckled to themselves, just itching for the buck to make a move so they could wallop him—"you ran off with Miss Mondeline here. Took her into Rattown. Tsk, tsk, boy." Schmitt's tone was heading past condescending into downright antagonistic. "What were you thinking, taking such a defenseless lady into a dangerous place like that? They teach you anything except how to make more rabbits?"

Rue got interrupted by Diana before the first word dropped out of his mouth. "Officer, with all due respect." Rabbit hand went to rabbit forehead. "Mr. Nicolades was escorting me at my request. It really is *my* fault we wound up there."

Schmitt rolled his eyes. "And with all due respect to you, missy, I don't really want your side of the story." The officer looked to Rue. "Your handlers here explained the whole thing to me before you even showed up. I figured a lowbrow thug like Cletus would bring you to trouble sooner or later."

"I'm tellin' you, Schmitt, she weren't never in no danger—"

The wolf spat on the ground. "I'm not gonna tell you again, son. You show me respect and maybe I'll go easy on you. You keep telling me stories and acting the fool, well." Schmitt hooked his thumbs in his belt. "I can't be responsible for what happens next."

If Schmitt wanted to sound like a sarcastic sleaze, Rue was happy to join him. "You see this guy, Diana? He sold out a hundred average Joes so he could get cozy up with the Chief o' Police." Diana kept her mouth shut, watching Rue glare in smug satisfaction up at the wolf who stood easily a foot taller and had more meat than a packing plant. "They call 'im Strikebreaker Schmitt. The Iron Boot. Y'wonder why we don't complain? 'cause this bootlicker an' his dog pack put us all in cuffs or in th' hospital." Schmitt's thugs growled but the boss wolf put his hands out, maintaining his stone demeanor. "An' 'cause the Chief is all chummy with the head o' the factory, well. Them benefits trickle down. Ain't life sweet, lapdog? You gonna be fetchin' slippers for the mayor next? Bow wow, puppy! Fetch! Good boy!"

The next words out of Rue's mouth were all foul and soaked in vitriol with a twist of asphalt against his teeth as he rolled on the pavement, clutching his left leg. Diana went to reach for him but one of her bodyguards grabbed her shoulder and pulled her back before she could move a step. The senior wolf put his nightstick away, whistling softly to himself and shaking his head like a child had done something stupid and, well, he got what was coming to him.

"Well dang, I dunno what's up with Cletus here, but he should get that knee checked out. It doesn't seem to be doing too hot. Petrezo, Daniels, get him up on his feet and give our man some new jewelry." The pair yanked Rue up to his feet with more force than was probably necessary; the one with the 'Daniels' nametag slapped a pair of handcuffs on Rue while mumbling things about his rights and attorneys. "Stick him in the trailer, boys. And Cletus, keep your head down." Schmitt put on the shit-eatingest grin imaginable. He'd've made a great politician. "Wouldn't want you getting an ouchie."

Diana scowled. "I am a Representative and a member of your *government*. I will report this misconduct to my superiors. Do you understand? I could have you put in prison for the rest of your life with just a word!"

"That's cute." Schmitt chuckled menacingly, arms crossed over his barrel of a chest. "She thinks she can scare me." Daniels and Petrezo tossed Rue brusquely in a trailer, jumped in the cruiser, and were on their way into the night. "You guys better get her out of here. This isn't a safe place for tourists." Diana shuddered. Schmitt's voice was pure *menace*, and it burned into her very core. "Have a nice day," he mumbled as he headed back off to the station.

Diana started to follow Schmitt, only to be again grabbed by her handlers. "Miss Mondeline, we're done here. It's time to go."

"Let me go!" She tugged her arm forward, stumbling on her injured feet. "I need to go help him!"

"Absolutely not. Your safety has been compromised, and I'm under orders to bring you back to the satellite." The nameless agent pressed his finger against his ear. "Bring the Representative's transport to my location for extraction." As much as she tried to resist, her body-guards quickly escorted her away to the waiting craft, and before the sun rose she was gone from The Eye.

***

Mornings were not Rue's forte. Within a few hours Schmitt had let him go—there was no one to charge him with anything, and the wolves had exhausted what they could do to the rabbit and get away with. The Limping Messenger was open as always, giving the few early risers a chance to knock the edge off their sorrows before the day started properly. Everyone ignored him, in fact.

"Ya think it was worth it, J?" Rue sat in the tavern, sipping the cheapest beer on tap on Jefferson's dime. The rabbit was properly broke.

"No way of tellin', man. Maybe she'll pull it off. But I ain't one of them claire-voyants."

Two weeks later, the lines were back up. Jefferson, O'Shannon, and

Rue were back in their predictable places, doing the same work they'd always done. O'Shannon had no spine, Jefferson had no restraint, and Rue had no concerns. The money was still bad, and more often than not Rue wandered through the alleyways to his apartment in the cover of darkness, dealing with all the citizens of the shadows. Just like he always had.

A month later, Diana Mondeline was on the television news. She had started some grand crusade in the halls of the DC Satellite, reportedly using the information from her tablet gizmo to show other people up there that the situation in Independence District was bad and the recoms needed help. She wanted the *truth* to get out. The general response in The Eye was apathy. It was too little, too late, and too much posturing. Rue at least had to give her credit for spunk. She'd put her heart into it, just like she said she would.

Six weeks later, Diana vanished. The news reported late one night that she had been travelling between regions when her craft simply disappeared. It was found a few days later, but no sign of any of the passengers. Most distressingly, her tablet was never recovered. Without a leader or evidence, the movement crumbled and was soon forgotten. President Trenton made a moving statement about her service and dedication. There were specials all over the news for a few nights. The Eye barely blinked.

The number of things that we failed to notice were precious until they were gone, consumed, sold, or burned away. Endless swaths of ruin now stretch as far as the eye can see, and nature's splendor is little more than a memory. Is there a lesson to be learned when that which one loses stands a chance of becoming attainable once more? Or are we set to squabble once again over all the things which we ruthlessly coveted but never learned to love?

A Road of Dust and Honey

Searska GreyRaven

Vex swore and leaned against her rig, tempted to pound her fist into the side. Broken bones hardly slowed down a bearkin of her size and girth, but she couldn't afford the time it took to tape them, or the clumsiness it caused while they healed, as if most of them hadn't been broken three times or more, defending what was in her rig.

Above, a vulture circled.

Vex pulled off her goggles, cleaned them on her threadbare shirt, and put them back on. *Fur's turnin' grey out here. Not sure if that's age or dust.* She tried to rub the grey off. *Nope, that's age.* She sighed and turned her attention away from her grizzled fur.

There were no road signs, no indication of where she was. She knew from her maps that she was somewhere between "middle of nowhere" and "the next Farm." The specifics were lost under the rolling dust dunes of the wasteland between them. Even the road was little more than a ghost, revealed by wisps of wind and buried again under tattered ribbons of blown sand.

The vulture cried out and circled lower. Vex grimaced.

"Not today, corpse eater. I got a green place to find and girls to feed."

She rummaged through the toolbox in her cab, sorting through several cases of repair spells before finally finding the right one. She popped the hood and glared at the dimly glowing engine, the verdigris covered tubes. A trickle of pale blue fluid dripped into the sand below, hissing when it touched dust.

"Not the best time to blow out a mana feed, you piece of shit," Vex grumbled.

Three hours and a heap of curses later, the engine roared to life. Purple smoke trickled from the tailpipe and something under the hood groaned in pain, but it was running.

From inside the trailer of her rig came a dull thrum, rising and falling.

Vex ambled to the back of her rig and knocked gently on the metal side. The drone intensified to a roar.

"I know, I know" Vex crooned. The roar changed in pitch, became plaintive.

"Just a little farther, I promise. We're almost there," she said. "Would a lullaby help?"

The drone continued.

"A swarm of bees in May is worth a stack of hay," Vex sang softly. The drone changed again as if humming along. *"A swarm of bees in June is worth a silver spoon."* As she sang, Vex put a little power behind the words, lulling the source of the thrum to sleep, sleep. *"And a swarm of bees in July ain't worth a piggy's sty."*

The hum continued a little longer and finally tapered off. Satisfied, Vex returned to the front end of her rig and checked it one more time.

It was a beast of a rig, twice as big as any off-the-line semi and more slapdash repair work now than original truck. Instead of a steady purr, the thing choked and shuddered. Rust puckered every metal surface, and the wheels were as cracked as the pads on the palms of Vex's paws. Here and there, scorch marks pocked the metal, patched with sheets of metal or held together with adhesive wards. Only the lock on the door at the back was shiny and chrome, its matching key on a barbed wire chain around Vex's neck.

If her rig broke down when she got to the Farm, well, someone would lend her a hand to fix it up. Might even be a proper magicanic who could recharge the AC and take a look at that mana leak in the front end. Folks traded a whole lot more for what she carried, but she'd settle for a hot meal, a safe place to camp, and a bottle of vitae.

Vex climbed into the cab and put her beast back in gear. The engine huffed, kicked, and finally the rig rolled forward. Her dash lit up, the fuel gauge tipping into the red for a moment before retreating back into the yellow once more. She tapped the glass bubble of the mana gauge a few times. That needle quivered but held steady in the yellow.

Vex frowned. She *really* needed a magi-canic to take a look at her rig. Hopefully, she'd be able to afford a decent one after this job.

"Damn mana tank leak," Vex grumbled. There wasn't much left, but it should get her as far as the next Farm. She shifted into gear. "Onward to green places, my girls."

Behind her, the rig rumbled and, faintly, hummed.

***

She rolled up to the next Farm just after dawn, dust settling on her long coat and boots as she hopped from the cab and shouldered Wilson, her rifle. Frick and Frack, her pistols, hung from holsters on her wide hips, polished metal gleaming in the sun. Tucked into her belt was a Y-shaped slingshot, and next to it dangled a small leather pouch cinched shut with a drawstring. Her rig shuddered as it shut down, letting out a wheeze and a belch of blue smoke. Vex grunted back, entirely unsurprised by her rig's outburst. She plopped a wide-brim hat atop her head and swept the gauzy veil back out of her eyes.

She frowned. Usually, the sight of her rig was enough to bring out at least one member of the local cavalry. Instead, she was greeted only by dust and sun, and the eerie wail of wasteland wind across the Farm's bubble dome. The Farm itself squatted just inside the dome, tired wood sagging and its roof tilted like a sombrero, shading the front porch.

Next to the road where she parked her rig, four freshly dug graves desiccated. The wooden headstones planted to mark the resting places were already fading to grey at the edges.

Someone's gotta still be breathin' around here. Graves don't dig themselves. Looks too green under that dome to be abandoned.

The garden within was protected both by magic and tech, the oiled surface of the bubble dome shimmering like a soap bubble in the sunlight. Vex squinted from the glare. As she watched, one of the vultures that soared constantly overhead dodged an attack from another and slammed into the dome. There was a crackle, a hiss, and the bird's body tumbled down the side of the bubble to the ground, a pile of greasy feathers and smoke.

Folks gotta protect what keeps 'em breathin. I get it. But God damn, how we got to this, I'll never understand.

She recalled vaguely that it had something to do with bombs, and something to do with a shortage of ice in vital places round the bottom and top of the world, but the rest was a long, hunger-filled blur. If not for magic and magi, she doubted anyone would still be breathing. Even tech couldn't keep up with the degradation anymore.

"You the Bee Mama?"

Vex blinked and glanced around the front end of her rig. Standing barely to her rig's headlights was a foxkin kit. Vex sniffed the air and smiled faintly. Overalls and baggy clothes might fool a human, but a bear's nose was too clever. The kit was a vixen.

"That'd be me, the Bee Mama" Vex replied. "And you are?"

"Kine."

"Kine. Pretty name. Where's your mama and pop?"

"They're, uhh. Sick. They sent me out, said I was a Big Girl Now and could handle it."

There was pride in the foxkin's words, and a small measure of deception. Vex's nose knew a lie when it passed her way, but for the moment, she had hungry mouths to feed and a rig that needed the attention of a magi-canic. Once her girls were settled, she could trade a bottle of honey or some beeswax candles for the use of the house phone.

"Alright, Kine, where do you want me to set up? Got a lot to unload."

Kine nodded and led Vex out to the domed garden, pausing just long enough to open the wards with a practiced gesture and a whispered pass phrase. The wards snicked shut as soon as Vex passed, making her ears pop.

"Hell of a security system you've got here," Vex commented.

Kine snorted and picked a small stone from the ground. With a flick of her wrist, the foxkin set it flying and it thunked against the center of a sun-bleached old target thirty paces away.

"Magic and tech is fine, but nothing beats a sharp stone to the face," Kine said. Vex was inclined to agree. Guns ran out of bullets. Stones though, stones where everywhere. She ran her thumb across the V of her slingshot and smiled.

Inside the dome, it was paradise.

Green and growing in every direction, right up to the edge of the bubble dome's curved wall. Row after row of corn, beans, peppers, and tomatoes. Boxes laden with bowing carrot tops, overflowing with potatoes, were spaced out here and there, with vines of squash trailing between. Coiling up the side of a decorative archway were vanilla orchids, green pods hanging low.

And everywhere, flowers. Coneflower, sunflower, zinnias, pusley, salvia. She could see cilantro and basil blooming, could smell mint and basil and sage. In the center of the ward, she saw fruit trees in full bloom, starfruit, lychee, orange, peach, even mango.

Vex looked around at the garden in amazement. "Your green mage has been working hard," she said.

Kine nodded proudly. "Papa always said, mama could make a stone bloom for her if she tried. She told me that she got some of the flowers to bloom out of season, because she heard you were coming."

Out of season my missing left toe, Vex thought. Some of these flowers and trees shouldn't be sharing the same field! And yet, here they were, blooming and thriving side by side.

"You mama is a hell of a mage, Kine. You should be proud."

Kine preened and puffed out her chest. "And one day, I'm gonna be just as good as she is. Better even! I'm gonna make the garden grow *outside* the wards!"

Vex chuckled and shook her shaggy head. "You do that, kid. Make the world green again."

"Somebody has to," Kine said. She picked up another small stone and tossed it into the air a few times, testing its heft. "Why not me?"

Vex didn't have an answer for that. She was looking for a place to set down camp for her and her girls. She picked a place where the ground was left fallow. Then, Vex returned to her rig and began the arduous process of opening it up. The chrome magi-lock gave at the touch of its matching key, but the other mechanical locks needed more coaxing. Some needed a healthy dose of swearing before they would give.

"Need a hand moving your…um."

With a flourish, Vex raised the door on the back of the rig and struck the foxkin child speechless. Within the shadowy interior of her rig, Vex had no less than forty white boxes stacked high. Many of the boxes bore new paint, but the faded black outline of something that might have once been lettering could be seen through it. Vex knocked on the nearest box, and the low hum that pervaded the air crescendoed into an excited drone.

"Morning, girls," Vex said. The drone raised in pitch, lowered again.

"You're a mage, just like mama," Kine whispered.

"Something like, though I have no affinity for green things. But bees? Bees like me just fine. Most of the time," she chuckled. "They have tempers, just like me. Prone to sting when you get on their nerves."

Kine took a few steps back from the rig, eyeing the boxes warily.

"You wanna meet them? Soon as they get some nectar in their bellies, they'll be right as rain and calm again." The drone picked up again. "My girls are hungry, and hungry makes 'em ornery."

Kine giggled. "Me too."

It took Vex a couple of hours, but she had all the boxes out of the rig and settled into the warded field. Years of the labor had hardened her muscles; she hardly felt winded this time at all. *Or maybe it's the sight of so much green in one place. Does a body good, after miles of dust and ruin.* Kine watched the operation from the limb of a nearby rowan tree, weaving lemongrass into a bracelet. Each time Vex entered or exited, Kine dropped from her spot and opened the wards for her. Vex didn't comment or try to get the password from Kine. Trust was rarer than water in the wasteland, and not a thing to be given lightly to a vagrant, even a Bee Mama.

Vex panted and surveyed her work, making sure everything was in order. The hives droned, scenting sweet nectar on the wind and clearly anxious to get to work.

"Are you gonna let them out now?" Kine asked.

Vex nodded and rummaged through her pack. She pulled out a floppy wide-brimmed hat with a veil and tossed it to Kine. "Put that on. I don't think they'll take exception to you, but hungry bees is tricky bees. Best to be prepared."

Kine put the hat on, veil draping down past her shoulders. Vex nodded, satisfied, and walked along the boxes, flicking one claw into the slot at the bottom and dislodging the metal screens that kept her girls boxed in.

Some hives came roaring out, swirling about. Some were more

cautious, climbing the sides of their home and stepping blearily into the sun before taking off. But eventually, they all took flight, circling and getting their bearings before investigating the bountiful garden.

"What's all that yellow stuff?" Kine asked, pointing to the yellowish droplets all over the ground.

"Bee poop," Vex replied.

"Ew."

"They've been cooped up a while."

A few bees came over to Vex and hovered in front of her veil. After a moment, they zoomed off. None of the bees paid Kine any mind whatsoever.

"So…that's it?"

"For the bees, sure. They know what they're doing. Gonna leave them to it now and take care of my own needs. I got stuff to trade, if'n you've the means to a hot bath and a hot meal. I'd also like to borrow your phone. Rig needs a magi-canic."

Kine bit her lip and looked away. "I'll have to… um…ask. I'll be right back."

Vex tilted her head and watched the foxkin trot off. Once the child was inside the house, Vex knocked on the nearest hive, her oldest one. Three bees came out and alighted on her paw. Each one was the size of a quarter and covered in fine bands of grey and buff fuzz, with black chitin beneath. One groomed her antennae, as aloof as a cat. "Keep an eye on that one, will you?"

A dismayed buzz from the bees.

"I don't need more'n one or two scouts. You can spare 'em. Just look at this place! You're gonna be rollin' in gold for weeks, maybe even months if they let us stay that long. Plenty to go around, and plenty of time to gather it all. That kid's mama has gotta be the best green mage I ever crossed paths with, and I ain't even met her yet. I can't blame 'em for bein' wary of us, but I got a bad feeling about this. Who sends their kid out to greet a vagrant? Something really ain't right."

A resigned thrum came from the hive itself, and the trio of scouts on Vex's paw shot off toward the house. Vex watched them zoom out of sight and nodded.

"Much obliged, regent," she murmured.

***

An hour passed, and Kine returned, bounding through the garden toward Vex. Before the kit could get too close, Vex dismissed the three returning scout bees back to their hive. *No one home,* they'd said. *Empty hive.* It didn't make any sense, but she didn't have a chance to press them on it.

Gotta be someone in there besides this foxkin kit, Vex reasoned.

"Mama says it's alright to use the phone. But be real quiet. She's napping."

Vex nodded and followed Kine into the house. The doorway was low, making Vex duck her head to get inside. Even though she'd had a lean time lately, Vex's body still barely fit through the doorway. *Foxes, gotta make everything feel like a burrow.* She took her hat off and looked around.

Houses out this far into the ruin of the world didn't have much, and this home was no exception. A battered couch and arm chair, ragged curtains, a scuffed up side table. The walls were sturdy brick, though, and the floor paved with smooth, red-brown tile. The scent of chilies and onions hung in the air, and Vex felt her mouth water again.

"Mama said I could offer you a taco, if you're hungry," Kine said.

Vex nodded and pulled from her long coat a bottle of rich, dark honey. "Make it three, and I'll trade you."

Kine's brows knit in confusion. "Molasses?"

Vex chuckled. "Nah, not even close. This is honey from the North, where the buckwheat fields bloom."

Kine didn't look convinced. "Looks like molasses to me."

"Bee Mama's honor," Vex said, holding up one paw, three fingers aimed skyward. "And everyone knows, if a Bee Mama breaks her oath, her bees will fly away and leave forever."

Kine nodded, accepting the oath with a child's solemn earnestness. "Alright. I'll be right back. The phone's in the room on the left."

"Thank you kindly," Vex replied, and ambled to the phone. Kine vanished through another door that Vex assumed was the kitchen, judging from the lovely scent of cooking food that wafted toward her. She wondered if Kine's tacos would have any meat in them. Been a good long time since she'd tasted meat.

Vex made her call on an ancient landline, sitting gingerly on a whicker stool that she feared wouldn't hold her weight. She marveled that the phone line still functioned and mourned how much of the world had been lost. *Used to be a call like that could be made anywhere, any time. Wireless connections, internet. It's all gone now, or nigh unreachable. How much more will we lose,* she wondered, *before we fight to hold on to what remains?*

It was a question with no answer. Vex herself had fought, had always fought, and had never stopped fighting since she was a cub torn from her mother's arms. She hung up the phone and stared at the battered thing, lost in her memories.

"You were in the war, weren't you?"

Vex startled and turned. Standing in the door was Kine, her expression wary and her ebon ears flat. The foxkin vixen had the grace and stealth of her vulpine ancestors, it seemed, and the gift for appearing seemingly out of nowhere. In her paws, Kine gripped a chipped blue plate with five tacos, laden with green and red stuff.

"What makes you say that?" Vex asked, eyeing the tacos. The scent of guacamole and cilantro filled her nose and set her mouthwatering.

"Your guns," Kind replied. "Those are army issue. My father had a pair."

"Had?"

"He traded them for seeds, for mama."

"Ah."

"He said it was a fair trade, death for life. He said, that's really all a garden is, a way to turn death into life. Mama only laughed, but she loved the seeds and tried to make them grow. That big rowan tree by the door of the garden, that's the only one that she was able to keep alive."

"Unusual, for a green mage to fail at keeping a plant alive," Vex commented. She pointed to the plate in Kine's paws. "Are those for me?"

"Three of them, as promised."

Vex nodded and handed over the honey. Kine took two tacos from the plate and handed the rest to Vex. The first taco, Vex devoured without tasting. The second, she took more slowly. The third, she savored. Warm corn tortilla, creamy guacamole. Then, the sharp bite of serrano pepper, and the sweet tang of tomato salsa, and buried at the bottom was a thin layer of pulled pork.

"I haven't had pork in years," Vex said, licking her claws.

Kine grinned. "We have a small herd here. We can't let them run in the garden or they'd uproot everything, so we have them penned up round the back," Kine said. She took a bite from one of her tacos. "Anyway, mama said the rowan tree seeds were from so far away that they refused to grow. They were homesick, she said. It hurt too much to be away from their home, so they chose to die instead."

Vex grunted, listening.

"She convinced one of them to try. Just one. It didn't want to keep going, even after she convinced it to sprout. She had to baby it for years. But once it finally decided to live, it grew so much. Mama w— is very proud of it."

Vex pondered Kine's hesitation but didn't comment.

"Are the bees your family?"

Vex choked on her last bite of taco and regarded the impertinent question with a curl of her lip.

"They're bees," she said gruffly. Vex licked the last of the sauce from her paws and set the plate down on the table next to her.

"I heard you talking to them," Kine pressed. "Like they could understand you."

"They're *bees*," Vex repeated, shifting uncomfortably. "Just bees."

"Papa said he'd heard rumors of smart bees once" Kine said. "They crossed 'em with wasps, somehow." She looked down at her toes, but her ears were perked forward intently. "He said the same people who made us, made the smart bees. Because they knew the world was dying."

"Ain't nobody made us *because* the world was dying," Vex said. "We were made *in spite* of it. Something had to carry on, I suppose."

A longer silence stretched between them.

"Last time papa came back from town, he said the humans were almost gone. That some plague was burnin' through them like wildfire."

Vex grunted. She'd heard the same, but she knew humans. If anything could be said of them, they were a durable lot. They'd manage. Always managed. Like weeds, or mushrooms, they always sprang back.

But nothing grows in the wasteland. Not even weeds and mushrooms.

Maybe this time, they won't either. She wasn't sure if it was a comforting thought or a terrifying one, so she set it aside.

Kine opened her mouth to say something more, but hesitated. She tilted her head one way, then the other, ears swiveling.

"Someone's coming."

Vex frowned, her own shorter ears flicking from side to side. "Can't be the magi-canic. Too soon."

Kine whimpered and dashed to the window. "Oh no."

Vex peeked through the window over Kine's head and growled.

Bearing down the road toward the house and its bubble dome was a dust cloud. The roar of engines rumbled across the barren desert like dry thunder.

"Kine, I need some things from my rig. Could you open the wards, please?"

"But—"

"Go get your papa, Kine," Vex ordered. "And your mama."

Kine opened the wards, and Vex charged out to her rig. If those raiders got inside, there were things she didn't want them to have. Things no raider—no one but a Bee Mama—should have.

Kine didn't run off for her parents. She followed at Vex's heels, whimpering. She stopped every few steps to pick up more stones, clutching them in her fist or shoving them in one of her various pockets.

"Kine, you need to get your parents. You said your papa was in the war. We're gonna need that if—Kine?"

The foxkin lowered her head and looked away, ears and tail drooping low.

"I can't."

Vex glared at the foxkin kit and growled in exasperation. "And why?"

"They're dead."

The words were so soft, Vex almost mistook it for the wasteland wind.

"They what now?" she asked, more gently.

"They're dead. A chupra got into the dome, bit 'em, and…and…"

Kine sniffled

Vex's expression softened. *The graves by the road. Of course.* Chupras, local shorthand for chupacabra, were clever and ravenous.

They could burrow right under a ward, given time and inspiration. The only farm sitting pretty in the middle of hundreds of miles of desolate wasteland would have been too much for any chupra to pass up. And once inside? She could figure out well enough what came after that "and."

"You all alone?"

Kine nodded. The bees' report suddenly made much more sense. *Damn it. Damn it to hell.*

"How long?" Vex asked.

"Two weeks now. I've tried to keep the garden alive. Mama taught me so much, but I'm no good at fighting. I can't...I don't..." Kine broke down sobbing.

Vex looked back over the field of green and growing things. Her jaw hung open.

"You kept this alive? All that time? All by *yourself?*" Vex looked at the foxkin, her eyes wide with disbelief.

Kine nodded miserably, her russet fur stained with tears. "It's hard, without mama to help, but she taught me everything she knew, or near about. They're gonna burn it, aren't they? Those raiders are gonna come, and take it all, and burn it, or *worse,* and I'm gonna die here!"

"No, you ain't."

Kine stopped sobbing and looked at Vex.

Vex looked at the foxkin, the corner of her blackened lips crooking up in what might have been a smile, twenty years and a hundred thousand miles ago.

"I...ain't?" Kine rubbed her eyes with the heels of her paws.

"Didn't anyone ever tell you, kid? You never mess with a Bee Mama." Vex's yellow teeth gleamed in the sun. "My girls are *hungry.* Now, here's what I need you to do."

Kine nodded, and listened, and the paw gripping the fistful of stones loosened.

***

The raider rigs approached the dome, spewing thick black smoke and filling the air with noxious noise. As they came close, Vex could see painted on the side of one rig a stylized M overlaid with a sweeping

V. The growl in her chest deepened. She knew that mark, and it told her all she needed to know about whoever was in charge of this raiding gang.

Of course. Humans dyin' of plague left and right, but the Vammatar Corp bastards that started it all are still alive and kicking. There's no justice left in the world.

The rigs came to a halt outside the dome, and six forms piled out of the three cabs. A human, and five canidkin. All six wore the patchwork clothing of the wasteland, but each wore the same stylized VM somewhere on their bodies, either as a tattoo (in the case of the human) or a brand (in the case of the houndmen).

I hate houndmen, Vex thought. *Of all the canidkin spliced into existence, nothing is as stupidly loyal as a houndman. Or as ugly.* She wondered what dog each of them had been cut with. Looked like a dingo, a beagle, two Chihuahuas, and a corgi. All of them bore scars or signs of mange. Vex's nose wrinkled in disgust.

"Looks like we got a live one here!" one of the houndmen—the dingo—yipped.

"Look-ee there, we got ourselves a bear!"

"Any lions and tigers in there with ya?"

"Oh my!"

"Get a load of this rig. What's a splice like that doing with a rig like this?" The beagle houndmen laid a paw on the hood of her rig, his dull claws scraping against the metal. A red tumor bulged from his neck, distorting his face and giving him a permanent rictus smile.

Vex growled. The beagle snatched his paw back. The other four houndmen howled with laughter.

A shrill whistle silenced the houndmen. They turned toward the human, clearly the leader of this pack, and Vex took stock of him. He had the rangy build of a man who'd been between good meals far too often, and the swagger of a man who was inclined to take that meal rather than ask for it. His thinning ginger hair was slicked back in a greasy ponytail, the knees of his filthy jeans shredded. He held in one grimy hand a tarnished dog whistle. He approached the sealed door to the dome and locked gazes with Vex through the film of the bubble dome.

"Let us in," he demanded.

Vex laughed and shook her head. "Move along, raider. This ain't a place for your kind."

The human smiled, a slight thing, but enough to cool Vex's blood. It wasn't the smile of a sane creature.

"Everything is our place, or have you forgotten, *splice?*" he said. Behind him, the pack of houndmen yipped and howled in derision.

Vex took a deep breath and returned the human's grin with one of her own. "Not forgotten, Vammatar scum," Vex replied calmly. "Just don't matter anymore. Move along."

The human rolled his shoulders and pulled a length of blackened pipe from his belt. "My kind built these domes."

"Your kind also built the bombs that damned us all. What's your point?"

The human ground his teeth and brandished his pipe. "Last time I ask nicely. Let us in."

"Or you'll…what? Huff and puff?" Vex challenged. "I got all I need in here. Food, water, power. Can't starve me out, can't bribe your way in. Kindly fuck off to whatever lab you and your bitches crawled out from."

The human rolled his shoulders, cracking his neck. "I'll take your rig apart, splice. You've done a fine job of hiding it, but that's a Vammatar Corp rig. I know that profile anywhere."

Vex shrugged and scratched her chin. "I'd wager you won't get past a good look, though. Not a magi-canic among your lot, and I rekeyed the wards to work only for me. Gonna keep you from doin' more'n spitting at it. Even if you can get inside, it don't run. Out of mana and gas, and the engine's shot besides. But by all means, go ahead and try. Been a dull time out here. I could use the entertainment."

The human narrowed his eyes. "What are you hiding, splice?"

Vex set her hands on her hips, paws resting on the butts of her pistols, and shrugged.

The human's gaze settled on the beehives, and his grin melted into an angry scowl.

"Oh, you aren't just a splice. You're a freak as well, aren't you?" he said.

Vex's black lips crooked upward. She twirled one paw and dropped into a mocking bow, sweeping her hat off her head.

"Boss, what's this we got here?" The corgi houndman kicked at the graves by the side of the road. He knocked over the wooden markers and started to use one to dig through the loose dirt.

The human turned and leered. "Looks like we got graves. Think they still got their skins? I hear bear hide is damned warm on a cold night."

"Don't you dare!"

Kine sprang from her hiding place and charged toward the dome's entrance.

"Kine! No!" Vex roared, but it was too late. Kine's nimble fingers had already finished the gesture to open the ward and she lunged through the doorway, closing on the corgi houndman. She barreled him over and clawed at him, snapping and snarling like a mad thing. Her jaws clamped shut on one tattered ear and yanked, shredding it further. He screamed batted at her, but she held tight.

The dingo houndman pried her loose before she could do any real damage and restrained her. "Well, look-ee here. Must be *your* family down there. Boss, fancy a new fox skin coat? Bet we got enough for at least two, and a hat if we count this little scrap. Or maybe a guard fox. She scared the piss outta the runt."

"Everything scares the piss outta the runt," one of the Chihuahuas snickered. Vex couldn't tell which. They looked alike enough to be twins. "Even baby fox kits."

"Shut up! She jumped me!" the corgi shrilled. "Let me eat her. Just one bite. Fox kits gotta be softer'n kibble." He licked his chops and slunk closer to her. "Been so long since I had fresh meat."

Kine snarled and tried to bite the dingo houndman holding her, but he slapped one mangy paw over her muzzle and pinched it shut.

"Leave off, runt. This one's more'n you can handle. Why don't you pick on something more your pay grade?" the dingo said.

"Something that can't fight back," said one Chihuahua.

"Like the dead," finished the second Chihuahua.

The corgi houndman growled impotently and went back to desecrating the graves, muttering darkly over his shoulder at the other houndmen.

The human turned to Vex, still within the dome, and his cold smile widened. "Open the door, splice. Or watch us skin her and whatever we find in those graves."

Vex ground her teeth. "I can't. Kid's the only one who knows how to get in and out."

The human bent down and looked Kine in the eye. "The throw rug telling the truth?" he asked. Kine nodded, her eyes squinted shut.

"You open that dome. We take what we want, and we leave whatever's left for you and the vultures. Agreed?"

Kine whimpered.

"Kine, the garden can be regrown. Can't fix the dead," Vex said.

"You should listen to your friend. Wouldn't want anybody to get hurt now," the human crooned. The Chihuahua houndmen snickered in eerie unison.

"Kine," Vex said, her voice soft. "Open the door."

Kine nodded, and the human raider dragged her to the door. Kine whispered the passphrase and gestured, and the gate irised open. The human whistled, and the corgi houndman desecrating the graves slunk back to his master's side. They stepped inside the dome, Kine still in the grip of the dingo houndman, the rest trailing in behind. Vex seethed. *Not how this was supposed to go, kid.*

A pair of bees came and checked out the new group to enter the dome. They quickly zoomed off. Moments later, the bees deserted the flowers and filtered back into their hives.

The drone of Vex's bees fell silent all across the garden.

The four houndmen not holding Kine captive all drew and aimed weapons at Vex. Two handguns, a rifle, and a shotgun. "Drop all your weapons, bearkin," the beagle houndman demanded.

Vex obliged, lip curled in disgust. Frick and Frack dropped in the dirt, followed by Wilson. Finally, she dropped her slingshot and its leather pouch. She kicked them all out of reach and glared furiously at the raiders.

"We're gonna eat like fat rats here for a good long time, boys," the human crowed. "Look at all that green stuff. And hives! Honey for days. Thanks a bunch, *bug mage.*"

Vex grimaced at the slur, but said nothing.

The human came closer, close enough that Vex could smell the rot on his breath. "I want honey, bug mage. Now."

Vex scoffed. "Bees haven't been here long enough to make the stuff. Even I can't change that. Sorry, but you'll just have to do without, company man."

The human's face reddened, and without warning he pulled out his gun and aimed it right between Vex's eyes. She swallowed; the only sign of concern she showed. Her paws were easy at her sides, her stance solid and sure.

"I said, give me some honey, splice."

"No."

The human's expression hardened. He dropped his aim and shot Vex in the leg. Vex bellowed in pain and dropped to one knee, clutching the place where the bullet bit.

"Leave her alone!" Kine shrieked, twisting her muzzle free of the dingo's grip. She chomped down, hard, on his paw. He howled and lost his hold on her. Kine shot off into the garden, vanishing from view.

Only Vex saw that as she fled, the foxkin kit had scooped up one of Vex's discarded weapons. Not the pistols, not the rifle, but the slingshot and pouch.

In spite of the pain, Vex smiled. *Clever kid.*

"I want some honey, bug mage. Give it to me, or I shoot out your other kneecap."

"You were a bit high for my kneecap, ass-jackal," Vex snapped, gasping. "And you'll have anything from my hives over my dead body." Blood ran in red rivulets from between her fingers. *Shit, did that bastard hit something vital? Can't stop the bleeding.*

From the hives, there came a low, angry drone.

The human pressed the still-warm tip of his gun against Vex's head, singeing her fur, but she didn't flinch. She stared at him, looking him square in the eye. "You'll get nothing, company man. You should walk away from this place while you still have your skin intact."

The human laughed. "I'm gonna walk away, alright. With my skin, your hide, and the hide of that whelp helping you."

From somewhere in the garden, there was a snap, and something small hit the human in the back of the head, splattering yellow gunk everywhere. Vex flinched back from the stuff like it was acid.

"What the *fuck?*" he snarled, swiping at the stuff. The air became thick with the cloying scent of—

"Bananas? The fuck is this shit? Poison?" He swiped frantically to get it off, but only managed to smear it around.

Another splat ball launched from across the thicket, hitting the human in the chest this time.

The hives roared louder.

"Ain't poison, hotshot." Vex said, pressing both palms against her leg, still trying to stem the bleeding. "It's something real special that only a Bee Mama like me carries with her."

Another volley, and three more splat balls thunked into three of the hounds. They yelped and whirled, but couldn't find Kine. She tagged the last two from somewhere off to Vex's left, but she never saw more than a flash of russet fur through the weeds. Vex was momentarily amused that the corgi houndman was tagged right in the crotch. *Kid either aimed or got lucky. My money's on aimed.*

From all forty hives, a steady stream of bees began to pour out.

The human pointed his gun at Vex again. "Call them off. Now."

"Nah. Ain't me they want. You messed with their Bee Mama. Bees don't take kindly to that."

Before the human could make another threat, the bees were upon him. A tornado of enraged insects enveloped him and each of the houndmen. He fired blindly at the swarm and managed only to hit his own houndmen. She couldn't see which ones through the furious storm of bees. She could only hear screams.

"Kine! Get over here!" Vex shouted. She yanked her hat over her head, smearing her blood along the brim as she tightened the strings around her face. Bees whirled around her but didn't attack. They knew her scent, her blood, and the reek of it on the air only made them madder. The gunshot had weakened her, but she still had enough strength to keep them at bay a little longer. *A swarm of bees in June,* she hummed under her breath, *is worth a silver spoon. Nothing to see here, ladies. Carry on, carry on.* She repeated it like a litany in her mind. So long as she stayed calm, calm as ice, calm as dust, they'd leave her alone.

Hopefully. Even a Bee Mama had a hard time calming bees in a blood frenzy, and she'd never seen her hives this furious. They knew her and her scent, but anyone else—

"Kine!"

The foxkin darted from the bushes, swiping at the bees zooming about her.

Vex swept the foxkin under her long coat and began to limp away. More bees pinged against her, their stingers bouncing off the hard leather of her coat. They dropped into the dirt and began lapping at the blood trail left with every step Vex took.

"Why are they going after you?" Kine whimpered. Already, her hands were swelling from three stings.

"I lost a lot of blood, kid. My girls were already hungry, and now they're *pissed*. We gotta get outta this dome. Ain't gonna be nothin' left alive in here when they're done."

Vex limped to door of the dome, leaning on Kine to keep her balance. More and more bees filled the air behind them, drowning out the screams from the raiders. A single bee came and hovered before Vex's eyes for a moment, made a series of short buzzing sounds, then flew off.

"Kine, honey, if you can get that door open, I'll be a very happy bear," Vex said. *Blood is in the air, Bee Mama,* it had said. *So much blood. So hungry.*

Kine tried three times, but her swollen fingers couldn't make the right gesture to unlock it.

"We're trapped!" Kine shrilled, panicking.

Vex cast around. "The tree! Get to the rowan tree. We can hunker down there and hope for the best."

Kine dove back under Vex's coat, and Vex pulled it tight, hoping it would be enough to protect the foxkin from the worst of the swarm.

The pair got to the tree, and Vex shrugged out of her long coat. She draped it about both of them and they huddled beneath, Vex's back to the trunk and Kine curled up in Vex's arms, listening to more and more bees test the leather, hitting it like hail.

"Get your paws into the dirt. They can smell the pheromone on you."

"I barely touched them!"

"Bees got a real good sense of smell, kid, and they stung you a few times. They're gonna go after anything with a whiff of alarm pheromone on 'em."

Kine did as Vex said, and the hail of angry bees tapered off. The roar continued, though, and Kine whimpered, snuggling against Vex's side. Vex grimaced, feeling Kine elbow a place where one of the bees stung her. Kine pulled back and tilted her head to one side.

"But you're their Bee Mama. Why'd they get you?" she asked.

"Ain't one of your plants ever bit you? Not their fault. Just how they are. Plants got thorns, bees got stings. Sometimes, squishy things like people get in the way."

Another swarm of bees plunked against their shelter, and Kine whined.

"It's alright, Kine. Bee Mama's got you safe and sound," she rumbled. "We're safe here for now."

"What's gonna happen to them?" Kine asked, clutching her paws to her chest. "Don't bees die when they sting?"

"Later," Vex replied grimly. The edges of her vision greyed.

Vex hummed her honey bee lullaby, and Kine eventually drifted off to sleep.

A swarm of bees in June is worth a silver spoon indeed, Vex mused wryly.

Outside, the roar of the bees went on, and on. And on.

***

It was three hours before the roar died down enough that Vex felt safe to peek her snout out from the shelter of her coat. The sun was near setting; ruddy light filtered through the seams in her coat. Three bees were camped on the bark of the rowan tree right near her nose. Vex froze.

The bees buzzed softly, almost ruefully.

"Y'all had your fill, I take it?"

An affirmative drone.

"Gonna be a bumper year for you, all that protein."

A proud and very satisfied buzz replied.

"You *can* talk to them!" Kine exclaimed. The three bees flicked their wings and turned to regard Kine, who shuddered and looked away.

Vex made a wry face. "The fewer people who know what these ladies are, the better."

The three scouts thrummed softly.

"You have smart bees." An accusation.

Vex sighed.

"They're my girls. I found 'em in a Vammatar lab, left to starve. They'd spliced honey bees with hornets and when they were done, just...left 'em. Locked 'em up in a dome to starve. I couldn't leave 'em like that, so I took the hives. Been running ever since with 'em, going from Farm to Farm. Most folks don't even know a true honey bee no more. They just think mine are kinda big, kinda weird lookin', but still just honey bees."

"But if they're smart, can't they just ignore the splat balls?" Kine asked.

"Can you ignore bein' hungry? The scent of fresh blood and the alarm pheromone was too much for them to ignore. You saw them before this. Usually, they're as sweet as bees come. But they're not *tame* bees, kid. Can't help but go into a frenzy when they smell that alarm pheromone. And when their Mama is hurt? Forget it. The Vammatar made 'em that way. I don't like to use it, but the bees trust me. Won't ever use that trick on something that didn't deserve it. The pheromones hit the air, and then like sharks and blood, they go mad. And unlike honey bees, my girls can sting again and again. Let me see your paws."

Kine held out her paws, and Vex sighed. "We gotta get something on those." She turned her attention back to the three scouts. "We gonna get hassled getting to the rig?"

A negative drone.

"Tell your regent I thank her kindly, and apologize for the inconvenience."

Another buzz, and the three scouts flew off.

"Now, they might still be grumpy. Stay under the coat, you hear? If you've still got that stuff on your fur, they'll frenzy all over again. I can keep 'em calm with a song, but I'd rather not need to. Throat's getting a bit sore." Vex checked her leg. It had stopped bleeding, mostly. She hoped it wouldn't be enough to rile them up again.

Kine nodded and tucked her hands under her armpits.

The walk to the rig was uneventful, save for Vex's quick glance at the place where six mounds of writhing bees crouched. She shuddered and moved on.

Kine showed Vex the gesture to open the door, and it finally opened for her. The pair limped across the dusty road.

Kine glanced just once over at the graves and shivered.

Vex unlocked the cab and pulled a tube of salve from the glove compartment.

"They didn't get the graves," Kine said.

"Nope," Vex agreed, tossing the tube of salve to Kine.

"The plan worked." Kine bobbled the tube and caught it.

Vex snorted. "That wasn't the plan," she said. "You weren't supposed to leave the dome."

"Still worked."

"Cocky."

Kine shrugged, and Vex sighed. She pointed to the tube of salve in Kine's paws.

"Should stop them from swelling up much more. Stings are gonna itch for a week, though," Vex said. "And it'll probably be two or three days before the swelling goes down."

"I'll live."

Vex chuckled. "Yeah, you'll live."

Kine grinned, and then the grin faded. "But what about the garden?"

Vex inhaled and scratched her chin. "Well, if it's all the same to you, me and the girls got no place to be for a while. Looks like you could use a hand around here. Gonna be at least a week before that magi-canic gets out this way anyhow. Mind if we stick around for a while?"

Kine's grin split ear to ear. "Yeah, I guess you can stay. As long as you don't mind doing the weeding for a week while these heal."

Vex plopped her hat with the veil over Kine's head. "Deal," she said.

Under the dome, the bees thrummed.

For some, bureaucracies are essential antibodies, protecting the organism that is the state from weakness and decay. Pay your taxes, sign the forms, and endure necessary pains to enjoy the fruits of a stronger, more resilient society. Nations are funny things, social collections of perpetuated truths, lies and crafted myths to make the whole machine run. So what happens when those tasked with making the machine work find its wheels grinding down upon them and those they love? When the truth wraps its tiny fingers around yours, will you truly learn what perfection cost you?

Protecting the Code

TJ Minde

"We had four approved births last month," the magistrate said, her brown head looking down as she stared at her notes. The pine marten wore long black robes that matched the fur on her paws. "And while all four were from approved pairings, the Research Institute is predicting they will not be of the quality they want. And if the RI isn't happy, we shouldn't be either."

Her eyes met Dixion's and stayed there for a moment.

While his dark ears fell, he held her gaze. "I understand how important it is that the best pairs mate. But don't blame my team if the approved couples didn't create the desired offspring."

"We don't have the space for useless people."

"I'm well aware of the shortages on space and food we have, Miranda. I'm just as affected by the rationing as you are. And I see the same reports from the front lines." Dixion crossed his arms.

With that, the room broke out in a murmur. Hushed tones carried along the words of "war" and "death."

"Yes, yes," she stood, glaring at Dixion and raising her voice over the din. "I know what the rumors are. But until the head counsel's directions change, we do our duty." She paused, waiting until she had their attention again. "We've received new guidelines for the Matchmakers." She shuffled through her papers, pulling one sheet to the front and sliding it to Dixion.

The magistrate clasped her paws behind her back as she paced her side of the table. "They want more brains *and* brawn from females; intelligence scores one-twenty or higher with above average health. From males, more brains than brawn; health is still a factor, but intelligence scores are more important around one-twenty range, as well. RI is hoping for some new blood for their science teams. The sooner, the better."

She stopped and set her paws on the back of her chair. "Is that understood, Matchmakers?"

"Yes, ma'am." The seven other martins around Dixion spoke as one.

She gave a curt nod. "Good. And make no exceptions; I don't want to hear about approvals for sob stories. And if there's the slightest hint someone of poor quality was approved, audits will begin again."

Dixion held back a sigh. "I trust my team. You don't need to worry about that."

"Good." She sat back down in her seat and collected her papers. "And one final note: there has been word from the Office of Intelligence. There are small groups trying to form a resistance of sorts, aiming to subvert the system that we've worked hard to build. They obviously don't know what they're doing." She clicked her tongue. "Stupid breeders."

Again, the whispers picked up.

The magistrate raised her paws. "You don't need to worry. As I said, this came from the Office of Intelligence. They're on top of the situation and are already investigating the issue. Now keep that out of your mind and carry on with your business." She stood. "Dismissed."

***

Dixion kept to himself as he made his way back to his chambers. He wasn't as social as the others in his department, and he liked it that way.

As he turned down the final hall to his chamber, three women sat at the bench waiting for him. He kept his head up as he walked past and they kept theirs down. Once the door was closed behind him, Dixion removed his formal robe and hung it on the hook behind the door, leaving him in his tight orange top and black slacks.

The marten sat back in his chair and pressed a button on his desk, accessing his small digital calendar. He scowled as the names and current job titles appeared on his screen.

"Cole, Janet," he called.

A moment later, the first woman entered his chamber. Her job title labeled her a farmer, as did her dark green shirt. She had the musculature for it: strong arms and legs and eyes that looked as if she was used to giving orders and directions.

She stood tall and confident, though her gaze affixed at the wall behind the pine marten. "My sister told me you were looking for strong women, Matchmaker." She slid her application across to Dixion. "People always said I have hips for birthing, and even a man like *you* can see that."

"You may talk up yourself however you like, Mrs. Cole." The matchmaker scanned the sheet for the fields he needed, checking boxes and initialing lines as he went. "But no matter what you tell me, the outcome will be the same."

She locked her paws behind her back. "Well, nevertheless, my husband was just approved for breeding and we're excited to start a family and raise a solider for our country."

He grabbed a stamp from the table and rolled it across the page. "I'm sorry, but your application doesn't line up with what the country needs right now." He held the paper out to her.

"What?" Her jaw dropped.

Dixion shook the page in the air. "Your application has been denied. You may try again next month."

"But my sister was just approved. And she's nowhere near as good as I am at what I do."

He sighed. "As I said before, Mrs. Cole, it doesn't matter what you tell me. You don't have the qualifications we need right now."

"That can't be right." Her rage grew. "If you don't approve me, it shows you queers don't know what a *real* woman is." She crossed her arms under her chest in anger.

"And if you really want to disrespect the head matchmaker—or any of us based on our decisions or sexuality, I can have it arranged so you are never *able* to breed." He laced his paws together on his desk. "Would you rather that?"

Her anger melted to fear in a heartbeat as her arms fell to her side. "No sir. I apologize. Please forgive me."

With a dismissive sigh he waved her off and looked at his calendar.

"Butler, Sarah."

As Mrs. Cole exited the room, Mrs. Butler slipped in and set her paper on the desk. The white shirt of a minor stood out against the shawl draped over her shoulders.

"Are you really here for approval?" Dixion said as he looked over her application.

She shook her head. "I need your help." She was almost whispering.

"You realize just being here could be bad, right? For both of us. And there's no way I can approve a minor for breeding. There's no exception to be had here." He rolled the same stamp across her page. "Even if there were, I couldn't approve you."

She nodded. "I understand. Come by the house. Please." She took the page and slipped out the door without another word.

Dixion rubbed the bridge of his muzzle before calling in the next woman.

***

The pine marten checked his watch: 7:03pm. *The walk didn't take me that long,* Dixion thought. The sun was setting on the quiet neighborhood, painting the sky with red and orange hues. Cookie-cutter home after cookie-cutter home stood side by side with the only distinguishing features being the number on the house and the tree in each yard that grew as it would.

He walked up the sidewalk to home 713. The building, accented with wood, felt like it belonged in a tree with large steps leading up to the door and a foundation that looked curved to fit into a massive oak.

I hope everything's alright. He took a breath, steadying himself, and then knocked on the door.

It didn't take long for a man about as tall as Dixion to answer the door. He wore a green shirt and a haggard look. "You came," he said in surprise. "Are you alone?" He poked his head out, looking around.

"That's an odd question, Dad. No offer of hug or shelter for your genetic code?" He raised his arms in offer of one himself.

The two martens locked eyes. Dixion, calm and hopeful; his father, jittery and nervous.

What's he scared of? He lowered his arms. *Me?* "Everything okay?"

Dixion whispered. "Sarah was in my office with an application today. She asked me to come but didn't say why. If she came to me at work like that, it must be important. Are you and Mom alright?"

"Yeah." His father looked down.

"Dad, what's wrong?" Dixion asked.

The older marten ushered him inside. "You'll understand in a moment." Once they both crossed the threshold, his father closed and locked the door behind them.

"You sure everything's okay?" Concern grew in Dixion's voice. "Is Mom having health issues? Trouble at work for you?"

"No, no. Nothing like that, Dixie." Dad sighed and offered a hug. Without a second thought, Dixion walked into his arms. "We're probably worrying your mother. Let's go." He held his son for a moment before leading them both down the hall.

As they walked into the living room, they found an older marten sitting on the couch, book in her paw and a steaming mug nearby.

"Coffee at this hour?" Dixion joked.

She looked up at him for a moment and her eyes went wide before bursting into tears.

Both men moved toward her.

"It's okay Mom, it's just me. What's wrong?" Dixion stroked her paw, trying to comfort her.

She threw her arms around him. "I'm sorry. I'm sorry." She sobbed as both her son and husband held her. "I've just been so nervous and tense and I thought your orange shirt was red for a moment and my heart stopped." As she brought herself under control again, his mother sniffed and pulled back, reaching for a tissue.

"Took me a moment to recognize you through the fear." She let out a nervous chuckle.

"What has you so on-edge, Mom?" Dixion continued to hold her paw.

She looked to her husband.

He looked to his wife.

Fear and nervousness was plain on their muzzles.

"What in the world is going on!" Dixion looked from one parent to another.

Before either could answer, footsteps came from down the hall. "Mom, are you okay? I thought I heard crying?" The youngest of his family asked as she stepped into the room.

Dixion saw her again, though this time dressed down. Sarah still wore a white shirt, but this one was larger.

As she caught sight of Dixion, her eyes went wide like her mother, but she didn't cry. "Brother, you made it." With a smile on her muzzle, she scurried over and wrapped him in a hug.

"You asked me to, didn't you?" Dixion held his sister for another moment before something odd pressed against his middle and his brow furrowed. He grabbed her by the shoulders, pulled her back, and looked down. Earlier that day, he was trying to get her out of his office so quick to avoid trouble that he didn't really look at her. Now, without the shawl and the immediate pressure of the law, he could.

Her middle was more pronounced than it used to be.

"Please tell me you've gained weight." A somber mood fell over the room. Dixion looked from Sarah to each of his parents and back to her belly.

A small bump traveled from one side of Sarah's shirt to the other.

"Oh my God, you're pregnant." He ran a paw through the fur on top of his head. "Do you know what this means?"

"Yeah," Sarah answered. Her eyes were locked on the floor. "I didn't mean for it to happen."

"'Didn't mean for it to happen?' How the hell *did* it happen?"

She smirked. "Well, when a boy and a girl like each other a lot—"

Dixion threw his paws up. "That's not what I mean and you know it."

Sarah sighed. "I talked my boyfriend into having sex—"

"Didn't you listen to the dating and breeding lectures in school? Why the hell would you do that!"

"Because we were stupid kids in love. Or we thought we were. And I assumed birth control and a condom was enough."

"Obviously not." Dixion pointed to her stomach.

Sarah crossed her arms. "Obviously."

"What's his name?"

"It doesn't matter. The second he found out I was pregnant, he split."

"I have ways to find out where he went."

"Dixie," she balled up a paw and set it on her hip. "It. Doesn't. Matter." Sarah accented each word with a jab at the air with her fingers. "He really doesn't care anyway. He and his family were more concerned about his own hide."

Dixion put a paw on the bridge of his muzzle. "And is that why you came by today? Trying to get approval and try to pass the kit off or something?"

"Kits," she corrected.

"*Twins*? Are you serious?"

His mother cleared her throat. "We think so. We can't take her to a doctor to properly confirm, but it feels like two."

"Have you thought about terminating—"

"No." Sarah cut him off. "I want to have some level of control over my reproduction, and I know the consequences for this," she said as she cupped her belly. "And I don't want to die in some back alley because an abortion went wrong. Besides," Sarah looked down at her stomach, "I care too much about them now." She kept her eyes down. "I went to your office today to ask you for help."

Dixion blinked at her in shock. "Help? What can I do to help?"

Sarah burst into tears. "I don't *know*. And that's the problem." She pressed her face to her brother's chest, hugged him as she cried. "I'm scared. Both for me and the kits. And I turned to you because big brothers help their little sisters when they need it, right?"

Dixion held her as she cried out her pent up fear, rubbing her back the whole time. After a short while, he guided her toward the couch. Sarah continued to cling to his side as tears still fell. Soon the anguished cries turned to sobs, and the sobs to silence as she fell asleep.

His mother sighed. "I think that's the first time she's let herself really feel all of this."

Dixion's mind wandered not just on his sister's situation, but around the words she said and her feelings tied to it all. "That sounds like her. She's always been the strong one." He sighed. "How far along is she?"

"We think she's late in the second trimester, or early in the third." Their mother reached out and pet Sarah's shoulder. "She doesn't show much yet, but she'll blow up the next few weeks."

"So she'll be giving birth in about two months." Dixion shook his head. "That's really not a lot of time."

"We know, but we have to ask: is there anything you can do, Dixie?"

She set a paw on his arm.

He looked from his sister to his parents, haggard and worried expression on their faces, and back. "I… don't know." He pet Sarah's arm. "I mean, I'm just the guy that approves women to breed. I have no idea how I could help."

Closing his eyes, he took a breath. "But, I can't just leave this alone. I'm not going to promise anything for anyone, but I'll at least think about it."

Without a word, his mother threw her arms around him. "Thank you, Dixie. Thank you so much."

***

"Dixion." The pine marten stood from the barstool he sat on. "I was worried you wouldn't make it."

"Yeah. Sorry Quinn." He leaned across the table and pecked the other marten on the cheek before he took the seat beside him.

"Started to think you stood me up for our second date." He reached out and grabbed Dixion's paw.

"Well, I'm here now." He sighed. "I had dinner with my family tonight and they live a bit further from here than I do. Turns out Dad may be sick and they wanted to tell me in person.

"Well, you could have sent a note or something." Quinn scolded. "I would have been there in a minute."

Dixion nodded. "I know; I should have at least let you know I'd be late. I got caught up in everything and forgot." He pecked Quinn on the side of his muzzle again. "Forgive me?"

Quinn smiled. "Depends. How will you make it up to me?"

"Oh, I can think of a few ways." Dixion winked as he rubbed his fingers under Quinn's chin.

"I *bet* you can." He yawned and stretched, making his back snap, crackle and pop. "But probably not tonight." Quinn tilted his arm reading the time on the watch. "It's already pretty late."

"Wait, wait, I hint at sex and you brush it off?" Dixion asked.

Quinn chuckled. "It's almost midnight, babe. And we both got work in the morning." He sipped from the glass in front of him. "And this might be my second round, so," he winked, "there's that, too. Besides, the curfew is coming up and you don't have my place registered yet. How about a rain check?"

Dixion let out an overly dramatic sigh. "Fine. We should register each other's places for check in." He looked down at his lover's drink. "You ready for another."

"My, my," Quinn said, sliding his empty glass towards Dixion, "saving the moving truck for the third date?"

Dixion snickered. "Please. It would just be nice to spend the night, maybe." He took the glass. "You're usual?"

"If you'd be so kind."

Dixion winked. "Be right back." He walked to the bar and, a moment later, returned with two fresh glasses of dark red wine. "Hey Quinn?" he asked as he took his seat again. "Have you thought much about kids?"

Quinn scoffed. "Beyond choosing who gets to make them at work, I don't see a point."

"Really? You don't want to pass on your genetic code?"

This time, Quinn laughed. "My code? I've gotten so much crap from people for denying their application; why would I want to go through all of that myself?"

Dixion sipped from his glass and shrugged. "I don't know. So someone remembers you when you're gone? Or so there's proof you were here once?"

"Dix," Quinn started as he reached out his paw to his lover's, "I'm happy without them. I don't care about passing on my name or anything like that. And I really don't see why breeders want them so badly."

"I never said anything about having our own. Nothing says we can't adopt. Might be easier to pick the traits the Research Institute is looking for and getting the best ones they want."

Quinn chuckled. "Are we really talking about kids on our second date?" He shook his head. "Well then, let me stop you there. I'm not against having my own kids; I'm against having *any* kids. They're such a drain on resources: costs for food, on time, additional stress," he counted the reasons off on his paw before looking to Dixion. "And then there's the biggest thing: we're freaking Matchmakers. Imagine how hard it would be for us to even start the process. I mean, they'd have us under a microscope, making sure we didn't subvert the system somehow." He sipped his drink. "Do you really want to have to deal with all of that?"

Dixion sighed. *Always thinking of things I miss.* "No, you have a point."

"I know I do." Quinn leaned over and kissed Dixion. "But what made you think about kids all of a sudden?"

"Huh? Oh, uh," Dixion scratched at the back of his head. "Just thinking about mortality and stuff with my Dad being sick. Like how I'll remember him and Mom when they're gone, but will anyone remember me?"

"Well, I wouldn't worry too much about it." He kissed Dixion again. "Now enough of the serious talk: did you hear about Jennifer in Fulfilment?" Quinn leaned forward to gossip.

***

Dixion scribbled on the notepad in front of him as the last woman walked out of his office. *Don't have any other appointments until after lunch.* He reached for the ever-growing stack of papers at the edge of his desk. *Let's see if I can't get some of this out of the way.* It didn't matter what the paper said; by the time anything hit his desk for approval, outside of an interview, it had been checked, double checked and triple checked for accuracy. It just needed his signature. The task was so simple, he moved on autopilot.

He scribbled his name and set the page aside. Again and again. *God, I wish I had a stamp like Miranda's for this. Though maybe one not as official.* Page after page, signature after signature, only paying as much attention as he had to.

He'd catch a word here or a phrase there, but never enough to care.

Until he saw "woman" and "child" on the same page and his thoughts went back to his family. *There has to be something to do for Sarah.* He pressed his paw over the bridge of his muzzle. *I mean, I've seen the results of this situation before: the children are taken away. No one knows what happens to them after that. And the parents are sterilized and locked up—punishment on top of a punishment.* Dixion sat back in his chair with a sigh.

And Mom and Dad would probably be taken too. Hell, they'd be seen as complicit in all of it. At best, they'd be locked up as well. At worst...

A knock at the door pulled him from his thoughts. Shaking his head, he sat up and put his pen to paper. "Come in." The door opened, but he didn't look up and continued signing.

"I have a few more for you, Dixion." His administrative assistant stood a few steps from his desk in her blue blouse. "The magistrate's secretary dropped them off on his way out."

"Thank you, Kim. I'll add them to the stack." He lifted the pile of pages up. "Here's fine," he said as he nodded to the desk.

She set the papers down. "You going to lunch soon?"

"Yeah." Dixion nodded as he aligned the edges and continued to sign again. "Just have some free time before my next appointment and these won't sign themselves."

"Well, you look like you've been working your fingers to the bone. Are you taking care of yourself? Eating right?" Her voice carried a softness of compassion he didn't get to hear often.

Dixion sighed again and set down his pen. "Yeah. I mean, Quinn and I were up late talking about... things."

"Talking, or..." Worry mixed in to her tone.

"We weren't fighting. I've been thinking about how my parents aren't getting any younger and how I'm not getting younger. Which brought on thoughts of my mortality and thoughts of passing on my code."

Kim chuckled. "Feeling your biological clock ticking a bit?"

Dixion rolled his eyes. "Not quite. But... sort of? We talked about kids some." He lowered his head and grabbed his pen again.

She crossed her arms. "And?"

"And he's not interested. Not having our own, not adopting. He just doesn't want kids."

"Well, maybe you can try to talk it though with him. Weigh some pros and cons."

Dixion shrugged. "Maybe. But I doubt it. It would probably just cause more stress, anyway."

"Well, in that case, try to not dwell on it too much, okay? Maybe get more sleep tonight. Remember you need to care for yourself." Kim set a paw on his shoulder.

"Thanks, dear."

She smiled. "You're welcome. Oh, and Miranda's secretary said the newest pages already have her stamp on them, so they can be submitted to Fulfillment once you're done." Kim turned and walked to the door. "When you can, leave home at home. Try to not let it affect your job."

Dixion nodded again. "I'll try. Thanks for listening."

The door closed behind her while Dixion continued. *Seems like she bought that.* He took a breath and shook his head before continuing. Order after order. Ruling after ruling. But when he saw the first document with Miranda's stamp, the wheels in his brain started to spin. *Well, there goes my lunch break.*

Dixion left his office and joined the collection of other pine martens at the elevator. When the lift going up chimed, he entered and pressed the button for the tenth floor. The ride was silent, but slow. *Is this a stupid idea? They'll have records...*

His mind ran as he waited. And when his stop came up, he pressed on and entered a small room.

"Hello, Matchmaker," the chipper pine marten in blue said from behind her desk. She typed faster than any person Dixion saw, and never looked at the keyboard. "How can Fulfillment help you today?"

His palms began to sweat. "I need a copy of travel papers."

She nodded. "Yes sir. And who's papers are you looking for?"

"I need a blank set. I think I have a forged page and I want to compare it."

She clacked away at her keyboard. "I can get you a duplicate but, for obvious reasons, it will be watermarked as an invalid document. Is that alright?"

He nodded his head. "I just need to see the true words on the page."

She smiled at Dixion. "And we can certainly do that." She continued to type away and a few moments later, the printer beside her whirled to life and spat out a page. "Here you are. I just need your signature for the document." She pointed to the digital screen pad at the front of her station.

Without question, he signed. "Thank you very much," Dixion said as he took the offered page.

"Any time Fulfillment can help, we'll be here." She turned back toward her screen, typing again.

With the page tucked safely under his arm, he returned to his office on the second floor and sat back in his chair, staring at the document. *This might work.*

***

The days turned into weeks, passing as they normally did for Dixion. Interviews, meetings and paperwork kept him busy day in and day out.

With a big yawn, the pine marten gathered up the papers from his desk and walked out of his office.

"Leaving for the night, Matchmaker?"

"Not yet, Kim." He smiled. "Just need to get the magistrate's approval on these documents. Worst case, I'll leave them on her desk. Then a stop to Fulfillment to drop the completed ones off. *Then* I'll head home."

The receptionist nodded as she made a note. "Sounds great. Have a wonderful night."

"You too, dear." He opened the door and made his way to the elevator. After pressing the button to call the lift, a chime emanated from the chrome doors and they slid open. In the carriage already was a fellow in a red shirt with gray fur in his muzzle.

"Afternoon Shawn. How's the Office of Intelligence treating you?" he asked as he stood beside the older man.

"Not too bad, Dixion. Kinda nice to not be working the streets, but it can get boring sitting at the front desk. Same shit, different day, right?" Shawn said.

"Tell me about it."

The older martin nodded to the folder in Dixion's arms. "Paper's for the magistrate?"

"You know me so well." Looking to the panel of buttons, Dixion noticed the twenty-second floor was already selected. "Heading up to the security office yourself, I see." he said.

"Yeah. Working a double tonight; was at the front desk for the first eight hours. Now they have me covering the floors for the second. Gotta make sure everyone here's safe and sound. You hear about the latest Breeder attack?"

"Nothing outside the whispers in the meetings."

Shawn nodded. "I've heard a bit more from higher-up's in OOI. Word is that they may be working with the wildcats."

"What? Pine martens *with* the wildcats?"

"That's the rumor anyway. After their last terrorist attack, a group of suspected Breeders were seen crossing the border into their country. Some think that means they're working together. Other say it may be a situation where, you know," he raised his paws in air quotes, "'the enemy of my enemy is my friend.'"

"And what is it they want exactly? Just to breed as their name suggests?"

Shawn shrugged. "That's what some people think. They haven't made any demands yet. All that's really been confirmed is their name. Anything more is as good a guess as any."

The elevator dinged as the carriage reached the floor. "Well, here's our stop." Shawn patted Dixion's shoulder. "You take care of yourself, okay?" Before he could reply, the older marten made his way into the hall.

"You too, Shawn," Dixion called after him and stepped out, heading in the other direction to the magistrate's office.

Stopping in front of her door, Dixion took a breath. *Please don't be in. Please don't be in.* He rapped his knuckles against the wood three times and waited. Five seconds. Fifteen seconds. No answer. He raised his paw and knocked a second time. Again, there was no response.

Dixion looked around. There was no sight of Shawn or anyone else on the floor.

He set his paw on the doorknob and twisted. *It's not locked.* His heart beat faster. *I got to be quick, but what if she's in?* The pine marten stood up straighter and held his breath. *I already have a plan. Just stick to it.* With an air of confidence, he opened the door expecting to see Miranda at her desk.

She wasn't.

The air rushed from his lungs. *Okay, work fast.* Dixion closed the door again and twisted the lock before moving toward her desk. *It has to be here somewhere.*

Her office, while larger than Dixion's, was very similar: desk and chair sitting in the middle of the room, short shelf of drawers behind it and bookcases flanking. Her desk was spartan, with no nick-knacks or other clutter. She kept a notebook resting atop a large desk calendar and a few bottles of brown liquor on the shelf behind her chair.

Well, there goes the hope for an easy find. He pushed down the thoughts and fears of getting caught and split the stack of papers into two piles on her desk before opening the first drawer. Inside were organized pens and notebooks, but nothing that looked like a stamp and inkpad. *Maybe it's under it?*

He reached a paw in, but pulled it back before touching a thing. *Would she notice?* Dixion balled his fist in apprehension. He closed the drawer and moved to the next.

Moving as fast as he could while still being quiet, Dixion checked drawer after drawer, moving the contents as little as possible. When the stamp was not found, he started checking the shelf behind the desk. *Crap, it's got to be here somewhere.*

He opened a drawer below the bottles and found short glasses and a boxy container. *Finally.*

The doorknob rattled.

Dixion looked over his shoulder. *Oh no.* He turned back to the desk, pulled a sheet from the bottom of the stack, then stepped back to the open drawer. Lifting the lid on the box, he saw a wooden handle attached to a rubber stamp inside.

The doorknob continued to rattle. Dixion grabbed the brand and the closed ink pad below and set both next to the paper. He flipped it to the correct spot before grabbing the inkpad in his paw.

As he tossed the lid open without a sound, the doorknob stopped rattling. *Dammit, is she getting Shawn?* With his other paw, he grabbed the stamp. Trying to keep calm, he pressed the brand from the inkpad to the page in a smooth, fluid motion.

With his heart racing, Dixion closed the lid to the pad and set it back in the box he found it in and set the stamp on top of it.

God, please let this dry quickly. He grabbed one of the two piles and, as he slid the page at random into the middle of the bundle, walked over to the door

He twisted the lock.

"What the hell?" he heard from the other side of the door. The marten's heart raced.

Dixion walked out and there stood Miranda with Shawn. The guard had a bundle of keys in his paw.

"What were you doing in my office with the door locked?" Miranda demanded.

"Oh, good evening Magistrate. I wasn't aware you were still here." Dixion forced what he hoped was a calm smile across his muzzle. "It must have been a habit. I lock mine when I don't have any appointments. Sorry about that." He bounced on his toes, trying to act aloof.

"I didn't ask *why* the door was locked." She crossed her arms and took a step forward. "What are those papers?"

"Completed files for Fulfillment. I just got finished with the morning's forms and the ones your assistance dropped off earlier. Wanted to give you the ones for your approval before I had these processed."

She held out her paw.

Dixion offered the papers. *Please don't see that page. Please don't see that page.* Miranda snatched them from his paw. He rubbed his writs anxiously and turned to Shawn. "Hope I didn't add too much excitement to your evening."

The guard shrugged. "All in a day's work."

Miranda shoved the papers back into Dixion's arms. "How have the Breeder attacks happened, Shawn? The reports said explosives, right?"

He scratched his head. "Yeah. Usually some sort of pressure trigger, or something like that. But Dixion's a matchmaker. He's gay."

She ignored his comment. "So, like, opening a drawer might set one off? Or sitting in a chair?"

"Possibly, but I don't think he'd do anything like that."

She turned to Dixion and pointed into her office. "Go open every drawer and cabinet in that room."

"I didn't, leave a bomb for you, Miranda."

"And I don't want to take any chances. Now go."

With the papers in hand, Dixion raised a paw to argue. "Miranda, I—"

"If you don't get your tail into that office in the next ten seconds, I'll have you arrested and interrogated as an enemy of the state."

His ears fell. "Yes ma'am," Dixion said in a small voice as he extended the papers to her. "Would you hold these for me?"

Without a word, she snatched them from his paws again. With his heart beating in his ears, Dixion moved about the room opening each and every cabinet and drawer he could find. About sixty seconds later, he rose from her chair and walked back.

"Could I have my papers back?" he asked.

She threw them into his arms. "Keep him here while I make sure nothing's missing." Before either Dixion or Shawn could respond, she stormed into her office.

Dixion watched from just outside the door as she moved around her space. She thumbed through the stack of papers on her desk, then through the drawers.

"Don't blame her," Shawn whispered. "Breeders have been targeting high officials in Family Planning. Everyone like her is on edge."

The two watched as she moved from drawer to drawer, and from cabinet to cabinet, before she walked back.

"Go about your business. But if I ever find you where you shouldn't be again, I'll have you arrested and questioned for treason." Without letting him respond, she slammed the door shut.

"Well, that certainly was exciting." Shawn bounced back and forth on his heels before walking on. "I'll at least have one good story for the night." He waved to Dixion without looking back. "Get going and have a wonderful evening."

Dixion raised a paw. "Thanks. You too."

He made his way down the hall and pressed the call button for the elevator again. Once the doors shut and he was on his way down again, he finally let out a sigh of relief.

***

"Hearfast, Juliet." Dixion sat at his desk with his day almost over as the young woman in a bright yellow shirt walked in.

"Thank you for seeing me again," she said as she stopped a few feet from his desk.

"Just part of the job. Let me get you your things." He made his way to the large filing cabinet. "I have your breeding papers, travel license and your leave of absence pass." He left the drawer open and dropped all three items into a manila folder and walked back to his desk. "I just need your signature and you'll be on your way." He held out a pen to her that she took without hesitation. "I'll admit I'm going to miss seeing you on TV for a while." Dixion smiled as he walked around his desk and handed her the folder.

"Don't worry, sir. I promise I'll be back after the kit is born." She beamed with pride and joy as she looked down, one paw around her middle and the other holding the folder tight.

"That's wonderful to hear." He gave her shoulder the slightest nudge and he walked her to the door. "And if there's anything else the Matchmakers or anyone else here at the Breeding Counsel can do, just let us know."

"I will. Again, thank you so much." She wrapped her arms around Dixion and walked out.

The smiled stayed on his muzzle until the door shut with an audible click. He sighed and looked at the clock. *Just enough time for my last meeting.* Looking around the room, he walked over to the open cabinet and grabbed a small card before closing the drawer.

"Banks, Sasha," he called as he sat. He waited for a moment before calling the name again. He rose from his chair, walked to the door and poked his head out. "Kim, did Banks, Sasha check in?"

"You're four forty-five pick-up?" She skimmed the check-in sheet. "No sir."

"Understood. Call her tomorrow and see if we can reschedule."

"Yes, sir."

As she made the note, Dixion closed the door and moved back to his desk. He took out a loose sheet of paper and scribbled the name "Sasha Banks" a few more times. *Has to be convincing.*

He took a breath and placed his pen to the logbook and signed the name before slipping the license into his pocket. *No turning back now.* Dixion closed his log and set it back in the drawer where it belonged.

Head held high, he grabbed his coat and threw it over his arm as he walked out the door. "I'm going to head home early, Kim."

"Sounds good, Matchmaker." She smiled up at him. "Though you may want to put *on* the coat; it's starting to get chilly."

Dixion shrugged. "Thanks, but I'm feeling a bit warm. Maybe it's just a cold setting in, but I like the breeze right now."

"Don't say I didn't warn you." She chuckled and waved. "Have a wonderful night."

"You too, dear."

He walked out the door of the building, doing his best to keep a slow, steady pace. He didn't want to look too excitable as he almost followed the path he'd been taking more and more. *Come on, Dix, mix it up. Just an afternoon walk; taking the long way home.*

Dixion meandered along and, about an hour or so later, walked up to a door and knocked. Three knocks, then two, and then another two. A moment later, he was greeted by his father.

"Hi Dixie. Good to see you." He hugged his son with a sigh. "Come on in, we're all excited you're here."

"'We're all?'" Dixion asked as he closed the door.

His father nodded. "Sarah had the kits this morning. A boy and a girl. You're an uncle."

Dixion ran past his father and into Sarah's room. She still laid in bed, looking exhausted, with a kit in each arm. "They're beautiful," he said in awe.

Sarah smiled. "Want to hold one?"

Dixion swallowed. "Can I?"

"Of course. Come on over." She nodded him towards her bed. "This is Roxie," she nudged the kit in her left arm, "and this is her brother, Hexion," then nuzzled the kit in her right arm closer to Dixion. Sarah smiled up at her brother. "Go on, you can pick him up."

He couldn't help but smile as Sarah raised her arm to him, offering up his nephew. The kit transitioned smoothly from mother to uncle, with Dixion cradling him close to his chest.

He rubbed a finger against Hexion's cheek. "They're beautiful," he whispered.

"You said that already," his mother chimed in. "But I've been saying it a bit myself." The three of them stood around, marveling over the miracle of new life.

The sleeping kit stretched out a paw and wrapped his digits around Dixion's finger. "He's so small." Dixion nuzzled the tiny paw.

His father chuckled "Of course. But children grow quicker than you think. The time will fly by."

"Oh, speaking of the kits: I was able to get Sarah's travel pass." Dixion cleared his throat. "Or should I say 'Sasha.'"

"'Sasha?'" Sarah and her mother asked at the same time.

"I faked a few documents and got you a travel license. That's how we're going to get you out." He smiled.

"And do you have it with you?" his father asked. "The travel license?"

Dixion nodded. "Tucked away in my coat pocket."

"But what about you?" His mother set a paw on his shoulder.

"I'll go with her. Give her an extra set of arms. And my government ID will smooth some things along. People shouldn't ask me questions. But we'll have to act fast."

"What about Quinn?" Sarah asked.

Dixion sighed. "I don't want to leave him, but I have to. He has no interest in kits and I don't know how he'd feel about breaking rules. Besides," he lifted his head from the kit in his arms and locked eyes with Sarah, "you're my code. I have to try to help."

"Do you have a plan?" his mother pressed.

He nodded, looking from parent to parent. "I've been slowly gathering information as I go. There's a cargo train that comes every third night. I was thinking we could try to stow away there and get actual passage on another train some ways off."

Both his parents had stern expressions as they held on to one another. "When does the next train leave?" his father asked.

"Well, the *next* train leaves in a few hours. But—"

His father cut him off. "You two should leave tonight."

"I—what? Tonight? Doesn't Sarah need to rest?"

His mother nodded. "Ideally, yes. But this situation is far from ideal. The kits will get fussy and they'll cry. People, eventually, will ask questions. We'll *all* get caught. But if you two leave tonight— while the kits are quiet—you might have a chance. Sarah can take a few of my blouses and your father and I could try to distract the OOI. Spin something about how rebellious our daughter was and ran away."

"Hold on, you realize what you're saying, right?" Dixion asked. "Sarah, talk some sense into her." He looked to his sister. She held Roxie closer to her chest, refusing to look at him or her parents. And as he understood, his ears fell. "You've already talked about it."

"They've thought this through, Dixie. A lot more than I have." She finally looked up at him with tears welling in her eyes. "Maybe even more than you have. They know what they're saying. And they understand the consequences. When the police find out they lied ..." She grimaced, holding back sobs.

"Dixion," his father said, setting his paws on his son's shoulders, "you and your sister are still young and full of life. And think of the kits and what lives they'd have here—if any." He pressed his forehead to his son's.

Dixion shook his head, keeping it pressed against his father's. "No. There has to be another way."

"Your mother and I have had joyous lives. And we know how special you two are. You deserve to have something close to what we had. And even better. So run, and live." He wrapped the younger man in his arms, hugging him. "And take care of your sister; she'll need you now more than ever."

"You really mean it? You want us to leave you here to die?" Tears fell down Dixion's muzzle. He softly cried, trying to not wake the kit in his arm.

As they stood there for a moment, Dixion's mother came up as well, damp tracks mimicking his along her muzzle, and joined in the hug. "No, baby. We want you to live."

***

They left the house a few hours later, still before check-in. The brother and sister, each with a kit in their arm and a bundle of clothes and food tucked in a satchel, snuck out of town in the middle of the night, avoiding contact with as many people as they could. The train depot stood on the edge of town and, with little issue, they were able to stow away in a dark corner.

Just as the red of the sun started to color the sky, they jumped off and walked into the next town like it was nothing. And with a flash of his ID and her travel license they were able to get tickets without issue.

Between their hidden sorrow and Sarah's exhaustion from new birth, the two of them sat in silence for a good chunk of the ride.

His sister rested her head against Dixion's shoulder. "Heaven's above, I feel dizzy."

"Close your eyes for a moment," He patted her head. "Mom said something like that might happen. She did say you needed to take it easy."

"Do you think they know we're gone yet?" she whispered.

Dixion nodded. "When we weren't home at curfew, the Office of Intelligence would have been notified. The police were probably knocking on Mom and Dad's door at seven am. Probably knocking on Quinn's door for me."

"Is he going to get in trouble?"

Her brother sighed. "I hope not. We weren't dating for too long and our history will show that. Hopefully he'll just be questioned."

"Do you think our markings have been posted yet?"

Dixion shrugged. "Can't be sure. But I'm hoping the kits will be cover enough."

"The *kits?*" Sarah hissed. "What the hell do you mean by that?"

"People won't see us. They'll be distracted by the cute."

"Please tell me you're joking?"

Before he could answer, a young woman in purple shirt held out her paw. "Tickets and travel licenses please."

Dixion handed her both "Sasha's" license and his ID.

"You don't have a license?" She asked, glaring down at Dixion.

"If you'd read the ID I handed you, you'd see I'm a Matchmaker," he said, glaring back. "And I am helping Mrs. Banks home as her husband is across the border fighting in the war."

The ticket taker's eyes widened. "I'm sorry, Matchmaker. I didn't know you did that kind of thing." She handed the documents back without staring at them longer.

"Just watch yourself in the future. Even here, I still have the leverage of my station."

She paled. "Yes sir. I'm sorry." Her paws were clasped behind her back and her eyes were down.

And almost as if on cue, the cub in Sarah's arms started to cry.

Dixion sighed and scooted closer to the child. "It's okay, sweetheart, you're almost there," he cooed. As Roxie calmed down again and stared back up at the ticket taker. "Do you need anything else?" His tone was softer, but the edge was still there.

"No sir. I'll move on. Just so you know we're almost to your stop." And on she went. Dixion and Sarah sat in silence until she entered the next cabin.

"Did you have to be so harsh to her?" Sarah asked.

Dixion shrugged. "I don't know. But she stopped questioning us, right?"

Sarah looked down at the kit in her arms. "Were you telling the truth? About having all your authority as a Matchmaker?"

"You mean if I was *actually* here on official business and didn't abandon my post?" He smiled and shrugged. "Maybe. I made most of that up on the spot with my work-voice. But that's in the past. I'm not going to be able to do anything like what I did again." Dixion sat back with Hexion squirming in his arms.

"So where *are* we going, Dixie?" Sarah asked.

He looked down at the kit in his arms. When Hexion let out a yawn, Dixion yawned back in response. "Oh man," he stretched as best as he could without moving too much. "Sorry. Not trying to ignore you." He sat up and looked around the cabin. Very few people were near them, and everyone was in their own world, either with their muzzle in a book, headphones in with music, or both.

"The next stop is a small military post. Not many civilians live in this town."

Sarah paled. "Is a military post really the best place for us?"

Dixion nodded. "I hope so."

"*Hope?*" she hissed.

"Hey, hey, calm down. Don't want to scare the kits." He scratched at Roxie's chin. "It's the closest town to the border I could find. I'm partly making this up as I go. I had a rough idea but didn't have anything really worked out. I was expecting to build the plan with you, but my timetable got moved up." Dixion sat back in his seat, taking a breath. "I don't think getting out will be too hard, but I have no idea what's going to happen after."

"Getting out? You mean to wildcat country? They'll kill us."

He pressed his head to his sisters. "Hey, let's not worry about that yet. One hurdle at a time; let's get out of the station first." A moment later, a chime pinged over the speakers announcing the next stop. "That's us." Dixion stood and handed Sarah her son. He draped a hip-bag bag over his sister's shoulder while he set a similar one on his lap.

As they pulled into the station, Dixion led them toward the door. The platform zoomed by, slowing little by little. Pine martens of all shapes and sizes with shirts of every color gathered around, waiting for the train to stop.

But the slower the train became, the more red was seen. Sarah squeaked.

"It's okay," Dixion said, tightening the straps on his satchel. "Deep breath. Could just be due to the conflict nearby. Head down and kit up."

After the train came to a complete stop, the collection of law officers asked for their papers when each passenger stepped off. One by one each marten flashed their IDs to those in red.

After Dixion and Sarah cleared the checkpoint, he took a breath. "Well, seems like they don't know yet."

Sarah didn't respond.

Maybe it's nerves.

Her eyes went wide and she looked to her brother. "The *screens*," she hissed.

Before he could look, the speakers in the station chimed. "Ladies and gentlemen, please draw your attention to the nearest monitor," a pleasant female voice said. "If you see either of these martens, please alert the nearing Office of Intelligence personnel.

Dixion look; "Missing and Wanted" read in bright white letters against a dark red banner on every screen along with detailed descriptions of himself and his sister. Their height and weight, eye color, even details of their markings. At the bottom was an additional note: parents arrested for aiding and abetting curfew violation; trial awaiting interrogation.

He stopped long enough to see the words for what they were but forced himself to keep moving. *Stay calm. Stay calm.*

"What are we going to do? Mom and Dad…" The faint scent of fear seeped from Sarah and a tear fell down her cheek.

"Woof," Dixion called loudly. "I think someone needs a change." He leaned closer to Roxie. "Yup. Definitely." He grabbed his sister by the arm and pulled her away from the monitors and towards a bathroom. "Go in, take a breather, and calm down," he whispered.

Sarah nodded without a word and slipped into the restroom while Dixion and Hexion waiting outside.

He kept his head down as he leaded against the wall. As the moments passed, the lack of movement stirred Hexion from his sleep and he grunted out in protest.

"Shh, shh, little one," Dixion soothed. "We'll be moving again soon." Hexion didn't care and wriggled his little arms free. "No, no, come on, buddy." He set a finger to the kit's chin before wrapping him back up and rocking him side to side. "Let's calm down and go back to sleep."

A deep voice chuckled beside him. "Newborn?" the gentleman asked.

"Yeah. He's tiny, isn't he."

"Eeyup. But he'll grow up quick. Enjoy tha time you have with 'im."

"Flies by, I hear."

The older marten sighed. "Like no other." He clapped Dixion on the shoulder. "Congratulations."

"For what?" He pressed his nose to Hexion's, playing up the act he fell into.

"Fer makin' a kit. Not easy to do these days."

Dixion nodded. "That's the truth."

He chuckled again. "Well, take care. Gotta get to the next train. Oh, and remember, you got this. From one parent to another." He turned away before any response could be made.

Dixion looked up and saw a larger marten in a red shirt blend into another crowd of Intelligence Officers. "Okay boys and girls, if you haven't seen the signs, we've have an additional directive: closer checks for the fugitives on the boards."

A cold chill ran down his spine as the group of officers cried out "yes sir."

Sarah stepped out of the restroom. "I'm still bleeding. I tried to take care of myself for a moment, but I'm worried."

Dixion nodded. "Well, our parents did say to take it easy. Hopefully we can."

"Yeah," she agreed. "Well, I think we're ready for whatever happens next."

"Then let's go."

***

They wandered through town, looking between each and every building for a way out. Over the lower homes, Dixion could see the trees stopped just out reached. *Probably to ensure someone couldn't jump from one into the town. Or the other way around.*

Down each alley was a tall wall. Most were cement. But Dixion happened to see one with a barbed wire fence. "I think I see our way out, but keep walking."

"Why not go right there?" Sarah asked.

Dixion shook his head. "We can't draw attention. We need to make it look as natural as possible. Once around the opposite block, then we'll go."

Sarah nodded her head and followed his lead. "I just hope we can stop soon. I'm feeling more and more tired with each step."

He wrapped a free arm around his sister's shoulder. "We have to go as fast as we can." And like that, the two made the way around the block before crossing the street again and heading down the alley with the fence.

"How are we going to get over, Dixie?" Sarah asked, looking up the ten-foot fence covered in barbs.

Dixion handed Hexion to Sarah and dug through his bag. "Dad gave me some tools. Wanted us to be as well-supplied as we could be." He sniffed at the thought of his father.

"I hope they're okay," Sarah whispered.

Dixion didn't reply. Instead, he pulled a pair of wire cutters from his bag. *We have to be quick. The sound alone could draw attention. Though I wouldn't be surprised if the first cut warns them...*

The pine marten worked as quick as he dared, snipping link after link while Sarah paced behind him. Once enough were cut that he could crawl through Dixion waved to his sister. "Hand me a kit at a time, then crawl through yourself."

She knelt at the fence and handed Roxie first, then Hexion. In the distance they could hear voices approaching.

Fear was in her eyes as she met Dixion's gaze. "Hurry," he whispered, urging her on.

She reached out her leg beyond the fence and cried out in pain. "Sarah!"

His sister began breathing hard as she moved to both of her knees and crawling through backwards.

"You okay?" Dixion asked as she took Roxie from his arms.

"Keep moving," she said. "What's the plan now?"

"We run." Without another word, he turned from her and charged through the trees.

The two of them slinked through the woods outside the border. "I saw movement over there," a voice called behind them.

"We got to hurry," Dixion whispered. "If we don't move fast enough, they'll catch us."

"Dixie, I want to. But I'm so exhausted and if I move much faster, I'll hurt myself or fall." Tears rolled down Sarah's cheeks. "I don't think I'm gonna make it."

"Yes, you are, come on." He wrapped an arm around her side, helping her along.

Sarah shook her head. "I don't think I will." She started to cry in earnest. "I can't do it. Take the kits and run."

"Sarah, I… I can't leave you. They'll…"

"I know. But I'm feeling dizzy and they're getting close. Either I take the risk, or the kits do." She pressed her back against a tree and sat down. "You *have* to run."

Dixion watch as blood collected on her pants between her legs.

She sat down hard before offering Roxie up to him. "Leave Dad's bag and promise me you'll take care of them. Promise me you'll keep them safe."

"I… I don't know what I'll do without you."

Sarah chuckled as her cheek ruffs matted with tears. "It's like Mom and Dad said: live." She pushed the kit towards Dixion. "Please promise?"

Matching tears rolled down his cheeks as he grabbed Roxie from her. "I promise."

The kits started to cry.

"I love you, brother. Now run. I'll try to buy you some time."

Dixion wrenched his eyes closed as he turned away from her.

"Hey," she shouted back the way they came, "I need help."

Dixion ran as quick as he could, dodging between trees as the kits cried in his arms. He had no idea where he was going but had no intentions of slowing down. He burst past a line of tree.

And almost plowed into a pair wildcats.

They were bigger than he imagined—large and muscular—wearing just enough fabric to cover their modesty. *Oh no,* he thought. Their eyes were on him.

The three watched each other, with the wildcats' gaze moving from Dixion to the kits in his arms and he noticed something strapped around their chests.

The two felines licked their lips before looking at each other. The one on the left nodded his head back the way the marten came. Without a sound, the cat on the right took off into the forest.

Once he was gone, the remaining wildcat kept his eyes unblinking on Dixion. He took a step forward.

The pine marten stepped back, meeting a tree. *What did the OOI tell us about them?* His heart pounded in his ears. *Prone to violence, dumb, cold and cruel creatures.*

The remaining cat licked his lips again. *Eats pine martens.*

Dixion looked down at the kits in his arms. *I must protect them.*

A loud, sharp scream cut though the silence. *Sarah!*

He made to turn back, but when the wildcat ran towards him, Dixion instead dropped to the ground, slamming his head against the tree, and arched his back, trying to protect his niece and nephew. *Protect the kits, protect the kits, protect the kits!* Tears continued to fall as he tried to prepare himself for the blows to come.

Instead, the world became darker as something covered him. No claws or teeth came. No pain.

The natural silence of the forest took over.

"Are you sure they went this way?" The voice belonged to the marten chasing them.

Dixion's muscles locked up in fear.

"Maybe. But the scream had to be from around here." At least one other marten was with the first. "Maybe a wildcat got her. Worse way to go, but with their barbaric scent-tracking, they could have found her first. It would have been the same outcome, no matter which of us found them. We both know it."

Dixion's stomach flipped, but he did his best to remain still.

The two men wandered elsewhere as Dixion heard them head back the way they came. But even as their voices became softer, Dixion didn't dare to move, hugging the kits tighter until they groaned in their sleep. Hearing that, he relaxed a little with a sigh. *At least they're okay.*

And the thought of his sister—their mother—hit him again and tears renewed. He continued to lay there, head against the trunk sobbing without a sound.

The cover rose and light poured over Dixion. He tried to compose himself as much as he could then looked up and saw the wildcat folding an odd shaped brown and tan fabric. Once the feline was content with its size, he rolled it up and bundled it tight, laying it between the strap around his chest and his back.

With the pack secured, he locked eyes with Dixion and licked his lips again and walked away.

He's just leaving us here?

Looking back over his shoulder and still seeing Dixion where he was, the wildcat turned back and took a step behind the pine marten. A second later, claws were pressed into his back, urging him forward.

"Okay, okay, I'm moving." Dixion said. The wildcat didn't respond. *What's going to happen to us?* His gaze lowered to the floor. *Well, if he's going to eat us, hopefully it's quick.*

The wildcat growled as Dixion began to slow, bringing him back to the present. *He's demanding. Maybe that's something they do? Push pine martens around?* His eyes went wide and his ears fell. *Maybe we're to be slaves? What did I bring the kits into?*

Dixion shook he head. *No. I'll run when I get the first chance. I'll try to find the Breeders and see if they can keep us safe. Even if it costs me my life, I need to do everything I can to keep the kits safe.*

The two made their way in silence, with Dixion's mind racing through different possibilities. The pine marten kept up with both kits still somehow sleeping in his arms; but cradled as they were, their weight was starting to wear on his back and shoulders.

Just as Dixion was about to try and rest for a moment, the feline moved ahead of him, holding his palm pads to the marten. Dixion stopped where was and watched as the wildcat pushed on through some trees. Waiting in silence, Dixion shifted from foot to foot. A few moments later, the foliage came alive and moved, making the path through easier to pass.

"What in the world?" Dixion took an unsure step forward and, beyond the tree line, he could see a small village built into the grove. Along the walls of the camp closest to him were a number of wild-cats standing side-by-side with their claws extended in a threatening manner.

And on a table near the closest hut was a body. Dark kakis stained red; a green shirt that was too big for her. "Sarah!" Dixion called. He ran to the table "Oh Sarah, I thought I lost you." He set the kits against her and pressed his head to hers. Her breathing was slow and shallow. "I don't think she's doing too well." Dixion looked around. "Is there a doctor here?"

The silence he received in response was deafening.

"Can anyone help?" New tears rolled down her cheek. "I already thought I lost her once. Please."

"What are you doing at this watch post?" A hooded figure stepped through the closest doorway, her voice soft like velvet.

"I'm trying to help my code. Is there anyone medically trained here?"

"Your *genetic* code?" She asked.

"My sister and her kits. Please, I'm begging you, is there anyone that can help?"

She moved her body towards another wildcat. "Take care of her and the young ones."

The large feline stepped forward with two others following.

"She just gave birth about two days ago," Dixion explained.

The hooded figure stepped forward. "So you're only goal was to help your family. Why?" She pointed back towards the city. "Aren't there doctors and hospitals there that can help her?"

Dixion looked down. "She's... a minor. She wasn't allowed to give birth. And as a Matchmaker, I knew what would happen if she was caught."

"Are you just worried about your sister? Your code?"

He thought about the question. *All the things I've done, the rulings I've given.* He signed. "I'm not proud of the life I've lived, but what else is there to do? We don't have the space to live or the food to feed everyone."

"What if you could expand?" she asked.

"But the wildcats—" He stopped and finally took in his surroundings. Huts were built along side and into the trees with wildcats of all shapes and sized looking down at him.

The woman in the hood chuckled. "Almost everything you've been told is a lie. There are other ways." She raised her chocolate brown paws and lowered the hood, exposing her small round ears and cream colored chin. "And we hope to open minds."

She was a pine marten.

Dixion's jaw dropped. "But we've been told..."

She stepped forward and kneeled. "I know. You've been told lots of things for too many years that are not true."

"Why?"

She shrugged. "Because change can be hard and scary. Your government officials didn't want to go the hard route. But we can teach you. Give you a new understanding to the world. And you'll find that both you and your code are safe here." She rose to her feet.

Dixion blinked. "I don't understand."

The female marten chuckled and raised her arms. "My dear, wel-come to the Breeders."

Empires die in stasis. They must continually grow to survive, conquer and spread and dominate. This takes more than cunning and will. The most basic building block of an Empire is bodies, soldiers to subjugate, and fresh replacements ever at the ready. No cog in the wheel of manifest destiny can rest, whether on the march or on the birthing bed. To resist the will of such a relentless machine is folly, until you realize whose paw really turns that wheel, and whose sacrifices keep it oiled in blood.

GILDED CAGE

Jelliqal Belle

How naïve I was to think this would be the easy life. I imagined that a place where every need was met and every want was gifted would be enjoyable. I was so wrong. I wish I could go back to the foul-smelling leather production houses where I worked my paws numb sewing leather chest guards and boots for the soldiers and leave this hell of a paradise.

At the full moon, all the new-women gathered to celebrate their crossover into adulthood after their first menses. For most, it was no big deal; you got to eat your fill for a change and a new set of clothes, but for a few, a different opportunity arose. The inspector picked some of the more athletic new-women for the guard, archery, or slings cohorts, rarely for heralding or scouting. A lucky few had the qualities wanted in a breeder. Intelligence, musculature, beauty, no one was ever quite sure what the selectors were looking for.

Me and my twin sister Tabs were shocked when we were picked. We are of the Airedale gens, family line. Tall and gangly with tight, light brown curly locks, a terrier's square muzzle with a too big nose, and droopy triangular ears; we never thought we were pretty. The inspector smiled and said we would be popular exotic beauties in the capital.

Everyone dreamed of becoming a breeder. It was said they slept on beds of clouds and ate honey-dipped bones every meal. It was hard to leave our family, but they were happy for our opportunity to better ourselves and wished us well with teary eyes.

We spent our first moon training with the other new breeders. We had a bed to sleep in, an actual bed with a mattress and a blanket, to ourselves, no sharing. No more sleeping in a puppy huddle to stay warm; a fire kept the rooms warm, a window kept the rooms cool. We could bathe every day if we wanted to, and our teacher actually encouraged it; groomers did our nails and styled our hair. We thought this was the life.

Our rooms were on an upper floor of a mansion with an amazing view of the capital, Omobono. We could see the hurry-scurry of the ant-sized merchants, the deliveries of armor, food, silks and spears. The bureaucrats and administrators buzzed about carrying armfuls of scrolls. We watched life happen down below and felt superior that we were here and not down there working so hard.

Mother Xaviera was an uptight Poodle gens who wobbled on two legs. There was no pleasing her. You were too loud, too soft, too brusque, too uninteresting, or too know-it-all. We mocked her funny walk behind her back.

Xaviera taught us the right way to howl the patriotic songs that we only half-knew from hearing the soldiers march by to fight the Catkin Celts, or the Tigris Tigers, or whomever we were battling at the time. The Empire had many enemies. That was the price of being the greatest empire in the world: everyone else was jealous of our greatness and wanted to tear us down. In those lessons, we learned my sister Tabs had a powerful voice. Who knew? Xaviera suggested that she could train for musician as her second vocation.

Mother taught us what would be expected. Honored males would be selected from time to time to come to the working girls' room where the women working to become pregnant stayed. Once the pregnancy was confirmed, they moved to the waiting rooms where they would help each other through their pregnancy, and then the nursing room until their pups grew enough to be weaned off the teat, and finally return to the working room to begin again.

Anything was better than the foul-smelling leather works with its caustic chemicals and piss-filled tanning vats. It took us weeks before our noses healed enough to begin to notice that there was incense in the air.

Midway through our orientation, the trainees were allowed to watch a promenade out on the balcony. Wave after wave of martial legions in gleaming armor left to go to war. We giggled and waved to the soldiers enjoying the respite from our studies. Some of the other ladies were blasé about the parade, but for me and Tabs, we had never seen anything like it. It was amazing seeing the army in their finery marching off to defend the honor of our Emperor.

"Look, Tabs, see the shields. I saw them delivered last week. The legionaries are well prepared to defend our Western border from those Catkin barbarians. So sad the Catkin don't have the wisdom to join the Empire and become civilized like the Libyan Leopards did."

Tabs just nodded absently. "I never realized how big the rexes were. Can you imagine how brave the men that ride them must be? I heard a full grown rex can snap a cow in two in one bite." Her stubby tail wagged in interest as the cavalry turned the corner in perfect precision.

I noticed Mother Xaviera stood stiffly, yet her tail snapped back and forth. She glared angrily at the procession. "Mam, is everything ok?" I asked her, afraid we had done something improper while watching the parade.

Xaviera looked around and noted the ever-present Shepherds. "It is quite the parade." She smiled and forced herself to appear to have a good time. Her scent didn't change though. We knew she was scared; we did not know why. Under her breath, she added, "Not here. Later."

When the parade was over, Xaviera headed straight for the wine in the central room and poured a chalice, drank it then refilled it. She gestured for me to follow her into her room. She sat on the edge of her bed and rubbed her hip. "That legion is led by Alpha Pilus Spike, a powerful Bulldog gens. He is cruel by nature, which makes him an effective officer and brilliant in battle, but that is not a desirable trait in a mate. He plays rough, sometimes too rough, with his "chew toys." That is what he calls us.

"Two years ago, he picked me. He wouldn't stop when I cried that it hurt. He laughed when I screamed as my leg dislocated and hip broke. He claimed it was an accident; he didn't know I wasn't exaggerating, so the old Matriarch had no grounds to ban him."

I felt bad for laughing about how she walked. "I'm sorry." I mumbled.

She dismissed the comment with a wave of her paw. "That is the past. Question is what to do now. When Spike comes back, he will come up to the breeding room looking for the new girls. We have at least a few weeks before he returns; I don't trust our luck that it will be longer than two moons." Mother chewed on her lip in thought. "We will advance your training so you new ones will have some experience before he returns. I will speak with the other trainers, too."

So our days were rushed, waking early and having lessons on various topics until the night's candles burned low: health, beauty, exercise, nutrition, and our important role in the pack. Some of our fellow trainees complained, but Tabs and I enjoyed it. The day soon came when we received our robes marking our status. Bright-colored silken robes from our Far Eastern provinces, cinched at the waist with a knotted belt, stopped only a little below our hips. I felt exposed, but also sexy. A black leather collar with a silver circle pendant finished the uniform.

We went in our finery to the temple to take our oaths in a formal ceremony. Even though we each spoke our promise binding us to work as breeders for the pack, did we really have a choice? Sure, we could work in the factories or on the farms, but what type of life would we have living near starvation, our backs breaking? Surely they would be short ones, away from the comfort of a warm bed and plentiful food. Our group had twenty new-women, but there were nine other classes, too. I was amazed there were so many.

I poked Tabs, "Look, on the dais, the Consuls."

She gave me a shush, but then turned and stared, wide-eyed. I wanted to hide before the Consuls, the advisors to Emperor Ignatius Nobilis himself. They were there, all of them: Aurumus Omnismin, Miles Colescaput, Mortem Aresson, Avarum Mercator, and Senem Severiorum. I felt like I was actually important and unworthy at the same time.

The shaggy sheepdog clergyman stood before us with his high hat and bejeweled robes. He blessed our wombs to be fertile and prayed that the Great Lady Mother Gravidam would help our pups grow. His acolytes walked through the rows and sprinkled us with scented water. It made Tabs sneeze.

The Consuls rose to speak. Each one read a passage. I did not listen much to what they said; the echo in the stone hall made my ears ring. Something about service to the pack, and honor and duty, I think. They droned on and on about the importance of our children, the future defenders of the pack, the future leaders. Afterwards, they came and walked the aisles. Most Consuls picked one or two girls to join their personal harem, to serve them and their bloodline exclusively. Senem Severiorum just watched with an amused grin.

Miles Colescaput, a black Mastiff gens, chose seven. He strutted past me to Afifa, an Afghan Hound gens with gorgeous tawny fur, then stroked her cheek with the back of his scarred paw. We all were so jealous. Mother Xaviera walked over to her, gave her a hug, and whispered something in her ear before adjusting her hair and sending her to line up for him. Xaviera must have been proud of her; I wondered what wisdom she imparted to her. Afifa had to be breathless in excitement being selected to serve one of the Consuls directly; however, as she lined up, I thought I noticed her tail droop.

Our training group was split up amongst the working girl rooms, which made up half of the upper floor of the Population Management Building. Tabs and I were kept together, as some men liked something called a threesome as a special reward for valor. The brief orientation included a tour of the decadent suites which even included a clinic, which I thought was odd until it dawned on it that of course that would be for the midwife. The women were friendly enough but seemed off: a lilt of the voice, flattening of ears, or a sagging tail here and there. Were they sad to see us?

Shepherds were stationed all around our floor. They were our servants to get us whatever we wanted and our protectors to keep us safe. The silent Shepherds were various breeds of muscular women trained as guards. I was comforted knowing they were looking out for us, yet I felt exposed and uncomfortable in my revealing robe. I kept trying to pull it down.

Matriarch was a grey-muzzled Labrador gens with milky eyes. She wore a long robe of pale blue with a hood; her leather collar had six gems on it and a silver circle pendant like ours. She walked with a cane to a cushioned seat and was obviously well-loved by the women. She spoke softly, so everyone listened attentively. She explained the rules. "The men will come every evening, and you working girls will entertain them. Anything they want, do it without question, lest it cause you great harm. If they go too far, send up a howl. Don't strike, don't bite, just howl. A broken breeder does the pack no good. The Shepherds will be near.

For every litter, you earn a gem on your collar. When you have seven gems, you have earned a diamond for your silver circle, then your work as a breeder is complete. You can either stay and continue to work here in a supporting vocation like nurse or musician, or you can leave. Your choice."

A yappy Husky gen with mismatched eyes asked, "But how are we to feed that many puppies? That's a lot of puppies."

Matriarch sighed. "You don't keep them. Once they are finished nursing, they go to state homes to be raised. When they are of age, they will be assigned a role which suits them, their abilities, and the needs of the pack when they are grown."

Horrified new-women whispered in shock. Even though they grew up poor in the rural areas, they were still there with their family that loved them. Brothers, sisters, aunts, uncles, cousins, all working together to try to survive the next winter.

"What did you think breeders do? You are here to birth puppies, to build our future. The strongest and cleverest soldiers come here to breed with you to strengthen our bloodlines. How could you possibly care for puppies? Do you have any idea how to raise a family? You are just out of puppyhood yourselves. There are others whose role is to raise the puppies. Trust that the pack will take the best care of them. Don't worry for them; they have a glorious future ahead of them. Your job is too important. For without you, they will never be."

"Mam?" asked a bright-eyed, lean Dalmatian gens from the farmlands. "How often does a woman earn her diamond?"

Matriarch looked down. "In the past, only a few a year, but we have improved our medical techniques thanks to what we have learned from our conquest of the Nile Crocodiles. We have hopes for better results from the recent trainees. Early indicators are promising. More frequently though, a young officer earns a boon for a victorious battle and asks for his favorite as his wife. So be nice to these men."

The room sobered as the new breeders considered their limited options.

"I encourage you to listen to the nurse; follow her advice on what to eat. Do the exercises you learned in training, even when you don't feel like it. You'll stay healthy longer."

"You mean have more babies," barked a cynic in the back.

Matriarch rose from the cushion, helped up by a nearby lute player, and leaned into her cane. "No, I mean it might help prevent your bones from shattering from the frequent pregnancies, or help you not bleed to death in labor. Having litter after litter takes a high toll on your body. I don't know what your life was before you came here, but you will be dreaming of it as paradise before year's end."

"Now, if you want a taste of what to expect tonight, some gem bearers have volunteered to answer your questions or give you a preview so it won't be so shocking. They will show you the pillow rooms so you can talk."

The curious and the brave went with the experienced women. Tabs looked at me, shaken. "You gonna go?"

I looked down, my tail between my legs. "No, I don't think so."

"We could go together," she urged, nuzzling me gently.

I shook my head.

"Okay, anything you want me to ask? Cause I am going to go."

"Ask what you can do to make it hurt less."

"Entertaining the men? Ok, I guess that is what the stretches do, but I will ask."

I shook my head no and whispered. "No, giving up your puppies."

Tabs leaned over, gave me a hug and a comforting lick. "You have me; we will be fine as long as we are together."

Tabs went and talked to a petite Cocker Spaniel gens with one gem named Chrissy. I felt alone and vulnerable in the center of the room. Seeing my discomfort, a musician came over. "Pick a room and take a nap. We usually nap in the daytime."

"Why?" I asked. I cringed as soon as I spoke because I knew the answer.

She gave me a friendly, melancholy smile. "Because we don't get much sleep at night." She helped me find a quiet room with a goose down mattress to sleep on.

I woke before sundown and went to find Tabs. Chrissy was in the common area eating some cheese and pointed back to the pillow room. The pillow room is just that, a small room, a bit over one arm's breadth by two arms' long filled with pillows and a small chest. The room stank of a pungent, musky smell. Tabs was tying her belt around her waist.

"So... what did you find out?" I asked. "Did you really have her show you?"

Tabs was fully relaxed and looked at me with her eyes glassed over and her tongue dangling to one side. She leaned against the wall for support. "Heavenly. Your body just knows what to do, and you react, and you want more and more and more, then suddenly stars, and your brain explodes."

"So it is bearable." I was relieved.

"No, desirable. I can't wait 'til tonight. I need to bathe and get some food cause I am famished."

"Great. Let's go." Encouraged, we went arm in arm to prepare for the evening. Maybe this wouldn't be too bad. Maybe the warnings were overblown.

My first was a quartermaster with some years on him. I didn't see stars or anything, but it was tolerable. He knew I was fresh and tried to be gentle, yet I still hurt when he was done. I ached between my legs, bruised by the experience. My insides throbbed painfully, stretched in a way they hadn't been before. Was this what I was here to do? Was this normal? I went to go and ask Tabs, but when I saw her, I realized I had been the lucky one.

Before I left my pillow room, I heard Matriarch barking at a soldier. Further down the hall, someone shrieked in pain. "You are banned and I don't care who your father is. I will explain to your CO exactly why, and if I need to, your father as well. Better yet, I'll offer to demonstrate on you what you did because apparently you think what you did is acceptable behavior. Shepherds, get him out of here. I have to see if she can be saved. You had better pray she doesn't die."

I could not help but go and stare from around the corner. It was shocking to see the soft-spoken Matriarch so mad. I saw the Shepherds dragging out a Dalmatian male. I guess he beat someone up because his paw was bloody up to the middle of his forearm. I was glad he didn't pick me, but my gut knotted up when I saw which room the clinic nurse raced into with her medical kit. Tabitha's room.

Tabs wailed in pain. Tears rolled down Chrissy's cheeks as she held her and rocked her back and forth. Tabs had curled into a fetal position, screaming, shaking. The sheets were covered in bodily fluids. Bloody paw prints on the walls. Oh My Lady, Tabs, what happened to you? Her room stank of urine, feces, and blood. I wanted to ask, but she was beyond all reason, mad with pain and horror.

There was no space for me in the tiny room. I collapsed in the doorway rocking back and forth, praying to Lady Gravidam in between my sobs "Don't let her die, don't let her die."

The clinic nurse forced a bitter-smelling fluid down her muzzle then tucked her in with a sheet. She pushed her hair back. "The tonic should help you rest and take away the worst of the pain. Try to sleep. It is over now. It's over. Sleep now." The nurse gathered the wet towels used to mop up the mess before she left. I fought back my desire to retch. So much blood. "I'll be back to check on you later. Chrissy, send someone for me if she starts bleeding out again."

Tabs shook her head as if in a seizure. "No, no, never again, no not never! I don't care what they do to me."

"Don't worry about that now, dear. Just sleep." The nurse motioned me to follow her. "Go see Matriarch. She wants to talk to you."

I stood up stunned, impotent, angry. This wasn't right. It made no sense. What did he do to her? My thoughts jumped from one half-formed idea to another.

Matriarch was in an animated discussion with Mother Xaviera, who had hobbled over when she heard what happened. She motioned for me to join them. She stood stiff as a board, tapping her cane in frustration. Matriarch growled her speech. "I was in a meeting with an administrator. This arrogant officer flew into a rage because his favorite was pregnant, probably with his pups. He had eyes for your exotic sister. The others tried to intercede, distract him from her, but he would have none of it." She half sat, half collapsed into her writing table chair. Her ears drooped. "He took his frustration out on your sister. I am so sorry. If I was here, the Shepherds would have intervened sooner. Since it was her first, they were not taking her cries for help seriously. With this behavior, I have banned him. He will never hurt anyone here again."

Xaviera's eyes watered. "I told her your sister sang. Tabs has to be here a year and a day to prove herself barren before we reassign her permanently, if she does recover. Many, who are used so cruelly, don't." She wrung her paws in distress and looked away, knowing her words were inadequate.

"So what do we do until then?" I managed not to bark, although I badly wanted to bite someone.

"We give her time to heal and see how she feels then. We can segregate her in the clinic when the men come until she is recovered. We take care of each other."

Someone stayed with Tabs during the first nights. Sometimes, she slept after a dose of the elixir, only later to wake up with screaming nightmares. Other nights, she sat in the corner, her tail between her legs, shaking and whimpering; a wool blanket wrapped around her like a shield, not letting anyone close. Over weeks, she grew less anxious. I realized she preferred Chrissy's company to mine, so I would check on her, but not hang around unless she asked. I was alone for the first time in my life; my twin was miles away in the next room. I was empty inside and trapped in this gilded cage.

Tabs' body healed, but not her mind. Tabs never wanted to be around men again. She shivered and paced as it approached dusk until she was sent into the untouchables room. The women on their cycle, hurt, or sick stayed in the clinic where the men couldn't touch them.

Chrissy and Tabs were always together—an odd couple, tall and lean Tabs and short, curvy Chrissy. I felt left out, but Tabs was slowly recovering; I saw her wag her tail for the first time in weeks. Over the passing time, I realized it was more than friendship and shared grief that bound the two women. I was glad to see my sister at peace and happy, but I missed her too. Tabs started learning the songs from the musician and helped with mending clothes in the laundry. Every night, she would return to cringing in the protected bower.

Two moons after we arrived, the next batch of new trainees came in. Our ranks had thinned by about a third as women became pregnant and were moved to the waiting room. I wondered if I had the same sad, tired expression of my predecessors when they had greeted us. Matriarch sat on the same cushion and calmly shattered their lives with her gentle words.

Later that afternoon, we had a surprise; Afifa showed up bedecked in fine silks and scented perfumes. Apparently, she had been demoted into the general breeder room. Most of the new bitches were cruel to her for having failed the Consul once they learned who she was. Afifa took the abuse, head down, shivering in perfect silence. They thought that she was horribly arrogant, too good to talk to us. I thought she looked thin and tired when I said hello to her. She just shook her head no and stared off into the distance. Her scent was off and her eyes strangely dilated.

Matriarch shooed the girls away and led the Afghan Hound gens to the untouchables room to rest unbothered. I noticed strips of fur missing from the back of her legs and wondered what could have caused it. In the morning, we found her body floating in the cold bath; she had tied silken sheets around her neck, then to the floor drain to hold her down. In her wet state, we could see she was with pup.

"How could she be so selfish as to leave us?" the new breeders complained. "Now we are short another woman and her burden falls on us." A few new-women went as far as to spit on her meat. I think they were taking out their first night jitters on her.

Matriarch barked at the naïve breeders. "You have no idea what this woman has endured. The Consul takes seven women so he can have one a night and they have a week to recover before it is their turn again. She is the ONLY one who survived this cycle. That means at the end she was his plaything every night. She was drugged so she could endure the pain. The fact she got pregnant probably had saved her life. And instead of finding support here, you attacked her like she did something wrong because she had the audacity to survive his abuse. He revels in causing pain to the body and the spirit. I hope the Great Lady shows you the same compassion when you have your first litters."

A few weeks later, I shared my secret with Tabs; I thought I might be pregnant. I felt full and my breasts ached. She hugged me, happy for my success, so I wouldn't get kicked out. I didn't want to tell the Matriarch yet; women were punished if they skipped out of their night work. I also did not know if I would still get to see Tabs if I was transferred. Tabs urged me to tell anyway.

Matriarch was happy to reassign me and said I could visit or that Tabs could come see me anytime. She smiled and said better to be cautious, especially with the first litter. She urged me to eat extra even if I was not hungry. Seemed strange to leave the pillow rooms for the waiting room, but it was not a day too soon.

The day the world changed, Spike's men returned home from their bloody excursion. They returned high on battle fever and lust for life. Spike had died a hero in a desperate rex charge flanking maneuver that saved the legion and ultimately won the battle.

The officers brought many riches for the nobles and the capital coffers. The legion had stumbled onto a key trading village on their return home. Hundreds of unclad feline prisoners paraded through the streets to be used either as production slaves or training dummies. They held their heads high and backs straight, sauntering with their feline grace, unashamed and unapologetic of their nudity, male and female alike. They snarled with disdain at the pampered citizenry lining the streets mocking them. The battle had been such a popular success that the Consuls awarded all the surviving officers passes to the working girls' lounge for the night.

This was unprecedented—never had all received passes on the same night—there were not enough women. Even the ones on their cycle were pulled out onto the floor. The men felt entitled and challenged each other on who would breed the most boys. The lust-crazed men ignored the sanctum of the untouchables room and started using them as well—even the ones who had been hurt earlier in the night and had gone there to recover. That is when things went bad.

My sister scurried away and hid in the dirty laundry early in the evening, so her scent was covered, but her lover Chrissy was not so clever. A drunken veteran with a scarred face found her hiding in a wardrobe, twisting her arm as he yanked her out. He cheered his good fortune to have found a fresh lass not yet worn out this night.

Then Chrissy panicked, tried to pull free, and struck him. Her desperate slap echoed in the halls. The vet in return smacked her so hard she bounced off the wall and crumpled on the floor, dazed and bleeding. The men who were not otherwise engaged ran over and held her down, shouting in anger and encouraging their brothers to teach her a lesson. They hit and kicked her in their frenzy. She screamed until she no longer had a voice, and then she cried. She whined throughout the night. Sometime in the early morning hours, silence fell in our defiled bowers. The Shepherds watched with hard eyes and kept the others away from helping her. Chrissy had broken the rules by striking a war hero, and she was paying the consequences.

The next dawn, the Shepherds woke us and herded us out of our chambers. The Shepherds—our servants, our protectors, our watchers—I learned were also our guards. The breeders were weary and worn from the previous night, the scent of sex still upon them as they were denied morning baths. I felt unclean and for some reason ashamed for them.

The Shepherds had gathered all the breeders, working girls, waiting women, nursing mothers, the staff and the servants, even the new girls still in training, to the equestrian corral. Normally, we never see the other groups. Women looked around to see who was where and give friendly nods to lost friends. I noticed netted carriages lined along the rail on the far side of the corral with the heraldry marks of the different Consuls. I guessed that even their private harems were present.

We sat upon hard wooden benches and waited to learn what this was about. The morning chill cut through our short wraps. An honor guard preceded Consul Miles Colescaput to a small dais. His scarlet and gold robes glistened under the early morning sun. The years had been kind to him; muscles rippled under his aged skinfolds. The Mastiff gens looked over us with calculating, dark eyes and nodded in approval. His jowls wobbled as he addressed us.

"To make it where we can be free, where our children and our children's children can be free, we have to all do our part. We sacrifice for you. We give you the best food, musicians and poets to entertain you. You have baths and massages and groomers. Is there anything else we can give you? I think not. We give you the softest down for your beds, the warmest wool for your blankets, and aromatic woods for your fires. Is there anything else we can give to you, for you are most precious to us, for are not within your wombs is our future as a people held? Is there anything more we can do for you?"

A few hesitant voices cried, "No."

"I can't hear you."

More cried, "No."

"Are their doubters? Truly, is there more we can do? Tell us how we can serve you." He raised his arms as he made his plea. It was humbling to see such a man beg before us women.

A boisterous "No!" was his answer.

"Are you then, our mothers, happy?"

A resounding "Yes!" from all quarters save one to my left.

He waited for quiet before he continued. "You have but one job— to become life-giving mothers. To make our soldiers forget for a moment the struggles they have been through, the trials they have endured, the horrors of war, to forget their lost brothers, to show them what they are fighting for-—for just a night. Is that too much to ask?"

"No." We barked back.

"Are there any among you who find their burden too great, who wish to surrender their place among the mothers and serve our people in another manner?"

"No!" echoed the mothers simultaneously in one voice. My sister remained silent.

"But yet one of you spat upon our sacrifices of our veterans. Dared to strike one who was there to do his duty as a hero of the realm to produce more heroes of the realm so that one day we might be able to overrun our enemies and live free. She broke our sacred trust, our law, our dignity. We disown her. We repudiate and renounce her."

Two of the palace guards dragged an injured prisoner from the side of the corral. She was shaved, naked. She was hobbled to walk on all fours like a beast, even though one leg was obviously twisted. Her lip was split. She bled from her nose and ears. Her eyes nearly swollen shut. Her tail dragged on the ground, broken. We tried to close out our minds onto who it must be, until her scent hit us. There was no doubt and no avoidance. Chrissy. A shiver went through the stands; women whispered to those who didn't know.

"This thing is nothing but meat. And meat it shall be, for 'tis no doubt any spawn of her blood would be equally defective. We were starving these rexes for the Colosseum games to hone their battle skills with the prisoners, but this is more pressing. We pray our citizenry will understand and forgive us." He watched our reactions as the meaning of his intent became clear. "You will stand witness and understand that even you mothers, our great treasure, are subject to the rule of law. Traitors will be hunted down and put down swiftly."

Chrissy was bound to a post near us like a sacrifice. Blood dripped down from open wounds. She tried to hold her head up, but she no longer had the strength. I was close enough to hear her labored breathing.

Two small rexes were brought out by their trainers, restrained by thick leather muzzles. These juveniles were only as tall as their handlers, their neck scales still green, showing their youth. My stomach turned; they were too small for a quick death. I prepared for the worse; I did not prepare enough.

All my days, I will never forget her death, her screams, the smell of her blood and fear. They started with her paws, then her arms, each taking a turn. We heard the tissue rip as they pulled her apart, the cartilage snap, bones crack and crunch. The rexes would take the small chunk of meat and toss it into the air. They opened their mouths like hungry baby birds with the meal falling straight into their gullet, then they took the next bite. The handlers used this as a training exercise, one bite at a time. They made it last as long as possible, even after she was dead.

I was close enough to see Consul's eyes gleam as he watched the carnage. Her screams and futile thrashing only seemed to please him more. I was quivering as I watched: fear, revulsion, disgust, sorrow, exhaustion, too much to process. I smelt fear and terror—death, but I also smelled his disgusting excitement. He watched the terror of the breeders, their horror and enjoyed it. Some even collapsed in fright. All stank of fear.

Gone was the fatherly consul, and back was the cruel Primus Alpha Centurion of the brutal battle of Kinsome's Plains, the great leader who sacrificed two legions of troops, ten thousand men, to win the day. His pleasure in pain made me think about Afifa. I wondered at the time, and I now wonder again, what she went through that had broken such a vibrant woman. I looked at the depravity and the lust in the Consul's face, and I knew I didn't want to know.

The mothers were beyond horrified. Some consoled the younger women who were shaking and crying. Others supported those who had fainted. My sister was stoically silent except for her left paw clenched into a fist. The Shepherds watched but did not help. I wonder what went through their minds knowing they were silently complicit with this torture.

When the rexes had finished eating, their trainers brought them to stand behind Consul Colescaput. He spoke to us again.

"Silence." He commanded, and he got it instantly. He looked over the tearful, frightened women with cold, predatory eyes. "Tonight, our officers will return and expect the open welcome that was denied them yesterday. They will reward any woman that pleases them a ring that you will then turn into your matriarch, who will keep tally. Those with the most rings will be rewarded. Those with none will be shaved and reassigned, as you will have made clear your selfishness to put your personal agenda above the needs of our society. Go now and prepare."

We lined up to leave, shaken and cowed.

"Oh, and by the way, the trainees will be joining you tonight. We want to be sure there will be enough girls to service all the officers that are stationed in the city tonight. We don't want a recurrence of last night, do we? Be ready by the first evening bell."

Matriarch was so distressed that two of the waiting women helped her to bed. I stepped up to organize the ladies. The Shepherds refused to serve today. They watched with contempt. We felt betrayed by them and did not want them about, anyway.

Some waiting women, who were not far along in their pregnancies, volunteered to do the Shepherd's chores. They straightened the rooms and aired them out while the working women bathed, rested, or saw the clinic nurses. They got permission to go to the kitchens and bring up food. The working women appreciated their kindness; they did not have to help. I suggested they meet the men in stages so no one would get too tired or too sore.

The younger breeders with two or less gems would meet the first wave. These men would be the most eager and energetic. Then we would alternate at each evening bell. The girls in training would service any men that wanted seconds or thirds as they should be too tired to really hurt them; they wouldn't knot up so big after the first time, if at all.

The men saw our worn faces and smelled our fear. A few felt entitled to do their part of punishing, but most did what was required and left quickly. For many, this was their first time up here and they did not want to risk getting banned. The moon was high and still the men kept coming. How many officers were in the capital?

A tentative new-man came up to me and asked if I would go with him. Pug gens new-man obviously had been drinking a little to get up his nerve. I had been focusing on keeping everything flowing, so I had forgotten I needed to get a ring for Tabs. We went behind a curtain to a pillow room. The heraldry officer seemed nervous.

"Your first time?" I asked as I opened my robe. I hoped my pregnancy would not show. I needed to do this.

"My first time here. My da said better to go with one as can show me the ropes. Ye seem to know what's about, eh." He fiddled with his drawstring.

"You don't want to be here?"

"Um, I never been with a woman, but I am no virgin if you take my meaning." He looked around anxious that someone might have heard.

"The walls here absorb sound well; otherwise, it would be deafening. Well, we could talk if you would rather, up to you."

"My da said if I didna come home with the stench of sex on me, he would beat me like a whipping boy." He cringed a little.

"Well, we can't have that. What does your lover do that you like?"

The nervous officer looked hopeful. Soon we were able to meet his father's requirement, and I earned the ring.

The night was long. Some men had been here before and went straight to their favorites. Others just took the first woman available. The men had clearly been told to punish the women for their lack of respect for the military, and many took it to heart. No Shepherd came to rescue the women no matter how loudly they cried out. I supposed special orders had been issued regarding them. I turned away. I hoped the other waiting women were safe.

Much later in the night, all the breeders were spent; some women just lay there as men pumped their seed into them, unknowing and beyond caring. Some girls were removed due to injury, too many, really. One of the trainees got caught by a fresh young Doberman gens, she might never be with a man again. He split her insides all the way up; young fool pulled out while fully knotted. She would have to be reassigned, maybe in the nursery, if she survived the blood loss and infection. Her tragedy reminded me to wonder where Tabs was hiding. I needed to give her the ring to turn in.

A gruff, older bloodhound with a bandaged, burned arm, still wearing his field leathers, came up near dawn. "Sorry mam, but my Centurion says I must be coming here. I ain't had time to clean up none. I be just in from the outer territory." I thought for a moment of getting one of the working girls for him, but I rather liked something about him. I was not so far along as it should be hard on my puppies.

"No problem at all, come along." I smiled wearily and led him into a resting room. They didn't smell as bad as the pillow rooms. I found an empty one, and he followed me in.

I helped him unbuckle his leathers and let them fall to the ground. He sat on the edge of the goose down bed, staring forward at the unadorned stucco wall.

I climbed behind him and rubbed his neck and shoulders.

He took my paw in his large scarred one motioning me to just be still a moment. "I am sorry, Mam, but I am not in the mood. I know I am supposed to come and pump ya solid, but I don't have it in me. I lead a scouting cohort. Or I did; don't know what tomorrow will bring. We gots caught by the Celts over near Isburria. They done figured out how to throw fire like the Greeks do. Most of the new-men in my squad is dead. The stench of their burning flesh is a smell I will never be able to wash off. These boys didna pick to be soldiers; they was told–like I reckon you was just told to be here, right?"

I simply nodded silently. I never considered that the men folk got selected and sorted like us women did. Or that they would not want to be soldiers to protect us.

"Well, one lad, a Gaul Bichon gens named Jacque. He was talented. He could carve anything. He could turn a stick into a rex or a hellcat that you would swear would walk off your paw and start hunting. I told him as soon as we got home, we'd get him reassigned as an artisan. Jacque was the first one hit, square in the chest. Least he died faster than some I guess, but such a waste of a life." He leaned over and shook in sorrow.

I held him and let him cry it out. I couldn't make it better, there was nothing to be said, but I could comfort him.

After a while he spoke again, wiping his tears with the back of his paws. "Thank ya mam. Here, here is the ring I am supposed to give you. I will deal with catching it from my Centurion for not coming back all sexed up. But let me give you this too, so you to remember him if ye would let me." He pulled out a small piece of polished wood that was a perfect hellcat. On the bottom was his mark, JB.

"No, I can't take this, this is your memory."

"Mam, I won't remember if I am dead. I lost my cohort; the few that survived are maimed or badly wounded. One even got hit in the face, and his eyes cooked in his head, leaving him blind. The army don't tolerate failures. I will probably be worm food by this time tomorrow. So please. Remember him, Jacque Bichon gens."

I swallowed in shock about to cry myself, for this man who cared so much and lost so much. I had a new appreciation for our charge to help them forget and remember what they are fighting for. "You are the first I have met that I wished I could breed with. I would bring forth pups with your wisdom and compassion. The world needs more like you."

The doomed officer looked up with sad, red eyes and touched my face. "Alas, mam, thems not traits soldier folk much want. My pa always said I was a softy. Tis why I'm a scout, less killin'."

We sat a moment, drawing comfort from each other. In the quiet, I had a thought. "I can help with the sexed up scent, so you won't get in trouble." I went and grabbed a wipe rag filled with the skanky smell of old sex from a nearby room.

He took the rag and rubbed it along his nether regions to prevent at least one element of chastisement. "You have a window round here?"

I nodded and led him to the small balcony. The men left in the rooms were all asleep; only we were awake. I wrapped a wool blanket around me as my short robe gave little protection against the cold. We stood together, waiting for the sun to peek out. He wrapped his arms around me, staving off the pre-dawn chill. I leaned against his warmth and sensitivity. He leaned into my compassion and strength.

We watched the autumn sun climb into the sky and heard the first day bell welcome the dawn. The whole world had faded away; it was only the two of us and the panoramic sunrise over the eastern mountains. I looked up into his dark brown sad eyes. I wanted to say something, something kind, something meaningful, but what do you say to a man about to die to give them solace?

He kissed me on each cheek and on the center of my forehead. "Well, perhaps I will see you again in my next life under better circumstances."

"That would be nice. I hope so too. What's your name so I know who to pray for on Memory Day." I felt so lame, so callous. I bit my lip as I knew tears were welling up in my eyes.

He looked up, surprised. "Prentis," he stuttered. "Prentis Bloodhound gens."

"Prentis, I am Meg Airedale gens and I will call you on Memory Day and sing to you and Jacque Bichon gens. You be listening for me." I stood tall for him, tears running down my muzzle.

He nodded gravely and gave me a truly tender kiss. The first I ever had. I thought my heart would burst. This touch was for me, to me, to my soul. "Do you have to go? Will you come back?"

"They are expecting me by second bell. My lady. I will come back if I can, at least send word." He took my paw and kissed the back of it.

"This happy memory I will carry with me as I leave this world. Thank you." He shook with emotion, then took control and stiffly headed out...like a good soldier.

I stood there in the sun, tears streaming down my face. I now understood war and understood that my children will either be production slaves, or soldiers, or be a breeder that makes them. There was no exit and no life for them or me.

After a while, Matriarch limped along to close the balcony doors and saw me. "Are you hurt too?" she asked, concerned when she saw my tears.

"Only my heart."

"That is the worst pain because it is slow to heal, if ever." She stood beside me, relieved we survived the punishment.

"What is the point in breeding children to become soldiers to die?"

Matriarch shrugged. "We all die. But did you do something worthwhile during your life that helped the pack? Then your life meant something, and you lived well."

"I suppose."

"You haven't seen your sister, have you?"

"No, why?"

"Tabs is the only one who hasn't turned in any rings."

"I am sure she just fell asleep and forgot."

Matriarch nodded knowingly. "See to it she brings it to me before the next bell. I am being watched and can't just give her a mark."

I went to go find her. She was in her usual place, hiding in the laundry. Her fist was bloody from where she had been hitting the floor. I woke her up gently. "Tabs, Tabs, you need to go give this ring to Matriarch."

"No."

"What do you mean, 'no'? You have to. Else you will be shaved and then who knows what. Since I'm expecting, I don't need one; I got these for you."

"No, you earned it; you turn it in."

"Tabs," I was exasperated. "I don't need it, you do. Here." I tried to force it into her paw.

"No, I am done. I don't want a man to touch me. It repulses me. I can't stand it, and I can't stand watching them touch you and the others. After what they did to Chrissy, I want to be gone from here."

"Turn in the ring, and we will get you reassigned as a musician. Move you to the waiting room or nursery."

"Sister, I know you mean well, but I want to leave here, here where I have memories of my love. My heart breaks as I look and see all the places where she is not."

I looked at her as tears ran down my muzzle and pooled on the floor. "You'll leave me alone."

She looked away and whispered. "Sorry...I am not strong enough to stay."

I gave Matriarch my rings. She took them sadly and made two marks by my name.

"She made her choice," I explained to avoid Matriarch's condemnation. Or was I trying to convince myself?

Two hours earlier, I would not have understood. I sat there and held Tabs and rocked her in my arms. I knew what it meant to lose someone you loved now, the emptiness of looking forward to a life with a vacuum where they should be. I was still holding her when the Shepherds came to take her away, tearing her out of my arms.

Tabs turned to me as they dragged her out. "I am sorry."

I went through the motions in a daze the next few days. Looking every time the door opened, wondering if they were the one with word for me...but none ever came. One morning I was watching the sunrise when the Shepherds asked me to come inside as they needed to secure the rooms. It was not a request.

I saw a light in Matriarch's room so I went in. "Why won't they let me be? I have done nothing but followed orders. This is my time. I am allowed on the upper balcony."

"Sorry dear, we are on lockdown. Would you like some tea?"

"Lockdown. Why?" I watched Matriarch. Somehow she seemed older today.

She was about to answer and then thought better of it. "This happens sometimes—never lasts long."

I cocked my head to the side. Matriarch's whiskers were twitching. "What are you not telling me?"

Matriarch raised her hands and turned away. "It is only rumor... from the Shepherds. They love to say things to cause us hurt. I don't know if there is any truth in it. I don't want to say 'til I do."

I rested my paw on her shoulder. "It is better to know. For even in the lies–there is truth and knowledge."

Matriarch nodded. She wrung her paws and looked at the floor. She spoke in a quivering voice, softly so others would not hear. "They say there was trouble in the jails. The Catkin rose up to escape and killed several guards. They said it was near where your sister and others awaiting verdict were held. Some inmates died too. But I don't know if she…" her voice trailed off into silent heaving sobs.

My legs gave out; I collapsed to my knees. Matriarch stroked my head and it soothed me, eventually. We clung to each other in silent grief. The day was nearly upon us, and breakfast had been served. "It was quick, her suffering is over. I think she would like that it is over now. Better than to wonder. Thank you for telling me." I dried my eyes and stood. I will survive, I vowed. I will earn my freedom, then my voice will not be silenced.

I lost my first litter in the following days, but Matriarch gave me my first gem anyway.

Since then, three years and two litters have come and gone. I have stood on the balcony and watched many sunrises, some days alone, some Matriarch stood with me in silence. Most days, I wouldn't think of Tabs. Some days, she was all I thought of, especially when I was waiting or nursing. I always thought of him. Often, my rest was tormented by horrors of men with melting faces and women torn apart piece by piece as laughing men watched.

I was at my lowest when nursing, looking into my pups bright eyes full of love and life, and knowing what darkness lay ahead of them. No one could prepare you for the pain of when they take your puppies away. The Shepherds have taken a dozen boys and six girl puppies from two litters from me.

New mothers are watched closely—not to see if the need anything but to keep them from killing their litters. It has happened twice since I have been here, and led to two more trips to the arena to see the Consul's rexes fed.

My recent litter, my fourth gem, was small and frail; only two boys and a girl have survived. I watched them sleeping next to me, wondering how long until they would be taken away. But for now I held them close, let them know love, comfort, and safety while they can. I had drifted off to sleep when I felt something grip around my muzzle.

"Shh! Don't be alarmed; it's me," said a voice with a familiar scent. I started awake and looked up into a face nearly the twin of my own. A different hair style and a big scar across her cheek, but I knew that face anywhere for it was my own. My tail snapped in happiness against the pillows. "Tabs!" I muttered through my closed jaw. I pulled her off balance as I reached up to hug her. We laughed like young girls again for a moment.

"Come on, I am here to free you and anyone else who wants to come." She grabbed my arm and pulled me up into a rib-crushing hug. She was thin, but strong.

"But my babies?" I had given up two litters. I would fight for these three sickly pups. They would not lose their opportunity for freedom.

"Bring them. Hurry!"

I tied my sheet into a sling, nuzzled them in, and grabbed my only possession, the small wooden cat given to me by the man I dream of.

I stepped out of the room; many Shepherds were dead with Egyptian beaded darts in them. Several Celt warriors were hunting the remaining guards. A scarred tabby with feathers in his braid seemed to be in charge.

"Is this the one? Let's go then." He growled.

"Tabs!" I clutched my babies to me ready to fight to protect them.

"They are friends. We broke out of the cells together three years ago. They have been taking care of me. They are here to help us, to free us." She gave my arm a supportive squeeze. "It is ok."

Seeing Tabs must have made me lose all reason, because I believed her. An odd, cloying smell in the air made me cough.

We stopped in the other rooms trying to get the women to join us. Most were too scared. A few actually fought us, called us traitors. A few joined us, maybe two tens of women. A few nursing mothers grabbed their pups, a couple just brought their girls, but most left them as reminders of a painful past or a burden which would slow down their escape.

The Catkin was getting impatient. "Hurry! We have to go. Guard change is next bell."

"You used Egyptian darts to attack the guards and the smoke?"

"Yes, don't want them following us west. The smoke has the partial effect of hiding our scents. The Empire has spread and taken most of our hunting land. Now we trade with the enemies of our enemy. The

Crocodiles have a trap waiting for the dogs of war when they go to seek their retribution."

We followed them as quietly as we could down the stairs and out into the night. We sounded loud compared to the stealthy felines. I still did not trust our ancient enemies. It made no sense for them to come and risk their lives to save a few women and children. The cold air finally snapped my mind awake. I asked Tabs in a whisper, "What is the other effect of the burning herbs?"

He hissed for silence but answered me. "It was the sleep herb added to the fires." He ushered us towards the water systems.

"The what?" I froze. "What does that do?"

"An herb which brings the endless sleep." He looked at me apologetically with his unblinking eyes. "It is painless."

"You are a monster." I barked, tears streaming.

His eyes jerked around looking to see if I was heard. "Quiet, you fool! Come on." He grabbed my arm and pulled me into motion.

"You are murdering the babies! How could you?" I pulled my arm away but kept running towards the sewer tunnels.

"Tomorrow, they grow up and kill my remaining children. I killed future soldiers so that maybe my kits or their kits won't have to war and make these horrific decisions." He looked away, troubled. "We did try to get them to come with us."

Tabs shook with anger, eyes filled with tears. "I didn't know. I swear I didn't know."

"We kept our word; we got your sister out alive. We are running out of time before being noticed. The sky is brightening, dawn is not far. Now are you with us? We cannot wait on you." Soft sounds of a new day showed the city was awakening. I noticed his hand on his knife.

One of my pups wiggled to get more comfortable in the sling, which reminded me of my priorities. "I will travel beside you, but I am not 'with' you."

"Good enough." He motioned for us to follow his tribesmen down the torchlit tunnels of the waterworks. He was watching for us to be followed; so far luck was with us.

As we passed along the sewage aqueduct's trail, I asked "What happened? I thought you were dead."

"I was imprisoned with others who decided they were not ready to follow orders and die quietly. So we found allies and escaped. But we were in bad shape, took a few months heal up enough to travel, then winter hit and closed the pass to reach his tribe. And well sorry, so long to get back."

The aqueduct ended at a steep angle to force the refuse down a shoot and away from the capital. The rushing water was deafening. "See you at the bottom." Tabs took a deep breath and stepped into the rushing water. The water deadened all sound but after a few minutes I saw a torch move back and forth at the bottom.

I secured the sling holding my pups and held my nose. The fall down the slide was terrifying. The wind stole my breath. I prayed to the Great Lady that she would watch over us. I wrapped my arms around my babies holding them tightly so they wouldn't fall out. We splashed into a shallow pond of sludge at the bottom.

I sputtered and tried to stand up with one paw as the other held the sling above water level. Tabs reached down and gave me a hand up.

"Now what?" I asked, shaking the water off and checking on my puppies.

"I guess now we live." Tabs took off in a slow jog towards the tree-line. "Choose a direction."

I grinned. "I like forward. See if you can keep up." I ran hard and fast on my long Airedale legs, savoring the feeling of the wind in my hair. No boundaries, no cages, never again.

Who are any of us in the grand scheme of things? The prostitute who is society's true messenger becomes the fool who comes to save us. In the end, all we want is someone to praise, someone to blame. We're all looking for scapegoats for the state of the crumbling world and nation's borders are drawn on that basis. But it's hard to wall off the worst aspects of a failing civilization when they may be inside each and every one of us. The great eye watches tenderly over us all, but in truth it's judging us, every second we draw breath.

THE TOWER

Gullwulf

The jackrabbit heard his panting breaths fill the space around him. He watched the ceiling fan above him rotate lazily, noting the dust that had gathered on the edge of the blades. Perhaps it was about time he dusted there. The lion was putting his pants on and there was still heat between the jackrabbit's legs. He flicked the pillow bracing his lower back away, rolling his shoulders into the mattress, kicking the sheets from his feet. The sheets would have to be washed. One ear flicked as he heard the clicking of a belt and he forced himself up. He watched as the lion slipped a shirt over his shoulders. The jackrabbit swallowed, working his dry tongue. "So, uh, can I call you?"

The lion laughed. The rabbit clicked his jaws shut, feeling the insides of his ears heat. Should have figured. The lion padded across the flat, opening the front door. He glanced once over at the rabbit and gave a big toothed grin. "Thanks for taking the thorn out, Thistle," he chuckled, and left.

The jackrabbit scowled, rubbing his front paw. "That was a mouse," he muttered, mostly to himself. It wasn't like Leonard would be back to hear it. Moving away from the mess on the bed, careful to keep his black tail from it, he was surprised to hear his identification bracelet chirp. He stretched across his bed and grabbed the device, flicking upward to let the message fabricate in the air.

+6507999999999
SENDER UNKNOWN
drop @ 7 am package sent pick up at young annes

Thistle sighed, letting the screen fade. Right. He let the message dissipate before his bracelet chirped again.

+777654867422
JAY ASTON
Hey cutie :P been thinkin bout that black tail of yours all last night.
u doin anyone later or just me? ;)

Christ did Thistle hate cats sometimes; even ocelots were just as insufferable as the lion who walked away. He slipped his bracelet over his wrist and grabbed his discarded pants. Getting outside and looking for a delivery was going to be better than staying in his flat and waiting for someone else to put his feet above his head.

Morning fog settled low over the city, dissipating the chill of the previous evening and combining with the thick smog of metropolitan pollution into a gray soup in the sky. Everything rendered hazy in the mist and it made figures in the distance indistinct. Proper dawn, the one that managed to breach the hills, was still a good few hours away. Most citizens were already up, shuffling to their jobs through the labyrinth of concrete and glass and filing into their respective buildings. Thistle had to avoid the swinging tails of the bleary-eyed morning workers, setting his hat neatly between his ears just as his bracelet chirped along with the bracelets of everyone around him.

Commuters paused, looking up to the tallest skyscraper in the city. The only building allowed to rise above five stories, it stretched to the low-hanging clouds with its digital eye projected and watching everyone, piercing through the mist. It was still in its sleeping position, eyelashes spread like a fan, but it opened bright and wide the moment that 7 am chimed on Thistle's wrist. The slit pupil contacted, the blue iris spinning until it filled up the eye, and everyone's head craned up at once. Text began to filter downward along the skyscraper:

GOOD MORNING CITIZENS! It is 7 am on this morning of March 28, 2059.
Currently the threat level is LOW. Thank you for doing your part to keep the FENCE in good condition and staying positive!
The weather conditions are SMOGGY. Anyone diagnosed with

asthma and canine species should wear their mask for any excursions over 30 minutes until 9 AM.

Please report to work on time! Attendance is slacking! A society which does not work together will not grow together!

Report any snags in the fence to maintenance immediately.

Keep your passwords protected! Reports of HACKERS using data from verified SECURNET accounts is on the rise. Remember, only messages delivered with SECURNET are legitimate, and SECURNET is the only network that you can trust!

The prices for stocks are as follows:

NAWQ, 45.67....

Thistle looked away from the display, as did a good portion of the population. A few of the more well-off folks continued to watch as the stock numbers filtered along the building screen. Thistle ducked around those who lingered and continued on his trek, keeping his steps light and his back hunched. As a jackrabbit, his stature made him near seven foot—in a crowd like this, it only served for him to stand out, which was something he took pains to avoid.

His identification bracelet chirped, and Thistle glanced at it. Text scrolled on the small device, asking him to "check in" with the central government system. A read of his index pad did the trick, and he continued walking down the street, flicking through the information appearing on his bracelet. Weather, the morning announcement, the current state of the skyscraper, and the status of the fence all came up. It was all information that hardly ever changed, day to day. Even the status of the fence barely fluctuated. He only gave it enough attention to keep anyone from getting suspicious.

These were not observations that Thistle would ever say out loud, nor would any other citizen of the city. If everything kept running, there was no reason to point it out. Just like how Thistle's function in the city was unspoken, but necessary for its survival. He rolled the thought around in his mind like a wad of gum, chewing it between paces on the grungy sidewalk. Was it too egotistical that he thought of himself in such a way? Hell, it wasn't like anyone actually *knew* what he did, or cared if they knew (if they weren't buying one of his services), just like how everyone would conveniently forget that the news they digested today was the same that it was yesterday.

Realizing his mind was leading him down a trap of its own making, Thistle shoved the thought aside as he traversed the now-empty pavement and turned deeper into the city for his pick-up location.

Young Anne's was tucked into the multitude of buildings on the south side of the city, against the second main thoroughfare. He ducked through an alleyway, strode past some of the pointed cameras, and soon after Thistle found himself in front of the little restaurant, its only identifying mark a neon sign with a red bowl and yellow noodles flailing outside of it. Thistle kept his head down as he entered the restaurant, the heat and steam flashing against his face.

The inside was just as dimly lit as the outside. Flickering bulbs of incandescent light bathed what little they touched in a harsh glow, while the heating lamps overtook everything else. There was only enough room in the restaurant between the greasy black bar and the tables to walk single file, and anyone larger than a deer was bound to have a hard time. Thistle was careful to tip-toe his way through the crowd, having to dance around the chairs that would push out, keeping his tail flipped up in the hopes that he wouldn't have to spend his evening with the ocelot. He slipped between the barstools and peered over the low plexiglass barrier at the bighorn ram on the other side, his hooved fingers working the ladles.

"Morning," Thistle said. "See the report?"

The ram flicked an ear, which was all Thistle got out of his presence. He scratched the back of his neck, running a paw over the tip of his ear as the silence stretched. He tapped his left foot, rubbed his wrists until he pushed the dust colored fur sufficiently to see his own pink skin. After a few beats in silence, wherein no one approached him, Thistle slid onto one of the proffered stools, hooking his feet into the rungs as he cleared his throat. "So, what's the special?"

Without breaking his stride, the ram flipped the knife in his hand and pushed a bowl of noodles, topped with brown herbs (the shipment day for herbs must have been moved, Thistle noted with a frown) and swimming in a brown broth. Thistle took it, making sure to grab some eating utensils designed to keep fur away from greasy food. He choked a few noodles down, swallowing hard at their cold, slimy texture sliding down his throat as he offered a warbled smile to the ram. If Thistle was lucky, these noodles had only been recycled from leftovers twice rather than the more typical five times, but

Young Anne's had a reputation to uphold. He coughed before he could get a sentence out to the ram. "Mn, good as always. Catch you during the lunch rush." As usual, the ram's flat gaze gave away nothing as he moved the brown herbs over onto the cutting board, using the flat of his knife to smash them. During their exchange, a waitress gazelle walked by, taking the bowl and leaving behind a small, twine-wrapped package, matching the clicking of the bowl to the thud of the package.

Thistle lifted a paw and turned away, sweeping the package under his arm. This one was small, but it weighed more than the jackrabbit estimated. He had to make an effort to hide what he was carrying. SECURNET may have been the premier messaging service that everyone used, but it didn't mean everyone was happy with it.

As Thistle's footpaw stepped onto the last squeaking board, a voice that sounded like gravel echoed behind him: "I wouldn't."

Thistle's ears shot up, knocking his hat off his head as they swiveled, straining behind him. The ram was still chopping decaying herbs, and there was absolutely no indication that he spoke. But he must have. No one else in the establishment would have spoken to him. A few bleary eyes were lifting up to look at him, horses lifting their long faces and wolves with noses twitching.

Thistle ducked to snatch the hat, sweeping the cap over his ears as he tucked his head underneath the door frame and dashed out, breaking one of his cardinal rules of never traveling faster than the surrounding citizens. Using the full length of his stride was always bound to cause undue attention, and as he sprinted along the edge of the sidewalk, several canines and felines were glaring at him in his wake for interrupting their meandering stroll. He didn't stop until the shadow of the skyscraper crossed over him, and the temperature dropped several degrees. The eye was unblinking now, the slit pupil sliding to and fro to keep a watchful eye over its citizens. Thistle shifted the package under his arm and folded his ears back as he shook his identification bracelet on his wrist, reviewing the message once more.

The message had to be from the civet. They were the only one who had continued to be a regular client of Thistle's. After the skyscraper had managed to see a few messengers getting lazy with their deliveries, most of the industry had been wiped out. It was a sure sign for

Thistle to leave it, but it was stable money, and it let him explore a different avenue of revenue than the one that involved getting passed around like a joint between men. Courier wasn't what most considered ideal, but it was better than dealing with any pressing matters in his life, and it kept him from being exiled to the low-income edges of the city.

The best pathway to the drop-off skirted the borders of the city. The monitoring from the eye lessened here, the sensors too covered in muck and grime to track citizens. It still wasn't a place that any sensible person would linger as even the patrols wouldn't cross here. It was too close to the fence.

Around him, the buildings morphed from the clean-cut office complexes of the industrial sector to the low-slung, grimy, abandoned buildings of the borders. He weaved through alleyways piled with debris and scrambled on top of shipment boxes. The thick smell of mold and mildew began to fill Thistle's nostrils, his ears scraping the wall until he stumbled out of the narrow corridor, catching his breath. When he looked up, the chain link fence was inches from him.

The fence ran around the entirety of the city, unbroken with no exit and no entrance. It stretched far above the jackrabbit's head, barbed wire curling atop to prevent even the highest jumpers from attempting to clear it. If he flipped an ear up, he could hear the hum of electricity crackling through the fence. The structure itself was bland to Thistle. It was what lay beyond that held his curiosity.

He padded closer, paw hovering inches from the fence as he felt the static crackle beneath it. Beyond, the landscape was featureless, brown sand and horizon whipped up into an eternal haze. If he squinted, the shadowed mountains in the distance cut jagged into the sky.

No one was out there. No one with their eyes that never blinked and their cold, bulbous skin. No one with their solid bone for muzzles that jerked and prodded with their every movement. No one with their tails that dragged across the ground and their flaps of loose skin that hung from their neck.

Thistle's breath caught as he stepped back. The fence was a good thing. It kept those others away. It kept those away whose diets had razed the land to the barren wasteland it was now, it kept those away whose needs had swallowed the precious resources for the collected whole, it kept those away who had gutted his ancestors over differences in blood and claw. It kept everyone inside safe. If he didn't look, the others wouldn't be there because they knew about the fence. The skyscraper watched and if anything approached from beyond, it would let the citizens know. They were safe under the skyscraper and its ever-watchful gaze.

His bracelet chirped, announcing that Thistle's pulse was reaching an unacceptable threshold for public outings. He took a steadying breath, feeling the smog whistle through his teeth and started to walk the border of the fence.

The fence was secure and stalwart, a contrast to the crumbling buildings beside it. It used to be the area for the lowest income housing, those who had specialized diets that the meal packets didn't always provide for, but even they too grew wary of eyes watching them from the other side, or so they claimed. All Thistle cared about was the fact that the cameras pointing inside were deactivated; another one of those dirty secrets. No one lived here, so there was no reason to waste power.

The abandoned apartment complex that Thistle used had a tiny mark at eye level, a shiny sheen on an otherwise dusty wall. Dried vines encrusted the dead garden out in front as the brick building clawed its way to four stories. Most of the windows had long since been boarded up and gated shut, the decorative lattice work choked by dying vines. He found the familiar footholds, grateful for his bounding jump as he scrambled up the lattice of pipework and dead garden terraces, wedging open the glass panels that made up the side of the building and wedging himself in with a grunt.

Other creatures had a hard time navigating these parts of the city. He had heard of a bear who, upon trying, had ripped open his spleen. Deer and rabbits made for the best messengers because of it, but fewer were around. There were rumors about what happened to those caught outside the sensors, but physical goods outside of SECURNET access had to be transported. It was work that was always available. Didn't mean it was the kind of good work like working in the gaze of the skyscraper, or in the eye itself, but it was always work and it would never run out, and Thistle could not imagine doing anything different.

As he moved the package under one arm, he heard a small noise. He lifted his ears, pushing his hat aside as his hearing sharpened.

Something was ticking. It wasn't the mechanisms of his identification bracelet (that whirred), it wasn't the crackling of the wires that spat just outside. He glanced down at the package.

"Jackrabbit!" The voice sounded like gravel, and Thistle jerked his head up, the tips of his ears brushing the ceiling. Eyes gleamed from the darkness, small fangs flashed as the figure spoke. "What are you doing? Put your damned ears down, you want to catch a goddamn signal in those!"

Like a scolded child Thistle hunched over, smartly replacing his cap and folding his ears along his spine. He padded through the darkness until he was eye-level with the civet, their coat wrapped around their spotted frame. Almond eyes glared at him from the popped collar, forcing Thistle to advert his gaze. Some claimed they could tell gender by scent; while Thistle knew what a male smelled like after his encounters, the civet remained a mystery. Thistle suspected they preferred it that way. Thistle wasn't even sure the civet was really a civet; he could have sworn that he had seen the civet with various implants, something to sharpen the ears or lengthen the tail, things that were banned given the trouble they had caused prior. Thistle was never sure if the rumors were true about things that could warm the blood or mimic raised hackles.

The civet huffed. "You have it?" Their voice warbled, modulated and pitched with static. It used to simply be rough with cigar smoke; probably something else that Thistle must have delivered to them.

He nodded, handing the parcel over. Something in its weight shifted, and he couldn't help but lift an ear enough to listen to a rhythmic click.

The civet snatched the package, leaning in until Thistle could hear the rasp of their voice modular kicking in. "Your payment."

Thistle nodded, not trusting his vocal cords. The civet took Thistle's identification bracelet and snapped something in it. The display fizzled for a brief moment, and then announced that credits had just been deposited. The chip would melt from Thistle's body heat in just a few moments, leaving him to scrub the metal from his fur.

This was the end of the job, but Thistle stayed put. His nose twitched as he watched the civet, their claws pulling on the twine of the parcel. The civet gave a sharp glance upwards and cleared their throat. "The money should be sufficient."

Thistle never asked questions. His job was to deliver the physical things that SECURNET did not account for and leave. Something tugged in his gut and made his left foot tap, but when he stopped trying to stare a hole into the ground to talk to the civet, they were gone. Thistle heard a metallic clang somewhere in the distance before he was bathed in silence.

***

He should be heading back. A cold finger of dread rested on the back of his neck, pushing against his nape as he climbed out of the apartment and started back to the industrial center of the city. Normally, the civet was brusk with him, but the impatience radiating off them had Thistle's stomach churning, and the ticking package didn't do anything to assuage his fears; since when did Thistle deliver anything that made noise and attracted attention to itself? Since when did the civet *want* anything that they didn't immediately take out from the package, to make sure Thistle didn't screw them over?

His thoughts didn't leave when he got back to his apartment complex. The streets were empty; everyone had shuffled into their office jobs and wouldn't be emerging until the designated lunch hour. He would slide in with the crowd then, blending in and checking the hotspots for another job. The civet's paycheck would keep him covered for another week, but having extra money was added security.

The dread slipped down his pelt and into his stomach. Normally, Thistle would simply hang around Young Anne's or any one of its sister establishments; all else failing, he could try to linger in front of the office buildings, keeping his tail flipped up as he pretended to peruse all the local news that would be filling up the skyscraper. He could also try to get ahead of one of the food shipments, if he was feeling particularly cheeky. Supplies continued to dwindle, even as the skyscraper reported "unimaginable gains". Right now, the very thought of hanging around other people made the sour feeling in Thistle's stomach turn to pure bile. By the time he was in the lobby of his apartment building, Thistle felt his stomach cramping up, doubling over, every breath scraping through his throat.

"Hey, uh, bunny." The huff from another creature had Thistle looking up. He was horrified to see the sharp blue uniform of the peacekeeping force, pressed tightly against the gray fur of the anteater. Black fur bobbed at her throat as she talked, tail loosely swinging behind her. "You are not looking well. Do you need a lift to the hospital?"

"N-no! I'm fine, I'm perfectly fine!" Thistle could hear his voice crack and winced. The anteater arched an eyebrow over her long snout.

"Let me see your bracelet," she said.

Thistle had to stop himself from thumping his foot on the ground as he lifted his wrist. Any sign of unease was going to be taken for suspicion, and that was exactly the opposite of what he wanted at this moment. The anteater brushed her huge claws over the bracelet, the readout displaying in the air between them: pulse, heart rate, and time outside. The anteater gave it a careful look, tapping a broad claw on a line of text. "Is there a reason you were outside for so long today, sir?"

"Well, ma'am—"

"Officer Diega," the anteater said, her voice clipped.

"Officer Diega." Thistle tried to put on his best smile and polite voice without breaking his muzzle. "I am a freelance worker."

"Freelance, hm?" Officer Diega pulled up her own bracelet, smoothing the display down to her arm as she began to scroll files projected into her fur. "Not too many of your folk around these days."

"No, ma'am."

"What were you doing so close to the fence?"

Thistle's stomach dropped. "I was. Uhm."

Officer Diega watched him. Thistle began to notice her claws, and build. She could do damage that Thistle had little defense against. He cleared his throat. "I was only following the morning announcements. About the, uhm. Snags in the fence."

"Regular patriot aren't you?" Diega clicked her tongue. "According to your travel records you do seem to be the adventurous type."

"That I am ma'am." Thistle took a step back, his paws flexing into the smooth tile. "Is there anything else you need from me?"

Officer Diega's eyes narrowed, but she said nothing, turning away from Thistle as her bracelet flashed, information overriding the display on Thistle's file. Thistle lingered for a breath before he began to amble up the stairs, even as his legs shook with every step that he took.

The walk to his apartment seemed to take ages, the hallway lengthening before him, stretching until he wasn't sure if he had even gone in the right direction, despite having taken this route for ages. He checked directions on his bracelet, cursed himself for his sudden indecision, and turned the corner to his apartment. In his mind, Officer Diega would have accosted him further and not let him leave if she really had any suspicions on him, but there was nothing to pin on Thistle. His job was untraceable, or so he told himself. Just as he lifted his bracelet to unlock his apartment, a cough sounded behind him. Thistle froze, his bracelet inches from his door. Officer Diega's shadow loomed over him. For an anteater she was fast.

"Going home already?" Diega's breath huffed behind him.

"Yep! I mean, as a freelancer I maintain my own hours." He drew his hand back, less he trip the door open. "Did you need something?"

"Yes." Diega shifted so her broad shoulders blocked Thistle's exit. "Your health records." She tapped her own bracelet. "I was reviewing them, and I noticed that your pulse had risen several times today to dangerous levels. What were you doing out there?"

"I ran, that's probably what did it." Thistle tried to smile, feeling his ears straining to twitch up.

"This wasn't exercise, Mr. Thistle," Diega said. The digital display was illuminated between them. "And it was close to the border too."

Thistle took a deep breath, and the display beeped. His heart rate rose, flashing as the pulse meter began to climb. His foot began to tap, his muscles bunching up as they prepared to do what a jackrabbit did best—run, fast and like hell.

Diega's thick paw landed hard on his shoulder, her claws curling into his fur. Thistle's ears shot up, hat falling off with them, but he only ducked his head. Diega's paw rested on the back of his neck.

"At least you ain't fighting," she rumbled. "Gonna look good for you."

None of it, of course, was going to look good the moment that they began to look through Thistle's records. He had to find a way to run—but the very act would only pull him deeper into trouble. He was frozen, caught between decisions and wanting to take none of them.

The rumble began in the floor. Thistle thought for a second that it was the filtration system kicking on until the tremors began to run through the walls. Diega's grip on his arm tightened moments before her bracelet flashed a bright red that Thistle had never seen. A couple just emerging from their apartment had their wrists light up like firecrackers. Words splashed across the walls, emergency lights appearing on the floor. Thistle caught a few scattered words from the rapidly scrolling phrase: "citizens report… danger… Eye speaks."

"Damn it!" Diega jerked Thistle along. Thistle tripped over his own feet trying to keep up and had to jump over the anteater's tail. She didn't take kindly to this and switched her grip to pinch one of Thistle's ears between her claws. "If you're really going to be this dumb to try to run on me—"

"No, I swear, no!" Thistle swallowed, even if his instincts fought his common sense. But if he kept his head down, everything would pass over him and he would be swept back into the current of people.

Back down the hallway and down the stairs he was dragged by the ear. They stumbled into the outside world, looking no different than it had minutes earlier, the sky the same choked gray and the skyscraper disappearing into the smog that clung to the atmosphere, however people were beginning to appear. Citizens poured into the sidewalk, many of the canine and feline ones having to wear their masks just to stand outside to see what was going on, leaving them leather faced in the sea of fur.

Thistle's foot began to tap before he had a chance to stop it. Diega glared at him, her small mouth set into a scowl, but he dismissed her in favor of trying to crane over people's shoulders and look at their readouts, comparing it to his own.

His was blank. Everyone else's read "Look to the eye." Thistle turned his attention to the skyscraper—and there was no eye.

It wasn't uncommon for the eye to close for brief periods, a rest while it processed the information it had gathered. Some people took it as a sign of good things—if the eye wasn't open, it meant security. But while the skyscraper danced with red lights, the eye was a small line in its blank surface. There was no way it could be interpreted as anything but ominous.

The eye opened, bloodshot. The clear blue of its iris was intersected with throbbing red LEDs, the eyelashes splayed and the pupil contracting wildly. The text began to filter then:

CITIZENS!
There has been a breach! A BETRAYER in our midst—someone who seeks to DESTROY and BRING DOWN our precious society! If you have any information about this TERRORIST, it is your DUTY to REPORT and bring PEACE to our great city!

Letters began to collide on the text as it scrolled. Thistle felt his knees begin to shake, shrinking as Diega's claws forced him partially upright. She had a paw pressed to the side of her head, trying to speak in low tones to someone. Her grip loosened for a brief second as she barked out "What?" and Thistle took his chance. He slipped out of her grip, and before she could even get a shout down her muzzle, he leapt, her claws missing him by inches as he bounded between citizens, jostling them in the crowded sidewalk. A few people gave him a strange look, but he pressed on. He jumped again, aiming for a blank patch of sidewalk, only to miscalculate and jam his foot hard into one of the storm drains. Pain shot up his ankle and Thistle bit down on a cry in his throat, muffling it to a whimper.

The gasps around him made his heart sink, everyone pointing paws and hooves up. Thistle followed their gazes, hoping his worst fears wouldn't be confirmed, until he saw them—a civet, poking their head out from a window as the eye convulsed around it, slowly stepping out onto the ledge. Everyone jostled for a better look, until the display of the skyscraper flickered behind them, showcasing the civet's leering grin as the eye slid down to the lower levels. The civet tapped something in their throat, their warbled voice amplified—Thistle realized with some horror that their voice now laced through everyone's bracelets.

"You live in the shadow of a lie!" The civet spoke. "And you have been far too content to stay in your bubble! You believe that you are safe, loved, and cared for!" The civet's body shuddered, and then pulled a paw down their chest. Fur sloughed off from their swipe, a dull glitter of bulbous skin shone where the fur once was. "You want to remain at the top, you think nothing can touch you—but everything you know is falling! Falling, falling, falling!" The civet's fur that continued to drop and peel off, his costume coming apart at the seams as spikes rippled from his spine, displayed in grotesque detail behind it, a split-second delay as the creature emerged from the shredded costume. The green scales shone through their fur made the wire that wrapped around their body easier to see as the rays of sunlight sliced through the smog. Hundreds of red-dotted lasers focused on the "civet's" body, and Thistle was certain he heard Diega's voice scream "Get down, get down right *now!*"

The muzzle was the only thing that still had fur, still looked like a mammal even if it wasn't. It tilted its head to the side, and then lifted its bracelet. The display behind the creature changed, showing a jackrabbit with dusty fur and a tattered cap—Thistle.

"Your prophet," the lizard said. "Your holy messenger. The one who has delivered your salvation!"

The creature fell. The wire trailed down its body and the deafening roar of ammunition made Thistle duck. He heard the hollow splat as the thing hit the ground a few seconds later.

And then the rumble.

Thistle looked between his fingers, frozen to his spot as everyone had backed up from him. The eye was bulging wildly, iris flicking around and the red veins expanding until the blur had turned violet. Its pixels began to break apart.

The explosion rumbled low in Thistle's bones, a slow echo caught on the lower levels, and the skyscraper began to fall. It crumpled upon itself, erupting dust and rubble as its shudders echoed across the streets. The eye blinked spastically up the skyscraper, trying to escape the shattering displays even as the LEDs in the eyes flickered, pixelated, and bled into red through the blue, swirling violet behind Thistle's eyes. Even that too broke, the eye turning into nothing but static that disappeared into the growing dust cloud that overtook the street. Bracelets flashed screens of purple and black, red text colliding on itself before going blank.

Dust coated everything, stung eyes and nostrils and through the screams Thistle could hear hacking coughs. He kept his muzzle shut tightly, hind legs coiled to spring only to feel a burly arm wrap around his torso.

"You," Diega screamed at him, "and I are going to have a very, very long talk!"

Through the haze of the dust, yellow lights began to pop up. Thistle's bracelet buzzed, and he looked down. Diega's bracelet matched the same sickly yellow. All muzzles looked down, their silence thicker than the dust surrounding them.

FENCE IS DOWN. SECTOR 1, SECTOR 2, SECTOR 3 …

Diega whirled Thistle around, shaking him, screaming. "What did you do? What did you do! Why? Why?"

Thistle felt tears choke him, and he wrapped his own paws around his throat, willing everything to go down. This wasn't his fault. This wasn't what he wanted. He was content with his life. He was content. It never should have fallen.

"I'm so sorry," Thistle's voice grated against his ears. "I didn't want this."

"What do you mean?" Diega's gaze was searching him, filled somewhere between utter terror and abject desperation.

Thistle shook his head. "I just wanted… I wanted it all to stay the same."

The citizens were watching him.

The sun was out, warming the concrete, the rubble. It would be warm enough for the others to come in, the ones with scales and feathers, one by one. The fences were down and in Thistle's mind he could see them lining against the fence, pressing, waiting to come in. They, the ones they forced out, would sweep over this city and drown them all in their pride.

"What do we do?" Thistle thought Diega asked him the question, but it was his vocal cords that bobbed between his pawpads. "Someone has to do something! The tower… the tower will tell us! Right? The tower, it's not gone, it's not!" He tore his bracelet off, shook it until it began to break apart in his blunted claws. "Answer us! Please, answer us!"

Everything they had known had fallen. He had delivered the bomb which felled their society, and now, they gathered around him, listening to him as he held the shattered remains of his bracelet. They waited for him to deliver.

"I'm just a messenger," he whispered. "I'm just…"

The city fell into silence.

His crying turned to laughing, his breaths choking out as he stood, higher than the crowd, ears swiveling.

"You did this," Diega hissed.

"We all did," Thistle muttered, closing his eyes.

Even though he was in the center of the city, he swore he could hear the scratching of scales as raucous cries began to echo across the city. The avian and the reptilian were coming to take back the oasis they had long since drained. There was nothing to stop them now.

What brings any world to grace, or to ruin? The souls that stray through it of course and leave one path for another less favored. Sometimes the consequences are small and contained, sometimes they're earth-shattering, but what to do when otherwise good people lose themselves?

The lost need love. The troubled need understanding, but some say that's not enough.

We need order most of all, order in a form above mere laws on paper. We need someone to turn to and rely on. And fear. Love alone for any God can't provide that.

THE PREACHERMAN

Stephen M. Coghlan

I peer through my cell's window and look out across the dusty wastes of the Australian beyond. The heat of the sun bounces off the scrubland and pierces through the bars that cover the open window of my chamber. The light collects in the dark bands that cover my eyes, making my face hot to the touch, but despite the relentless heat, I cannot look away.

The first indication that the Preacherman is on schedule is the plume of dust that rises like a pillar of smoke over the horizon. It grows larger throughout the day, steadily moving forward as if there is no force on earth that can halt its inexorable advance.

I am interrupted by a rattling of keys that announce the keeper's return. Upon entering his office, the kangaroo speaks to no one in particular, although I am the only other occupant in the building.

"Preacherman's never late."

Remaining mute, I turn away from the fiery air of the window and slump into the shade of my bunk. Dust from the straw filling of my mattress floats into the air and dances in the dim light. I watch the shimmering motes with a clarity and fascination that I have never had until now.

The door to outside opens again, and in steps the woman that I both long to see, and dread to face. Maria wrings her paws together. The ebony fur has peeled from her knuckles, and her usual stoic face is run with lines of worry and tears of fret. My keeper does not acknowledge her presence, nor does he stop her from walking to the bars that separate my cell from the rest of the office.

"Why?" She squeaks to me in her small voice, which trembles with rage and loss. "Why did you kill him?"

She waits for an answer, but I have none that I wish to give, and none that she deserves to hear.

"Please, give me a reason." She begs, but I remain mute.

"I need to understand." She pleads as her fur stands on end and her tail swells. I leave my mouth sealed, but the scents of her mixed heritage, the colors of her father, a ship rat, conflict then merge with the undercoat from her mother, a brush-tailed rabbit rat. She is beautiful.

"I swear that if you stay silent, I will cast my vote for your life." She changes tactics to threats, but I do not reply.

"Goddamn you, Joshua Ezekiel Thompson." She curses my name as she takes her leave. "May your badger hide burn in Hell!"

She slams the door behind her, and only when she is gone do I find words to say. I whisper them, fearful that speaking them any louder will immediately bring God's wrath upon my head.

"I did it, for you."

And so the pillar grows, until the shadows are lengthened by the setting sun, and the time of dusk arrives. That is when the gang of convicted sinners marches into view. The last rays of daylight burn into their fur and flesh as they are paraded along, joined at the ankles by links of chain. They all walk in different ways. Some drag their heels, some stumble, and others march along almost proudly towards their fate. Some of them are crying, some are smiling, but all keep moving, for behind them struts the Preacherman. His face is obscured by the tall top-hat that he wears, and his black suit and onyx duster seem to absorb what light remains about him, but the giant cross that hangs from his neck, and his starched white collar, and the bullet that he wears as a pin over his heart, gleam brightly.

He does not ride in on a horse nor other beast, but saunters alongside his captured quarries. Across his broad shoulders rests a large announcer, and two smaller ones, with pearlescent handles, glimmer at his waist.

An antechinus stumbles and falls, and when he does not rise fast enough, the Preacherman is there to deliver swift punishment with his heavy boots, which look so worn and aged that they may very well have been inherited, passed down from father to son.

The others in the gang help their fallen member to his feet, but he is already dazed and bleeding, and he stumbles along with his companions, guided only by the chain that joins them together. I watch them until they march out of sight.

Only then do the bells of the town begin to ring. Their desperate sounds echo away into the hills. It is a call, a command to gather. I see as others leave from their work and homes and begin to make their way to the center of our settlement.

The keeper stands and collects his keys. He offers me a cursory inspection before he makes tight the shackles about my wrists and ankles, then I am escorted out of my holding cell and towards the gathering crowds.

By the time we make it to the center, the jury has already been assembled. They sit at the front, along the one bench, side-by-side. They had been chosen by random lots immediately after the last Preacherman departed, and so they are prepared for their duty.

I am not to be tried tonight, so I am shackled to the pole of judgement, alone. From my place I cannot see the Preacherman through the crowd, but I hear his booming voice.

"Praise be to God."

"*Praise be to God!*" My neighbors and peers respond. The quartermaster's wife, a dingo bitch, throws up her hands and begins to babble in tongues.

"Thanks be to Jesus Christ, our Lord and Savior."

"*Thanks be to Jesus Christ! Our Brother! Our Salvation!*"

"Praise be to the Holy Spirit."

"*Praise be for the water we drink, the earth we stand on, the air we breathe!*"

"Praise be to the three-in-one, who redeems us from our sins."

"*Praise be to the merciful, who save our wretched souls from eternal damnation. Amen.*"

Done with the customary introduction, the Preacherman bypasses the typical sermons and gets directly to his other duty.

"Brothers and sisters of Christ. We *are* gathered here today to pass *earthly* judgement on those *we* believe to be wicked. May we be granted the Wisdom of Solomon, and may our decisions be right in the eyes of God, Amen."

The crowd's cheer is deafening, and I catch a glimpse of the Preacherman at his place before the pulpit. His dark fur is dust coated, although I can see that its once dark coloring is now peppered throughout with grey, and the skin underneath is tanned and weatherworn. Eyes, darker than the pitch of night, take in all about him. A faint scar runs from his forehead, down the bridge of his muzzle, and ends at the edge of his left lip, leaving him a permanent macabre grin. The Tasmanian Devil's shoulders are wide, and his bare hands are calloused from the desert sands. His tail remains still and idle as he speaks, with one hand still holding his large announcer, and the other grips the side of the podium.

"I have brought you both the charges and their papers. Jury, we will allow you until the sun has vanished entirely, for the night, to review."

The deciders of earthly law stand and leave for the privacy of the interior hall. Only once they are out of earshot, does the Preacherman continue.

"We shall sing, together, our praises to the almighty."

All but I begin to chant. I am quiet because I do not deserve to join the rest. I am an outcast, made so by a mortal sin, and so I feel rejected and absent from the glory of our Lord.

When he sings, the Preacherman's voice carries above all others, as it is trained to, and it pulls the rest along with it, leading the masses until the jury returns. They take their seats as the final notes drift away into the dark sky.

The Lord's Prayer is muttered in hushed murmurs, and then the first of the charges is brought forward.

"Lithany Evans McGrath" The Preacherman addresses the female hedgehog at his front. "Has been charged with coveting another woman's possessions. Two witnesses produced evidence. Jury, did you review her case?"

An elder echidna rises to his feet. He is nervous and appears to sweat from the pads of his hands, even though the night air is rapidly cooling.

"We did." He squeaks, before he loosens his tie and collar.

Looking back at the accused, the Preacherman whispers to her, but all can hear his words. "And how do you plead?"

"Not guilty, your honor." The hedgehog speaks as fast as she can, the words rush together. "Iwassetup, Iwa—"

"Silence!" The Preacherman's voice booms into the night. A baby begins to cry, scared from its slumber by the powerful vocals.

Ignoring the child, the Preacherman looks at the jury.

With a cough, the echidna continues, "And we find her guilty of petty theft."

The hedgehog begins to cry. She pleads with the crowd, but her voice falls upon deaf ears, and any who do pay her heed remain quiet on account of both fear, and sick anticipation. Almost tenderly, the Preacherman takes the hedgehog's left paw in both of his, and the crowd grows silent. The devil's eyes stare into the woman's weeping ones, before he speaks in a voice that is soft and sad.

"May God grant you the mercy that mortals have not. Your earthly punishment is thus."

When he crushes her hand, the sounds of breaking bone are loud and sudden, piercing through her own scream of pain and horror, and with them, the crowd roars its approval.

"Thanks be to God!" An owl yells.

"Praise be to our all-knowing Father!" A bat joins in.

"Blessed be the King!" Maria's voice carries over the crowd, and I begin to cry.

"Sylverster Richards!" The Preacherman's voice quiets the celebrations. "Has been charged with rustling herds. Ten witnesses have submitted their findings. Jury, have you reviewed?"

"Yes, your honor"

"How do you plead?" The Preacherman addresses a young sheep dog, who looks starved and hungry.

"Guilty, with reason." The pup speaks back. "My family was cheated. We paid for nine healthy heads, but only received the weak and sickly."

"Judges?"

"Guilty of rustlin', but we also find the farmer who sold the beasts guilty of extortion."

"So be it." The Preacherman decrees and swings the butt of his large announcer into the pup's abdomen with such force that the youngling doubles over and coughs up blood.

"You shall keep ten healthy heads, and consume one further for your troubles, but you must return the rest." His voice is for all to hear. "Your punishment has been dealt.

And so it goes, until all that is left, are those whose sins force them to be judged by those not of the earthly realm.

That is a job for the morning, a morning that I wait for with mixed emotions, as I watch the stars slip across the nighttime sky.

***

It is the time of the Morning Star, and it is already getting hot. Even with the growing heat, the Preacherman appears unaffected as he finishes the benedictions, before he takes his place in front of the four condemned.

He no longer carries the large announcer, but instead wields one of his small ones. The ivory handle of his tool is inlaid with a gold cross and is available for all to see as he paces back and forth.

"Does anyone here, on this earthly realm, believe that the charged should be allowed to plead their case again?" The devil asks of the crowd.

Silence.

"Does anyone here, now, believe that any of the charged should be spared?"

The antechinus that the Preacherman had kicked the evening before, breaks down sobbing. He falls to his knees and begins to pray in a mantra as loud as his lungs will let him.

"Father, please forgive me! Father, please forgive me! Father—"

Taking three bullets from his belt, the Preacherman loads only half of his announcer's chambers. When he is done, he spins the magazine, and stops its rotation without looking.

He faces one of the accused, a fallow deer, and asks the woman, "How do you plead?"

"Not guilty!" She yells. Anger warps her face as the barrel of the announcer is placed against her head.

"May God find, in his infinite wisdom, mercy for your soul."

The Preacherman squeezes the trigger.

The announcer speaks with a crack, and the doe's head disappears into a fine red mist as her body falls forward and lies still.

The spent round is replaced with fresh ammunition, the cylinder spun again. A Vesper bat is next.

"How do you plead?"

"Not guilty."

The announcer speaks again, and the flying mammal collapses to the earth. One leg twitches about in a mockery of life; rippling the wings.

The chamber is loaded again, and then spun, and then put to the weeping antechinus' head.

"How do you plead?"

"Guilty!" The crying marsupial replies. "I am a worm, I am a wretch!"

The Preacherman stays his finger. "Does the jury accept his plea?" He asks, and for a moment, the twelve chosen talk amongst themselves before they hurry to reply.

"Yes."

"Then mark this this man, for he withheld guilt until the end, and so he shall be punished, and so he shall be made to pay for his sins, but then, shall he live to the end of his penance, he shall be made free. Twenty years' hard labor." The Preacher's command is sound.

"Thank you, all merciful!" The antechinus falls prostrate to the dust of the floor. "Thank you, Father!"

He does not resist nor complain as he is dragged away, but instead breaks out into a loud and off-key hymn of praise.

The last one in line, a Goana, does not wait for the Preacher to ask, but instead yells out defiantly, "Not Guilty."

The announcer is put to its head.

The hammer falls on an empty chamber.

Proven innocent by God, the monitor lizard raises its arms and cheers to the heavens. Its shackles are hastily removed before it walks through the crowd. Accolades and apologies are lauded upon it.

Once order is restored, the Preacherman looks me in the eyes.

"Bring the accused to me."

My shackles are undone from the pole I have been secured to all night. As I am brought forward, I am pelted by mud and debris; mocked for having soiled myself during the hours I was left exposed to the elements.

The wrinkles about the devil's eyes deepen as he leans forward until our noses almost touch. I can smell his hot breath, and I cannot escape his piercing gaze.

"Joshua Ezekiel Thompson, you have been charged with the murder of your best friend. How do you plead?"

Before I can answer, my former friends and neighbors begin to jeer, and Maria steps forward, a rotten cabbage in her arms.

The other announcer warns her to stay back when the Preacherman draws it faster than the eye can follow. She freezes, as the hammer is drawn back, but Maria gets the hint.

"Ready this badger for travel." The declaration is for all. "He shall be judged at the next town."

***

The sun is not at its zenith before we begin to tread the dusty trails. We march together, just us, in silence through the blasting heat. The daylight feels as hot as a smelter's oven, and it burns through my clothes and singes exposed flesh. My fur offers some salvation, but it is not much.

The night is worse. With little moisture, the air falls into a bone-numbing chill that sets muscles twitching and bodies shivering until the great light rises again.

Throughout it all, the Preacherman seems unaffected. The devil does not loosen his collar nor tighten his duster.

It is on the second night, while we rest at a billabong, in front of a fire built of twigs, that the Preacherman breaks the silence.

"Drink." He orders and tosses me one of the canteens that I have been forced to carry for so many miles.

At first I do nothing. I am too tired to understand.

"Drink." He growls. "Or I'll shove it down your throat myself." He removes a knife from his boot. "I'm gonna get you to town one way or the other, but I don't want to have to carry you the rest of the way there, so drink."

Pulling a hard sausage from his gifted provisions, he cuts himself a slice.

I drink until the vessel is drained.

A piece of bread lands in the sand at my feet, and then so too does a slice of traveler's cheese. I am so famished that I do not wipe the dirt from my food before I devour it.

A smile creases his face, and the puckered scar lifts his lip. Looking back into the flames, he gnaws on his supper, pausing every few mouthfuls to throw more food at me, until our stomachs are quenched from their gnawing hungers.

Cold winds sweep across the ground and I shiver. I am chained to a boulder, and I am too far from the fire to find any warmth from the flames. Noticing my discomfort, the devil stands, and opens my shackles before he returns to his spot.

The food and water have restored my mind, but I am confused by his actions.

"Why did you free me?" I wonder.

"Because if you run, I can catch you, and if I don't catch you, I will shoot you." The Preacherman answers.

The moon casts its bluish light upon the scrublands as I make my way to the warmth of the flames. Tired from the journey, I try to fight the fatigue, but fail.

I am awoken by the Preacherman's voice. The devil of God sits by the fire. In his hands, he is cleaning another announcer, one that I have not seen before. It looks old, but regal. On the ground beside him is the parchment that holds the details of my crime.

He speaks again.

"So, did you do it?"

I shiver as I remember.

Tobias was my friend. He, like me, was born on the island, from parents who had been deported from the mother country, whether the punishment befit the crime, or guilt was certain, was another matter of its own.

Both of us had been raised to work the gold mines, which were owned by the land barons and squatters. Since we were the children of criminals, we were forced to work, rather than seek our freedom at other mines, which were open to the immigrants who flocked to the land voluntarily.

And, like me, he had fallen for Maria, but unlike me, he earned her love while all I had of her was her friendship. Jealousy and rage simmered for long, until I could not take it anymore, and challenged Tobias for the right to woo her. Although he was a stoat, and weaker than I, he rose to face me.

I felled him with one blow, and he fell against a stone, and his head cracked like an egg, and his brains and blood leaked out across his fur, staining the ivory purity in horrid and unforgiving crimson.

Wrath turned to guilt, and I called for help, but it was too late.

"It was an accident." I falter but continue. "It's all there on the paper. You can read, so you must know."

"A few written words do not talk." The Preacherman exclaims, his whiskers shifting as he growls. "I want to know from you, did you kill him with your own hands?"

"Yes."

"No weapon."

"None."

"Impressive." He chuckles.

Indignation rises within me. "Are you mocking what I've done?" I asked in horror.

"Hardly." He answers with another laugh. "You've never shown any indication of violence before, and you have no formal combat training, yet you killed someone with one fatal stroke."

"I killed my friend!"

"You say it was an accident." He becomes serious again. "We all make mistakes."

"I broke the holy law."

The devil's laugh is full of bitter mirth. "The laws exist to be broken. They are only there to show us that we are imperfect. We are meant to fail, and then we are meant to beg for clemency."

"How can I be forgiven for a mortal sin?" I implore, hoping for an answer.

"He moves in mysterious ways. His decisions, His grace, are beyond our mortal comprehension. We must beg for forgiveness, with our entirety, and He *WILL* judge us. He will weigh us. If we are found wanting, then we shall be damned, but even the most wretched of sinners can sit by His golden throne."

"My best friend is dead by my hand. My paws are stained with his blood. I let lust, a deadly sin, lead me to worse. Every beat of my heart feels like a curse, a blow. Can you even wonder how I feel inside?"

The rattling chuckle that originates from the Preacherman sounds like bones clinking together. Content that his weapon is clean, he tips back the engraved barrels, and begins to pour a blackened powder from a horn.

"I know far more than you could ever fathom, boy. I was a bushranger before I was a beast of the cloth. Preachers like me, we aren't saints. There is no one in their right mind who wants to be one of us. Do you know what makes us different from others?"

I shake my head as he drops balls and shots behind the special dust, packing them tightly with a rod.

"We accept that we are sinners, and we embrace that fact. We are not recruited but are chosen by God himself to carry out his work. He chooses only those who have committed mortal sins, and have accepted their guilt, and gives us our penance, which is to serve Him in all means.

"And we only exist because the church and state are entwined. Our beloved Queen needs her income from the lands, and authorized our creation, while subduing her foreign subjects.

"Tell me, have you ever read the Bible?"

I nod.

"The full Bible? Have you ever heard the words of Matthew, Mark, Luke and John, of Paul and Peter?"

The names are unfamiliar to me.

"Of course you haven't." The devil laughs. "Why would they let you hope? Why would they let you hear words of encouragement and why would they cast a man as a son of God?"

We sit in silence that is only broken when he rolls the paper of judgement and replaces it into its tube. Tilting his hat, my captor covers his face and in moments, he is snoring.

The announcer he has loaded and prepared, sits on the ground, between us.

I reach for it.

It is large and heavy, solid and well-built. I marvel at the intricate carving, and the majestic metalwork.

How could he have been so foolish to leave it so exposed? I imagine pointing it at him, pulling the trigger, blasting his black fur into oblivion. I imagine running away, starting anew, moving to another land.

I remember Tobias falling, and the sickening crack as his head splits at the seams, and out pours his brains.

I hesitate.

I return the announcer to where I found it.

The twisted smile returns to the devil's face. He has been watching me and has always had a small announcer aimed at my chest.

"Do you know why we only load three bullets when we go to trial?" He asks, opening one eye.

"For the Father, Son, and Holy Spirit?"

He snickers, clicking his fangs against each other. "Heaven, Hell and retribution. When we spin the cylinder, we are firing blind. We do not see where it lands, and so God guides us. If it falls on a bullet, God has called the wicked home, if it falls on an empty chamber, God has spared you."

He safeties the weapon and slides it back into its holster. For a moment, his hand returns to the bullet he wears above his heart as he murmurs, "There, in God, is always three."

He takes back the announcer he left at a test. "Do you know what the true miracle of God is? His salvation is available for anyone, even the likes of me and you. He gives grace to the worms of the earth, the scum of the land. He gave me life anew.

"Do not think I lack understanding, brother. You suffer in the guilt of your actions, as I once suffered for my own. I will give you one final option: If you remain in the morning, I will take it that you have accepted your guilt, but if you are gone, I may lie and declare you dead by my hand. There are no witnesses. The choice is yours."

And, in moments, the Preacher breathes the deep sighs of one asleep.

***

The sun is rising as we march into town. The first who see us send their children running to spread the news. As we march towards where my fate shall be decided, the Preacherman whispers to me through his fangs, "Last chance."

I set my jaw, straighten my fur, slow my tail, and continue, resolute in my decision.

"It is late, and we must have the trial. I can postpone your death for one more day." He tempts me, but my decision has been made.

We make it to the hall, and I do not wait, but stand at the foot of the podium while my companion greets the others. I do not know them, they are strangers to me, but they are the last faces I shall see, and I love them all.

"*Amen!*" The crowd roars, and I realize that I have become lost in my thoughts.

"We are gathered here today to bear witness. The one who stands before you has pleaded guilty of murdering his friend in jealousy." The Preacherman's voice is sullen, and distant, and unlike anything I have heard him use before. "He asks that you witness God deliver him to his just punishment."

I watch as my captor walks before me, and in those moments, we meet eyes, and he is my brother. His black fur seems to reflect the light, and he burns brightly. My flesh is cool despite the heat.

I am at peace.

As per my request, the devil loads all six chambers. He spins the cylinder still, before he presses it to my skull. I feel the cold of the barrel against my ear. It is gentle and caressing.

I begin my final words, my epitaph.

"Our Father, who art in heaven, Hallowed by Thy name." I spread my arms. "Thy will be done."

"Thy will be done!" Roars the crowd.

It is comforting when the hammer is pulled back until it clicks into place.

"Thy will be done." Whispers my companion, who has seen me to this shore.

The hammer falls, and the ringing of metal is clear through the air, but I am still alive. Has the announcer failed?

I feel the barrel leave my head. I see the Preacherman point the weapon into the air. I see him pull the hammer back again, and I hear the cylinder rotate once more

The crowd is silent, save for a few voices that whisper, but they sound like the wind blowing across the lands.

BANG!

The announcer speaks in a booming voice for all to hear.

The chamber is breached, and the first round is pulled from its chamber by calloused fingers, unfired.

The voices in the crowd grow in wonder and amazement.

Taking my paw, the Preacherman places the bullet upon my palm. Leaning close, he whispers to my ear. "In God, there is always three."

Then I am standing, and the devil's voice is booming louder than the announcer ever has.

"Arise, brother. You are neither forgiven nor reclaimed. Your penance shall be paid, and only when you have made what is due complete, will God collect you."

His voice becomes hushed, almost sad, as he stumbles out the last words. "Today, you no longer owned by a corporation, or a crown, but by God himself, due to walk the earth and carry out His will.

"You are a Preacherman."

Stunned to silence, I rise, gripping the symbol of His mercy, His salvation. My mouth opens to protest, but the only words that spill forth, are the same I have heard spoken, and the crowd, my brothers, my sisters, carry the cry.

"Thy will be done."

When Mother Nature gave out on us we found our true selves, didn't we? The hoarders, the thieves, the oppressors...all stood apart from those who proclaim they just want to help.

The last essential commodity of any dying world is heroism if you think about it, the promise that bold people will save us from the ravages of all that sprawls beyond the walls.

In their shadow stand the humble ones who just want to help without fanfare, those silent saviors who seeks to bestow us with the truth.

How dangerous they are...

Forbidden Fruit

Detroit

Everything and everyone within Turner's shop was tired. Four large deputies in patrol gear shuffled indifferently through the store while a corporal watched. The tightness of the aisles made it hard for them to maneuver. Turner stared blankly into space, only generally aware of their existence. He kept his paws flaccidly on the counter, an unlit cigarette hanging from his lips. He could not reach into his pocket for a light, having been ordered to keep his paws visible for the duration of the search. The corporal, a puma who appeared desperately bored with the whole affair, tried to engage Turner in conversation. His thick tail waved aimlessly through the stale, musty air.

"You want a light?"

"No."

"It's not a trick." The puma produced a silver lighter from his breast pocket and held it up in front of Turner. The bobcat gently shook his head no, his whiskers wobbling ever so slightly. It seemed almost as though he denied that the lighter existed. The cigarette could not be lit by a nonexistent object. The puma shrugged and put it back in his pocket. He wasn't old, but his face showed lines under the eyes. Even his relatively thick coating of fur couldn't hide the dark bags. He closed them for a moment and sighed. Turner kept staring straight ahead. Plastic and metal clattered weakly in the background as the deputies continued to root ineffectually through the bins.

"Enough." The corporal called out to the deputies. They stopped skimming through the endless sea of odds and ends and began to head back to the front. A general air of relief pervaded the scene. They had play-acted enough. The puma turned to face Turner and began to give him a canned speech.

"The selling of illegal parts… a great danger to our community… civic responsibility… a serious crime…protecting our youth…" The words ran together in Turner's head. He'd heard all the boilerplate dozens of times before. He didn't hate the corporal for it; they all knew the game. Everyone would roleplay their assigned part, and when the show finished they would go about their business. It always worked this way. Turner nodded along almost imperceptibly, waiting for it to be over.

"…keep our city strong. Alright. Let's go." The deputies and the corporal slinked out of the shop, probably in the direction of some coffee. They all seemed bedraggled and exhausted under their mountain of protective gear. Turner lit his cigarette, inhaled, and coughed. The packs in his current carton had been terrible. Usually during a leaf shortage, they would cut the missing tobacco with something less harsh. But these smokes tasted like drain cleaner. Perhaps the bureaucrats in the Agriculture Department were just trying to kill off the smokers faster. He stepped around the counter and began wandering the aisles of the shop, straightening the stock that the deputies had disturbed.

Like most of the peddlers in Commercial Zone 13-S, Turner worked as a junk dealer. He specialized in electronics. He had crammed his shop from floor to ceiling with castoffs of every type and description: game consoles, laptops, radios, even tape decks and record players. He had huge bins of bricked smartphones and watches, charging cables of every description, computer parts of various degrees of obsolescence. Three decades after the upheaval of the Enclosure Movement, Turner had become one of the few who could keep the exhausted technical infrastructure of the city limping along. Lower-tier cities like Memphis were dependent on the Turners in their midst: the animals who could finagle solutions to critical problems out of decades-old castoffs. That explained why his weekly harassment by the authorities had such a shadowbox character. The powers above hated ragged technical impresarios like Turner, but they needed them. They knew too much and were perennially seen as potential sources of trouble; yet their existence was grudgingly tolerated, because the city could not function without them. They could be called upon to repair hydroponic farms or hospital life support systems in a pinch, or to discretely maintain the ersatz devices of the privileged. Turner and the rest of his class understood that they adhered to an unwritten code. The regime gave them enough room to breathe, but not to yawn. Push it too far, and the Security Squad would pay you a very unpleasant visit.

Turner returned to the counter, satisfied that the deputies hadn't stolen anything. He pulled up the project that he had begun before the corporal paid him a visit. In a tray, he had partially disassembled a very old smartwatch. It had been an expensive and powerful device in its day, but now lay battered and forlorn. Cracks split across the glass screen, but he had reason to hope that the touch pad lay undisturbed. Cigarette still in mouth, he delicately pried it apart with a set of miniature tools. His seasoned paws moved swiftly. With the bezel apart, he could see that the touchpad remained intact. He sighed with relief. He put out his cigarette to avoid contaminating the panel. With a tiny plastic wedge, he popped the part out onto a clean cloth. He quickly wrapped it in protective gauze and inserted it into an envelope. He carefully slid it into a bag below the cash register. He'd be taking it to a special job in a few days.

As he put the envelope in his secure spot, his paw brushed past the photo that he kept there. He paused for a moment, looking around to see if anyone was loitering in front of the shop. Satisfied that he was alone, he pulled it out and sat it on the counter. He stared at a very old three-by-five, mounted behind a piece of glass in a plain wooden frame. In the picture itself a cheetah stood by the edge of a river. He was shirtless in a pair of waders, with a massive grin on his face. He held up a massive river catfish with his left arm and a fishing pole in his right. The water swirled reddish with mud, the same color as the clay in the riverbank. Tall yellow pines framed the scene, with blue sky beyond. Though faded, that blue still touched something deep inside of Turner. He didn't have to take the photo out of the glass to remember what was written on the back of it. He silently mouthed the words as he traced the sky with his finger. "Cat and fish on the Chattahoochee. Tim, '97." He repeated the words in his mind. Now he pressed more firmly on the glass, the tip of his claw making a scraping noise as he slid it back and forth. He realized that his emotions were slipping out of check, yet he did not pull back. He wanted to feel the pain, the anger, the desperation, the fervent desire to grasp pawfuls of green grass and mud and pine straw on a warm afternoon with a friend under a clear blue sky, to really remember that such things had once been possible and were not mere delusions he carried in his mind, to know that he was not alone in remembering such things, even if the kits and cubs of today were taught that such things did not exist and never had. He exposed his yellow fangs as he pulled back his muzzle. His paw shook and the glass rattled in the frame, as his whole body trembled with the fury rising up inside of him. He lost his grasp, slipping into a rage that he couldn't control. The blue of the sky blurred away into the red of unabated fury and longing as his eyes swam with tears.

A loud electronic chime buzzed in his ear. It echoed throughout the mall, through every dingy shop and storefront. Closing time, nine o'clock. Turner jerked violently, snapping to his senses. He suddenly felt exhausted. He slumped back on his stool, consumed by a coughing fit. He listened to the chime ring again. With great effort, he placed the photo back underneath the counter. He grabbed his bag, his coat, and set of keys. Turner wearily checked over the shop one last time. He flicked off the fluorescent lights, and then turned the two deadbolts shut. Pulling his coat around his hunched shoulders, he headed for the exit. His fingers still trembled as he fished for another cigarette, the fur stained yellow with nicotine. He slinked crookedly under the red glow of the emergency exit sign, a half-specter in the cold haze of the night.

***

The heaters never worked right in the commuter buses. When they had been bright yellow school buses forty years ago, the heaters were more than adequate for a southern climate and a load of rambunctious kids. Now they were almost totally dead, leaving passengers to shiver as the autonomous heaps juddered and shook down the road. As a bobcat, Turner was better off than most with his generous winter coat. Even so, he still felt the bite of a cold January morning. He sat near the front of the bus, staring out the window at nothing in particular. He had the touchscreen piece carefully tucked inside of his satchel, as well as what he hoped were enough tools to complete the repair job. He stroked his yellowed whiskers with his cold fingers as he looked out the filthy window.

Turner lived in South Memphis, and he would have to take three separate buses to reach his destination. They were rolling north now along Riverside Drive, headed towards downtown. They'd passed the old exit for the I-55 Bridge into Arkansas, which had collapsed into the Mississippi River a decade ago. The river itself had disappeared from view well before that. The lack of plant life meant hellish erosion of the river's watershed, rapidly worsening the already notorious flooding of the Big Muddy. Now Riverside Drive traveled alongside a massive dike built of dirt and rubble. Here and there, recognizable pieces of debris poked out from its ugly sides. Memphians had been so desperate to stop the flooding that they had piled whatever could be spared into building the wall: smashed homes, old trailers, cars, and the constantly eroding, infertile dirt. Turner had traveled this way enough times that he instinctively knew where to look for the most recognizable pieces: a hunk of an airplane fuselage, half of a faded beer billboard, the burnt hulk of an old dump truck. The bus shuddered and jarred as it rattled over the long trails of eroded dirt snaking across the crumbling road. Soon the bulldozers would be back out, pushing the dirt up against the dike yet again. Massive walls of compacted earth and rubble surrounded the rest of the city, offering some protection from the hellish dust storms that regularly swept the denuded countryside. The walls allowed Memphians to cling to life, but they kept much of the city shrouded in darkness.

They were within sight of downtown now. On the right, the most unavoidable scar on Memphis' battered landscape loomed. An immense tower, one hundred stories high, jutted into the sky like a burnt match jammed into the earth. Crump Memorial Tower stood on the site of the old U.S. Bankruptcy Court. It was a sort of do-it-all centralized warehouse of authority, housing both the city government and numerous federal offices besides. The uppermost levels were a mystery to all but a few, and wild rumors circulated about its subterranean extent. That it functioned as a Panopticon was an open secret. Memphians feared and loathed the Crump, as it was colloquially known; yet the trickle of resources that flowed out from it was one of the few things keeping the city alive. It was the only helicopter landing spot for a hundred miles in any direction. The bus turned dark inside as it passed through the tower's shadow. Turner shivered slightly in the cold, the tips of his whiskers shaking.

The bus hit an enormous pothole in the road, and everyone bounced up in their seats. Turner crashed back down and immediately collapsed into a violent coughing fit. He hacked and hacked, nasty wet coughs underlain by two packs a day for many years. Turner felt his embarrassment rising as the other passengers glowered at him. Embarrassment quickly gave way to anger. He couldn't breathe, and yet these assholes felt compelled to treat him like he had the plague. The fit finally eased, and he spat a big glob of disgusting effluent on the floor. He stared at it while he pondered his inability to quit smoking. He'd never been a big smoker until after Tim had gone missing. Once he had disappeared, Turner had fallen back on nicotine and gin as a coping mechanism. He'd tailed off the liquor eventually, but the cigs stuck with him. He knew that it was a crutch, and he hated himself for it. But now, he felt nothing. It had become a purely automatic habit. As soon as he got off the bus, he would light up without even thinking about it. He checked his battered watch as the bus groaned to a halt. Turner stepped out into the cold air as the other passengers eyed him with suspicion. He ignored them, shuffling off to find his next connection.

Another bus ride and an hour later, Turner was finally within a few blocks of his destination: the old Botanical Gardens. He felt for his satchel and opened it. The envelope laid there undisturbed. It was almost nine in the morning. He reasoned that he should be able to get the job done in an hour or two. Underneath his jacket, he felt the outline of another tool: his stun gun. He was headed into a rough place in an already tough city. Although he cut an inconspicuous figure, he knew that he had to be careful. The Gardens became a densely packed squatter settlement during the chaos of enclosure. Refugees from the outlying suburbs had packed into the city core, slapping together new dwellings wherever they could find an open spot, or built on top of existing housing. As the gardens in Memphis died off, a massive shantytown took their place. Now it had become one of the hardest places in the city. The puppy that needed his help lived somewhere within the dark and dirty confines of the former park. Exact addresses were hard to come by in such a place, but he had a plan to find it.

The bus groaned to a stop, and Turner shuffled off of it. He was still several tough blocks away from the Gardens. Shadow reigned; overhead lights were intermittent in all but a few areas of the city. The dust suspended in the atmosphere meant that most days passed by in a perpetual haze. He lit a cigarette and began making his way toward the Gardens, plodding slowly down the sidewalk. The street was mostly empty. Two bears sitting on the front stoop of a partially collapsed townhouse eyed him as he walked past but said nothing. In the doors and stairwells of other buildings, feeble vagrants lurked. None of them looked like they had the energy to attempt anything more than a half-hearted plea for change, but Turner still kept his eyes open. He felt the lump of his stun gun again on his right side. A hundred steps ahead, a dark figure rose from a stairwell and toddled unsteadily into the middle of the sidewalk. Their shape seemed ill-defined, as if they were a swirling cloud of dust and shadows that vaguely resembled an animal figure. Turner could feel his body tightening as he approached. A few steps away, he stopped. The shadow was really a very old raccoon, his facial fur gone almost completely gray. He had a black rag tied around his blind eyes, and he wore an incredibly tattered military jacket. Turner wondered whether he might have been wearing that same jacket continuously for thirty years. The raccoon said nothing but proffered a chipped mug. Turner pulled a dollar piece from his pocket and dropped it in his cup, where it rattled like a suitcase full of bones. The raccoon tipped his head in a gesture of gratitude. Turner decided to ask for directions.

"I need to know where Harrison's Store is in the Gardens. Can you tell me?" The raccoon put his free paw up to his chin. He only had two fingers. After a minute of reflection, he remembered.

"South edge. Near the old art gallery." His voice creaked, as though he hadn't used it in a long time.

"Thank you," Turner said. The raccoon nodded again. The bobcat continued his journey down the sidewalk, leaving the raccoon standing there with his cup still outstretched. At the next corner, he paused and looked back. The raccoon had disappeared, melting back into the shadows. A few more blocks, and the Gardens came into view.

It seemed to have grown in the months since Turner had last come through this place. The shanties were piled on top of each other in a great haphazard pyramid, six stories tall at its highest. A rusting old broadcast antenna marked the middle of the settlement. Narrow and twisting alleyways snaked into the mass of shanties, with most of them remaining permanently unexposed to the sun. Many thousands of animals lived here, most in miserable poverty. Yet the resourcefulness of the residents made it more livable than it appeared at first glance. Running water and electricity for many dwellings had been successfully appropriated by tapping into the city's decayed infrastructure. There were denizens with links to the Undernet as well; that was how one of them had contacted Turner in the first place. He ran through the contents of that message in his mind as he pondered the size of the shantytown.

It was a plea for help from a desperate father: a dog who had heard through the grapevine Turner could work miracles with old electronics. His son lived in the Gardens: a pup with a greyhound mother and a shepherd father. He'd been born with diabetes, and his family struggled at first just to get insulin. They finally secured a steady supply from a sympathetic street pharmacist with inside connections. Even then, the young dog's condition fluctuated wildly. At times he had been near death. A doctor doing charity work finally fitted him with a second-hand insulin pump, which saved his life. But after a year, the control panel on the outside had finally given up the ghost. Now they were stuck manually adjusting the settings, hoping and praying that the pup wouldn't be under- or over-dosed. That's where Turner came in. The father pleaded with Turner to work his magic, hoping and praying that the bobcat could fix it. Come to Harrison's Store in the Gardens, said the message, and you will find us. The old smartwatch arrived in his shop that same day in a part exchange. That sealed the deal. He would do what he could to help.

Turner made his way along the southern side of the squatter encampment. A massive pile of scrap and trash formed a sort of de facto fence along the park's southern border. The remains of cars, trucks, street sweepers, appliances, buses, and vending machines were piled thirty feet high. Many of the hulks were deeply scarred and pitted by fire; they'd probably been dumped here after one of the riots that periodically convulsed the city. Most of them had been raided for parts or had sections of steel cut away with torches. He heard dull hammering sounds echoing from the other side of the pile. Now he remembered: the impromptu ironworks on the first level of the Gardens built and repaired many items from trash. The wind shifted, and Turner smelled the pungent odor of burning coal and garbage. He rapidly approached a break in the wall. Several thin characters were milling around. As he came within view, they seemed to stiffen. Turner tensely puffed on a cigarette. He pulled his satchel close, reaffirming that he still had his stun gun. As he came up to the break, a caiman in dark overalls marched up to him.

"Watchu want?" He was young, but many of his teeth were broken or missing. He had the thin, hungry look of someone well acquainted with living paw-to-mouth. Turner tapped his cigarette out.

"I'm here to see the Collison family. I need to go to Harrison's Store."

"Never heard of 'em. Who are you?" Others were gathering around them, forming a sort of half-crescent. A tomcat with a missing ear gave him a hard look, as well as a mutt with tattoos covering his neck. Turner's heart beat faster.

"My name is Turner. I own a parts shop. I'm here to fix an insulin pump for Dale Collison's child."

"What the fuck is 'in-soo-lin?' You a dope dealer or somethin?" Turner's fear turned to anger.

"I'm not a goddamn dope dealer. There's a puppy that's sick, and I'm trying to help."

"Well you don't look like a fuckin' doctor!"

"That's because I'm not, asshole!"

"Shut the fuck up!" The caiman grabbed the front of his jacket and yanked Turner violently forward. He lost his balance and fell, his satchel clattering to the ground. The pressure was too much. Another coughing fit seized him at the worst possible moment. On his paws and knees, he desperately tried to cough away the tar and mucus clogging up his lungs. It so consumed him that he couldn't even reach for his stun gun. The other animals surrounded him while the bobcat hacked away on the ground. The caiman sneered at him, showing the teeth in his long snout.

"What a bitch."

"Let's dump his ass." The coughing eased just enough for Turner to grab the thick leg of a Rottweiler that stood over his prone form.

"Please," he pleaded wheezily.

"Don't fuckin' touch me!" He kicked Turner's paw away. The caiman grabbed the back of Turner's neck and yanked him to his feet.

"Listen, bitch. You got no business here. The Gardens ain't got nothin' for you. Get out less you wanna fight bout it." The caiman clutched the special spot in every cat's neck; Turner couldn't move. He balled up his other fist, as though he wished to sink it deep into Turner's face. The bobcat winced and prepared for impact.

A loud siren suddenly hit the group from behind. It was the squawk of a patrol car. All of the animals surrounding the bobcat scattered instantly, sprinting back past the scrap and melting into the shantytown. The caiman unceremoniously dropped Turner and promptly disappeared. The bobcat collapsed in a crumpled heap. Still gasping for breath, and unable to focus his sight, he heard the open and shut of a car door behind him. Tramping boots followed the door, steadily nearing him. In a panic, he began to weakly gather up his spilled tools into his satchel.

"Stop! Paws where I can see them." It was a firm command from a familiar voice. The bobcat whipped around. The puma corporal from last week closed in on him, his gun drawn. Turner raised his paws, praying he wouldn't be shot. The corporal seemed to recognize Turner as well.

"It's you! That junk dealer from the mall."

"Yes." The corporal paused, looking past Turner to see if any of his tormentors were still lingering. Satisfied that they weren't, he holstered his weapon. He grabbed one of Turner's free paws and helped him to his feet. This flummoxed the bobcat; he expected to be beaten, or worse. He brushed some of the dirt off his clothes while the puma eyed him, his tail flicking back and forth.

"What're you doing here?" Realizing that he could think of no better cover story, Turner decided to tell the truth.

"I got a message from somebody that wanted me to help fix their kid's insulin pump. He said to come to the Gardens and look for Harrison's Store. He said to ask for Collison." The patrolman seemed to relax, slightly.

"So you came out here by yourself?"

"I wouldn't have believed him, but he sent pictures. It's a sick kid. I can't say no." Turner began to reach into his bag, but the puma grabbed his arm and wrenched it painfully. He winced.

"Stop right there! Keep your goddamn paws where I can see them."
The corporal grabbed the bag off Turner's shoulder. "What is all this?
Tools? Parts?"

"Yes. That's it." Turner remembered the stun gun with a lump in
his throat. Getting caught with that would mean a trip to the Crump.
Maybe he could avoid a pat-down if he could convince the corporal
that he wasn't lying. The puma let go of Turner as he sifted through
the contents of the bag.

"What's in the envelope?" He pulled out the brown packet with the
touchscreen carefully wrapped inside of it. Turner yelped. "Be careful with that, please! It's fragile. It's the part I need to fix the pump."
The puma slit open one end with a claw and peered at the contents
inside. Turner feared that he might confiscate it. The Memphis cops
were notorious shakedown artists; many of them would take anything they could fence later. After what seemed like an eternity, he
slid the envelope back into the satchel. Turner sighed with relief. The
puma handed the bag back to him. The patrolman looked around,
confirming once again that the Garden punks had been chased sufficiently far away. He then began speaking to Turner in a low voice.

"Listen to me. I was the one who told Collison about you." Turner
was stunned. He opened his mouth as if to speak, but the puma put
a thick finger over his lips to silence him. "He's a janitor at one of the
substations. I overheard him when he was talking about his kid. I
don't know anything about any of that electronic garbage, but I figured that if anyone could do something about it, you would."

Turner gave him a sour look. "I'm trying."

"I'm sorry. Look, I'll take you to the store. They won't fuck with
you as long as I'm around." It was hard to argue with that. In addition to his sidearm, he had a submachine gun strapped to his chest,
and plenty of equipment around his waist. In contrast with Turner's
asthmatic frame, the puma looked like a star linebacker. The bobcat put another cigarette in his mouth without thinking. The puma
offered him a light, and this time Turner accepted. Up close, Turner
finally read the name on his badge: Wesley. They started walking
through the break in the junk wall, towards the shanty pyramid. The
sounds of hammering grew more distinct, as did the smell of noxious smoke. Here and there, Turner caught sight of more thin animals eyeing them from the shadowy nooks and crannies.

"Why did you tell Collison about me?" He took a stiff drag in the cold winter air. The corporal looked confused.

"Because his kid was sick and he needed help. I know you're good with fixing all kinds of bullshit, so I told him. Why else would I?"

"You know I'm not exactly our city council's favorite feline. Or anybody else up in Crump. That's why you and your boys visit me every other week."

"What does this have to do with helping Collison's kid?" the corporal said, his voice rising slightly.

"I'm asking why somebody like you would do this, when it could get you fired. Or worse. You have something to lose."

The bobcat got no response from the officer. Turner was hobbling along slightly behind the puma, so he couldn't see his face; but the agitated flicking of his thick tail told him everything he needed to know. Turner realized he'd crossed the line, and he decided to let it go. They trudged along in silence for a few more minutes before the puma suddenly stopped. He spun around and stared Turner down.

"Listen, asshole. I know what you're getting at. You think I'm just another scumbag doing the dirty work for the goddamn bloodsuckers that run this place." He spat out the words in a pissed stage whisper while jamming a stocky finger in Turner's chest. "And you know what? I don't blame you. I know why people hate us. But I'm from here too." Turner could feel the tip of the puma's claw poking uncomfortably through his thin shirt. Wesley turned away from the bobcat, and his bad-cop snarl broke into a quavering plea. He gestured towards the shantytown. "This is my city. No trees, no grass, no flowers, barely any sun or sky, but I was born here. I'm not giving up on it. I'm not quitting on the people that live here."

"I'm not either," Turner said quietly. The puma turned away from him and stared glumly at the dirt. Turner could tell he was embarrassed, but he understood now.

"Good. I didn't think so. Now let's find Collison and get his kid fixed up." They resumed walking, heading towards a low cinderblock building with a rusty metal roof. To their right, a variety of animals in heavily patched, filthy coveralls were working on pieces of metal. Some wielded ancient welding torches on bits of washing machines and cars. Others were more like blacksmiths, hammering away on makeshift anvils in front of smoky furnaces. It was an almost medieval scene. With their heavy coveralls, boots, goggles, and other garb, the animals had become practically indistinguishable from one another. Only the occasional peek of a tail or hoof gave away their species. Watching them work, an emotion filled Turner that was not quite hope but close enough. Who was to say what the city would look like two decades in the future; but for now, they would survive. Day by day, the Garden residents would eke out an existence from the barest scraps they could find. Perhaps they would live long enough to give another generation a chance to redeem what was left of this country.

"We're here," Wesley announced. They'd come to Harrison's Store. It stood in the middle of a clump squat cinderblock buildings, which Turner guessed might have once been a food court. Most of them were burnt out or badly damaged. Harrison's was the only one with any perceivable activity. The lit sign read "Harrison's Store" in a jumble of salvaged letters, their different colors and shapes nailed together on a wooden board. He could see an old wolf inside behind the counter, standing next to a jumble of mostly empty shelves.

"Alright. I'll go ask if they know where Collison is at." Turner threw his cigarette butt on the ground and headed inside. Wesley stayed outside, lighting a cigarette for himself.

The puma pondered the Gardens as he puffed. The place where he had spent much of his youth had grown substantially since those early days; yet the parched brown dirt that surrounded it appeared much the same as it had been twenty years ago. When it rained, it turned into hideous mud. He was too young to remember the Enclosure; he had been born three years after the walls had started rising around the majority of the country's cities. He had missed the violence and trauma that had accompanied that momentous event. Yet his generation had been the first to grow up without any real exposure to what might be called "nature." He'd spent his entire life in the city without seeing any plants or feral animals of any kind, besides the rats and raccoons that lived in the sewers. Nothing green existed within the Memphis city limits outside of the sprawling hydroponic food factories, not even house plants. Every animal lived in a maze of concrete and dirt, permanently bereft of any outside influence besides the sky. Only the few that worked in the Agriculture Department had the privilege of gazing on the lowly plants that kept the city fed and alive.

In his entire adult life, he had seen plant life in the Memphis city limits only once. One time he had been called for emergency duty to a fire in the Agriculture Department. He had seen row after row of hydroponically grown potato plants in dingy troughs. He remembered the bright green of their leaves, straining to grow under buzzing fluorescent lights. They were humble things, but the mere sight of them had led to a deep stirring inside his psyche. Impulsively, he reached out and grabbed a pawful of leaves. He had sudden visions of wide-open grassy savannahs, steaming jungles, rugged mountains covered in forest timber. He knew consciously that these memories, if they could be called that, must be false. He had never once set foot in any of the places that he now recalled in vivid detail. Yet in a much deeper place, beyond the shallow frontispiece of his conscious self, he knew that they were true. These were the places that were meant for him and his kind. They were the places that his ancestors had dwelled in, places that he had been hardwired to covet and desire as his own natural habitat. He remembered that he had released the leaves from his paw and realized that the floor was soaked with his tears.

As a cop he was supposed to be an enforcer of law and order, but these days he felt more like a repairman scrambling to keep the city from crumbling into nothing. When he joined the force, he'd bought into the propaganda that he was the one keeping the city from falling into chaos. It was true, in a sense. The men in his unit were constantly called out to push-start buses, to shore up dikes with ancient bulldozers, or unclog storm sewers choked with mud. In between, they were tasked with cracking the skull of anyone who stepped too far out of line. He was no saint in that regard, having roughed up a number of animals for the crime of skirting the establishment. His guilt over those excesses led him to try and make up for it on the sly, including this current venture with Turner. Deep down, he was exhausted and scared. Things were always getting worse as time wore on. The dikes eroded faster; the downpours were more furious; food tasted bad and was harder to come by. He knew they were fighting a losing battle to keep the city alive, and he wondered how long it could go on. Sometimes he lay awake at night, staring at the ceiling, wondering if the next day would be when it all finally came crashing down.

The wind ruffled the puma's long whiskers. Wesley heard the door of the store opening behind him. He wheeled around to see Turner shambling down the concrete steps in front of the door. He looked satisfied.

"The store owner got in touch with Collison. He's going to bring his son down here. So we just have to wait."

"Yes." The puma seemed preoccupied. Turner looked at Wesley searchingly.

"Are you alright?"

"I'm fine. Let's get this done."

***

Turner held his breath as he pushed the power button on the top of the device. After a second, it beeped. The indicator lights flashed green. His nervousness rose as the screen remained dark; but after about ten seconds, it lit up brightly. He breathed a sigh of relief as he scrolled through the various submenus. The touchpad seemed to be working properly. The pump clicked and whirred amid the clutter of screwdrivers and electronic bits on the workbench. Turner looked up at Collison and nodded. Anxiety melted away from the father's face as he squeezed his son's shoulders.

"Is it fixed?" The young dog sounded hopeful but tired, as though he couldn't muster any more energy. His sunken cheeks betrayed a long struggle to control his blood sugar. Turner smiled and motioned for Collison to bring his son closer.

"Yes, Randy. It should work fine now." Turner offered the pump to Collison, who accepted it with palpable gratitude. Turner could see the tears welling up in both of their eyes. Wesley, keeping watch at the back of the room, struggled to keep his own emotions in check. Collison leaned in to whisper to his son.

"Randy, thank Mr. Turner for what he's done."

"Thank you so much, Mr. Turner."

"That's just fine, Randy." Turner crouched down so he could be face to face with the pup. "Make sure to take good care of it. It'll help you grow up tall and strong." The pup nodded earnestly. Turner paused for a moment. Something about the mottled brown and grey of the pup's fur brought back an old memory. "Tall and strong. Just like an oak tree." The words flowed out before he could stop himself. Randy looked confused.

"Mr. Turner, what's an 'oak tree?'" Turner looked up at Collison, filled with regret. The elder shepherd gave him a knowing look, a dark smile that betrayed inner pain. In the lines of his face, Turner could see the frustration of a father who could not give his son the life he deserved at any price, the life to which all animals had once been entitled. He gently mussed his son's ears with his paw.

"Don't worry about it, Randy. Mr. Turner is just kidding around."

"Oh. Okay." Randy smiled innocently. Collison gently tucked the pump into his satchel.

"Ok, Randy. Let's get you home so we can get this set up." He faced Turner again. "Thank you."

"Any time. If it malfunctions, you know how to get ahold of me." The shepherd nodded. He gently steered his son toward the back of the room, past Wesley. The puma mustered a smile, for the child's sake. The door shut, and the father and son were gone. Turner immediately sank onto a battered wooden chair and put his head in his paw. Wesley drew up a chair opposite him. They sat in silence for a few minutes. Turner stared at the floor, while Wesley gazed off into space. Eventually, automatically, the bobcat began fishing for a cigarette. This time, he offered one to Wesley too. The puma accepted. They lit up and puffed in the semi-darkness of the grungy back room. Turner finally spoke.

"I lived in west Georgia in the 80's. I worked for a pulp and paper outfit as an engineer. It wasn't glamorous, but it paid decent. I didn't do much besides fish and ride my Harley on the weekends. Just a really simple life. It was smooth sailing for a while, but then something strange started to happen. It was like the trees started to dry out for no good reason. Every year we would get a few more off the company land that were weird inside. The wood turned to powder at your touch. The arborists hadn't seen anything like it. Eventually they found out that all these trees came from the same plot of land." Wesley listened intently as Turner went on. "This went on for a while. Then we began to hear from other forestry guys in the rest of the country that they were having the same problem. They had all these little patches of land full of diseased trees, and when they cut them down, they wouldn't regrow anything. Like they were totally barren. But the biggest surprise was that these patches seemed to be growing."

"The Die-off."

"Yes. That was the beginning of it. But it happened so gradually that we didn't realize how screwed we were until it was really out of control. We always assumed that whatever it was, the land would heal and we could replant. But, here we are."

"Yeah."

"I fought with the other execs about getting the EPA or anyone else to help us. They didn't want outsiders involved, especially not government people. But eventually we couldn't hide it. We needed help. I called in some people that our arborists recommended, and the EPA. That was when I met Tim." Turner paused. He took a long drag on his cigarette and gradually blew the smoke up towards the ceiling.

"Tim?"

"He worked as a plant biologist with the EPA. We became friends." Wesley sensed that Turner held back something about his relationship with Tim, but he decided not to pry. It wasn't any of his business. "Tim and his team worked on the barrenness issue for two years, and they finally figured out that there was something wrong with the soil chemistry. Any plant you tried to grow in the bad dirt would just crumble because something was eating them up inside. The cell walls would collapse."

"It was the nano-something, right?" Wesley remembered vaguely now, stories that had been passed down orally. He'd never been one for science stuff, but Turner had jogged his memory.

"Yep, that was it. Nanomirrors." Wesley looked confused, so Turner kept explaining. He gestured with his paws, forming a sort of bowl in the air. "To try and keep the planet from warming, they started mass-producing these atomic-sized mirrors to catch light particles in the upper atmosphere and bounce them back. They were supposed to be held up there by satellites that generated a magnetic field. The oil and gas companies thought they'd found their savior. They put quadrillions of them in in the exosphere. They promised that if they fell down, it wouldn't matter anyway. The only problem is that they kill cells that photosynthesize when they get in the plants. The satellites couldn't hold them in place after all. They started falling back to Earth, and we were screwed. Tim was one of the first ones to report the findings. It blew up in the media then; everyone started calling it the Die-off. And that's when things really went downhill." Turner finished his cigarette and drew out another. Wesley lit it for him.

"I remember looking out the window of my office and realizing that all I could see were dead trees. Just miles and miles of dead trees and clear-cut land. Pretty soon even the dead trees were gone, because they crumbled to dust. That's when I knew that it was going to get rough. The grocery lines started soon after that. So did the refugee convoys. It only took about three years from the beginning of the Die-off for everything to come unglued. Tim lost his job, because they voted to disband the EPA. All of the political bullshit just made everything worse." Turner waved his paw in the air, as though dismissing some bad memories. Wesley nodded silently. His cigarette was just a stump now, but he still held the butt of it in his paw. Turner coughed a little and then took another drag. He looked bitter, jaded. Wesley finally spoke.

"I remember something from when I was little. There was a tree left in a park near downtown. It was dead, but still standing. I remember a big crowd of people around it, and they tried to keep it from being cut down. But then a bulldozer came and pushed it over. I remember that it was loud and I was scared. Then my mother grabbed me and we had to run, because the police were rushing the crowd."

"At least you got to see one." Turner stubbed out his cigarette. "Of course, that's all over now. The walls are the only reason the dust and wind doesn't kill us. Wonder what it looks like from the top of Crump these days." Wesley's ears twitched. He was picking up vague traces of some commotion going on out front. He wanted to go check it out, but he had one last question for Turner.

"What happened to Tim?" Wesley feared offending Turner, but his curiosity compelled him to ask. Turner didn't respond for half a minute. He let Wesley's words hang in the smoky air. He suddenly stood up and began gathering his things with his back turned to the corporal.

"We were trying to get from Atlanta to Birmingham. I made it. He didn't." He threw a screwdriver aggressively into his bag. "I left Birmingham a year later. I've been here since." Wesley could see now where Turner's limp had come from. His left leg was warped, as if it had been badly broken once and never healed properly. The bobcat turned away from the bench and frowned.

"There's something going on out there," he said, jabbing a finger at the door.

"Yeah, I know. I heard it." Wesley tensed as he put his hand on his gun. There was the sound of clattering cans and shouting behind the locked door.

"Is there any other exit?" Turner said, panicking.

"Nope." The door suddenly rattled with a huge bang. Wesley realized what was going on. "Fuck. It's me. They've come looking for me," Wesley said. Turner was stunned.

"What?!"

"I'm not supposed to be here. We're not supposed to go to our home neighborhoods. They musta traced me." Wesley gritted his teeth.

"Shit!" Turner's eyes were as wide as a full moon. The door rattled with another huge bang. More shouting.

"Don't say anything. Don't make any moves. Just sit." Wesley pleaded, but Turner was already panicking. His eyes were huge as he frantically scanned the walls for another way out. There was another huge bang and the door finally burst open. There was chaos as a half-dozen officers poured into the room. With an angry snarl, a black jaguar brought his truncheon down on Turner's head.

***

"Hey. Wake up. Wake up, cat." Turner stirred slightly. He felt an aching throb in the center of his skull. Someone was gently rubbing his face with their pawpads, but he couldn't bring himself to open his eyes. He began to sit up, but then started to cough harshly.

"Aw, damn. Here." Somebody was forcing a nebulizer mask over his snout. Instinctively he began to suck in and felt a rush of vapor into his lungs. "Good. Just keep on it." Although his eyes were still shut, Turner could tell that he must be sitting on some type of bed or cot. There was a gentle rocking as the person with the inhaler sat down next to him. They put an arm across Turner's lower back while the cat sucked down albuterol. "Okay. Just keep breathing. Jesus, they messed you up." He could feel the unknown person gently brushing at the fur between his ears. They grazed a particularly tender spot with a claw, and Turner screeched.

"Agh!"

"Jesus! Sorry." Turner's eyes were open now. With his vision still blurry, he began to take in his surroundings. He was sitting on a narrow cot at the edge of an enormous, dim room. Two massive concrete pillars in the middle stretched up to the ceiling, which was maybe fifty feet above his head. He couldn't see any windows; but there was a profusion of control panels and displays lining the walls. He looked to the right, and he could see a narrow corridor of electronics that stretched all the way to the darkened corner of the room. To his left, there was a metal stairwell that reached some twenty or thirty feet up the wall. He was still thoroughly bedraggled and wary, but nothing about his surroundings suggested imminent doom. The nebulizer was doing its job; his airways were opening, and he stopped struggling to breathe. He turned to face his unknown caretaker.

"Hey." It was a young female badger, her face winnowed with concern. She was stocky, with a finely tapered snout and bright-white stripes. She wore medical scrubs, and her free paw rested on a portable nebulizer machine. "My name is Holly." Turner stared at her, not sure if he should say anything. "It's alright. Just keep inhaling, there's plenty left in the capsule." Turner nodded slightly. She rubbed his back slightly. "I know you've been through a lot. But when you're done, we need to go upstairs." She gestured towards the metal staircase.

"Where are we?" Turner spoke out of the side of the nebulizer mask.

"Crump Tower," she said.

His stomach churned. She tried to comfort him. "I know. But it's not bad. I promise." The nebulizer shut off. Turner pulled the mask off.

"Where is Wesley?" She looked confused. "The police officer." Her face lit up with understanding, but she was crestfallen. She replied haltingly.

"I know he's in holding somewhere. That's it." Turner squeezed the nebulizer mask tightly. "I'm sorry."

"Not your fault." Turner was still wary, but he could guess that she was just a cog in the machine. She was only here to make sure that he didn't cough out a lung. "I'm fine. Take me upstairs.

"Okay," she said, and Turner slid gingerly off the cot. They began making their way towards the stairs, as Holly supported his still-shaky frame. "Easy now." She flicked a light switch, and fluorescent lights slowly buzzed into life across the room. As he limped slowly upwards, he could see over the banks of panels and computers that had obscured his vision. He was stunned by what he saw as they ascended the clanging stairs.

Between the two concrete pillars was an immense machine that looked like a cross between a giant paper shredder and a Borg cube. A profusion of thick cables and pipes sprouted from the sides. An enormous conveyor belt descended from a hole in the ceiling, terminating directly over a wide slot in the top. Another conveyor belt snaked out from underneath the machine, cutting a wide path over to a dark slot on the side of the room. He could see brightly-colored signs that warned of high pressures, extreme temperatures, and killing voltage all over the scaffolding that surrounded the machine. They reached the top of the stairwell, and Turner stopped to stare at its full extent. Holly tapped him on the shoulder.

"I don't know what it is. They just said I was supposed to show it to you." She sounded worried.

"That's alright." Turner's brain rattled with questions. The purpose of the machine mystified him; but even more so, the reason that it had been shown to him. Holly seemed scared, as though she had witnessed some dark secret that was forbidden to all but a few. He looked behind them and saw a thick metal door embedded in the concrete wall twenty steps behind them. Directly above it was a security camera, its lens trained directly on the two of them.

"Do you have somewhere to take me?" Turner said gently. He sensed Holly's foreboding. He took her paw in his and squeezed it.

"Oh, yes." She was slightly embarrassed, but he felt her squeeze his hand back. They made their way to the door. It swung open, revealing a long dimly-lit hallway. Doors marked with inscrutable combinations of letters and numbers lined both sides. At the end was an elevator.

"We're going there. Up." Holly pointed to the end of the hall. Turner's mind continued to spin as they made their way towards the elevator. There had to be some logic behind both the machine and his exposure to it. He knew he had mechanical skills that were in short supply, but what was he supposed to do? As they came up to the elevator, the doors opened on their own. Turner glared up at yet another security camera. Someone was watching. They stepped inside and the doors slid shut. They began moving upward without touching any of the buttons.

They glided smoothly upwards. The only sound came from the dull hum of the motor. The thick carpeting and the dark wood on the walls suggested totalitarian luxury. Turner counted the seconds internally. He had already guessed that they were somewhere underground, but the interminably long elevator ride confirmed it. They were headed somewhere very high in the building. Abruptly, the elevator slowed and stopped. A disembodied voice suddenly burst out.

"Nurse 179-A, exit the elevator." The doors slid open to reveal two muscular jackals in suits, their eyes hidden behind polarized lenses. Holly shot Turner a quick glance of fear. She stepped tentatively forward, still clutching the nebulizer. Turner raised his paw, as if to catch her one last time; but the voice barked out again.

"Bobcat, do not move." The two jackals suddenly lunged forward and grasped Holly by the shoulders, their long claws flashing. She yelped as they yanked her out of the elevator.

"Hey!" Turner yelled, but he wasn't quick enough to grab her. The jackals pulled her into the hallway and the elevator door shut abruptly. The gondola began to ascend again. Turner seethed.

"You can do whatever you want with me. But you better not touch her." He spat out the words. Teeth-clenching rage had displaced his fear. "I know you can hear me. Whatever shit you're planning, you better make a good pitch." There was no response, just more of the same steady upward ascent. After a few tense minutes, it finally began to slow again. Turner looked around instinctively for something that could be used as a weapon but saw nothing. He gritted his teeth as the door slid open.

There were no suited toughs, but the light was blinding. Turner blinked as his eyes adjusted to the sunlight flooding the room. He stepped forward cautiously and was promptly struck dumb by what he saw. Plants were everywhere in the sprawling room, which was bounded on all sides by soaring glass walls. All around him were more planters, filled with an enormous variety of greenery: shrubs, flowers, even juicy tomatoes ripening on the vine. And the most extraordinary part was that the plants all seemed to be growing in dirt. He walked up to a planter filled with ferns and dug his paw into the soil. It was warm, soft, and moist, staining the fur on his digits a muddy brown. He watched it crumble back into the planter, his jaw slightly open. He closed his eyes and sniffed. His nose, desensitized though it was from all the smokes, still picked up a rich bouquet of aromatics: roses, ferns, violets, tree bark, pollen. He sneezed. Suddenly he heard footsteps behind him.

"Don't sniff too hard." The same voice from the elevator rang out behind him. Turner slowly wheeled around. "Turner, I believe?" A tall ocelot stood in a ray of sunlight, his dark suit cutting a sharp profile. The sun glinted off the watch that adorned his left arm. He had the serious expression of an accountant or an undertaker. He began to walk slowly towards Turner.

"Yes." Turner responded warily.

"Did the nurse show you the machine in the basement?"

"Yes, she did. What are you going to do with her?" The ocelot waved his paw in the air dismissively.

"That's not important."

Turner balled up his fist but decided not to push the issue. "So what is the thing in the basement?"

"It's a soil-cleaning machine."

"Holy shit." Turner whispered softly to himself. They'd finally figured out a way to get the nano mirrors out of the soil. That explained the conveyor belts; they were carrying massive amounts of dirt in and out of the room. And the room full of plants; it was real soil after all. He wandered down the aisle, touching the plants and feeling their cool green leaves in his paws. The ocelot trailed a few paces behind, apparently content to let Turner take it all in. He came upon a large wheeled pushcart covered with potted trees and shrubs. Turner leaned over and sniffed a delicate miniature magnolia, his nose filling with the pleasant vapors. The ocelot piped up.

"There's a catch, though. To make it work, we have to basically turn off the city." Turner swallowed hard. "That's the only way we can get the amount of power and water we need. We can't run the hydroponic plants and the fresh water system at the same time as the cleaner. We can't run the rest of the electrical grid either."

"Can't you rotate them? Run the machine at night and the rest of the city during the day?"

"No. Once we get it running, we can't just turn it off. It's a huge process. We had to plan a month ahead of time just to test it." Turner remembered a particularly vicious citywide blackout from a few months prior. Even the hospital hadn't been immune. Now it made sense. The ocelot leaned over against a planter and raked his claws through it. He flicked the dirt away, and then extended a paw to Turner.

"Roderick is the name. I helped design it. I'm an engineer, too." Turner warily shook his paw. The ocelot's grip was firm. Turner decided to cut to the chase.

"Why am I here? Why are you telling me all of this?"

"Your police buddy couldn't keep out of trouble. He's the reason you got your head split open." The ocelot grinned fiendishly.

Turner hocked and spat in a planter. He spoke through gritted teeth. "What are you going to do to him?"

"That's not up to me."

"Isn't this the part where you're supposed to say that you'll spare him if I help you?"

"Why do you care about him? Isn't a chance to save your own pelt good enough?" The ocelot seemed slightly bemused. Turner's anger simmered, but he kept a calm exterior. Now that he was coming down from the high of being surrounded by so much luscious foliage, he forced himself to think. He made a quick visual inventory of his surroundings. They were standing at the end of a row of plants, with the pushcart full of pots directly behind Turner. He glanced down and noticed that it had foot brake on the rear axle. Looking towards the back of the room, he had a clear path directly towards one of the floor-to-ceiling windows. He couldn't sense any other presence in the room; they seemed to be alone, although he could see security cameras hanging from the ceiling. A few were trained directly on the two of them. The ocelot continued on.

"Here's the deal. We, by which I mean Uncle Sam and the people who actually have useful skills, want to build more soil cleaners. We can start building colonies on clean dirt once we have enough to go around. But we can't do that and keep the rest of this city on life support, or frankly any of the others. And I'm fine with that. There's a whole lot of gutter trash out there who don't need to be kept limping along forever. This is a chance to start over, and they don't need to be part of the picture." Turner cringed, but he kept listening. "But you're in luck, Turner. Because you have skills. Anthros that still know something about production engineering are a rare breed indeed. We could send you off to Seattle or San Francisco to supervise the set-up, and you'd be a king. You'd get to have whatever you wanted." The ocelot leaned in uncomfortably close and tapped Turner on the chest. "Oh yeah, about that: you'd be first in line for some chemo and a new set of lungs. Because you're gonna need those." Turner looked up at Roderick as the realization dawned on the bobcat's face. "They gave you an MRI when you came in. Not pretty. Some big lumps you got in there." Turner's stomach churned. Deep down inside, he had known instinctively that something was wrong. The coughing had been getting worse, with his spit-up occasionally going bloody. Now he knew. He backed away slowly from the ocelot, his whiskers and ears drooping.

"So there's the deal. And really, you don't have a choice. We're not letting you back on the street now that you know." There was a menacing edge in Roderick's voice now. Turner kept his head down. In his mind, the faces of everyone he met on the way here flashed: the passengers on the bus, the raccoon in the street, Wesley, Collison, Randy, Holly, the jaguar that had clubbed Turner over the head. All of them flawed, surely; but also animal. Flesh and blood. Filled with their own thoughts, fears, loves, losses. No number of beautiful flowers or fresh breaths would ever erase their faces from Turner's memory. He looked up at Roderick and smiled.

Turner pushed down on the cart's foot brake with his own paw, releasing it. It began to roll backwards. He knew the ocelot was much stronger, and that he'd lose a brawl—he only needed a quick surprise to execute his plan. Summoning all of his strength, Turner lunged forward and gave the ocelot a firm shove in the chest with both paws.

"Ugh!" They both toppled backward, and Roderick's head smacked the edge of a concrete planter. Turner saw his eyes roll back in his skull. The bobcat scrambled back up and headed for the cart. It was still rolling. He got behind it and began pushing with all of his might. He could feel his chest tightening as he gasped for breath, but the cart was gaining speed. The plate glass window loomed at the end of the hallway. His heart raced and his chest felt about to burst. At the last moment, he leapt aside and let the cart fly forward.

There was an enormous crash as it punched a hole in the window. Huge shards of glass rained down on Turner as the cart toppled over the edge of the building. The full load of potted plants sailed out into the sky, before quickly heading downwards. Covered in glass shards, bleeding and wheezing, Turner struggled to his feet. He staggered towards the broken glass window. The wind whipped violently past the jagged edges of the broken glass. He clutched his constricted chest as he peered over the ledge. Dozens of stories below, he could see where the cart had landed. The whole load of plants and soil had crashed into the middle of the street. Animals were starting to gather around it. He smiled; the secret was out now. Behind him, there was a vague trampling of boots. He turned to face a squad of security officers running towards him.

"Put your paws in the air!" Turner smiled but didn't comply. "I said put them up!" The lead officer, a German Shepherd, barked the command threateningly; but he was suddenly shoved aside by a staggering Roderick.

"You'll never see daylight again," the ocelot screeched.

"We all will," replied Turner. With his back to the broken window, he calmly spread his arms. He smiled at Roderick, the officers, and the security cameras. "Tim," he whispered to himself, as he fell backwards out of the ninety-fifth story window.

Revolutionaries and Collaborators never truly think about posterity in their moments of truth, when hard choices have to be made that will shape their own lives and the lives of so many others. Sometimes that's bravery, sometimes that's foolishness. Sometimes it's both.

People often forget that the hardest part of any revolutionary action is figuring out what to do with the legacy you've built for yourself after the dust settles.

We can't break free of the choices we've already made or the actions we've taken. Is it foolish to even try?

Photographs

Televassi

I remember the heat; flames curling up into the night sky, the sirens from the Spires above. I remember the feeling in the air.

I snorted when they forced me to the ground. I kicked wildly when they cuffed me. You don't forget how the crunch of bone gets the heart pumping, how you have no room for guilt.

'Keeping the peace' kept things the same.

It's odd; I didn't remember kissing Kira as they dragged us away, but that's the photo everyone recognizes. Two people, paused, before their world was pulled apart.

A little romance helps colour the failure of that night, after all.

***

I am not the revolutionary I once was. I have grey streaks in my mane and brown spots on my thighs that have turned black. I used to have a rowan tinge to my coat that helped my firebrand tongue; now it's a dull brown. The firm muscles in my flanks have gone flabby. My gut sticks out. I wear glasses. Each morning in the mirror it gets harder to see the resemblance to the photograph; you have to know I was there.

I am tired, worn out, waiting for change that I could not grasp. Perhaps if I had claws I could have dug in, but maybe that's the thing, us horses already had domesticity bred into our DNA. Thankfully we are good at carrying weights around.

The Chimera District Council doesn't see it that way; a token collection of fools and dreamers tossed a scrap of power so the Spires above could continue to make all the important decisions. They seem to think I make a good History teacher considering how much of it I saw firsthand. I suspect that actually, having the old agitators on payroll helps bring the younger ones into the fold.

I don't notice the time pass as I make my way to work. The Haven; its gleaming white spires and squat concrete foundations have this effect. It's the artificial light and sky above. I've never seen the sun move, and though I don't notice it as much, the fact that the shadows never move still disturbs in that 'tingle on the back of the mane' way. There's a lot I forget to notice now, like how I don't pause to look up from the grey maze at the elegant Spires above. There are classes to run.

It's September. Every year, the students turn Campus Central Reservation into a crucible of scent. Societies clamour for membership fees in exchange for freebies or Council subsidised perks. The campus itself is a CDC initiative (authorised from above); the first step to liberation is in the mind, not the body. In reality it serves as the one meaningful place among the Districts where divide and conquer doesn't apply; where the three Chimera breeds can mix.

My back's aching already and my hooves throb from standing here for so long. It's only been an hour. The sports clubs, as usual, have the crowds, but I can't blame them If you're good enough you've got a shot at playing at the very top, both senses. Turns out our animal physicality makes quite the engaging display.

Second to the clubs is the Post-Apoc Soc, as ever, already assembling a decent band of colonisers, mostly scrawny wolves with eyes lit up with the 'lone wanderer' mystique. They're a society of fantasists allergic to multiple syllables and the realities lying outside the Haven; nothing but greasy clouds, ash, and dust. Yet compared to them we're fighting over the scraps of crowd that hurry past our way.

Maybe the dream is still that powerful?

"When Jesus Christ died, he sacrificed himself to save all souls," Edna proclaims by my side, smiling earnestly at a fallow deer who'd accidentally caught her gaze. The doe returns a polite smile, biting her lip as she skips away. I guess she knew the mantra of the centuries that proceeded; that the scripture spoke of mankind's redemption—not our own.

I always find standing here difficult, but every year I come. I was never a true believer, but I'm here to give my wife the support she believes she needs.

The next one to fall our way is a wolf. Ears pricked up, he steps out from a group of his peers. He's got a smirk stretched across his grey muzzle, sharp teeth to compliment the rough, angular patterns on his clothes; his tail is full of bristles. There's always a couple of troublemakers every year.

"How can you stand there?" he snaps. Not at her—at me. His eyes go sharp, but then blurry at the edges. "You died in detention."

Edna steps in front of me, in that way people of faith have limitless capacity for self-sacrifice.

"You should be ashamed—if the others could see you now." He grapples with Edna's attempts at a comforting embrace. "I bet you think of your old doe when you fuck her!"

In days gone by, I would—I should—have shouted back. Instead I just stand there, silent. I can feel the weight of my wife's eyes upon me, heavier than the scrutiny of God. A single movement would betray me, but in doing so, I knew I only betrayed her. The truth has a way of sapping away your rage. So like everything else here, I stood there and took it.

"Sell-out," he snarls. Then he disappears into the crowd. After a minute everyone is back to milling around; the new faces totally unaware of what just happened, wrapped up in their own little lives.

"You okay?" Edna asks, squeezing my hand. Bless her, she doesn't even question the mention of Kira.

"Yeah," I reply. It's a lie but she doesn't question it. I'm already trying to figure out who he could be. He can't have been old enough to have been there that night, but he could remember a room in the family house where the door was always shut. Maybe a sibling, a mother, a father? Plenty of wolves wound up dead that night—just because they have a muzzle full of pointy teeth that looks so threatening when shouting.

Unlike the unmoving shadows or spires about, I think about him for the rest of the day. I notice every wolf that crosses my way. Maybe he knew Rey, or Freja? I can't even picture them. What about the others I knew in passing, who looked up at me for a word of encouragement? I wish I had a wolf's nose, then I'd be able to know. Trawling through my faded memories, trying to match up pelt colours doesn't get me anywhere.

When we pack everything away for the evening, Edna, thankfully, doesn't ask me to come say prayers. I don't know if she read the name of the goddess on my lips.

***

I sometimes wonder what cosmological joke it must be that I still know Kira. In the years since Settlement and the creation of the CDC, we'd both found our way onto Reservation staffing. We're both surgeons in our own way; I try to stitch together the fragmented records of history, she operates on our unhealthy understanding of our own biology. She's good at it too; the Haven purpose bred her batch to pull out ball bearings, nails, and bone fragments.

I remember those nimble fingers.

I'm thankful for the small blessings, like how the dim light of the bar makes it harder to distinguish the dimples in my coat and hides the grey streaks. I want to know how she still looks so beautiful. Her dainty legs, muddy brown eyes, cream patches of fur on her forehead that show just from underneath her long, hazel hair; just like when revolution was on our lips.

"Right now my research focuses on Chimera's physical imperfections. We all know wolves lack the hand structure for delicate work thanks to the dewclaws, but it's not actually a purpose bred trait from their design. We need to stop believing our genetic engineering is so perfect. It's a neglected interaction between the human and lupine alleles, that causes roughly two-thirds to get them instead of thumbs—in short, they were made to be the unfinished product."

Instead of sharing her indignation I'm just staring at her like a dumb puppy.

"I'm glad to hear one of us is still making a difference," I joke. "Nobody, not even the bureaucrats up in the Spires know what happened after the 21st century." As a result, anyone and everybody had their own agenda. Purists on both sides claimed it was the other race that started it, realists and moderates shifted the blame to someone and somewhere else, while the few remaining just saw it as confirmation that life is inherently destructive.

"I wouldn't hold your breath. My findings effectively confirm that the wolves were bred to die; that it was cheaper to make a gun to fit rather than give them actual hands." Kira sighs, brushing my hand. "That's some legacy."

We pause for a moment, recoiling from each other.

"You always were the optimist though," I add.

She leans back, taking a sip from her glass—the vodka brewed behind the black doors in the cellar downstairs. Officially, Chimera weren't meant to have access to anything over 5% due to 'beastly' natures. It's amusing how the Haven lets me teach Prohibition though—they tried that before the Havens and they just drove it underground, which is exactly what's happened.

"If I can just understand the allele's interaction, then someone can fix it. Then that's something mended." She shrugs, rolling her eyes. "Never mind. I heard Reika caused a bit of a scene for you," Kira stiffened, taking another sip. "That wolf's a good student—a good person."

I shrug, but the doe isn't convinced.

"Look, the thing is, he's already on his final warning for behaviour," she says quietly. "And you know as well as I that the faithful can be a bit touchy—"

"Edna's not like that" I counter. "I mean, she knows I don't even believe anymore."

"I know," Kira pressed, "but if anything were to happen it'd tear up the progress he's been making for one weak moment. He's got a sharp mind, and a set of hands too."

"If you're so worried that something will happen then why not drop the proxy and speak to Edna yourself?" I challenge.

She ignores me and continues her argument. "That pup—and I say pup because he's still not mature enough—can actually make something of himself. But if he gets registered he can kiss that hope goodbye." She pauses. "Besides, you know he's nothing like what we were. We had our own fair share of reckless behavior, and it was arcing bottles at faceless police."

I bow my head, conceding to her like I always did. "I'll keep an eye on things. For you."

"Sorry Val," she huffs, leaning closer. "I know he wasn't what you wanted to talk about."

"He kind of was. It got me thinking." I chuckle, taking another drink. "I mean, did agreeing to Settlement make us cowards?"

"Hindsight is wonderful," she muses. "So too is the luxury of being able to ponder 'what if?'"

"Come on, you're not being honest with me. You'd love to not just be flirting with me." She shoots me a sharp look—yes, someone may hear, but I don't really care. I press further. "I mean, look. We went from showing off bruises to standing in theatres lecturing in monotone, looking at monthly paychecks. We're still stuck down here, and we still can't be together."

"Settlement is better than nothing. We've got a process going. You do know the other Havens don't even allow chimera inside them, right? They still see us as volatile weapons in need of decommissioning, not housing!" she snaps. She only looks more beautiful when angry. "I wouldn't want to be out there. I've seen the figures—six minutes of sunlight in months! You couldn't grow anything out there."

I couldn't argue against fact. If you didn't believe it, then you could just go to places at the edge of the Haven's reach. There you can glimpse the outside, through the gaps in the dome's dead pixels, and see what lay beyond. I think they never fixed the display on purpose, just to prove that our collective captivity was no choice of theirs.

"I know, I know," I surrender, partially. "But we fought to get this far, and then what? We stopped. What have we seen change since then? The Spires drag their heels about anything meaningful, the CDC does nothing, and each year we send off students back to their Districts, busy doing grunt work that'll break their backs so they won't be able to look up anymore." I pause. "Maybe it's just me, but that wolf did get to me."

"You sure it's that?" she says, narrowing her eyes at me. Her hand is creeping across the table again, teasing my fingertips. So many times I've dreamt of slipping a silver ring over one.

I sigh. God, she just knows my outrage was never so selfless and noble.

"Freedom is a fine dream," she says, "but reality is full of compromises. I'm sure things would be a lot worse if we didn't live in here." She looks away as she says that, checking her watch. "I've got to head off—my time allocation off-District is almost up. Wouldn't be good for my research if I can no longer swipe through because my ID has been flagged on the system for running over."

"I wish I could come home with you," I blurt out.

"See you at work."

Woefully, I watch her little white tail bob away.

***

My reflection in the tram's windows stares back at me as gaze out into the night. I don't appreciate his sullen look, so I lean back and look up. In spite of the darkness, I can see the white Spires of the Haven's upper reaches glittering above, divorced from their stocky foundations. I wonder if the people up there ever look down. Then again, I don't look at the earth unless something's caught my hoof.

The Districts were only meant to be a temporary fix. Unlike most of the Havens built to preserve humanity after the war, this one was built with that conflict still in mind. While the Spires had become beautified achievements in the time since then, the lower levels remained a maze of reinforced concrete, a convenient dumping-ground for all the Chimera they bred for a purpose that never came. The result; a sprawling, bestial underbelly that those in the white Spires above are determined to keep under heel, because beasts can complete menial tasks cheaper than fancy computers.

I got off at the stop before my own, thinking it best to walk some of the booze off before Edna opened the door. While I hadn't told her that I'd be out past recreational hours, she has grown used to me being out at the same time as the nocturnals.

She just prays about it, like every other problem.

I pause mid-step, shaking my head. I apologise to her, refusing to excuse myself by blaming the alcohol. Really, I am jealous of her. Her coping strategy for all of this doesn't come in a bottle. In spite of all the world's darkness, she has found a way to be happy.

I find her lying asleep in front of the television, its static screen repeatedly showing a message that programming would resume at 6am. I'm disappointed really; I want someone to talk to. That's what she offered, the faith included. You could talk and they, she, would listen. It was listening, it was being heard that I needed, not the feeling that I needed to be saved.

Gathering Edna in my arms, I carry her to bed. She doesn't even stir as I let her down on the sheets. As usual I have the option of joining her, but instead I lie down on the floor and stare up at the ceiling.

***

Edna was out before I woke up—early morning prayers, then charitable work in the District. She'd left breakfast on the table, but I wasn't hungry. I gulp down the juice and scrape the rest into a plastic bag which I throw in the bin before I reach campus. No need to make her worry.

Campus is like most of the buildings down here, a squat concrete block that serves as a solid foundation for the elegant skyscrapers above. The ribbed walls are stained with black lines of runoff, while here and there are patches of brightly coloured graffiti; abstract forms and birds in flight.

The entrance has plenty of security; tall walls, big gates. My ID runs through the waylocks fairly easy—faculty members at least get a decent privilege level to mixed species grounds, so the two uninterested humans wave me through. They're typical Napoleons; short and fat compared to the Chimera, and to other humans they're probably the dregs of their generation. Why else would they be down here? We knew it and they did too—explaining why one of them keeps spraying some sort of cheap perfume about themselves for every Chimera that passes his way. If you take a sniff, the bad odour comes from her companion, specifically the oily sheen on his skin. I don't know how they find all that bare skin attractive.

Just as I clear the gates they pull a wolf behind me inside their booth, yanking him by the long tufts in his fur. It's guilt that forces me to stay and watch, because I was party to this system, because my compliance allowed this to happen, day in, day out. Five minutes later they kick him out; his thick pelt shorn, and his claws clipped aggressively against the skin. They did it simply because they could, because they wanted to put him in his place. Instead, he strides off, aloof, bearing the indignity like a badge of honour.

I dip my head in shame and bite my tongue.

***

The rest of the morning is dull. The faculty insists on holding one-on-one meetings with all students, regardless of year group. The first years are especially useless; one asks whether they need to read everything for the course. Another admits she doesn't like history. After them, I'm certain I appear like a grumpy, haggard old horse—which at least ensures the meetings run short.

And then Reika strolls in.

He wears scabby leather boots that come up below the knee, patched jeans that have pockets of brown fur pushing out from the holes, a black shirt, and a dirty, ripped leather jacket—black also—with brown patches of fabric sewn over the elbows.

"Remember me?" He smiles with a faux-friendly manner; sitting down on the empty chair; putting his feet up on my desk. "I remember a lot about you."

I say nothing.

"Question is, do you? Do they let you say how we got humiliated by Settlement?" he says, knocking one of the books onto the floor with his feet. And then a stack of papers.

"What do you want, Reika?" He smirks at the mention of his name.

"I want to talk to you about last night," he says, producing a folded up photograph and throwing it onto the desk. There I am, reaching across at Kira, dreamy eyes betraying me.

"You followed me?"

"You'd have noticed me if I was there. Let's just say old friends haven't forgotten about you, even if you've forgotten about them." I turn over the photograph. There's a black three-pointed star on the corner.

Fuck off. Does he really expect me to believe he's part of the Underground? They've been silent for years. Most, if not all of them are locked up for various crimes—arson, assault, theft. They certainly were never the railroad out of the Haven that they claimed to be. Besides, their mark is easy enough to make; any kid who plays on the streets knows about it. As if reading my expression, the wolf tuts, flicking his lighter against a cigarette.

"Don't smoke in here!" I snap.

"What makes me think I'll listen to you?" He grins. I'm already sick of it, the way those black lips peel back to reveal those sharp, glistening points. "If you shout, they'll come running in and I'll show them what you've been up to."

"Stop wasting my time!"

"You've wasted enough of it by yourself."

I yell, slamming my hoof against the floor. I don't care about the threat; I'm not here to be humiliated. "You'd better give me a bloody good reason not to turf you back to whatever slum you came from."

"That's more like you." He stabs his cigarette against his paw. He doesn't even flinch as the embers touch his skin. He sighs, running his yellow eyes up and down me. "It's quite a relief to see you're not happy, even with such a… cushy lot."

"Is that why you're making a scene? You jealous of someone who's made something of themselves?"

He doesn't smirk. His eyes soften and his breathing slows. "No, I'm not jealous," he admits, his ears drooping slightly. "I feel pity for you," he says wistfully, tapping his paw against the photograph. With a shrug, he pushes it over to me. "Pity, that it comes to things like this."

"What do you want?" I press again.

"You've got old friends. They still keep an eye on you. They'd also like to see you again."

I snort with full thronged contempt, in that way horses only can. "Last time I checked, friends didn't go about threatening to have me dragged up in front of the authorities."

"You think we'd go to them about this?" The wolf frowns; enough in the ensuing silence that I believe I can hear the fur on his forehead bristle. "You think you should be trusted still, after all the years?" He leans closer. "Maybe for the right tip, they'd turn a blind eye to you seeing her at odd hours of the night."

"Fuck off!" I snort, kicking at his chair. I send it spinning against the wall with a dull thud, but he's nimble enough to leap out before I ever make contact.

"That's the spirit," the wolf growls, standing tall. A wildness flickers about his mane, and for a moment, he seems free. "Keep hold of that photograph for now. Think on the past—ours, not their version of it," he says, flicking his black, braided tail about. The metal beads within catch the light, shining like silver. "Then think of the future."

***

I stay late that night. It has been years since I've heard from anyone else who'd been part of the protests, longer still since I'd even heard of the Underground. They've existed as long as Chimera have, but none of us was really sure what they did. It was always a loose coalition of disparate political ideals. Occasionally various thugs and arsonists would invoke the name to justify their desire for disorder. Perhaps they existed simply as a phantom to make District patrols look over their shoulders at night.

For a moment, I wonder whether Reika is pulling my tail. Maybe he needs to see a psychologist. That would be convenient, if it were not for the photograph. I cradle my head in my hands, running my fingers around my muzzle, tracing the patterns her light fingers used to take. I sigh, accepting that I'd noticed nothing that night.

It is dark outside when I leave the office; the shadows long as the lights above struggle to reach down here. The Spires twinkle like stars but feel like eyes. I probably can catch Kira before she leaves her office; that way I can at least warn her without it looking like anything beyond work. Of course, the Underground—if it were true—would know, but for anyone else it wouldn't be out of the ordinary.

I catch her in her lab—her white apron speckled with a fine mist of blood. Instinctively my nostrils flare, my breathing becoming quick and my movements skittish.

"It's only a dissection," she says dryly. "Not like there were any fragments needing to be removed."

"Doesn't it make you feel sick?"

"They removed the gene for that," she sighs.

"Can I have a word?"

"Now? Or do you want me to scrub down first?" she queries. I wait in her office until she finally comes through, smelling of citrus and pine needles.

"What can I help you with?" Professional as ever, she places her hands neatly in her lap. I place the photograph on her table. She sniffs, tracing the scents lingering upon the paper. "So Reika gave you this?" she asks.

"But he wasn't there last night."

She stiffens in her chair. "This is blackmail."

"Yep."

"And after I gave him a chance—"

"He says it's from the Underground."

She swears, laughing forcefully as she spins around on her chair. "What could they want?"

"He didn't say, but he says they'll be in touch."

"It's because of that night, isn't it? That night where we thought we could change the world by burning some tyres and waving some signs. I bet they're wanting to stir things up again—get us to plant some ideas in impressionable minds, nudge some kids who don't know better their way so they can get incarcerated so the Underground can make some point." She runs her hands through her auburn hair, scratching her scalp.

"You know as well as I we burnt police cars and threw rocks," I added.

She shot me a sour look.

"First we were bred to fight their wars, which thankfully ended before we started bleeding for them. They didn't plan on having to house us, but why should we be grateful that they didn't kick us outside of the Haven's walls? We didn't ask to be made!" Kira snaps.

"You almost sound like one of the Underground," I retort.

"The difference between us and them is that we don't want to be out there. The Underground is deluded. They're all fire and revolution but they have no plan for afterwards. There's nothing outside the Havens but brown skies, black water, red earth. I like having a decent life expectancy. I like not having to take iodine pills. You do too." She replies, her shoulders sagging. "Chimera and Humans, neither of us had a choice about this mess."

"What shall we do?" I nudge her shin with a hoof, urging her back from the past, to the present.

"We don't really have a choice, Val. We don't know what they have, but well, I bet they wouldn't bluff." She sighs, then catches my look. "We'll wait and see. He said they were old friends, yes? Hopefully they remember that, at any rate," she finishes, standing up and striding down the hall past me. Her hooves clack against the white linoleum with such authority. Each tap beckons me to join her. I hesitate for a moment, standing alone among the white halls, the smell of disinfectant strong. I know I can't though.

"I hope they remember too," I say, to no one in particular.

It's odd. For that entire time, I just wanted her to kiss me and say she'd figure things out. Just like before.

**

That evening I go to confession. Even though the conclaves in the Spires above haven't come to a ruling about Chimera, there were still those devout enough to believe they could forgive our sins. As a result, it's just a nondescript building with some sealed booths, complete with voice distorters and sealed vents between sides so no one can identify by scent; a weird cross between a phone booth and an ATM.

I've never wholeheartedly gone for these things. A lot of people don't, but there's a strange comfort in knowing that you can empty your guts to someone, have them listen and not judge. There's a fine line between ranting to yourself or to someone, and that same line makes the difference between going crazy or not.

I look for a booth with an amber light on the switchboard, indicating that someone was present and ready. Sealing the booth, the light flicks green as I turn the audio on.

It's weird hearing the distorted voice as you speak—loud enough to overpower your own.

"It's been a while since I've used one of these," I begin, aiming to cut off a lecture on how things worked.

"How long since your last?"

"I lost track after a year."

"Well, it's good that you're here now," the voicebox replies. "What do you wish to talk about?"

"I need advice," I hold my head in my hands, massaging my temples.

"We tend to find the two go hand in hand. How can you hope to have good advice if you don't give the whole picture?"

"Because I don't believe anything can be done."

Silence. The light flicks back to amber momentarily. The only sound that made me sure my companion was there being the sound of their breathing.

"Don't be afraid. I'm not here to judge."

"Where could I start? I'm married to someone I don't love because the breeds can't marry outside of their species. I've all but lost my faith. I've got a bunch of criminals blackmailing me about the one I do love. And I'm stuck in this God-forsaken prison we call a District, reminded more every day I look in the mirror at how I failed to make a change. What's your advice on that?" I snap, flicking the audio off. Sometimes it feels good to shout.

Deep breaths, get yourself together.

"I'm sorry. I didn't mean that. It's just… I don't see a way out from all of this." I add. I wasn't sure if my sincerity conveyed across the distorter—there was a long pause.

"Why are you here?" comes the terse reply.

"Because I've not quite yet given up hope on changing things for the better."

"For yourself, or for others?" The audio is quicker than usual.

"I don't trust myself to know that answer."

"Then how can anyone help you, if you don't know how to help yourself?" The audio finishes, the light turning red and the door opening. I sigh and grind my teeth before leaving, stepping out of the building into the street and waiting downpour.

Rain is a strange simulation in the Haven. When there was more space, the vast network of irrigation pipes tended to the once green fields. Swallowed up as the city grew and written off once the labs could meet their agricultural targets, they found a new lease of life in maintaining ideal atmospheric conditions. Perhaps more importantly, the simple trickle of raindrops helped to diffuse the tension of living in a giant bell jar.

I trot along, trying to keep out of the worst of the deluge, only to recognise the wolf on the pavement. Reika laughs as he stands in the rain, waterdrops curling about neatly as they run off his mane. He does a little spin for me, waving a radio between his paws.

"That was a fun little chat wasn't it?" he calls, flashing that grin of his.

"You were eavesdropping?"

"The other option, Hoofer. It's not in my nature to be so passive." He skips over towards me, his tail flapping about behind him. "I didn't think the past bothered you."

"Just one more thing you've got wrong about me," I huff.

"Come with me then." The wolf grins and took the lead, eyes goading me to follow.

***

Against better judgement, I follow Reika down to the promenade. Unlike the rest of the Haven, it was an attempt at terraforming, sometime between after the war and before the Spires rose. A seafront built in mock Victorian style, it was promptly abandoned due to its proximity to the Districts, but officially due to its inability to circulate a current in the lagoon, leaving a mess of stagnant water and boarded up buildings.

We duck under crooked railings and wander across the beach, following the sea wall. I guess at one time they'd planned it to hold back the waves; instead it stood a silent reminder over our futility to shape the earth. Every so often I catch the scent of urine and stale beer. Reika comes to a halt underneath the stilts of a pier, where a single black door stands sternly bolted into the sea wall. Producing a key, he quickly unlocks it and pulls me through, slamming it shut. I wince as I hear the faint clack of a lock falling into place somewhere behind me.

Red light glows from neon tubes attached to the ceiling, following a tunnel that curves downwards. I blink and rub my eyes, listening as I hear noises from deeper below. Beside me, Reika grins, his teeth a deep red in the light. He pushes me forward, chuckling to himself.

"Go on," he whispers, nudging me again. Placing my hooves gingerly on the uneven steps, I go, listening to the wolf's quick breathing behind me. After a couple of minutes, the floor levels out, the concrete changing to tiles covered in some obscure floral pattern. Mattresses and soft furnishings lie thrown down in a haphazard fashion, with various mixed breed couples lounging together, the scent of their taboo accented by the acrid wisps of incense drifting in from some shadowed corner. I hadn't been to a den in at least fifteen years, not since I met Kira, and certainly not since my stint in containment. That certainly closed a lot of doors in disreputable circles, but neither was cowering underground for a quick stay of reality truly satisfying.

"Keep going," Reika breathes, sounding distant. He skips in front of me, beckoning as he disappears behind another door, down another flight of dimly lit steps, until the air becomes cold, and the ambience behind us gives way to the sound of dripping water. He pops the latch of a derelict fire door, and walks into a small, cosy room littered with scattered pages from ripped books and waxy marks from spilt candles.

"I wonder how long it will take for them to close this down."

He shrugs my words off, eyes flashing up to meet my own, reflecting the dim light. "They? Do you honestly believe those above us care what we do?" He shook his head. "They'll never come down here—Humans forfeited the earth, reaching instead for the sky." He snatched a dark bottle from a shelf, lapping his tongue across the top before gulping it down. "The purists won't find us all, and when we move on, another one will pop up to replace this one." He sounds nothing like he does on the surface; much calmer, less confrontational. Vulnerable even.

"They'd lock you in containment though. I was in containment, and believe me you don't—"

"Chimera can't lock each other in containment." He glares at me. "Even then, you were soft. You gave in. You believed they couldn't be beaten." I say nothing as he brushes his hands over my faded scars. Fur can cover a lot, just like time and words of change.

"No," I huff, flicking my tail about behind me with an audible swish. "I believe we can beat them another way."

"But who is 'they' now?" He shifts about, pulling at the silver beads in his tail. "Who enforces their law? Who keeps the breeds in their districts? Who decides to allocate our time off district? The day we agreed to settlement was the day we agreed to police ourselves."

For once I don't ignore the pull in my stomach; I don't ignore my instinct. I knew it was true. The CDC drew up the districts, plotted the boundaries, made the policies. We put together the plan; the Spires simply signed it off.

"Why though?"

Reika simply handed me a scrap of paper. From the blackened and blotched verse, a simple phrase caught my eye.

'Better to reign in hell, than serve in heaven.'

The wolf sighs, looking at me with forlorn eyes, pulling out a photograph from behind a cushion. It's dog-eared and crinkled, but the image itself is still recognisable—that one of Kira and me from that night. He crooks his head to the side, nodding.

"It's still a powerful image," he sighs. "Your generation may remember it, mine doesn't. We both know it's not printed in the new history books." He looks up at me, no longer fierce—ears drooping, eyes wide. That sharp, amber tone is gone. "What were you thinking then?" His gaze goes back to the photograph. "I'd like to know."

"What do you think?" I reply softly.

"Nothing else but her."

We stay silent for a moment, listening to the murmur of air somewhere above us; the distant drop of water echoing from somewhere below. I feel half-tempted to have sympathy for him. Then he pulls his head back and laughs, long and loud.

"God, I haven't even had much to drink and here I am being all sentimental." He paces about, his tail brushing against my thigh as he stalks past. "Wait here," he commands, before disappearing somewhere behind me. There is a rapid knock, and the door swings open. Reika motions someone to enter but remains outside on his own.

It's hard to make him out in the red light because his fur is black, so too are his eyes—no colour in the iris. Kira told me it was a rare flaw that shows up in wolves only; another tidbit I remember from her talking about her research. His footsteps are quiet and deliberate and he sits down before me in one twisting, fluid motion without as much as a sign of effort.

"Old friend," the wolf rumbles, inclining his muzzle.

Toro has kept the quiet intonation that made everyone lean in to hear his words. He still has that mystique about him that the girls found so enthralling, and that I confess had gotten the better of me some nights too.

"I thought you were dead," I whispered, struggling to keep control over my tongue. I hadn't seen him since he fell from the bridge.

"You could say that for a long time, I have been," he counters. Though I can't see it, I know he is giving me one of those thin, fangless grins that were his signature; something he developed to keep the other breeds at ease. "Surprised?"

I sit down next to him on the couch. "You can smell that. You do know they were pretty keen to know where you were while I was rotting in containment." I chew my lip. "You could have said something, sent some message."

"What would that've achieved?" He smiles.

"I mean when I got out."

"You had changed. You thought in spite of the sacrifice, we had won. You seemed happy with the settlement process, saying your prayers, setting up a home. You wanted to stop fighting and start living, and I get that." I feel his breath rush past me as he exhales, punctuated with some spicy tones from his last meal. "Everyone has to suffer for their cause." He leans back, scratching the ruff of his neck with a paw. "You thought you had paid your dues."

"I believed the other leaders were either dead or locked up. Besides, if you really believed I was done then, why drag me into your mess now?"

"You and Kira were never the leaders of our little revolution," he retorts, flicking a tuft of loose fur from his claws. "But you knew better than them how to capture hearts, and I'll admit I have missed talking with you," he laughs. "Please, don't waste anymore of my time. You could have done more, I could have involved you sooner—but neither of us are here to argue about the past." He runs his tongue over his lips, wetting them again, still careful not to show his fangs—quite the courtesy. "Remember, I could ruin things for you if I wanted," he says coldly.

"Toro—"

"Enough. We both did—do—what we need to," he growls. "And I need you to do something." The old wolf leans against me, angling his back so he rests against mine. I feel him shift as he tilts his head up, his muzzle coming within inches of my ears, which swivel round to meet the sound of his breathing. The rise and fall of his chest matches mine, and I can feel the thud of his beating heart against me. I remember how he used to do this just before he fucked you.

"I know you love Kira. I know she loves you. I need you to speak to her." I hold back my question—why not yourself? But then again, she never liked Toro; 'full of tricks and creepy movements,' she said.

"You know the Underground. You know we've been smuggling people out of the Haven for decades now. The world's changed like you wouldn't believe out there. The other Havens have opened up and trade with each other; there's tracts of land now that've been scrubbed clean. Not by man, by nature itself. We have clean water. Fertile soil. Low counts. In short, there's a place where we can be free.

We just need more doctors."

"Oh no—you do not seriously think I can convince her to drop everything—"

"It's not dropping everything when it would let the two of you finally be free," he says smoothly.

"What about this Haven then? Have you given up on them?"

"Why would you think I want that?" he replies. His wolf-accent is really quite thick; if I close my eyes it almost sounds like a cat purring throatily. Almost. "We were so close, but we never got past the bridges. Sure, there's some change, but I won't risk my neck for those who are satisfied to live with a trickle of it. We can smuggle one or two people out, sure. Not three Districts."

I stand up, but the wolf was already on his feet and in front of me. God I'm out of shape.

"What about the humans? Are they really going to turn a blind eye to Chimera settlements?" I counter. I couldn't believe such activity went unnoticed.

"Their answer to their past is to forget about the earth. They look to the stars," he chuckled, shaking his mane. He grips my hands, squeezing them gently, as if trying to transfer his strength into mine. "You can stand here and lie to me how you're both happy with your classes and your waylock privileges, but I'll cut you short," he snaps, darting closer, resting his fangs against his lips. "I'll remind you, all I have to do is hand things to the right people and your little house of cards will tumble down." He growls, snapping his jaws loudly in the space next to me.

"My son will show you out," he grumbles, and at that call Reika came swiftly in.

***

At first Kira refuses to open the door, but once I remind her that her refusal to let me in will only arouse further suspicion, she lets the waylocks draw. I brush my hooves on the cute owl doormat, but she still snaps at me.

"Do you have any idea what you're doing?" She shoots at me the old, familiar glare. This is against our rules—we do not, ever, meet at home.

I shrug. "We have to talk," I reply, cutting her off. "It can't wait."

"Oh, I'm sure!" she huffs, throwing her arms up—as if to say, come put me into containment now.

"Don't be angry with me—please, just listen." I snap back, trying at least to steer the conversation in the direction I want, that really, I believe we both want.

"Angry? You just barge in here in the early hours of the morning—I can't even imagine how many violations you've just clocked," she retorts, sitting down at her desk. My eyes wander around the single room; the messy bed in one corner, a sink and microwave on a counter in another. A gnarled wardrobe stands ajar, showing her few clothes; plain, without colour. Only her desk gave the room any sense of personality; bits of paper, annotated print outs, and photographs of various birth defects in the breeds lay strewn across it. She stacks them to the side, massaging her temples.

"I saw Reika tonight—"

"Of course this is about Reika," she mutters, folding her arms. "I wish those idiots would realise I've got better things to do with my time—my research, my teaching; it all helps."

"Actually, it's kind of about us." I whisper. I am not entirely wrong.

"No, I'm not even going to entertain—" she begins, grabbing hold of my arm to try and shove me away, but instead she kind of just collapses inside them, her attempt morphs into a hug. I feel her shudder as she holds me close to her chest. It's hard to keep the act up forever.

"You know I don't love Edna," I admit. "Look," I shrug, holding her tightly. "I can't lie, I have been speaking to Reika. Yes, he *is* with the Underground. The thing is, they—Toro—has an offer—"

"Of course," she grumbles, "he's too stubborn to just die."

"If you believed there was a way out, somewhere other than here, would you take it?"

She stirs in my arms, taking a deep breath.

"We all have dreams."

"Kira. They've found a place. Turns out the reason things have been so quiet is that they've spent most of their energy building out there."

She giggles. "Do you really believe the Havens wouldn't notice, let alone allow Chimera to settle outside the domes?"

"Apparently, as long as we're not penned in on the same side of the wall as them. We both know they don't care for the earth anymore." I chuckle. "Kira, they need someone who can do more than just bandage cuts and set bones. You'd be helping people, doing what you do best."

"What I was bred to do," she counters. "I'm doing good here. I'm teaching the next generation, passing down what I know, doing research."

"You could still do it out there. You wouldn't have to worry about CDC approval."

"It's not just that!" She grinds her teeth. "In here, as much as I hate to say it, we have security. Stability. You ever wonder why Toro needs another doctor—did you even ask? Because call me a cynic, a coward or whatever, but I bet it's no paradise out there."

She has me there. Maybe I'm forgetting that this is blackmail, that Toro has made threats otherwise, but standing there in her study, seeing her in her pale nightdress, I'm only thinking about the two of us. At the end of the day, love and self-preservation are hardwired as two selfish instincts.

"What about the list of things we've never done?" I murmur, running my hand lower down her back.

She shivers. "You're such a manipulator."

"Not when the feeling's mutual," I tease, my hands trailing softly across her thighs. Hers still linger upon my shoulders, but I could feel them twitching as she tries to resist. Surely, they begin to wander, reaffirming themselves with where they used to roam. "I'm tired of keeping up appearances. I'm tired of lying. I'm tired of looking in the mirror and seeing a stranger staring back at me, of having to pretend that I don't love you, and then when I'm with you, being unable to surrender to how I feel."

She laughs softly, kissing me breathlessly. "I was waiting for you to put it that way. You never really needed to convince me," she murmurs. "That's the sad thing. In spite of everything; the progress, the research… I just want to have something for *me*." Her pupils dilate. "Don't you hate yourself for being afraid—for not having the spirit to stand up. I know mine gave out long ago, and I just covered it up, saying bravery was going on as normal."

"All those people thought that picture of us meant something. I've spent a good portion of the quiet hours of the night not knowing whether to laugh or cry about how pathetic it all is."

"We did what we had to. Not everyone can make big changes."

"Well, we don't have to," I whisper. "Tonight we can start where we left off," I grin.

"After all these years?" She smirks, pulling my hand as she takes me to bed.

***

Toro skulks in the shadows. He squints, shielding his eyes, unaccustomed as they were to the daylight from below the Spires as he stands by the service door.

"What a welcome party," I scoff, surprised that he'd deign to show his face above ground.

"I wanted to see it for myself," he replies, the faintest sliver of a smile appearing at the corners of his muzzle. "I see you packed light," he sniffs, raising an eyebrow.

"We took what we needed," Kira says, ignoring how the wolf's snout glistens as it quivers in the air.

"You're here now," he shrugs, disappearing behind the door.

"Only you today then?" I ask, wondering where Reika lurked.

"For where we're going, two's usually a risk," he sighs, the black ruff about his neck shifting slightly. "It stands to reason that the more you try it with, the more likely someone will get caught," he growls, his mane pricking at the nape as he slinks back into the darkness.

"Well…" Kira exhales, holding her hands up. It's not like we have much of a choice, but at least this time it is, in part, our fault. "You coming then?" She grins at me, reminding me of that youthful smirk she'd shown thirty years ago.

At first the tunnels are familiar—we go down, following the black wolf who pads on ahead silently. I recognise the den—the remains of it. The red bulbs are shattered, leaving an array of glass that crunches under my hooves as we walk on ahead. Even though his pads are soft, Toro doesn't ever flinch; he treads on ahead all the same. The mattresses are empty, the walls peeled bare. Here and there, a needle or two gleams as it catches the light, but there's nothing to make sense of. All their scents are garbled up into one; impossible to pick one out.

"We move on every so often," Toro says, breaking the silence.

"Reika will burn it out, and when they come sniffing around here, there'll be nothing."

We continue down, deeper into tunnels that become less and less accommodating. They are no longer shelters but cramped maintenance tunnels, filled with hissing pipes and dripping water that snake and twist like mad roots. In some sections we squeeze past burning metal, crawling, scraping, shimmying, following some path deeper into the bowels of the Haven—a route that only Toro can make sense of.

All the while my mind begins to wander about what lies outside. I was born inside the Haven, raised in it, fought for the right to live in it. I've never seen the world outside; my dreams of it were full of ruddy haze and oily colours. Now I will get to see it, and I don't know what to expect.

"Look," Toro whispers, pressing a button and pointing up. A single shaft of pale light trickles down from a speck up above, illuminating the cramped shaft—and a ladder—leading all the way up. "The surface," he breathes, the sound catching in his throat. "You go first," he says, stepping aside. "It's important for you to be the first to see it."

Without as much as a protest, I push Kira forward. She grips me by the arm, trying to shove me back, but instead she just pushes me back against the pipes. Her breathing flutters erratically against my neck; matching mine.

"Please." I roll my eyes. "I'm not getting hung up over it." She relaxes for a moment, running her eyes over me. "It's not like it won't be there for me to see either."

"More to the point, it's not wise to hang around here while the vent is open," Toro mutters, his tail flicking about impatiently behind him. Kira gives the wolf a sour look, then starts her climb. I follow behind, with Toro moving softly below me. It is slow—hand over hand, hooves clipping the metal bars loudly, the sound reverberating all through the shaft. Slowly the light grows stronger. Then white sphere swallows Kira as she scrambles up the final rungs.

For a moment, I hesitate.

"Don't bail on me now," Toro growls. "I don't want to die because of you," he finishes. He nips my legs, forcing me upward—they of course bred out the urge to kick.

When I get to the top, Kira's arms reach down to grab my own. It's hard to see. I try to peel my eyes open, but I keep on squinting, trying to adjust from the dark. God, it's bright. I feel the wind on my shoulder, it's a cool, pleasant breeze. I can smell Kira next to me.

Then I realise. The brightness—this is a white spire. I see the blue sky ahead, sealed in by glass that glints in the light above. And as I turn to run back to the shaft, Toro slams the cover shut.

Bastard.

I don't recall swearing, but I could feel my rage ripple through my voice, through the air.

"I'm sorry." I could hear it rising up from beneath the cover, a low, pitiful whine. "This is the only way."

"For what?" Kira shouts, sinking to her knees as the sirens wailed away in the distance. I stand up, looking all around. The bridge. It has barely changed from that night. On one side the sealed gate of the upper District, the other the smooth white bases of the Spires, circling up towards the sky, caught in a moment of dance.

"When people saw that photograph, you were their heroes. We had a sign; a clear vision, a just cause—something neither I, nor the Underground, could ever be. And for a time, the people held to that through your detention. But when you came out..." he trails off, as if—I think—he sobs, "when the icons of the revolution supported settlement, they stopped fighting too. They settled down. They gave their way a try, and look where it's gotten us. Still looked down upon. Still sub-human. Because of you, the struggle died out."

"So you what, you sacrifice us so you don't have to bleed yourself?" Kira screams, pounding at the metal cover with her fists.

"I died when I fell from this bridge. You became the lifeblood of the movement, and you squandered it. The people allowed themselves to be cowed because their idols were cowed too."

"You're sick," Kira spits.

"This world's sick," Toro roars. "It's always taken the sacrifice of good people to make it better."

"Pity it couldn't be yourself."

"I wish. Sacrificing yourself is easy. Sacrificing others is hard. Only this way they'll see. They'll feel anger. Outrage. A tragedy to remind them what needs to be done."

I remember holding her in my arms.

I remember wishing for another second, grabbing her, pulling her behind me as I kiss her.

And finally, I remembered that kiss from the photograph, all those years ago. In response, something seemed to click.

I'm having trouble boosting the signal, so if you can pinpoint the nearest working tower on your set, lock onto it with the code I've included and that will smooth out the transmission feed. That's better. I was worried I'd lose you.

Where was I? Oh yes. There's an order to things, they say, a way things have always been. Rising tides and rising ire can't shake the bedrock upon which society is built, or so some assume.

But you can only pull the wool over someone's eyes for so long. Complacency with the status-quo is a master's weapon, but it can also belong to the downtrodden as well. Listen to this, sister...

GLOVES

James L. Steele

I stepped inside my husband's house for the last time and closed the door. I set the blue lunch bag on the carpet, making sure it was still zipped, and unclasped my wrap. As I unwound the single piece of thin cloth from my body, my eyes wandered down to the lunch bag. It was identical to mine, but it was not mine. I hadn't even looked in it since I met Ant today, but it had been on my mind as I worked on the factory line and during the bus ride home.

One of Ant's questions came back to me now: "Eighteen. Why are you required to cover yourself in public, but he is not?"

I had always believed what I was taught in school: that my fur was too thin for this climate, so we wrapped ourselves in cloth to be more comfortable. I had never once thought about why my husband never wore one until I attended the meetings.

I hung the cloth on the hook by the door, picked up the lunch bag and strolled through the hallway, keeping an even composure and hopefully an even scent.

From the living room I heard gentle moaning. Mouse had come home earlier, and our husband was on top of her. Mouse glared at me as I walked past the couch and into the kitchen. I met Mouse's eyes, flashing hate at her, making sure she knew she was not the only lioness in this house and I could challenge her whenever I wanted.

There had been a time when it would have occupied my thoughts all night, when jealousy would run through me and I would do everything I could to be the better wife so Rocke would be with me instead. It had consumed me for so long I felt embarrassed by how much time it had taken out of my life.

As I listened to them from the kitchen, several more of Ant's questions came to mind.

"Four. Why does your husband have his own room, but you live and sleep in the living room with the other wives?"

"Twenty-two. Why do you spend your free time fighting with the other wives for your husband's attention?"

I opened the refrigerator and slid the lunch bag onto the lowest shelf. Rocke might open it, looking for food, but that was a chance I was willing to take. If he discovered what I had brought home, I figured I could simply flee. I only had the gloves, but I did not have to use them. All day at work I did not imagine myself using them.

I walked back to the living room and sat on the couch opposite Mouse and Rocke. Mouse glared at me, growling and moaning extra loud, making sure I noticed she was under him, not me. I growled back, trying to sound full of fury and pushing it through my scent. I was acting the part now, but just a few months ago, I did not need to act. Back when the emotions were real and I desperately wanted to be where Mouse was now, all the time, and no other wife would take my place. I did not miss those years.

Minutes later, Meek walked through the door. I heard her unwrapping, and then Rocke's third wife pranced into the living room. Mouse growled at her, moaning extra loud to show Meek her place. Meek growled back, sat beside them, slipped a piece of paper between two of the cushions and immediately began doting on Rocke. Our husband nuzzled Meek as he thrusted into Mouse.

I watched them. I had been watching them for months, keeping the questions in mind. The nuzzle had nothing to do with affection. It was a subliminal reminder that he would get her next if she were good. The sight disgusted me even more today than usual.

Rocke finished with Mouse. The large lion climbed off her and sat on the couch facing the television. Mouse continued licking Rocke's muzzle, feeling his chest. Meek sat on the other side of him and began straightening his mane for him.

"It's your payday," Rocke said to Meek.

"It is!" she said, reaching behind her, pulling the piece of paper from between the cushions and presenting it to Rocke. "All the overtime paid off! I made one-eighty this week!"

"One-eighty. Nice." Rocke tuned to Mouse. "You hear that, Mouse?

Meek brought in one-eighty. What was yours last week, one-twenty?"

"I begged for overtime," Mouse said, still cuddling up to him, feeling his fat body up and down. "But they told me they didn't need anyone else."

"Sounds like you just have to try a little harder next time," Rocke said, nuzzling her. He then fixed his eyes on me.

I saw what was happening. Rocke kept his wives in constant competition. He told everyone who made what in a week, and for most of my life I had been driven by intense desire to have the biggest paycheck.

Mine had been inadequate compared to the other wives' for a long time. Instead of begging for more hours, I went to the meetings. At first I had been terrified of losing favor with my husband, and it had given the other wives an advantage over me, but as time went by, I discovered falling out of favor with Rocke was not such a horrible thing. It had allowed me to step back and observe what was happening and ask questions.

Rocke never said anything to me about my checks. He never had to. He let the other wives' reactions move me. Knowing they would rise in rank as I slipped down—knowing he would favor them over me—it was more than enough to keep me in line back then.

"It's your payday, too, Flora," he said.

Meek paused feeling our husband up and glared at me. "Yeah, Flora, what did you bring home?"

Mouse also faced me. "Did you even work at all?"

I played my part and growled at both of them. "I work every day of my life to keep this house going. Not my fault they won't let me work more."

"So where is it?" Meek said.

"Let's see it!" said the other lioness.

"I think I left it in my wrap."

I had done it on purpose to give me a reason to leave the room for a few seconds so I wouldn't have to watch the other wives destroy themselves over this lion.

I stood and walked back to the door, reached into the cloth that covered me during my workday and pretended to hunt for the paper. I took much longer to find my paycheck than I needed to. I expected Rocke to mount Meek while I was gone, and the jealousy still rose within me, but now I knew where it came from.

When I was ready to be in the same room with the lion and his wives, I pulled out my check. I hadn't even read it. I knew it would be low, and I knew what Rocke's reaction would be.

I returned to the living room, sat down and handed Rocke the paper. The male took it, letting his claws peek from his fingers just to remind me of what I lacked. He read it over.

"You only put in forty-eight hours this week."

"And you only brought home ninety-two!" Mouse said.

Upon sight of my paycheck, the other two wives felt and cuddled up to Rocke even harder.

"How do you explain this, Flora?" Rocke said.

"Work is cutting back. They're making us work off the clock for part of our shifts until things improve."

"Sounds like you need to find a new job," Rocke said.

"It's difficult to look when I have to work."

Rocke smiled at me, showing me the sharp teeth. It was not a smile of affection. It was a smile of being aroused by the two wives on either side of him. Wives who brought home more. Wives who had done so much more to earn his favor.

I remembered entire years when the mere sight of this would have made me scared to lose my place in the family. I would have doted upon Rocke even harder, begging him to be patient and promising to do better next time. I would have gone to work early, begged for more hours, begged for a promotion, begged to be moved to a different line where they had more hours, or even to do something hazardous so I could compete with Meek, Mouse, and Kept.

Earlier this year I pleaded with my boss. His name was Stalk. He ran the line, walking around naked among an entire factory of clothed lionesses. His signature was on my late-commuter's passcard, alongside my husband's. I begged him for favor the same way I begged my husband. That's when I first met Ant.

As soon as Stalk was out of earshot, Ant leaned over and whispered. "Question number one. Why do you do all the work, but your husband stays home?" And then she walked away. Left me to ponder that for almost a week.

When I met Ant again, she gave me question number two. "Why are males always the bosses, and the females always on the assembly line?"

Another week went by. I began to notice it was true. The males were always in authority, and the females were the workers. No exceptions. I found Ant during lunch break, and this time she told me to meet her after my shift.

We met in an alley a few blocks from the factory. Several other lionesses had come, and Ant began to ask more questions. Some of the females had been there before and were called upon to recite specific numbers. The meetings consisted of repeating these to one another. Never answers. Never discussion. Just us standing in an alley, reciting questions. Back then I didn't understand why the meetings were run this way.

Rocke watched television. Meek and Mouse sat on opposite sides of him, stroking and licking and doting on him. I didn't feel the need to try to work my way to the preferred position anymore. It had once occupied my entire existence outside of work.

An hour after I came home, Kept walked in the door, removed her wrap, and knelt in front of our husband. Her last paycheck was only slightly higher than mine, and I shuddered watching her try to keep her rank in the family.

Three females feeling up one male at once, each begging to be the preferred lioness, to be the first to have his cubs. All four of us had been doing this for years.

We had been talking about raising children for quite some time, but Rocke was not ready for it yet. I remembered entire years going by yearning to have his children, hoping he would pick me over them. Now I asked for my pill every week.

As I watched them, I shuddered thinking about number sixteen: "Why do they compel us to take a pill that keeps us in heat year-round, but prevents eggs from being released?"

Kept continued trying to raise her rank in the family. I watched. Because my paycheck was the smallest, I was expected to be the distant one, not worthy of her husband's attention. I accepted my place. I had no right even to ask for attention until my paycheck was third highest.

Kept rose from Rocke's crotch and tried to lick his muzzle. Meek and Mouse both growled at her. Kept growled back. They both lunged for her, knocking her down and rolling around on the carpet. They mouthed necks, swiped barren paws at muzzles and eyes. Rocke sat on the couch and watched, flexing his hands, making his claws slide out and in.

I idly flexed my hands. No claws came out. That was number twenty-eight: "Why are females required to be declawed upon birth, but not males? Why must females have their teeth filed blunt, but not the males?"

I had been taught that lionesses were a danger to each other, and it was for their safety. Fights like this were common, and we couldn't have lionesses hurting each other. I had been part of many scuffles over the years, and now I wondered how I never saw the underlying reason behind all of it before.

In moments, the fight was over, and Kept knew her place in the family. Mouse and Meek took their positions on the couch at either side of their husband, and Kept took hers on the floor, at the lowest position, nuzzling Rocke's feet.

The late-night meetings in the alley had filled me with all kinds of questions. So many things to think about. Nothing but questions. So many questions for months that helped me see my life in entirely new ways.

Then Ant began taking me aside at random moments of the day and asking these same questions, but this time her scent told me that she did not expect me to repeat the questions. She wanted to know if I had answers.

The first time was during lunch break about a month ago. She had sat next to me and repeated number twenty-four. "Why do they give us diminutive names?"

I did not even have to think before I spoke. "Because it's how they think of us."

And we talked like nothing was different. I had plenty of questions I wanted to ask Ant, but the timing never seemed to be right.

The next day Ant asked me number eleven. "Why is it law that a lioness can't go outside city limits without her husband?"

"Because males make the laws to keep us in our place."

The next day Ant asked question number nine. "Why are you in competition with his other wives?"

"To keep me so busy I won't have time to think."

"Why is it illegal for a female to be without a job?"

"Working keeps us busy and thoughtless."

"Why is a female forbidden from interacting with a male other than her husband or boss?"

"It's a way for males to keep us from leaving the pride."

"Why do females go to different schools than the males?"

"They teach lionesses how to work. They teach the males how to own us."

The meetings had continued as usual, introducing the questions to many new lionesses. Some I never saw in the meetings more than once, but many others stayed and memorized the questions. I never gave any of them the answers I had come up with. The meetings were designed to produce the one thing the males did not want, and each lioness had to become that on her own.

A commercial came on. My husband rose from the couch, bent Meek over and mounted her over the armrest. Mouse and Kept sat on the floor and watched, growling at one another. Meek glared at both of them, moaning extra loud so the others could hear, subliminally reinforcing the feeling that they could be under him right now if only they had worked harder and brought home more money. Mouse and Kept would be driven to put in more hours, do more dangerous work, anything to earn Rocke's favor. I watched for a few minutes, pretending to be jealous, but feeling only disgust.

The longer I watched the angrier I felt. Prior to the meetings, I had only aimed it at the other wives in the family. Anger for surpassing me, anger for bringing home money, anger for being under Rocke instead of me. Now for the first time I realized this was exactly what I was supposed to do with the emotion. Exactly how males wanted me to feel.

But this anger was new. It was not directed at Meek, Mouse or Kept. Somehow Ant had known it would be time, and she had given me what I needed to act on it.

I stood and walked to the kitchen. I opened the refrigerator and unzipped the lunch bag. A pair of gloves lay inside. I slipped them over my hands, one at a time, then fastened the buckles around my forearms. They became part of my body. A part that had been taken from me at birth, more than merely my body, but my ability to do anything myself.

On the tips of the gloves were metal claws. Seeing claws on my hands felt right. The anger within felt right, and it flowed into my hands. There was never a happier marriage between mind and body than what I felt that night, that moment.

At lunch today, Ant had asked me the final question. Number thirty. "Are things different?"

I whispered my answer to the cold interior of the refrigerator, emptied daily by my idle husband who took all the food my years at the factory had bought.

"Males tell us we're living in modern times. Our factories make computer systems and automobiles. Medicine has saved countless lives. Technology eliminated the need to live in prides, where females did all the hunting and males merely guarded their territory from intruders. Now we herd the animals we used to hunt and we have leisure time to pursue our interests. But we still live in prides. The lionesses still do all the hunting, and the males do nothing but sit at home and collect wives. They keep us in this role because they benefit from it. We have not advanced beyond our primitive nature, and things are worse than ever because now they know what they are doing. Before, it was instinct. Now it is deliberate."

Ant stood up. "A job is waiting for you on the other side. Fifth and Broad tonight if you're ready."

Ant switched lunch bags with me as she walked away. I knew what was in the bag without even opening it. These gloves were only a rumor, but I had a feeling they would be waiting for me when I could answer all the questions.

Many lionesses never reached this level, the moment their anger was finally aimed at the right person, and they were ready to have their power back. When I first started learning the questions, I never imagined I would.

As the sound of Meek moaning and the other two lionesses begging for our husband's attention found me through the walls, trying to make me feel guilty for not working harder and earning my place under my husband, I looked at my new claws and relished my anger and the means to act on it.

I wasn't just a female. I was a lion. Instead of a desire to please my husband, hunt for him more, bring home money, I now created questions and answers of my own. It was my money. I earned it. Why couldn't I spend it? Why were males only allowed to deposit checks and make withdrawals? Because everything was set up to give me no way out of this. I wanted to make my own way out, and now I had the means.

I took the lunch bag from the refrigerator, turned and dropped it in the hall by the front door. Then I walked into the living room. Rocke was still on top of Meek. The other two wives looked on, growling, threatening one another, wordlessly reminding Meek that her position was not permanent. Our entire lives were wasted this way, and these females did not see it. I couldn't take it anymore. I opened my mouth and roared.

Everyone paused and turned their heads. Before they could recognize the gloves, I leaped over the couch and landed on both Meek and Rocke. My first instinct was to wrap my teeth around Rocke's neck, but I remembered my teeth were rounded and would not pierce his thick flesh. Instead, I shoved the claws into both sides of his neck.

My husband roared, thrashed, rolled over, taking all three of us down to the carpet with him. I held on and pushed the claws deeper, and then away, ripping them out of his neck. I had hit both the vein and the artery.

In just a couple swipes, it was done. I separated myself from Rocke and stood back, watching him panic. Watching him bleed. He was gazing up at me.

"Flora! What…? Wh…"

Meek, Kept, and Mouse cowered on the carpet, screaming and crying, keeping their distance from us.

"Flora…" The life was fading from his eyes already. "You were my… favorite. Why?"

I knelt down, held my bloody claws up to his eyes and screamed in his face. "We don't need you!"

Then I turned to the other three. "We don't need him! We don't need any of them! We do the work! We hunt! We bring home the meat! We bear the young! It should be us in control of everything! Why do we let them control us?"

The other wives glared at me, shaking, crying.

"Remember the questions I asked you? Didn't any of you think about them? If you stay, they'll put you with another husband, and you'll have to compete even harder for his attention! It won't end! This will change nothing unless you come with me!"

But there was no comprehension in their eyes. Only grief that the center of their lives was dying, and all their work had been for nothing. There was no convincing them. They had never asked a question in their lives other than how to make their husband happy. Beyond this worry that consumed every waking thought, they did not know how to ask questions, let alone answer them. They were the victims of this order I had to fight for.

"If you change your minds, find me."

I looked down at Rocke one last time. He was still breathing, but the carpet under his head was soaked and more blood still rushed out of his neck. I turned and walked to the door. I quickly unbuckled the gloves and shoved them in the bag, then I walked out and down the street.

It was illegal for a female to be out this late without her husband, or a work permit signed by her husband and her boss, so I was asking to be arrested. The officers would be female, but they, too, were unconscious of this system they were trapped in, and they would not listen to me. I walked down the dim alleys between the apartment complexes and row houses and abandoned factories, clutching the lunch bag close to my chest.

I stopped at the corner of Fifth street and Broad. I couldn't stop thinking about what he had said. I was his favorite. The whole time he had been rooting for me. The thought made me shiver.

Moments later, I caught a familiar scent approaching behind me. I turned around and met Ant's eyes. She was unclothed, and the sight of an unclothed female who was not my husband's wife made me nervous. I averted my eyes from her.

Ant embraced me. That's when I noticed she was wearing a pair of gloves of her own.

"Welcome to the revolution," she said.

I cried. "Why did I do that? How am I going to eat? How am I going to live!"

"That's what happens when you're allowed to be what you are. I will lead you out of the city. There are places you can go."

"Then what? I've been living to please him so long... What am I supposed to do now!"

She held me tighter. My husband had held me like that, always making sure to extend his claws, scratching me, reminding me who was in control without need to say a word. The gesture felt different now. Ant did not touch me with her claws. She had known the same gesture and treated me like a lioness, not merely a female.

"Anything you want. You can become a recruiter, an assassin, a saboteur, or anything else. Eventually we hope to start a nation of our own, where everyone works, and her work benefits herself. Not them."

I cried again. "I loved him. I loved him so much. He said I was his favorite! He said it with his dying breath!"

"He didn't love you. Even if he didn't know it, he was only using you. It's their nature. Before we go, you have to choose a new name."

"A new name?"

"My name outside the city is Runner. It was my husband's before I killed him. I gave it dignity. You are not Flora. You will not be trampled and subdued anymore. What is your name now?"

I thought about that for a long moment. I disliked standing here in this cold alley, naked and shameful in front of this other female. But these were old impulses. They would pass soon enough.

"My name is Rocke," I said. "I will give it dignity."

Runner released me and met my eyes. I did not turn my gaze from her now.

"Follow me." Runner dashed down the alley. I chased her tail.

Going somewhere other than the factory without my husband was a new feeling for me. Even while running, I was not cold. I did not need the wrap. I would never wear one again.

So much goes on behind the worlds we build, so many things to maintain, so much decay to battle.

As the weariness of keeping it all going sets in, you outsource your struggles and leave unimportant things to unimportant tools.

With all the strife and toil moved behind the scenes a nagging feeling creeps up.

Just what did we discard?

And what if the perfect world we seek isn't for us at all?

THE RECLAIMERS

Joseph Vandehey

It happened in a city I will not name, on a road I will not describe, out in the myriad identical desiccated East European ruins that humanity long ago abandoned. "Manufacturing output has dropped," my orders read. "Assess." So I packed my bags and left the gleaming mid-Atlantic megalopolis on the first flight I could to Berlin.

The landing, on a cracked, rarely used tarmac, was rough. The drive through the streets even rougher. My body, unused to such discomfort, was glad when we arrived at the station. The train, at least, was high-speed, cushioned, modern, meant primarily for shuttling items made inland to the coast where they could be shipped to the great sea cities, but they had a passenger car attached for when assessors like me needed to travel across land. I was the only person aboard the whole automated rail line that day. Likely the only person in months.

My colleagues—no, my friends—I do not wish to bore you with a travelogue. I did not take pains to send this letter confidentially to regale you with tales of my adventures. But it is necessary, truly necessary, to express to you the magnitude of what has happened by way of comparison. Please indulge me, be patient, and, above all else, swear to me your secrecy in this matter.

My fellow scientists, how long has it been since we have truly discovered something new? How long have our papers been rewriting and reconfirming what was already known? True, we delight in learning, but how long, my friends, since we have experienced the joy and the terror of the unknown?

That is what I offer you.

And that is why I demand your silence.

To return to my narrative, once I was past Berlin's city limits, beyond the last direct connections to human habitation, the only living beings I saw were livestock and the Vermin. Most of you, living comfortable lives asea, have never seen one of them. Perhaps you have never even heard of them. But in the cities, menial tasks are performed by expensive robots and we all know that someone or some*thing* far less costly must be toiling on the continents to provide us all the goods we require. The Vermin are genetically engineered rats, ferrets, raccoons, and otters with the occasional badger or other species thrown in. They stand a meter tall, with hunched shoulders, and brains pre-programmed with a certain task and enough intelligence to carry it out. A Vermin farmer waters a cornfield. A Vermin plumber fixes the water pipes when they leak. A Vermin picker harvests the corn. A Vermin loader monitors the corn being packed into crates. A Vermin driver takes the crates to the train. A Vermin stevedore offloads the crates onto boats. They are the new domesticates, the wheels by which humanity lives a life of luxury.

But their minds are limited. The same farmer who happily waters corn would be flummoxed by wheat. They have no inkling of the world beyond their pre-programmed task, the most basic of problem solving, and the necessities for survival.

And yet...

We scientists should not be surprised that simple programs could lead to complex results. The honeycombs of the bee, the mounds of the termite, the intricate networks of ant tunnels—all come from tiny brains following tiny sets of instructions. And are the results not magnificent?

You can see the same among the Vermin. Assessors have long noted what we call the spiderweb paths. As I looked out from the train, I could see them all across Europe: generation after generation of thousands of little feet creating pathways through the countryside. These paths had started as side-trails, but became bustling highways of Vermin, often improving on the efficiency of the old, abandoned roads. Each time I have gone past them, they have grown subtly more intricate; out in the country, old asphalt roads are reclaimed by plants, while the Vermin use their own trails exclusively. It is the law of unintended consequences at work.

I spent two hours on the train, until it stopped in Warsaw, the first destination in my tour of Eastern Europe. Although I was the only human in the city, there was an apartment ready for me at the station (maintained by the Vermin, of course). Where the rest of the city had fallen into decay, the room, like the train before it, was a marvel. I was told they rebuilt the station apartment once every five years precisely for the comfort of assessors. The constant chattering and squeaking of the Vermin made it hard to sleep at first, but my body, unused to such travel, soon succumbed to the soporific pull.

In the morning, I had the robotic kitchenette prepare me a hearty meal and some snacks for the journey. I wasn't too keen on relying on what the Vermin considered food: nutrient cubes of compressed algae. It was an unusual feeling. I was so used to being able to stop on any street corner and ask for any meal that came to mind. To go for miles without a proper kitchen was positively barbaric.

With my pockets stuffed with things to nibble on, I began to wander. Most of downtown had been razed to the ground to be replaced with a single factory. It stank of smoke and musk and grease and sweat. I found myself gagging for a few minutes until I acclimated. The noise was another matter. The Vermin were everywhere, constantly wandering the streets at all hours, pressing in from all sides, and they were constantly making sounds, squeaks or chirps or growls or hisses. A true cacophony, unceasing and unyielding. The smell I overcame long ago, after my second assessment trip. The sound I could never deal with. After my third visit, I had noise-cancelling earpieces made.

As strange and curious as the Vermin are to us, they, in turn, are indifferent to our presence. They treated me as little more than an obstacle in the road, and I had more than a few ferrets try to take a short cut by climbing right overtop of me. One cheeky fellow snatched a piece of my granola bar from my pocket and carried it on home, looking—if I may anthropomorphise them—especially smug.

Sometimes my duties require weeks of careful hunting to determine what is happening. It is like a puzzle, requiring knowledge of many areas to tease out the one thread of causation. Not so this time. I found the source of the manufacturing decline long before I had even reached the factory. Indeed, barely more than two blocks from my apartment at the train station.

You see, my friends, many of the old streets and buildings of Warsaw are still there. In their heyday, they must have been a wondrous sight (although they pale in comparison to today's aquatic cities). Now, though, the streets were paths for the Vermin, and the buildings repurposed into homes. Badgers huddled on the floor of restaurants under upturned tables. Rats nested in the shredded remains of beds in otherwise empty apartments. Otters sprawled over the counters of groceries, underneath signs saying "słodycze"— that is, "candy." (Wandering the ruins is an emotional experience, but few things have rent my heart like seeing a bookstore filled with great volumes be covered in shredded paper as it had been transformed into a home for weasels.) If one looked closely at all of these places, the cause of the manufacturing decline was immediate: it was winter, Warsaw was cold, the buildings were crumbling, and the Vermin needed insulation. They had nicked scraps of fabric or cotton—whatever was available—to use for themselves rather than recycling them as their programming had intended.

The law of unintended consequences had struck again. I theorized at the time that this was due to a conflict in their instructions. They had been commanded to recycle unneeded materials, but they had also been commanded to ensure their own survival. Warmth is critical to survival, so the two commands had battled in their minds until survival won out.

I would like to think Asimov would have been proud of that little deduction.

And yet I was concerned. No, I was worried. For there were two facts that this explanation did not cover. First, the Vermin should have been automatically given enough blankets to ensure they stayed warm. And second, the current winter was a mild one and should not have required any extra insulation. Why then were they gathering it?

The only reason I could give for their behavior at that moment was that they were stockpiling.

And yes, yes, I know what you will think. Impossible. Far beyond what they should be capable of. And if they were capable of this, what else? There was a moment, a fleeting moment only, when I wondered if the Vermin might be dangerous. But I had seen no evidence of that. I put it out of my mind and continued on.

I made a note to request that more such faux insulations should be ordered than used in manufacturing so that the Vermin would have a surplus. Alas, an assessor's job is not so easy. It would not do to guess that this was the whole source of the decline. I had to press on.

So out I went, first to the factory in Warsaw, and then farther, winding my way by train from city to village and village to city, working my way north and south in broad strokes and creeping my way ever further east. I had a Geiger counter in one hand as I approached the Russian wastes, leery of staying too long in those radioactive lands, even inside the shielded buildings that had been constructed for the Vermin.

The farther I went, the more the law of unintended consequences reared its face. More and more Vermin co-opted their duties to do something else, useful but unintended. In one town I noticed new construction work. No Vermin were trained to build, but they were made to maintain the factory there, and I found evidence that some of them were taking sheets of metal, the same that they would use to repair the factory walls and repairing walls of their homes. It gave the buildings an odd patchwork look: ancient red brickwork up against pure white structural plates.

And on and on it went. It was awe-inspiring and terrifying in equal measures. Vermin, who in theory should be unable to do more than maintain their base needs and attend their jobs, were beginning to repair the cities, little by little. Roads were repaved. New pathways were built. Bridges were fixed. Canals were dug alongside roads when sewers failed. New irrigation pipes were laid instead of repairing the old. Homemade awnings shielded the Vermin from rain. The programming we had left them with, which we had thought too simple, was in fact far more versatile. This too, I put in my report, couched in language to make it seem a benefit: it meant there was even less we had to worry about maintaining on land. My superiors are like most these days: people of luxury rather than people of study like ourselves. They were not trained to see the concerning questions that lay beyond my words.

Alas, I am a scientist and not a poet. I wish I had a better tongue for description so that you, my friends, might at least marvel with me. For the things that the Vermin built were new. In the cities on the sea, every building that is ever built is the same as every other building ever made. Endless copies. And yet, out here are new designs, new architecture. It was marvelous.

And then it happened.

Again, I will not say when or where, for fear of exposing them. Even to you, my friends.

It began as I was wandering a town, on a rarely used (even by Vermin) side street. I was taking notes on the frequency with which the Vermin were appropriating materials for unintended uses: how many items of faux clothing I noticed, or how many of them had wrapped cloth around their feet as makeshift shoes. I was ducking my head into buildings here and there to examine the interiors. And there, as I looked into an old jewelry store, I saw it. It was a long thin piece of gray cloth, hung from a rafter and pooling on the floor. A badger was there, and with deft movements he was sewing with some bright red thread. This was an unusual arrangement, even by the standards of what I had witnessed already, so I took some cautious steps closer. (The badger, like most Vermin, was unperturbed by my presence.)

The badger was sewing a square close to the bottom of the cloth, and as I looked up, I saw that the whole cloth was covered in such squares, some with a ball of bright blue in the middle. While the boxes were neatly arranged, the pattern of the blue balls was highly irregular, with clusters here and there. I stood staring dumbly for a half hour before in a flash of inspiration I checked the recent weather. Sure enough the blue balls corresponded exactly with the days on which there had been rain.

A calendar! My friends, they had made a calendar.

Every new thing I had seen from the Vermin prior to the point seemed a natural extension of their duties, but not this. I knew some Vermin managers made note of the weather to double-check the amount of water needed for irrigation that day using basic geometric pictograms. I knew some Vermin overseers had to make daily records of the amount of things they shipped. I knew, of course, that there were Vermin seamsters and seamstresses. I could see bits and pieces of how such a calendar could be created, but how—and more importantly, why—they combined their efforts to do this was beyond my comprehension.

This I could not put in my report. There is no way to paper over an act of original creation. To repair a few unintended things is of no big consequence, but for the Vermin tasked with one thing to do something wholly different… No, I could only imagine the result of such a report. Concern. Danger. Suspicion. Destruction. How could it be anything else when even I—yes, my friends, even I and I am not proud to admit it—felt the icy prickle of danger when faced with something alien. I wanted to tear apart this calendar and stamp on it until it was in tatters. I wanted this new thing destroyed utterly and completely. I wanted to run away and hide back where things are comfortable.

But I did not. I steeled myself and pressed on.

For, my friends, I did not write to you just to tell you of this one small thing of a calendar. There is still more. I wandered out from the jewelry store and its calendar with my head spinning under the possibilities. I paced the streets like a man half-asleep. Then, out of the corner of my eye, I saw a flash of yellow, an otter wearing a bit of color around her head like a veil. I had no immediate explanation for it, and despite the potential for danger that lurked in the recesses of my mind, I followed her on a hunch.

Like all the Vermin, she was quick, slinking and dodging through the throngs at a break-neck pace. I had to jog to keep up, far more than I usually do. I was worried I would lose her just because I would get exhausted. But just as suddenly as I had seen her, she stopped. It was at a church, small and provincial, presumably Roman Catholic. The roof had caved in, and the walls held only due to the ingenious masonry of ages past. The otter slipped past the broken front door, which I had to shove a bit in order to follow.

As I entered the main sanctuary of the church, I saw the light explode into colors. An old stained glass window had miraculously survived. It was a picture that I had my wrist-comp identify as St. Francis of Assisi. He was surrounded by animals, including, most prominently, an otter with a golden halo. The otter I had followed had a bed made just under the window, and she rested there with her equally golden veil.

As I looked closer, I saw the window had not just survived, but had been repaired. Some elements of the window were heated plastic from the factory in town.

I was still reeling from my encounter in the jewelry store. And this was something else. A calendar had a practical useful purpose. But what could art mean to the Vermin?

I wandered further into the church, around the massive bulk of the collapsed roof, and there, at what would be the altar of the church, I beheld what I could only describe as a shrine. There were icons of a dozen different religions and ideologies collected there, some in truly sacrilegious arrangements. A Christmas tree (plastic and eternal) stood in the center, a star of David at its pinnacle, garnished with ornaments of burnished red Buddha statuettes and pennants with hammer and sickle on them. The ground was covered in painted yin-yangs and Khandas, and along the walls were hung a hundred copies of the old flag of the country we were in.

I took a step closer, my hand reaching out to touch, and from behind me came a screeching. I spun to see the Vermin, who normally would take no notice of me, all gazing intently at me, mouths open in various growls or barks. I froze in place, with a feeling of fear crawling under my skin. I had never seen such behavior. Could they—would they—turn violent?

And the answer I knew in that moment was yes.

I am no expert in animals. What few beasts we keep in the cities are in zoos. All I could think to do was shrink myself down. Look small and unimportant. And slowly, they quieted. But even as I inched away from the shrine, torturous step by torturous step, I was aware of every eye in the building fixated on me. I fell into one of the pews, one of the few objects in the church neither destroyed nor in use. I swear to you I spent hours sitting there in silent contemplation, attempting to understand. How had the Vermin, whose minds were so simple, created this? Why had they created this? Why had they cared enough about it that they would not let me touch it? And what should I do?

As I sat, I thought of all the ways which we had over the years broken down intelligence between us and the animal kingdom. There were those who were the tool-users, and those not. There were those with complex social systems, and those without. There were those who were self-aware, and those not. There were those with detailed communication systems, and those without. In every case, humanity was never alone on one side of the spectrum. Chimpanzees themselves joined us in most measures of intelligence. The one thing we declared ourselves unique for was the very possibility of culture and history. And here there was culture, used and possibly understood in a rudimentary way by the Vermin.

Perhaps we humans have once again been too full of ourselves. We believed that culture set us apart, yet the Vermin have coopted it without even needing much intelligence of their own.

It made sense that they used these icons and flags: they were symbols that were constant over large areas of land, common enough to be seen across the land, but rare enough to be recognized as objects of importance. And the Vermin recognized that they were important things even if they understood nothing else. Perhaps that was all culture was. How many of us could, in an instant, explain the significance of a cultural icon other than, "It was important to others, and so it is important to me."

Or perhaps a better analogy was that of children, children too young to put complex thoughts into words, but who could still understand that an object was somehow meaningful.

We had, thinking we were only creating domesticated laborers, produced something new and original, beyond our wildest hopes and dreams.

And so I sat. And I thought. And I wondered what I must do for the longest time. Because one question above all others had to be answered and that same question above all others I did not know the answer to: what would happen when these children grew up?

And then I thought of us, of humanity. Has what we have done been so different?

Humanity is the ultimate integrator. The ultimate syncretist. Our modern monoculture contains elements of all the cultures that are no more: German, Japanese, Russian, South African, American, Peruvian—all can be found in bits and pieces still. Languages became loanwords. Cuisines became dishes. Religious dogmas became once-a-year observances. In that, the Vermin are as we are: reclaiming bits of our culture that we had tossed aside.

But then humanity has also been the great destroyer. Beyond those loanwords and dishes and observances, those cultures are gone forever.

We have destroyed everything else. I have seen it in my travels. Asia is a barren wasteland. South America is not long behind it. We spend our times on floating cities creating nothing that was not created before. There is no new art. There are no new scientific endeavors. There are no new buildings. We are stagnant, doing nothing more than prolonging our existence on this planet. We are a dying people and I do not know how much longer we can last.

We cannot keep the true nature of the Vermin secret forever. Nothing stays secret forever. And if what is left of humanity were to learn of it right now, they would feel the same terror I felt at first and these Vermin, the first new thing to happen on this planet in a century, possibly two centuries, would be exterminated.

Perhaps that terror is justified. Perhaps the Vermin will become violent and destroy us. And perhaps, given what we are now, this is no longer a bad thing.

And my friends, I know what you are thinking. You are scientists like me.

You are thinking we should go out to the Vermin, to the church where I sat and thought. We should observe them, dissect them, understand them, and claim them for ourselves once again. You might think that in our study, we are immune from the desire to destroy, but we could easily be the worst.

So I will not tell you the city where it happened, or describe the road.

I only write to you, quietly, secretly, and plead with you to help me find a way to save them. Maybe all that can be done is to find a way to keep them secret long enough to let humanity quietly die out. Or maybe we can finally convince our people to do what we have so often advised others when regarding something new and beautiful:

Let it be.

Let it be.

Please just let it be.

It gets to you, sending these signals out over and over again. I wish I could have just one sip of coffee to push past how tiring this sometimes gets. I'm just so glad that you're out there, listening to this. Of all the things I miss—well, that's not important. Here's what is: a King needs jesters but jesters don't need Kings. Lucky for Kings most jesters don't know that, or certain things better left unspoken would be shouted to the heavens.

COFFEE GROUNDS

Thurston Howl

Some say the world will end in fire; some say in ice. They never would have guessed it would end in coffee.

The year is 1946, and the world, or at least society as we knew it, is no more. I'm the local Chronicler, so it's my job to report things as they happen. Usually, I just write for the locals, but this time, I'm writing to you. Things are changing. And I hope that someone will be able to read this if something happens to me. This is the story, unedited, uncensored, and written more or less in one sitting. It is the truth as I know it. So, if there are survivors after telling this tale, then maybe the truth isn't as scary as I think it is. But if you're reading it…there may be one less survivor than at the time of my writing this.

As I stare out at the wandering souls in the Arena, my thick black tail flicking in the wind, I think back to how this all started, how it all began. Five years ago, Germany sent their planes over much of the world, contaminating most of the major freshwater sources with a chemical known as cobisticine. What internationally became known as the NZ-Plague—named such for the Nazis who had funded the toxin's research—could survive in water without risk of dilution and could kill anyone who had ingested the chemical within a week. It targeted the heart and made it slow down to a gradual stop. Chief, the leader at the Arena, suspects that the toxin was based off some canid genetic material or something. That would be the only thing that can explain what happened to us.

I had drunk the same water as everyone else, but it had no effects on me. I watched as everyone around me died, gripping their chests in pain, and I cringed as the streets I walked down to get to work thinned each day. While most of New York had died within the first month, I had survived. That's when the news started changing: there was hope. It wasn't a cure, but it was a half-immunity of sorts. It seemed that some people, people like me, had developed certain chemical structures that altered the toxin, which activated the canid DNA and instead of killing us morphed us into…

Well, look at me. I am a six-foot-tall black wolf with abs even Hercules would envy. I have paws instead of hands, and my voice is deeper, often turning to a growl when I speak. It turns out I can thank coffee for this. The only survivors were those who had had a coffee addiction of at least four or five years. Coffee did something to our hearts…or our blood…something like that. The surviving scientists had speculated about caffeine and other chemical structures in the heavenly drink, but now I'm not sure there are any scientists left. Then again, not everyone made it out here to the Brazilian colony, simply called the Arena.

Why Brazil, you ask? Simple. A few miles north of the Rio de Janeiro, before the NZ-Plague of course, was a string of coffee bean plantations. Brazil was one of the first coffee capitals of the world, you see. To those of us who survived, it made sense: go to the thing that's keeping us alive; go to the *source*.

There are eighteen of us here, all of different ages, and we all look different. But we are all canids: jackals, wolves, coyotes, dogs, foxes, some mutts even. All of us stand on two legs, talk (some even howl), play, work, mate (the only person who knew what a "knot" was had been a veterinarian before this all happened; figures, damn fur-lovers), and, of course, drink coffee. Chief set up a mechanical stream that constantly runs down the middle of the Arena. He says it's too dangerous to leave and makes us stay here at all times. We've erected walls that not even we know how to get out of. But the sky is our ceiling, and it's beginning to cloud over…

"Hey, Lawrence!"

I turn my head to face the coyote who's approaching. The kid goes by the name Axl, and he always has these comically huge, wide-framed glasses balanced on his snout. I don't think he actually needs them, probably a demonstration of what he always calls "practicing the aesthetique." The way he clicks his tongue against the roof of his muzzle when he pronounces that final syllable "*teek*" irritates me. But I'll just sip my coffee. What do I know?

"Hey, Axl, what's up?" I say, already wishing he would leave.

The kid comes up to me and leans forward, heaving from loss of breath. "I've been trying to find you. Chief w-wants to see you!" he pants.

I raise what should have been my brow. "Oh? What does he want to see me for?" In this little colony, everyone has a place. It's not perfect, but we all trust Chief. My place is the Chronicler, the writer. Chief gets me paper, tells me the news, and I write it down in an interesting and believable way. Chief was once bold and always in your face. Everyone would see him out in the open, working on repairs in the Arena or sorting out some small dispute. But he seemed to change over those first months. It's not that he became less bold…not really. It's more like he fell back into himself. At times, I wonder if he had become *more* animal through all of this. But even so, I am the one he trusts. I am the Chronicler. Just as I trust him, so too do the others. When I come and post his words on the wall, everyone heeds the demands as if they were speeches from the Chief himself, his form almost tangible from the ink on the page. I know that for those who harbor certain fears toward the Chief that this lettered form is looming and foreboding, but, for me, even knowing how his eyes sometimes glow in the dark, I see the form as one that simply demands respect, inspirational in its own way.

Sometimes, I've questioned the things he tells me, but I know he means well for everyone. He wants to keep everyone calm and not panic. Each of us has a sad story about watching the people we loved die. So, it's best for us to just move forward.

Axl manages to stand upright, and I see his tail swaying excitedly now. "He says he has a big project for you! A big story to cover!"

I eye him over. He's one of four in the colony who has decided to go clothesless in this apocalyptic time (I at least have the decency to wear some comfortable pants or jeans even). His fur is all brown and white, and I can make out small coffee stains on the white fur near his wrists. He's always so energetic, and I still can't decide if he was some kind of runner before the NZ-Plague hit or if he's just coffee-drunk. I smirk inwardly. He's cute, but couldn't be more annoying: in essence, he is easily my closest companion in the colony. "What's the big story this time? Did someone fall in the stream again?"

Axl blushes and rubs the back of his head at the callback to his past accident. "N-n-no. He says it has to do with something on the Outside."

This time, my eyes widen, and I brush past Axl, making a beeline straight for Chief's chambers. The Arena is a mostly stone temple in the forests of Brazil. Yet, it's so adaptable. It has tunnels and passages, rooms for each of us, a ravine that runs through the center of the temple both outside and underground, and access to a small breeding ground for food Chief was able to secure for us. When the cities lost all their power and civilization fell into ruin, we needed a place that was simply safe. Chief was the one who made broadcasts regarding the haven on radio and TV before the power completely died in the world and helped all of us meet here, this one safe haven. It was only right that Chief had the largest chamber in the temple. And when he had asked for it, a loud growl in his voice, even those who didn't think it was right submitted to him. Together, we are stronger for it (or are we?). Before entering the stone entrance, I turn to look back out at the Arena. When had the walls become so high?

I suddenly realize Axl has been following me. "Now, what do you want?" I snap.

He looks down and starts shuffling his paws. "I...um...I was wondering if I could join you?"

I turn back toward the entrance to Chief's chambers and keep walking, knowing Axl is following right behind me. I just don't have the heart to tell him no.

This tunnel always seems to swallow me up. While most of the colony use small heat lamps to keep our tunnels lit, Chief prefers the darkness except...I can see the orange glow of his lamp. My ears prick backward, trying to judge how closely Axl is following. The lamp produces a single pool of amber light, pouring over the massive gray fox as he reclines on a black mat.

"Oh," the deep voice starts. "My favorite *author* has come to visit."

I can't help but shiver. I know how much Chief has done for us. But still, every time I have to see him, his sheer presence is just overwhelming. The chamber smells of sweat and long decayed food, of damp fur and rotten breath, of week-old urine and even of death. "You wanted to see me, sir?"

"Yes," the fox hisses. "Is Axl with you?"

My ears listen carefully, and I can tell he stopped a few yards away, hiding right behind the opening to the chamber. As much as I trust the Chief, I know he is a disciplinarian by nature—quite harsh at times, true, but that's what's needed to keep us strong and safe, right?—and Axl has not earned any such rebuke. "No," I say, my tail tucked between my legs, revealing my lie. "He came and fetched me and then went away." I trust the old fox's senses are nowhere as good as they might have once been. Knowing he cannot read my body for the clues of my dishonesty just makes me feel even guiltier.

"Good." The fox raises a gnarled claw and beckons me forward.

Swallowing nervously, I oblige.

"I have news from the Outside that I want appearing in your little paper this week."

My heart leaps. So it is true. "What news, sir?"

"There is another, smaller colony of survivors not too far from here. They have made contact and want to connect."

I almost fall to the ground right there. Surely, he sees my tail wagging. "Are you serious, sir? That's excellent! I cannot wait to spread the word."

As a low growl fills the chamber, the lamp glow seems to flicker. "I need you to tell them exactly what I tell you, *wolf*." My ears flatten instantly at the sharp rebuke. "The Arena doesn't have the space for another ten or even five people. We don't have the food either. But these foreigners have claimed they will come here whether we invite them or not."

"So…" I hazard, "what are you going to do, sir?"

The fox laughs. I hate it. The echoes fill the chamber, and it sounds throaty, as if he is going to cough up his lung in the middle of his roar. "It's not what *I'm* going to do, wolf, but what *you're* going to do."

My tail immediately goes between my legs again. Damn, I hate how telling animal gestures are. I couldn't be more thankful for the darkness right now. "What do you mean…sir?"

The gray old fox is sitting up now, and his silver eyes are shimmering in the amber light. "We've worked together a while now, haven't we? I've shared secrets with you that no one else in the Arena would dream of. And you've always been loyal to me. Now is no different." In my head, I keep thinking how different this really feels though. It's not the first time the Chief has asked me to distort the truth a little. It has always been in everyone's best interest. But for some reason, right now, this feels…different…self-serving even. "You're going to write a story telling everyone that the people who are going to come knocking on our walls are the people who started the NZ-Plague, and that they are *not* canids, no matter what they claim."

"But…" My fists clench as I gradually start finding my confidence again. "If we don't let them in, what do you think will happen to them?"

The fox waves a paw. "Who cares? We're happy here, right? That's all that matters." In that moment, Chief seems a lot less chief-like. "I need a draft in front of me by tomorrow. Think you can manage that, wolf?" When did he start calling me that? His name for me has always been "Chronicler," a lot more regal than a species denigration.

"Yes," I whisper.

"What's that?"

"Yes, sir."

The fox laughs again. "Good wolf. Now get to it. I expect to hear from others that you've been hard at work at the coffeeshop, yeah?" The coffeeshop is just the main pool the stream runs into. There are some stone tables there that, truth be told, are pretty damned good for setting up to write, but at the moment all I can think about is stopping myself from vomiting in Chief's chambers. I remember the things he's done to those who disobeyed him in the past. One newcomer begged the Chief to turn him back into a human. So, the Chief snapped his tail. Another time, a young wolf begged the Chief for something else to drink besides coffee, crying that he couldn't sleep at night. So, the Chief had told me to hold him down while he poured bowl after bowl of coffee into the cub's open maw. At the time, it was hard for me, too…but I saw it as a necessary evil. Now, questioning my leader for the first time puts all of this in a sharp retrospect. Maybe our leader is just a tyrant. And maybe I've been gullible enough to believe he was anything but. I kept justifying it. After all, didn't cops use violence from time to time? Hadn't the law always exercised violence when needed? When had I lost sight of the limits…

"Yes, sir," I repeat. When he waves his paw again, I turn and start walking. I know I walk past Axl at some point as his fear permeates my nose. Entering the sunlight again, the rich, dark smell of the coffee stream hits my nose, and there could not be a more welcome aroma after being in Chief's chambers. I breathe it in and sigh. My tail wags a little as I start to relax again. Maybe this is for the best.

Then, Axl taps my shoulder. I do not turn to address him. His voice is a growl, "You don't intend to write it…do you?" I can hear his clenched paws and his set jaw. For the first time, Axl seems the stronger of us two. He's angry, and I wish I could calm him. I want to tell him to be quiet, to not be heard. It might have made a difference if I had. But I didn't. I fed his fire. I argued.

I lower my head, and my tail goes back between my legs again. "I don't know that I have a choice, Axl."

Axl's voice turns sharp then, and I can feel his brow is furrowed without even turning. "You can't do that! You know it's a lie!"

I do face him and put a paw around his muzzle, clamping his jaw shut. "Be quiet! Do you want the whole Arena to hear you?"

He pushes my paw away. "You can't write it, Lawrence. You just *can't*." He storms off, running. His tail bristled, and his ears are pinned back. I've never seen him so angry before, and deep down I know he's right. I clench my own jaw. *I know he's right.* Yet, I have to write it. I didn't get to where I am today by fighting the system. I did it by following orders." I imagine my loneliness when everyone around me died. I remember obeying the call on the radio as the only hope for a future, one with others like me. I remember hopping a couple of cars over until I managed to make it to a port where the Chief had stationed a plane to pick up survivors. I remember being among two others when I made it. "I did it by surviving. If I fought Chief on this, his goons—he only had three or four, but they are terrifying as all hell; just imagine the most terrifying werewolves you can—would make short work of me. Then, I could join the expansive list of writers who did stupid things to get themselves killed by higher powers. I know Axl is right, but I have to do this. I start walking toward the coffeehouse.

***

After the paper was circulated, the anger spread through the Arena. Even the calmer residents were sharpening sticks and stones to prepare for the foreigners, the Nazi regime that really wasn't. People came to me for all their questions: *What should we do for armor? How many of them are there? What color do Nazis bleed?* And as Chief instructed me, it was my job to create the answers that would most incite their anger. They didn't need coffee for energy; my words did that plenty.

At first, things were all going according to Chief's plan. But the one thing that neither he nor I anticipated was Axl's interference. He started telling people the truth as I knew it. I remember thinking, *This is our chance. Chief will have to confess everything now!* But everyone called him a fool, a liar, and even a traitor.

Here in the Arena, I market our way of life as a utopia. I always brag in my writing about how much better we have it than some cities even before the NZ-Plague. Hell, coffee is a billion times cheaper now. I'm sipping a cup even as I write. But as perfect as utopia sounds, a perfect society doesn't handle rebels very well. As a utopia, we ostracized Axl. We ridiculed him. And then, Chief's goons killed him. They drowned him in the river. His body was found face down, tail up one morning. And can you guess what the headline for that morning's paper was? "Village Fool Died Drunk!" It was supposed to be my most comedic piece yet, and you can bet it was. It still is. Now, the guilt is too much to bear. I know the truth. I have been telling people lies. Axl knew the truth. He told people that truth, and because he wasn't me, he was killed for it. If I tell people now, I might be killed for it too...but people would believe me...I'm sure of it. I might have lied in the past, but...blame the message, not the messenger, right?

I think back to when I first came to the Arena. The Chief was still organizing things and assigning roles. He found out my love of reading and knew I'd be the perfect Chronicler. Having written orders made it easier for him to, in essence, be in multiple places at once. Plato once said that all art was a mere imitation of that which is Truth. Yet, for all of that imitation of reality, people flock to the written word more easily than the oral. When the word is committed to page, it becomes concrete. It becomes visible, re-readable, memorisable, bound in physical space in a way that spoken words can't be. I realized one thing above all else: the way to instigate change in this corruption was to abuse the very beast of burden that had created it.

So, today, the day before the war with the foreigners is supposed to start, the headline I posted to the Arena walls reads thusly, without the Chief's approval and without his knowledge: "The Chief of Lies." Within hours, the Arena's utopia crumbled. That is right. With my words alone, I have dismantled perfection. I did not go back to the coffeeshop after delivering. Being the coward that I clearly am, I hid in Axl's old room. I am taking in his scent now. Yotes, as I'm sure you know, have this unique stench. It's dirty, filthy, and earthy…but it's not unpleasant, not really. It's warm. It has the reek of a desert, the sweetness of baking asphalt, and the saltiness of too-dry biscuits. That would be what I would like to write on Axl's tombstone. But he never received a burial. They threw him over the temple wall—I realize now that some of the people had been tasked with building the wall up at night while everyone else was asleep. The Chief, after all, was a creature of the night. Now, I sit here in Axl's scent, the last collection of his cells in the Arena. It's comfort.

The War the Arena was expecting has changed. Outside this chamber is a civil war. Considering how few survivors there are on this planet, it may as well be a third world war. Those who support Chief…and those who support themselves and freedom, those foreigners only a day's march outside, and even me. I don't know who's actually winning. I'm just a writer, the Chronicler. I'll sit here with my cup of coffee and drown in the aromas of a coyote.

My heart feels like it has stopped. In the tunnels that connect to this room, I hear hacking. Not hacking as in with a sword, but as in someone is coughing up a lung. There are voices accompanying it. The old fox has found me.

I hope that the Outsiders find some people to open the door for them when they arrive. I hope they find the river of coffee and some hope of survival. I hope they are welcomed with sad smiles and open, furry arms. The Chief of Lies may finally silence his writer, but I do not think he will last through today's war. I think of Axl, the one person that makes this apparent lack of a future worth it. I shall dream of him when I pass. I hope these actions are enough, enough to let him forgive me. My desire is not a fiery, passionate one. It is solemn and cool and quiet. I seek only forgiveness.

The hacking approaches. This time, I'm not sure what kind it is.

I've chronicled our story as best I can. Were we ever really safe here? Did we ever escape the dangers of Hitler's plague? Or did we just replace fear of one tyrant with fear of another?

He's here. I see his silver eyes in the final tunnel before the room. They're piercing. Another sip of coffee. He's not going to deprive me of—

The first steps toward unequal worlds are always taken with complicity, aren't they?

Those downtrodden bring it on themselves, or that's what you're supposed to think. There are flaws in some characters, it's just the way some are. It's in their blood. No matter how noble some of us are some others are just bad people and really isn't everyone a kind of bad when left to their own devices? Aren't we all looking for authority figures to raise up, to protect us, reveal that some deserve their respective lots in life?

To teach us who's a good dog?

And who's not.

Not All Dogs

Mary E. Lowd

Lucky was a good dog. He'd been a good dog all his life.

So why was he standing in an office supply store, watching his three adopted kittens run wild, while trying to figure out how to make protest signs for a rally to free his tabby cat wife from prison?

Two of the kittens, Allison and Pete, kept bringing Lucky glitter pens and eraser sets designed to look like spaceships, piling them up on the floor around his paws, while he and Robin, the quiet kitten from the litter, stared at the different types of poster board. Some were flimsy. Some were thick like cardboard. There were even neon green and yellow ones.

"Mama would like a green poster," Robin meowed. His ears hadn't unflattened since Lucky had picked the three kittens up at the police station. "We should make her green posters."

Right now, Lucky would do anything to keep his kittens happy. If buying some extra junk at an office supply store would distract them, then so be it. The terrier grabbed three pieces of the green poster board and several white ones of different weights. Then he balanced all of the cutesy eraser sets on top, grabbed a rainbow pack of extra-thick pens, and headed for the checkout counter. Before he got there, Allison slipped the glitter pens onto the top of his pile as well.

The dog behind the counter was some sort of lab-spaniel mutt, all smiles and wags. As she scanned the items for their prices, she looked over the counter at the kittens and woofed, "Doing a school project?"

Robin hid behind Lucky's legs, and Allison was too busy counting the colors in the glitter pen set to answer. But Pete announced loudly, "We're protesting that the bad cops locked Mama up." His tiny orange-striped face was almost hilariously serious. Almost. Except there was nothing hilarious about their situation.

The lab-spaniel's jowls strained; she looked stricken. She must have finally recognized them—the family of Petra Brighton, that infamous orange tabby. Petra's case had been all over the news. According to the big news stations, Petra had assaulted a police dog who'd pulled her over for a routine traffic check. The smaller indie news sites were more measured in their coverage, pointing out that video footage of the arrest hadn't been released yet, and maybe they didn't have the full story.

Lucky didn't need to see video footage. He knew his wife; Petra had a temper, but she wasn't stupid. She hadn't assaulted that cop. She couldn't have. He was sure. Pretty sure.

"Could we have a bag for this?" Lucky asked, gesturing at the pile of pens and erasers, hoping to hurry the checkout process along and not wanting to talk to a random retail worker about his personal life.

The checkout dog packed Lucky's purchases into a bag, handed it over, and woofed, "Good luck."

She sounded sincere, and Lucky smiled at her, warmed by the sympathy. A tired smile, buried under his scruffy terrier beard. "Thanks." He gathered the three kittens around him and walked them out to the car. It wasn't until he was driving home, all three kittens strapped into their car seats in the back, that the words "good luck" started to sour in his mind.

Why should he need luck? He needed justice. Petra had been wrongfully arrested and was being illegally detained. Justice. Not luck.

Was the checkout dog saying that he'd need luck because cats can't get justice? Was she saying that she believed the big news stations, that Petra had assaulted the copper dog?

Or was she just wishing him luck because he was a dog with cats in his life—his wife and his kittens—and cats are unreliable, unpredictable, erratic creatures? They can flip from purring to hissing at the drop of a dime. Any dog dealing with cats must need luck to get by, right?

Good thing his name was Lucky.

Lucky seethed, grinding his teeth, as he drove. He hated cat stereotypes. His kittens were no different than any litter of puppies. They squabbled over toys, begged for treats, and drove their parents crazy by being adorable trouble-makers. They swished their tails when they were angry and purred when they were happy, instead of wagging their tails when they were happy and growling when they were angry. But so what? A kid's a kid, pointy ears or floppy, they all need love and patience.

After a while, Lucky realized he'd been driving in circles, looping around the local playgrounds, instead of taking his kittens home. That was probably what Petra had been doing when she got arrested. He hadn't been able to ask her, because the cops wouldn't let him see her. But he knew she liked to take the kittens on a drive when they were being restless. Once the trio was strapped into their car seats, they had to settle down, and it gave Petra a moment of peace. Sometimes the kittens even fell asleep.

But not this time. They were too busy brainstorming ideas for their protest signs.

***

Once they were home, Lucky set the kittens up at the kitchen table with the poster board and pens. He claimed one of the thicker white pieces for himself but let the kittens run wild with the rest.

With a big, thick, green pen in his orange-striped paw, Robin scrawled, "L3t MaMA gO." Green pen on a green board. Not the easiest to read, but sweet and sincere.

Allison seemed to lose sight of the objective and filled most of her white board with a glittery rainbow. She grabbed one pen after another with her gray-striped paws and added one line of color after another to the bottom of the rainbow until she'd used every single one of the pens, glittery and otherwise. She had to squeeze the words, "Equil Rights 4 Cats & Dogs," into the lower right corner, squished and hard to read. Still, the rainbow was eye-catching.

Pete, on the other paw, drew a shockingly good caricature of his mother behind bars, reaching towards a cartoon version of himself. Two orange tabbies, one big and one small, separated by cold iron. It was cute, funny, and heartbreaking all at once. That boy was going to be an artist.

For himself, Lucky wasn't sure what to put on a sign. He knew that ARFF—All Rights For Felines—staged protests every couple weeks for cats who'd supposedly been wrongfully arrested. Like most good dogs, he was sympathetic, but he'd never actually been to one of the rallies or paid much attention to them. He hadn't needed to. He wouldn't even be preparing for a protest now if one of the ARFF coordinators, a calico named Cassandra, hadn't cornered him as he was leaving the police station and asked him to say a few words at tomorrow's rally for Petra. He had no idea what he would say.

Eventually, Lucky wrote "Due Process Knows No Species" in big black block letters. As he stared at the finished sign, he wondered whether they were all making a big deal out of nothing. Surely, the cops hadn't been serious about refusing his demands to see Petra. It must have been a misunderstanding. They weren't done processing her; they wanted him to get the kittens out of the way; and that Cassandra cat had been riling everyone up with her threats of a rally. If he went back alone, he could get everything sorted out.

***

Half a day wasted on phone calls, babysitters, and the police station waiting room proved that idea wrong. No one but the president himself would be getting in to see Petra.

The wolfhound at the front desk was warm, polite, and apologetic to Lucky, but she couldn't help him. Even when he lost his cool and barked at her, furious at the bureaucracy of it all, she stayed patient with him. She even asked after the kittens, wanting to be sure they were okay after seeing how shook up they'd been.

By the time Lucky gave up on seeing Petra for that day, he was utterly confused. He hadn't believed the sensational speculation on the news about Petra slashing a cop's nose with her claws, but all the dogs at the police department were being so reasonable. Firm but reasonable. And one of the cops was even a cat. Maybe if they were holding Petra for observation there was a reason. Maybe her temper had finally snapped? She had been really run down and stressed out lately. Maybe she had attacked the cop.

Just a small scratch, of course. But still, it would explain better how the cops were acting.

Lucky wouldn't know until he saw her.

On his way out of the police station, Cassandra cornered Lucky again. Somehow, the calico from ARFF had managed to gather a half dozen cats with signs in front of the building, even though the rally wasn't until the morning.

"They're still giving you the runaround in there?" Cassandra asked. Her black-and-orange splotches gave her face a lopsided look.

Lucky shrugged, feeling beat. He'd barked himself out at the wolf-hound already.

"Don't worry yet." Cassandra's triangular ears kept twisting, and her golden-eyed gaze darted about as if, even while talking to Lucky, she was more focused on monitoring the crowd. "We're working on forcing them to move Petra to a shared cell. That way she won't be alone. There'll be an observer for anything they do to her."

Lucky frowned. He wasn't sure what Cassandra thought the cops might do to Petra. If there was any truly safe place in the world, it would be a police station. The cops here were good dogs. And the one cat, of course.

Lucky was more worried about the fact that Cassandra had somehow learned more about Petra's situation than he had. How much trouble were she and these ARFF cats giving the cops? Was their trouble-making part of why he couldn't get in to see Petra?

He just wanted to see his wife.

"Do you want to go over your speech for tomorrow?" Cassandra asked.

Lucky did not. "Are your protesters going to be here all night?" he asked, looking over the motley collection of tabbies, torbies, and various solid colored cats. All moggies, no purebreds.

"Petra will be," Cassandra answered. "So we will too."

Anger flared in Lucky's chest. Was this cat implying that these strangers cared more about his wife's comfort than he did? He'd been arguing—politely and deferentially—with cops every minute that he hadn't been watching his kittens since he'd heard about the arrest. It had been the longest two days of his life.

"I need to get home to my kittens," Lucky woofed. "I'll see you in the morning." He didn't like this cat, but maybe her protest would pressure the police into working something out—some way for him to get in and see Petra. It wasn't much, but right now, he'd have to take what he could get.

***

Bright and early the next morning, Lucky packed a backpack with snacks—tuna jerky, salted cod biscuits, and candied sardines—a couple bottles of water, a few favorite lightweight toys, and extra jackets for everyone. The backpack was stuffed full by the time he was done. Then Lucky packed the kittens and the protest signs in the car and drove them all over to the police station.

They parked a couple blocks away, and Lucky led his kittens like a tiny parade along the downtown sidewalks, each of them carrying a sign. The kittens carried their signs proudly. Lucky felt awkward and conspicuous with his. For better or worse, there weren't too many cars driving by at this time in the morning to see them. The morning air was crisp and chill against Lucky's scruffy fur and light clothes, and the sunlight slanted between the buildings in a way that glared off of car windshields, blinding him periodically.

Just as Cassandra had promised, the rally cats were still protesting in front of the station. Nearly a dozen cats now, and also a few Chihuahua mixes. Chihuahuas always seemed to be more eager to support cats' rights than other dogs. Usually, big dogs assumed it was because they were small like cats. But Lucky—a terrier mutt—wasn't much bigger, and yet here he was at his first rally today. First time for everything.

It wasn't that Lucky didn't support cats' rights. Of course, he did. He was married to one, wasn't he? But there's a difference between voting for equal wage laws and standing outside with a poster board sign. Democracy depended on voting; protests were for when democracy broke down. And as far as Lucky knew, democracy hadn't broken down in the Uplifted States since the Dark Times after the humans left Earth. In fact, given that they'd elected their first feline president last year, democracy and cats' rights seemed better than ever.

"You're here early!" Cassandra meowed, marching out of the crowd to meet Lucky. "And you've got all three kittens! That'll look great on camera."

"You sound surprised…" Lucky woofed. "Were you not expecting me this early? Or to bring the kittens?"

"Well, kittens are a handful at protests, and the local news station won't be here for a few hours." Once again, Cassandra's wandering ears and eyes made it seem like she was only half paying attention to her conversation with Lucky. "But if you're up to the challenge, that's great! Like I said, it'll look great on camera—three kittens missing their mama."

Lucky was annoyed. He'd given Cassandra his phone number. She could have called him to let him know when to come, and he'd had the kittens with him when she'd cornered him day before last. What did she think he'd do with them? Leave them home alone? "I didn't bring my kittens to look good on camera," Lucky grumbled. "They're not props."

Cassandra didn't hear him; she'd already drifted back into the crowd of protesters to scold a chocolate-furred Chihuahua who'd climbed up beside a stone statue for a photo. The statue was of a human police officer, and the Chihuahua was posing next to the granite human as if the two of them were holding her protest sign together. It read, "Humanity Loves Us All" along the top, and under that, "Cats' Rights are Canine Rights."

It was an explicitly religious First Racer sign with that reference to the long gone human race. Lucky figured the calico must have a problem with First Racer signs at her protest.

The chocolate Chihuahua got down from the statue and started loudly barking scripture at Cassandra. A lot of feline ears in the crowd flattened. Lucky didn't have a chance to see how the altercation turned out, however, because the kittens were ready for snacks. Already. It was going to be a long day.

Lucky propped his sign up against a trash can, took his backpack off and dug around inside it. The snacks were buried under the extra jackets, and he practically had to unpack and repack the whole thing right there on the sidewalk to get at the coveted fishy morsels.

The morning passed in a strange haze of stress mixed with boredom. The kittens staggered their demands such that Lucky finished putting his backpack on after getting Robin tuna jerky right before Allison asked for a drink; after he got the drink, Pete was cold and needed his extra jacket. As soon as the backpack settled on Lucky's shoulders again, Pete changed his mind—the jacket was too hot. Can you put it back in the backpack, Daddy? And so on. It felt like a bizarre obstacle course, except without the exhilaration of running or jumping.

For a while, Lucky led his trio of kittens from one end of the block to the other. It made the kittens happy, and they sang a song about parades while waving about their signs. Until Cassandra asked him to stop.

"Why?" Lucky asked, upset that she wanted him to stop the one activity that was making the kittens happy. But once again, the calico's attention had strayed from him before he thought the conversation was over. "Will you listen to me?" Lucky snapped. "Why don't you want us parading?"

Cassandra's ears skewed, not fully flattened but clearly unhappy. She looked at Lucky with enigmatic gold eyes. "We don't want to cause too much commotion."

Baffled, Lucky woofed, "I thought that was the whole point of this demonstration."

But Cassandra was gone again. This time, the calico had rushed off to talk to a police poodle who'd poked his floppy-eared head out of the station to check on the protest. He was a tan-furred standard poodle, nearly twice the height of most of the protester cats.

Lucky wanted to check in the with police officer too, but suddenly Allison desperately needed her rag-cat with the green button eyes and yarn whiskers from the backpack. Lucky tried to keep an eye on Cassandra's interchange with the poodle as he knelt down on the sidewalk and dug through the backpack. The tan-furred poodle kept fiddling with the handcuffs and night stick strapped to the belt on his deep blue uniform. That didn't seem like a good sign. Why was he so nervous? Was there bad news about Petra?

Lucky found the rag-cat and held it out for his gray tabby daughter. "Here you go, Allison."

The kitten squeezed the doll tightly, purring and happy. "Raggedy Kitty says thank you for getting her out of the backpack!" Allison meowed. She wrapped the rag-cat's arms around her sign's picket and said, "Look, she's helping me hold up my sign!"

Lucky smiled at his daughter's adorableness, but he was still distracted by wanting to talk to the police poodle. "Come on, kittens," he woofed. "Let's go hold our signs over by the statue for a while." The statue was closer to the station's entrance, and maybe Lucky could beckon the officer over to talk to him there.

Crossing five sidewalk squares of concrete with a troupe of kittens holding signs can prove to be a far more complicated production than seems possible. First Pete saw a colorful leaf he wanted to pick up—it was only a few steps out of the way. Then Allison showed off that her rag-cat could fly—by throwing it in the air. The rag-cat landed several steps out of the way in the other direction. And Robin simply decided to be mulish and complain that he didn't want to stand near the human statue, because humans look creepy with those flat, knobby faces. No muzzles and barely any ears!

By the time they made it over to the base of the statue, the police poodle was busy talking on a cell phone. Lucky didn't want to interrupt him.

Lucky wondered if the poodle was the officer who had pulled Petra over. The wolfhound at the front desk hadn't been able to give him any useful specifics, but if he could talk to the actual officer who had pulled Petra over, then maybe he could finally get some answers.

Lucky wanted to know why Petra had been pulled over in the first place. Had she run a red light? Missed a stop sign? Forgotten her turn signals? He wished she had been driving more carefully. Then they could have avoided all of this.

Lucky had asked the kittens, of course, but all three had been asleep in the backseat when their mother was pulled over. They'd only woken up when the cops moved them to the squad car—a different squad car than their mother was in. They'd been petrified by the time Lucky picked them up at the station.

In fact, when Lucky had told them about the protest, at first Robin had refused to come back to the station at all. He only agreed when Lucky had explained that the protest would be held outside the station, and there would be a bunch of other cats there. That part had seemed important to Robin.

Lucky was pulled from his reverie by the caterwauling sounds of angry kittens. "Hey, hey, calm down, guys!" Lucky barked, almost reflexively. "What's wrong?"

Allison and Pete had climbed up on the base of the statue; an orange tabby and a gray tabby squabbling beside the knees of a granite human. Pete had taken Allison's rag-cat and was holding it above his head, keeping it away from her. Allison was practically spitting, trying to get her beloved rag-cat back.

Lucky didn't have a chance to sort their quarrel out. The police poodle's voice rang out like gunfire, the kind of booming bark that startles and stops everyone in their tracks, the kind of bark only a big dog can make: "GET OFF THE STATUE!"

Pete dropped the rag-cat on the statue's base and scrambled down right away. Allison was still picking up her rag-cat and checking to make sure the doll was okay when the police poodle made it over to her. He grabbed the rag-cat out of her gray-striped paws. "I SAID GET DOWN!"

Allison yowled and reached for the rag-cat. Lucky tried to step forward and smooth the situation over, but the police dog threw the rag-cat down on the ground and Allison hissed at him.

The police dog drew his gun. At the sight of the pistol, Lucky's sight blacked out. He'd never seen a gun in person before—certainly not being pulled on his kitten. When his vision cleared, he was standing between Allison and the police poodle. He didn't even know how he'd gotten there.

"Get that kitten off of the statue," the poodle barked, still pointing the gun, now at Lucky.

Lucky's paws were shaking, and he made sure to keep his body between that gun and his baby. But he got Allison down from the statue.

Allison tried to cling to her daddy, but Cassandra had come up beside them and Lucky pushed her into the calico's open arms, away from the gun. He never took his eyes off of the gun, as if looking at it could stop it from firing. He could barely breathe until the poodle had holstered it again.

"You pulled a gun on my baby," Lucky woofed, out of breath and ready to burst into tears.

"She scratched me!" the poodle barked.

Lucky realized that he was still hearing his heart pounding in his ears. His vision had blacked out for a moment, but he knew what he had seen: "She didn't scratch you." It was hard to put words together in this state. "She hissed at you."

"Same thing," the police poodle woofed. "Cats gotta control their tongues. Even kittens. Gotta show the proper deference to police officers."

The police dog was acting like nothing strange had happened, but Lucky felt like the entire world had turned upside down. He'd never felt afraid of a police officer before.

This must be what Petra felt all the time.

Other cats too.

In that moment, Lucky realized that Petra hadn't done anything to get pulled over. Other than be a cat, behind the wheel. He hated himself for doubting her. He thought of all the times he'd thought she was being crazy or paranoid... How many of those times were justified?

"Just stay off of the statue," the police poodle barked, "and everything will be fine."

Lucky watched the poodle stride back into the station, tail swishing. Had it been fun for him?

Then the distraught terrier looked at all the cats, holding their signs, watching him. They'd all been living in this upside down world where the police were a force of danger all along.

Three kittens rushed into Lucky's arms. The terrier held his feline babies tight.

***

Three days later, Lucky was allowed in to see Petra in her cell. It would be another two weeks before the protests built to the point where the police were pressured into releasing her. Even then, it was only because of her powerful family connections. Many cats weren't so lucky. They became statistics.

Behind iron bars, Petra's orange fur didn't look fiery like it usually did. She looked faded; yellow-stripes instead of crimson. Lucky wished he could have protected her from this. But that would require changing the world.

"I didn't do anything wrong," Petra meowed to Lucky.

"I know," Lucky said, reaching a scruffy-furred paw toward the bars. Petra came forward and held it. He was too ashamed to admit that he'd doubted her. She would forgive him. She must have already forgiven him hundreds of times already, without him even knowing it, for all the times he hadn't understood.

Lucky clutched Petra's paw between the iron bars. If a cat and dog could fall in love, adopt, and raise kittens together, then dogs could learn to respect cats. But it would be a long road. A road that he should have been walking down for a long time. He would start now. For their kittens.

"I'm so sorry," Lucky said.

Pledge allegiance to a flag, to an ideal, to a cause. The call to something greater comes to everyone, but too often we fail to heed. When the perfect citizens we envision to represent the very best of us don't exist we find ourselves forced to create them.

Therein lies our nation's greatest curse and blessing. Those unfortunates whom we fail to protect will be part of our legacy. Those whom we deliberately misuse will stitch our sins in spangled cloth for the world to see in the fullness of time.

A Better America 501(c)(3)

NightEyes DaySpring

The coyote morph, X35670, stopped on the edge of the manicured lawn to scent the air. It was dark; most of the street lights that once lit this area long ago had died. With his keen eyesight, he could make out a huddled figure about 50 meters away on a park bench. Twenty years ago, tourists used to come out here to see the monuments, even at night. Now they barely came during the day.

Some of the humans called him Hunter, but he preferred X35670; it was unique. Anyway, having a real name didn't mean much anymore. The people in front of him had real names. Perhaps that was why they were here. He had been created as a single genetic variation in the Coyote-X morph line. He wasn't like the people he helped.

He walked toward the huddling figure, keeping an eye out for the cops. The coyote couldn't afford to be noticed going about his rounds. His job was to get in and get out quickly.

As he approached, he realized it wasn't one person but two. "I'm with A Better America. Are you in need of assistance?" he asked.

The woman looked up at X35670 with shrunken eyes. She had a young child pressed against her who was wheezing. "Do you have any food?" she asked.

"Yes," said X35670, dropping to his knees and pulling two nutrient gel packs out of his satchel. He gave the woman one and the child one after ripping them open. "Take it slow," he advised, "You don't want to get stomach cramps." The gel would keep them moving.

"Thank you," mumbled the woman as she carefully helped her daughter eat some of the gel.

X35670 pulled out four more packs and handed them to the woman. "Where are you from?" he asked.

"West Virginia, coal country," she said, taking a mouthful of gel herself. She didn't ask him where he was from, but that didn't matter. All the morphs originated from a laboratory in Texas.

If they were from West Virginia, there was a good chance both of them would have heavy metal poisoning. A lot of the ground water out that way was toxic now, so he pulled out a packet of pills to help with that and handed it to the woman. "I have to go now," he said, "before anyone notices."

"God bless you, coyote," the woman said as he moved off.

It was illegal to feed the homeless in public spaces, so he couldn't stay with one person too long. He worked in a gray area though. They couldn't charge him since he was owned by A Better America and thus considered property, but that didn't mean they wouldn't haul him in. It always took a month for the charity to get him released if he got picked up. In the meantime, people would go hungry.

The next person he came across was an elderly man lying on a park bench. He had a small cart sitting next to the bench, piled high with bags of clothing and other odds and ends. The man reeked strongly of alcohol, and he wearily watched X35670 as he approached. The coyote paused a few meters away to try and ascertain what was wrong with the man before he asked.

"Do you need assistance?"

"No," said the man, turning away. "I don't want a handout from you."

"I have food," offered X35670.

The man sprang up. "Go. Beat it!" yelled the man, as if he was trying to get rid of a wild animal. "Shoo!"

The coyote lowered his ears. He encountered people like this sometimes. Not everyone would accept food from a morph. He learned to just move on if they wouldn't talk to him. There were always others further along his route.

He continued down the sidewalk along the edge of the lawn. The next person he found didn't even stir when he approached them. He slowed his walk until he noticed the strong, rancid, unmistakable scent of death.

He sped up to get past the lifeless body and took a turn at the next junction of the sidewalk to head toward one of the memorials that honored the fallen of past wars. He often found veterans there, and it was on his list tonight to check the area. Depending how empty his shoulder bag was, he'd return to the charity to refill before making more stops. On a given night, he sometimes visited up to thirty different people before his paws became too tired to keep carrying him and it became too late. Around 1 AM he'd return home and log his night's activities before falling sleep.

***

A Better America was located off N Street, in a converted brownstone the charity had bought not long after it had incorporated ten years prior. The building was over a hundred fifty years old. It had been built by a successful railroad man for his wife and kids. Successive tenants and institutions had modified the home, each adding their own touch to the structure representing the era they lived in. These successive remodels gave the house an eclectic feeling with elements of different styles coexisting together. In the front foyer alone, art deco sconces competed with the original segmental arch doorway to set the mood against modern chairs and a built-in 1950s receptionist desk designed to fit in the tight space.

X35670 shared the front room of the basement with another morph. A little window high up on the wall looked out on the sidewalk. From his cot, he could see the feet of everyone who walked into the building. It was tight, but it was home, and he could decorate his side of the room however he wanted. So far, he just had put up some desert posters, but it gave him a sense of his own personal space, something he never experienced until he came here.

"It's getting worse, you know," said Samantha, going over the log of their recent activities. The tigress, his roommate, was seated on her own cot across the room.

"Is it?" he remarked, pulling his attention from the window. He liked to watch the feet go by on the sidewalk.

"Well yeah, you've had a seven percent uptake in stops this past month and I've done four percent more. We're seeing twenty percent more people than we were a year ago."

The coyote yawned. "I hadn't really noticed. There are just so many of them. I try to reach as many as I can." The tigress was always checking the stats, but he just focused on doing the job. Their stats tended to be comparable, and the charity seemed happy with his work, so he didn't see a need to worry.

She put the tablet down and stretched, her fur rippling. "It's good work we're doing, Hunter. Beats what I did before."

He laid his ears back.

She noticed his reaction. "Not the name bit again. You don't complain when Shandra uses it."

X35670 nodded softly. "I like my serial number. No one else can call themselves that. It's a unique name."

She rolled her eyes. "If you call me Z45069 again, I'm going to sock you a good one. You don't mind walking around in here nude with me, but you get embarrassed when people call you by your name?"

They both preferred to be nude indoors, but that was only because humans kept their homes too warm. "It's only been two years. You've had your name much longer. Your first owner gave it to you."

"She was nice. She said I reminded her of her granddaughter." Samantha paused before asking the question. "What did he call you?"

The coyote looked down. He used to be owned by a man who used X35670 for sexual purposes, buying him at fifteen to help fulfill desires he could not legally get elsewhere. He had been a powerful man, a politician, and X35670 had hated him. Eventually, when the coyote morph reached twenty, he had been discarded and sold to a third-party seller.

"I didn't have a set name them. He'd call me whatever fit his mood." He stopped to take a deep breath. This wasn't something he'd told her yet. "Slave. Slut. Boy. When he was horny and feeling aggressive, I was just Fuck Toy. To other people he called me 'The Morph.'"

"Holy shit," She growled. "He wouldn't even give you a name? I hope we get that asshole someday."

The coyote sighed and pulled the blanket around himself. He tried not to talk to Samantha about his previous life, but she still occasionally brought it up. She knew enough of what had happened to understand him. He preferred not to think of that man anymore, but it was hard. "Shandra wants to legally go after him, but he didn't break any laws." Shandra was their coordinator and worked for their director. She oversaw their street outreach.

Samantha grumbled and got up. She walked over to the chest where she kept her clothes to fish out a shirt and a pair of shorts. "He better hope I never get him alone."

X35670 nodded and went back to staring out at the window. All that was in the past now. He wouldn't have to see that man again.

"Hey! Are you going to get ready for the staff meeting or not?"

"It's always the same," he remarked, getting up to fetch some clothes. "The job doesn't change much."

"Yeah, but it's good for us all to get together and talk things over. Shandra wants us to work as a team."

Shandra was nice, but X35670 had never really figured out how he should feel about her. It had taken him a while to trust her, and even now, two years later, he felt he wasn't quite part of the team.

"I know," he remarked, pulling a shirt over his head and then putting on some pants. He checked to make sure he looked presentable in the mirror. Some of his fur was matted, so he quickly started fluffing it up. It made Samantha happy to see him engaged with the others, and he didn't want to disappoint her.

***

The storeroom in the rear of the basement was always cramped for these meetings. The wolves, Fang, Claw, and Paw, were leaning against a pallet of water bottles in the back. They had sequential serial numbers and were the closest to brothers morphs ever could get. Their fur patterns were slightly different smoke gray and tan patterns. Samantha and X35670 took position off to the side, while the other two morphs on the team, Janice and Thomas sat on folding chairs in the middle of the room.

"All right," said Shandra, pulling up a map of the city on the screen against one wall. "You guys have done amazing work, but the current legislative agenda threatens to make things worse. They're also trying to close down another homeless shelter. I'm hoping we can step up our game so we can attract more donations."

"Do they ever do anything right on the Hill?" asked Janice, a sandy colored jackal who only recently joined the organization. Next to her was Thomas, a field mouse who was the first morph to join the charity.

"They used to," Shandra said with a frown on her face. She had been doing charity work since before X35670 was born, and she was well versed in its many issues. She wasn't a tall, statuesque woman, even with her close cropped curly hair having given way to gray now. She'd fought off muggers and counter protesters before and could hold her own in a fight.

"Can't they see what the consequences of their actions are?" pressed Janice.

"If they did, we wouldn't need A Better America. I don't know if anyone is going to wise up at this point, but I keep hoping."

The room murmured agreement and Shandra went back to her map. "It's a big city, and we only have seven of you. We've also got another cease and desist letter threatening legal action this morning for feeding the poor. You don't know how much it frustrates me I can't join you out there, but they would lock my black ass up the moment I stepped out of here with a help satchel."

X35670 nodded and listened as Shandra went over their routes for tonight. She wanted to bump up their start time by an hour to 7:30 pm, just before sunset, and that brought up a discussion on police interference. Besides the capitol police, he didn't see the cops out much, but he kept a look out for them. It was always a game of not being too noticeable while trying to cover as much ground as possible. Janice had a run in last night with an officer, and the team discussed how she handled it. She was still fresh and too idealistic to realize some of the danger she was putting herself in, but she would learn.

He listened, but he already had his route planned out for tonight. He had a few regulars to check on he hadn't made it out to in the last few days. As long as he kept his head down, things would be fine.

***

It drizzled that night, the cool rain keeping the streets fairly empty. The damp on his fur didn't bother X35670 as he made his rounds. Knowing that most of the open areas wouldn't be occupied because of the rain, he altered his route and stuck to the streets and some back alleys away from the National Mall. He shot a quick text to his compatriots to let them know his plans, and the team agreed.

Everyone he found was huddled out of the rain, so he quickly ran out of the few waterproof space blankets he had on him.

He was only two hours into his run, when he encountered a woman with long matted hair avoiding the rain under a store awning next to an alley entrance.

"Hello," he said, coming up to the woman slowly. "I'm with A Better America. Are you in need of assistance?"

The woman looked up at him. She'd been staring down at the street. "Who is that?"

"We're a charity that helps feed the homeless," he said calmly. "I have food if you need it?"

"You do?" she said with surprise.

The coyote nodded and reached into his satchel, pulling out a nutrient gel pack for the woman.

"Hey! Stop!" growled an angry voice from behind him.

He froze, and carefully turned around. Two men in dark clothes were heading toward him. Were they cops? They didn't look like cops.

"Don't feed that woman," yelled the first man, coming up to him and trying to grab his bag from him.

"That's my job," the coyote said, as he jumped backwards.

"She doesn't need your help. You're only hurting her by feeding her," snarled the man as he lunged at him, knocking the woman aside.

X35670 panicked and tried to flee, but the second man had circled around him and pulled out a knife. He froze as that man came forward. With a quick slice, he cut the strap of his satchel and pulled it away. X35670 was knocked to his knees by the first man who punched him in the gut. Gasping for breath, he tried to fight back, but the man slammed his fist into the side of his muzzle before kicking him backwards.

He hit the ground and rolled into the alleyway, crashing into a pile of trash bags. While he was stunned, his assailants tore the contents of his satchel apart, spilling the contents onto the street. The nutrient gel packs they ripped open and poured into the puddle, while the energy wafers and pills they stomped into powder. When they were done, the first assailant threw the torn, damaged satchel at him.

"Go home to your owner, you filthy animal," he said, teeth bared in a snarl. Together the two men walked off, high fiving each other.

When they were gone, the woman came over and helped pull him out of the trash.

"You okay?"

"Yeah, but he got me good. What the hell is wrong with these people?"

"They don't see either of us as human," said the woman, picking up a gel pack that survived the violence intact. "Thank you for what you could give me."

He grumbled and looked through the shoulder bag. Everything left inside was ruined and covered in gel. "I'm going to have to go back and get more supplies."

The woman didn't say anything else, but she clung to the gel packet as if it was the most important thing in her life as he walked off. X35670 clenched one hand into a fist as he rubbed the side of his muzzle, tail and fur bristled. He got why they didn't see him as human, but couldn't they at least see the people he was trying to help as human?

**

He texted Shandra and Samantha to let them know about the encounter on his way back to the brownstone. Both asked him if he was okay, and he had to reassure them he was. He also informed them he was going for fresh supplies and then heading back out. He wasn't going to let this get him down.

Back at the charity, he tossed his ripped satchel down and grabbed a new one. After packing some extra thermal blankets and texting the group channel he would be out late, he took off again.

The streets were quiet, but he still kept checking over his shoulder before he approached anyone. Slowly though, the rain picked up, and it soaked into his fur. The weight of his tail helped ease some of his tension by tiring him out. The part of his genetic markup that was pure coyote once hunted in the rain, so why couldn't he? Of course, he wasn't out here seeking food, but it was similar to what his ancestors had done.

It was already past midnight, and he was overdue on his scheduled return time, when he got a text. He fished out his phone and saw a message from Samantha on the group chat: *Abort return! Raid!*

He stopped dead in his tracks. A raid? Against the charity? He tapped a quick reply. *What's going on?*

Hunter, stay away. I'm trying to find out, came a reply from Shandra.

What the hell was he going to do now? Confused, he found a diner that was still open and ordered something to preoccupy himself. The staff gave him a look but didn't say anything. They passed a steaming cup of tea to him, which he sat in the window with, staring out at the wet streets. No one who came in after him sat near the coyote. X35670 hoped it was just the wet dog smell keeping people away, but he had a feeling that wasn't the reason.

Finally, after what seemed like forever, a message came in from Shandra. *Meet Samantha by Washington Circle. Turn off your phone!*

With panic, he shut down his device and headed off to the rendezvous point. It took him twenty minutes to get there, but he found the tiger under a street lamp, waiting for him.

"Come on," she said, the moment she spotted him. "We need to put some distance between us and here. Is your phone off?" She took off in a random direction.

"Yeah. What's going on?" he asked, scrambling after her.

"I don't know," she whispered, as they walked. "I came back late just as the cops showed up. I had to jump the fence behind one of the neighbor's properties to get away. I think they're shutting us down," she said.

He blinked. "How can they do this?"

"I think they're calling it a social stimulus. It supposed to encourage more workers to return to the work force."

He barked a bitter laugh out. "That's hypocrisy. There aren't jobs for them to go back to."

The tigress nodded. "It is, but no one seems to care. The police have a court order, and they're seizing the charity's assets right now as we speak."

"They can do that?"

She nodded. "Civil asset forfeiture."

Fuck. "That includes us."

"Actually, it doesn't." she said stopping to pull a small envelope out of the shoulder bag she was carrying.

"The charity bought us."

"They did, but A Better America is run by smart people. They transferred everyone's ownership to a shell company out of the Bahamas." From the envelope, she pulled out two small needles for injecting microchips. "I went to Shandra's apartment after I left the charity, and she gave me these. All we need to do is rechip."

X35670 looked at the needles. "Can't they find out who owns us by our serial numbers?"

"Yeah," said the tigresses. "These are coded under different serial numbers for siblings who died already."

Each morph gene line used slight variations of the genetic code to create unique specimens. While each morph was unique, their serial numbers referred to where in the gene line they came from.

"I..." the coyote gulped. "I don't want to be someone else."

"You're still y—"

"No!" he shouted. "I am X35670. I don't want to be a different serial."

"You would still be you."

"That number is the only thing I own. If I let that go, who am I?"

"Hunter?"

His ears splayed, and he backed up against the building they were passing. "That's just a name."

She leaned over and put her hand against the wall, so she could whisper to him. "The government is trying to seize X35670. If anyone scans your chip, they are going to see that you are on the seize list. Now, do you want that hanging over your head, or do you want to keep some semblance of freedom?"

He looked at the package. Until the politician had bought him, he had just been X35670. They were discouraged from having real names before they were sold, and each was addressed only by their serial number. "Your owner will give you your name," he had been told. When his owner had first called him slut, he felt his heart stop. He knew then what was going to happen before it even occurred. Now he was going to lose the one thing only he owned.

She grabbed him by an arm and started dragging him down the street. "I try hard to work with your hang-ups, Hunter, but we don't have time right now. Trust me on this one."

He yelped to get her to stop, but Samantha kept going.

***

Their destination was a little bodega on a corner in one of the poorer neighborhoods of the city. Apartment buildings fronted the street, most with darkened windows, but the neon lights of the bodega were still on. Samantha slipped a piece of paper to the cashier who told them to wait. They milled about for a few minutes until an elderly man came downstairs and waved them over to the back room of the store.

He took the piece of paper Samantha had and glanced at it. "You have the needles?"

She nodded and pulled the chips out of her bag. She handed them to the man.

He glanced at them and nodded. "You're with A Better America?"

"Yes," said Hunter.

The man nodded and walked over to a desk in the back room and tossed the paper into a shredder. "No need to leave any evidence behind. All right, this will be quick."

"Will this hurt?"

"Not at all. You might feel some warmth, but that's necessary to burn out your existing tag."

"You aren't taking it out?" asked Samantha.

The older gentleman shook his head. "Too risky and too obvious. Your chips use electrical induction in order to function. All I need to do is pump enough voltage into the chip and it fries out. Unless someone X-Rays you, no one will notice you have two chips. Should someone ask, tell them your initial chip died and you had to be retagged. It's the same tech we've been using on our pets for decades."

"I am not just a pet!" growled X35670.

"Hey, easy there. I'm just the messenger." He held up a device containing coils of electrical wiring attached to some batteries in a 3D printed case. A small screen was on the back of the device. "The fact they're cheap makes this easy."

"All right, do it," said Samantha.

First, he used a scanner to locate the chip in Samantha's shoulder blades. "Z45069," he said when he found it. He then brought the device close to her skin and clicked a switch. It made a little pop as it pushed current through the device. He then checked with the reader, and when satisfied, he used the needle to inject a new chip into her.

He checked with the scanner when he was done. "Looks good. Your serial is now Z32893. You're next coyote."

Hunter tensed up as the man walked over to him and scanned him to find the chip. "X40871," he said when he found it.

"Wait, what?" said the coyote.

"X40871. Isn't that you?"

"I'm X35670"

The man frowned and checked again. "It says X40871."

"That's not what his paperwork says," said Samantha.

The man frowned. "Have you been rechipped before?"

The coyote shook his head.

The man did another read on the chip, and then clicked a button, pulling up the chips information in the online database. "Serial X40871, property of Bethel Biotech. You don't have a name entered."

"Who the hell is Bethel Biotech?" X35670 asked.

The man shrugged. "Do you still want me to rechip you?"

"No."

"Hunter, if you don't get rechipped, they can find you," said Samantha.

"No... Someone had me rechipped so I couldn't be found, and I think I know who."

"You'd remember the injection," said Samantha.

He thought back. There were parts of his memory that were blank. Periods where he couldn't remember what had happened exactly, but he knew after waking up from the smell and where he was sore what had happened. "Not necessarily. Can you look up my original serial?"

The man shook his head. "This reader only passes the key embedded in your chip to get your data."

"All right," said the coyote getting up. "We better go, but if I need to, can I come back?"

The man handed back the unused needle. "Ask for Raoul. Tell the cashier you need to discuss a delivery."

"How much do we owe you?" asked Samantha.

"It was prepaid," he said, as he looked over the CC TV screen sitting on the desk. "Now get out of here before anyone comes looking for you, and good luck."

They walked through the store and stepped out onto the street. It was well past 2 AM now and nothing stirred, but that didn't make them less nervous. They walked without a destination in mind.

"It was him, wasn't it," said the tigress, after a few minutes.

He stopped. "Yes. He must have done it one of the times he drugged me."

"He drugged you?"

The coyote scuffed the ground. "He liked me to be pliant. If I resisted, he'd use drugs to get what he wanted."

She flexed her claws, digging them into her paw pads. "How could anyone do that to someone?"

Too easily was all he could think. He quickly learned that fighting back was useless, but he still did it. Maybe that's what eventually caused him to be sold. "I don't know," was all he could muster.

She growled and glanced around. "Let's find some place to lay low before I start cursing out here."

"Good idea."

***

They slept in an alley that night behind a Chinese restaurant, shoulder to shoulder. The smell wasn't pretty, but it was dark and quiet. The ground was decently clean too. It seemed safe at least, and that was all that mattered.

In the morning, they turned their phones on to find a text message from Shandra saying the coast was clear.

Returning to the charity was tough. The front door was propped up, having been kicked in. Inside, the offices had been looted and bits of paper were scattered on the floor. Odd things were broken, not because they were valuable, but because someone thought them too nice and intentionally destroyed them. His home, his little place in this world, was in shambles. Their cots were overturned, and their clothes scattered everywhere. He walked from room to room in disbelief.

In addition to the overwhelming feeling of violation, there were news media covering the raid, talking to charity staff outside, even interviewing some of the morphs. He spent some time listening, but when one of the reporters wanted to interview him, he opted to instead slip away into the desecrated brownstone. In the middle of the front office he found Shandra, sitting on an overturned file cabinet. She was scrolling through text on a tablet.

"What were they looking for?" asked the coyote.

"Who knows. They seized most of the paper records, and all of the food supplies. Our public relations guy has been posting all morning about this on social media."

"Won't the government notice?"

She glanced up from her tablet and shrugged. "Maybe, but I've seen this before. If we're going to rebuild, we need to solicit donations from the community. So far, the numbers I've heard sound good."

He sat down on the floor. "This is wrong."

She flipped across the screen. "How so?"

"The raid, the way we're trying to come back, it all feels like a game. No one really cares, they're just trying to keep the status quo going," he said angrily.

She put down the tablet and gave him a serious look. Shandra looked both empowered and tired at the same time. In that moment, he could see the dark wrinkles in her face, the gray of her hair against her ebony skin as a testament to her years of service to the public good.

"The work you've done has helped people, Hunter."

There was that name again. His name. The one he'd let Shandra give him when he couldn't think of one for himself. "Has it really changed anything?"

"In a small way, yes. We can't reach everyone though, so there is always going to be more we could do. There has yet to be a period of human history where there hasn't been suffering."

"Yes, but the raid, the government, they don't care about the people."

"Not anymore."

"Don't you see though? It's a game they're playing with us, to keep us from moving up."

She laughed. "I forget sometimes for all you've been through, that you still have traces of naivety. Of course, it's a game. It's a cycle. It's never quite the same, but it keeps repeating."

"Then why are we playing it?"

She swept her hands around the office. "Do you want them to win?"

"We've got to break the cycle."

"Trust me, if I knew how to break this cycle, I'd be doing it. Over the course of my career though, power has swung more and more away from the people. I'm here to help push that pendulum back."

He propped his muzzle up on his hands. "You knew this would happen. That's why you sold us."

"Transferred. It was an administrative precaution only. We will never sell you, Hunter. My ancestors were bought and paid for. Trust me, I would never allow it."

"But I'm not free," he said softly.

She sighed. "You are as free as we can legally let you be. If you want to pursue a more rewarding career path, I will support you. You've never asked about this before."

"I know." He hesitated. "My chip, the original one, what happened to it?"

"The one you burned out last night? It's still there."

"No. I was rechipped before."

She frowned and picked up her tablet. "Let me see. They should have the digital records online already." She tapped at the screen and pulled up his file.

"According to the," she grimaced, "bill of sale, you are X35670."

"I know, and that's who I always was. That's not what my chip says. It says X40871 and I'm owned by Bethel Biotech."

She frowned. "It's not our policy to verify chips."

"Right, but who is X40871?" he asked.

"That is indeed a good question." She tapped into the screen. "Bethel Biotech?"

"Yeah."

She pulled up some information on the firm. "They're involved in genetic research." She kept looking for a minute. "There are a number of ethics complaints against them."

"Don't all the companies involved with morphs have pending lawsuits."

"Oh god, yes. There are tons," she squinted at the screen. "They're tied to the Strong family."

"Senator Strong?"

"Yeah. His brother is CEO. I'm surprised that I haven't heard of them before. Their market capitalization must not be too big."

"Marcus…" he said with a low growl.

"Yes, Senator Marcus Strong, your past owner." She frowned. "What was the serial the chip said again?"

"It was X40871."

She tapped it in and stared at the screen, frowning. She scrolled down.

"What?"

"Well I see part of what they've done. They've reported you as stolen property."

***

He hadn't been in a medical office so clean and neat since he'd left the biotech facility, but they had managed to pull strings and find a doctor willing to work with morphs. The MRI machine was loud and being inside it felt like being buried alive. The noise made Hunter want to crawl out of the torus and get as far away from the machine as he could. After what had seemed like forever, they'd gotten the images they need. Now he was sitting in the office of the charity's lawyer while Shandra went over options with the lawyer.

"You can clearly see the second chip implanted in Hunter's shoulder," she said. "From what the doctor can determine this one, appears to be the one functioning."

"Can we get the original out?" the lawyer asked.

"Carefully. It's not so deep to be a complicated operation, but the doctor will have to go dig it out. Why do you want a dead chip out?"

"Evidence. Each chip has its serial micro-printed on it. The surgery will need to be recorded though so we can present it as evidence in court." The lawyer smiled and flashed his perfect teeth. Hunter had met the man only yesterday, but if he could think of anyone personifying a shark it would be this man. "I want to be prove beyond a shadow of a doubt that they tried to defraud us by selling us a morph they illegally rechipped."

"Please don't use the word 'sell,' it has bad connotations," said Shandra.

The lawyer glanced at hunter. "First forgive me for speaking about you like this, Hunter," he said to the coyote, before he turned to Shandra. "Legally, and I know it hurts to think of this, but Hunter is just a product we purchased. He has no more rights than a dog we buy at the pet store. In order to pursue this, we're going to have to go after the angle that they tried to defraud A Better America by using deceptive business practices."

Even though it was true, Hunter could feel his ears lower.

"Hunter, Samantha, and all the others are my employees, Mr. Wallace. Just because we can't emancipate them doesn't mean we treat them like they're property. They're as human as you and I."

"I agree, but we don't have a case to challenge Senator Strong and the Senate Bioethics Committee he chairs. We can backdoor morph rights into this, but I can't use that as the basis of the case. Taking out the chip would give us proof to show they committed fraud. I can file a legal brief as soon as we get the chip out to push our claims."

"What about the three that got picked up, Janice, Thomas, and Fang? We can't just let them sit in jail."

"I'm already working on that. That should be easy since we transferred everyone's ownership. I'm hoping by pushing the case with Hunter we might be able to scare Bethel Biotech enough to exert some pressure to get the others released quickly. If you want to push this into the public consciousness, it's going to take time. The senator's political position against morphs could let this get picked up in the national news."

"What about Samantha?" asked Hunter.

The lawyer glance at Hunter. "Rechipping her and the others will keep them out of jail, if the cops do bump into them. Bethel Biotech isn't the only one who can play games. Once things settle down, we can file paperwork to transfer their serial numbers and everything is kosher. I'm most concerned about how to handle you, Hunter. You are our chance to get them to back down and give A Better America some breathing room."

The coyote cleared his throat. "They're only going to back down if they want to."

"Legally, we've got them where we want them."

"They have more financial resources to fight this than we do. Senator Strong will find a way to waylay this if he wants. It could take years to resolve it. If you want to take Senator Strong down, we need to play at his level."

The lawyer frowned. "We can only assume the senator is connected to the raid right now, but I think we can find a link if we look closely. I've gone up against politicians before. I'm not scared of the senator, Hunter. I've got my own tricks up my sleeve."

"I'm sure you do, but he wants me back right?"

"That seems so," said Shandra.

He glanced at the lawyer and leaned forward to Shandra. "Then let's give him what he wants."

Shandra cleared her throat. "You know what he's going to do to you."

The pain flooded his mind and he nodded. "I know." For years he endured it. For years he'd cried only to himself at night. Even now, he still worried he was just a toy for the senator, but he was more than that. He was X35670, and X35670 had a name with a meaning. "But to get to Senator Strong we're going to need a lure. He's been pushing this anti-morph rights position for years since morph rights contradict with his religious views. Family values voters are the people who keep putting him back in office because they think he is doing something about the morph issue. They don't realize he's just exploiting them as a base for his campaign. If he thinks he still owns me, I know how to use that against him."

"I don't follow," remarked the lawyer.

"The senator purchased me for his own sexual gratification. He raped me whenever it suited him, starting when I was fifteen."

Shandra gave him a sad look and nodded. The lawyer looked like a ghost. The coyote didn't know if they'd told him about that, but the thought obviously sickened him.

Hunter smiled, showing his fangs. Humans didn't like when you showed too much fang, and the lawyer drew back. Shandra wasn't fazed by it. "I suggest we do a little hunting of our own and use what we know against Senator Strong. It's time people really saw how he has been 'benefitting' off of morphs."

***

The surgery had been an in and out affair. The removal of his original chip had been quick. The doctor had used the same incision to implant him with a low powered locator beacon that worked through pulling energy out of his blood stream. The range was only half a mile, but it was enough. After that it was easy to get himself picked up by the cops.

"X40871, your owner is here," said the police officer, coming to the door.

"Owner?" asked Hunter. He had been waiting a week in jail for this.

"Yes. Mr. Strong. He's here to pick you up," said the cop.

He felt his chest tighten, and he swallowed before he could nod. The man opened the cell and put handcuffs on him. He was then led through the jail, but they turned once out of the cell block and went down a different corridor than the one he'd entered through to a side entrance.

Out in the alley, a man wearing a dark trench coat and a car waited. The officer and the man exchanged words, and then the officer took the coyotes cuffs off. As the jailer walked away, the other man opened the door to the limo. "Get in."

Reluctantly, Hunter got in and the door was closed behind him. On the other side of the compartment sat Senator Strong. The stared at each other for a minute as the driver got in and started to drive away.

"Didn't think you'd see me again, did you?" asked the senator.

"You sold me," Hunter said flatly.

The senator chuckled and leaned forward. "Sold is such a vulgar word. Let's just say I loaned you out. Why don't you have a little something to drink and we can talk this over?" He motioned to a cup in the armrest of where Hunter sat.

"I'm not thirsty." Hunter knew what was in the cup.

"I insist."

He glanced down and picked it up. He took a big gulp, of the drink. In the back of the throat he could taste the saltiness of the GHB he already knew was in the drink over the alcohol.

"Why am I here?" asked Hunter.

The man frowned. "I know two years is a while, but you don't get to ask the questions, slave."

Hunter squared his shoulders. "My name is Hunter."

"Is that what they called you? I don't like it."

He wanted to scream, but he kept his voice back. He didn't need to be here forever, just long enough. "It doesn't matter what you like. I like it."

The man lowered his voice. "I see you've got some fight in you now. I'm going to enjoy breaking that out of you." He pulled out a leather strap. "Now do I need to do this the hard way, or are you going to smarten up quickly?"

The effects of the drink were starting to take hold of him, but he didn't care. "Make me," he slurred at the Senator.

The senator laughed. "I already have."

***

He awoke bound, with his head spinning. His body hurt, especially under the tail where a crust of fluids had developed. The senator hadn't been gentle this time.

"Oh god," he moaned. "Why did I agree to this?"

"Agree?" came a voice, one he knew but could not recall who it belonged to. He just knew he didn't like that voice.

He turned his head to try and focus on it. He knew from experience the drug would sometimes affect his eyesight. "Yeah, agree." In the distance, there was a sound his idled mind couldn't quite make out.

Someone came up and grabbed him by the scruff of his neck. "Agree to what?"

His eyes tried to focus, but his senses were just starting to come back to him. "On letting Senator Strong rape me. I knew he would."

"You agreed to nothing."

He laughed and closed his eyes. That mysterious sound chimed again. "Actually," and the memory came back stronger to him, "I suggested it."

The slap across his muzzle startled him and he was shaken and his eyes flew open. "Don't try and play with me."

He blinked until they would focus. It was the Senator who was with him. The fog in his mind had lifted enough for him to recognize the man. "You didn't think it odd I let the police pick me up?"

"No one knows you're here."

The distant sound came again, and this time his mind was able to process it. It was the sound of a doorbell, followed by someone banging on the door. "Oh, they know, and they brought friends."

Coda

So that's it, or as much of it as I've been able to scrounge together. I've worked really hard to catalogue all that's happened, sort the sins from the triumphs, figure out where the ideal, perfect society that we thought we were on the brink of went so horribly wrong. The myths come together to reveal truths. Or perhaps various truths collect to become essential myths. In any case, thank you so much for sticking with me.

At last, here's where it all comes to fulmination, you the hopeful soul who has remained with me through all these remembrances. I desperately need your help which is why I now bring you this warning.

The scourges of the old world, the dominant, the arrogant, and the well-meaning despots didn't die, they merely scattered, and seek to reform and try to save us from ourselves a second time.

I've tracked their signal, and I've tracked yours. They're converging now because they want you. They want to take you under their influence, whisper more of their same honeyed lies, convince you to vest your faith in them, concede your power, make them your protectors and patriarchs and Gods. The foot-soldiers of the next world order are already on the move, following my moving signal, trying to pinpoint those who are receiving all my warnings.

They want you, and their acolytes, their disciples, their badged, ordained, and deputized slaves are coming as I speak with promises in one hand and fetters in the other. If you've seen lights on your horizon then you honestly don't have a lot of time.

They're heading straight for your camp and no doubt they'll reach your firelight very soon.

Now would be a good time to start running my friend.

And if it's too late for that, resist.

About the Authors

When the Ministry For Acceptable Thought kicked in the door to **Faora Meridian**'s domicile, he thought himself doomed. But when brave members of the anti-government resistance spirited him away from the Ministry's cruel clutches, he discovered his calling in life: the creation of anthropomorphic fiction that would help give the masses hope in these dark times.

Okay, so he wasn't very good at giving HOPE per se, but at least he's found some modest success through publications such as *Heat*, *Hot Dish*, *FANG*, and now here, as part of a team of brave, animalistic propagandists fighting the encroaching dark.

Mog Moogle has been lurking around the fandom since the early 2000's. He started writing furry stuff just for fun in 2004. Since then, he's posted several free stories on SoFurry.com and his first printed story released in 2016 in *Fragments of Life's Heart* by Weasel Press.

When not doing furry stuff, he's usually trying to figure out how to do more furry stuff. He loves to travel and see new places, and really enjoys furry conventions.

Mog's had a few interesting experiences that lend to his writing, an Army veteran and former police officer with an adrenaline junkie mindset has led to more than one interesting adventure in his day.

He's usually a friendly type of critter that enjoys hugs and loves talking to readers and fellow writers. Feel free to contact him and let him know what you think of his stories, (or his terrible bio.)

George Squares is an author currently living in the Virginian mountains with his husband. He has training in creative writing from UNCW and majored in undergrad Biology.

Tyler "TD" Coltraine brings his twenty-something years of experience to another anthology, waxing into the socio-political world for a bit. Occasionally a novelist, often a smut-smith, always a slacker, TD spends afternoons with his cats, his video games, and a lot of ideas that ever-so-slowly make their way to the light of day. Look him up on SoFurry and feel free to say "hello".

Searska GreyRaven has been telling tales for as long as she can remember. She makes her home in southern Florida, sharing her lair with her bee hives, assorted wild reptiles, and a hoard of books. She was most recently published in the anthologies *ROAR 9* and *What the Fox?!* Her work can also be found on her SoFurry page, searska-greyraven.sofurry.com and she can be followed on Twitter (@ SearskaGreyRvn).

TJ Minde found the furry fandom after moving to Ohio almost ten years ago. It is there, he picked up the pen—or grabbed a keyboard, as it may be—and started creating characters and worlds. TJ is incredibly grateful for the community of artists, writers and friends he found; they helped him discover something that he cares about—writing. TJ has grown to become more passionate about the craft of writing and enjoys creating new worlds and aiding others with projects of their own.

TJ's other works may be found in *ROAR, FANG*, and other anthologies both in and out of the fandom. For thoughts, comments and replies in bite-sized chunks, he can be found on Twitter @TJMinde.

Jelliqal Belle is an abuse and rape survivor. *"Gilded Cage"* was a purgative story, channeling nightmares of buried fears. If you or someone you know is in a toxic relationship, there are choices; please get out to build a better future. Read about codependency and break the cycle. When Jelliqal is not loving on her pets, working in her garden, or running with her guild in a MMORP, she is passionately avoiding housework by writing. Jelliqal is the writing facilitator for Furry Weekend Atlanta and a member of Furry Writers Guild and Sisters in Crime. Jelliqal writes fur fiction, mysteries, and poetry. Her stories are published by FurPlanet (*ROAR 8* – Ursa Major award finalist), Thurston Howl Publications (*Breeds: Foxes*), and *Werewolves Vs.* (*Fascism & Hollywood*). Twitter @Jelliqal or Telegram as Jelli Qal.

A seagull wolf transplanted from the sunny West Coast into the chilly Midwest, **Gullwulf** has only recently become a furry but has held a fascination with the anthropomorphic arts since she was a child. She's thrilled to chase a dark future in her fourth published story *The Tower* and has previously been published in the biannual

Werewolves Vs. online zine as well as Thurston Howl's *Seven Deadly Sins: Furry Confessions* and FurPlanet's *Dogs of War*. With a love for history, the 80s, and Ancient Egypt, there's no telling where her next story will take her. Find her in the frozen wastelands, or on social media with twitter @gullwulf.

Stephen M. Coghlan is an ever-expanding author of speculative fiction who inhabits a small area of the great, and oft-frozen, national capital region of Canada.

Predominantly a Furry Writer, his works include *The Genmos* and *The Nobilis* series, as well as a myriad of short stories.

He can be found lurking on Twitter or Facebook under the handle @WordsBySC, or on his website and blog: scoghlan.com

Detroit is a writer who discovered the furry fandom in 2013. His interest in how people use (and misuse) technology is a key theme in his work. As a professional historian, he's also fascinated with how people remember and commemorate the past. This is the first time he's published a story in a furry anthology, but he has an extensive background as a historical writer and researcher. He's currently based in the American South and enjoys sports in his spare time.

Televassi writes, naturally, to give his habit of staring off into space some legitimacy, as well as that of routinely frequenting coffee shops to fuel his chai latte 'problem.' His poetry, prose, and non-fiction have featured in publications such as *Heat*, *Furries Among Us*, and the Ursa Award winning *Gods with Fur*. Televassi is currently working on a novella that he hopes to finish by the end of next year, but then again he said that to himself the year before. Outside of writing, Televassi likes to rock climb, wander about in the woods, frequent furmeets, and generally be a well-socialised wolf.

James L. Steele is a writer in Ohio. He is often asked to sum up his life's story in a single paragraph. James is very depressed by how easy this is. He has been published in *Gods with Fur*, *Claw the Way to Victory*, *Solarcide*, *Tall Tales with Short Cocks v.2*, *Bourbon Penn*, and *Fictionvale*. His sci-fi novel *Huvek* is published through FurPlanet.

Visit his site at JamesLSteele.com, his blog at DaydreamingInText. blogspot.com, and his twitter @JLSteeleAuthor

Joseph Vandehey, often known in the fandom as Fugue, is a mathematician by day, a writer by night, and a tea addict at all hours.

Thurston Howl is the editor-in-chief of Thurston Howl Publications, an editor for Weasel Press and its imprint Sinister Stoat Press, an occasional formatter for Armoured Fox Press, a reporter for *Between the Lines*, and the founder of both the Furry Book Review program and the Leo Literary Awards. Under his humansona name of Jonathan W. Thurston, he has published sexual horror novellas *The Devil Has a Black Dog* and *Straight Men*, multiple fantasy novels, and short stories and poems in *ROAR*, *Heat*, *Civilized Beasts*, *Passing Through*, *Typewriter Emergencies*, *Dogs of War*, *Vagabonds*, *Lupus Animus*, *Wolf Warriors*, *Orange and White and Tweets All Over*, and more.

Mary E. Lowd writes stories and collects creatures. She's had more than one hundred short stories published, and her novels include the *Otters In Space* trilogy, *In a Dog's World*, and *The Snake's Song: A Labyrinth of Souls Novel*. Her fiction has won an Ursa Major Award and two Cóyotl Awards. Meanwhile, she's collected a husband, daughter, son, bevy of cats and dogs, and the occasional fish. The stories, creatures, and Mary live together in a crashed spaceship disguised as a house, hidden in a rose garden in Oregon. Learn more at www.marylowd.com.

About The Editors

NightEyes DaySpring is a known troublemaker who is currently wanted for crimes against literature and excessive coffee consumption in public. His over twenty counts of crimes against literature include appearances in *Werewolves vs. Fascism, Seven Deadly Sins,* and *FANG,* along with other anthologies. *Dissident Signals* is the first anthology he has helped edit. Currently, NightEyes is believed to be in hiding somewhere in Florida with his boyfriend. For updates on his writing, visit <u>nighteyes-dayspring.com</u>, and for day-to-day nonsense, follow @wolfwithcoffee on twitter.

Remember, war is not peace, slavery is not freedom, and ignorance is not strength.

Slip Wolf is a hard-working writer and occasional editor who stockpiles literature for the coming apocalypse in steel-sleeved books that will not burn at 451 Fahrenheit. The dark future better love furry fluff is all he's sayin, cause nobody's steel-binding any science books. He waits in Canada for that knock on the door from the corporate doomsday cult with his mate, son, and dog Whiskey, who has a ham radio and is starting a necessary mutation.

Stay tuned to Slip's tweet-waves at: @Slip_Wolf and check other stuff through: <u>furaffinity.net/user/slip-wolf</u>.

Keep your lit sharp, friends. Read, Write, Resist.

About the Artist

Teagan Gavet is a professional illustrator, graphic novelist, and freelance rambler. Find more at: http://www.teagangavet.com
http://www.furaffinity.net/user/blackteagan